Techno Ranger

A Sam Harper Military Thriller

Thomas Sewell

Dedicated to my (unbeknownst to them) mentors for this one:
Tom Clancy, Robert Ludlum, and David Drake.

And as always and forever, Christi.

For a current list of related books and short stories, please visit SharperSecurity.com.
Email TR@catallaxymedia.com for news about future books.

Cover Design by Aaron Leavitt.

ISBN 13:
978-1-952242-00-7 (Paperback)
978-1-952242-01-4 (Hardcover)

Published in the United States of America

Catallaxy Media, Charlotte, NC
http://CatallaxyMedia.com

Contents

PART ONE

OPPOSITION TEAM

Chapter One:
Surfin' USA

Two minutes left.

Few Army engineers are brilliant enough to risk more deaths than the bombings of Hiroshima and Nagasaki combined just by surfing, but Michelle always insisted I bottled-up a genius for destruction.

It all kicked off in an HH-60H Seahawk helicopter.

Utilitarian.

The Navy is all about ships and planes. By comparison, their Spec Ops budget might as well be a rounding error. Only one active Special Warfare Sea Combat unit in the Navy.

HSC-85, the Firehawks.

Our pilot and crew chief took every opportunity to brandish their flaming-bird-over-golden-trident emblems. Everyone at Naval Air Station North Island in San Diego was suitably impressed.

Even a noob 2LT like me knows to learn patches and badges. Especially when your life may depend on them.

Michelle acts clueless about uniforms, but she's a wise wahine. Notices more than she lets on.

Ninety seconds until drop.

Our Firehawks pilot shoved the cyclic forward. Dipped the copter's rad flame-painted nose down.

Picked up speed. Doors already open. Bare to the sky and sea.

Below, ocean waves crashed into a blur of black-rock cliffs. We flew down the Southern California coastline. Through salted air.

One minute.

Adrenalin pumped. Amplified the waves. Blasted them against my eardrums.

Ready to go.

Michelle and I bounced into the air like we'd hit the peak of a roller coaster.

Stomach soared. Lousy turbulence.

We slammed back into the aluminum cabin floor. Black neoprene wetsuit material compressed below us.

My spine shrunk. Stomach dropped.

Thirty seconds.

Dude! No need to kill us during the insertion.

Grabbed the back of Michelle's parachute harness. Felt where the five straps combined. Double-checked they were still hooked to a safety line.

Secured beats dead.

The setting sun highlighted the tangled city hills on the far side of San Diego Bay.

Lit up the hill my family lived on the day I was born.

The hill where twenty years ago today, Child Services regretted to inform me my mom and dad died from collateral damage.

I was seven.

That taught me to hate collateral damage.

My first trip back since Army ROTC. First since putting on second lieutenant's bars. My first love was the epic surfing at Lowers or off La Jolla.

San Diego held jumbled memories, sour and sweet.

Shook my head. Refocused. No time for nostalgia.

Fifteen seconds.

"Better make out on this trial run." I forced my words through the wind. "Or my REMF colonel will rake over my career."

Michelle turned her head. Tilted her lips toward my ear. "Pretend it's a surfing contest. You used to win those."

Not cool dude! Used to? I just shook my head.

Five seconds. Years of my team's work to validate.

More than a surf competition. Our test reduced to the ultimate evaluation process: soldiers in combat.

Simulated or not.

Target reached. Green light. Leaned forward, ready to propel myself outward.

Left hand on one rubberized edge of the opening. Right hand on the back of Michelle's wetsuit.

No more time to prepare. To back out.

The Firehawks crew chief doubled as our jumpmaster. Unhooked our safety cables.

Now nothing kept us in the whirlybird.

He tapped Michelle's right shoulder. "Go. Go. Go!"

Naturally, she hesitated, so I pushed her.

She slid out of the cabin. Plunged toward the ocean.

Michelle was never into unquestioning obedience. We got along that way, although that attitude doesn't optimize my Army life.

The Seahawk's four-bladed main rotor whomped the air outside the cabin. Drove it more vertical than horizontal. That gust propelled her away. Yellow static line unspooled behind her.

She'd be fine.

My bare legs dangled out the open cabin door. Blond leg hairs danced in the draft. Courtesy of Uncle Sam's logistics, my black Aqua-shoes matched my shorty wetsuit.

The jumpmaster stepped away. Hit the quick release for the tie-downs holding our pair of eSurfboards in the cabin.

I plunged forward. Dropped after Michelle.

Fought the rotor wash. Peeked back for a second.

He pushed the two eSurfboards out the opposite door, attached to their own static lines.

So far, so good, but falling doesn't kill you.

Needed to escort Michelle, the High Value Target (HVT) for today, from here to the USS Midway aircraft carrier docked on the east side of San Diego Bay.

Ideally, without the dozen Ranger Reconnaissance Company (RRC) dudes waiting in ambush below, shooting us.

My ears popped. Extended my hands, arms and legs.

Dove through the air buffets. Tasted the offshore breeze.

Controlled my descent. Twisted to face the briny deep.

The sunset to the southwest reflected in the five foot swells off Point Loma. Golden rays turned the swells a luminous green.

Seafoam. My favorite color.

WARCOM, AKA *The Center*, stationed in the Amphibious base on Coronado peninsula, stretched between the bay and the ocean, making this SEAL home surf. They'd evaluate our tech test mission. Determine if my eSurfboard was useful.

See if it totally destroyed their existing equipment's capabilities, like I'd promised.

Michelle reached the end of her static line. It jerked the deployment bag off her back. Her chute streamed into the rushing air.

Opened with a whoosh.

She only had to manage her wetsuit. I carried thirty pounds of tactical gear, plus an M4A1 carbine with I-MILES for use in the exercise.

The SEALs brought in Rangers from the 75th RRC as a Special Operations element. They could both use some water training and would provide a neutral OPFOR during the exercise.

Nobody wanted a biased result.

Chute deployed with a pop and a jerk. Harness transformed into a giant playground swing.

Prefer for safety to pack my own chute, but either way it's a relief when it opens properly.

I tugged on a control line. Oriented myself toward a point in the ocean a hundred meters away from the breaking waves. Followed Michelle through the air.

The steady offshore breeze wanted to push us into the sand, but we needed to keep water below us.

Michelle hit the water like a cannon-ball under a dandelion.

I plunged into the ocean swells 20 meters from her. A sphere of water sprayed into the air around me.

My exhausted chute settled into the drink downwind. Left alone, it would act as a sea anchor. Drag me through the waves.

Bobbed up. Deep breath. Salty air tasted like heaven.

Popped a pair of quick-releases. Cut my chute loose.

The underwater kelp jungle grabbed at my legs.

Couldn't get tangled or this mission would end faster than a shark who swallowed C-4 and a blasting cap.

Turned west. Shielded my eyes from the glare of the sunset with my left hand. Paddled against the water with my right to stay afloat.

My carbine, strapped to my tactical harness, dragged me away little by little with the motion of the crashing whitecaps.

Only so much weight a baby life-preserver can help with.

Our pair of prototype eSurfboards splashed into the rolling waves about 30 meters farther from shore.

Michelle released her own chute, so I ignored her as safe enough for now. How much trouble could she get into while floundering in the ocean?

Equipped with waterproof GPS trackers, a spec-4 would come collect our chutes once the surf pushed them up on the beach.

A series of waves smacked me in the face, but I duck dove through. Swam for the prototype boards. Held my breath with each submersion.

Facing white breakers just before dusk, I raced across the green waves. Dodged seaweed tentacles. Was at home here. I'd surfed since age ten, but lately I'd missed the inner peace of riding gnarly waves.

I'm a soldier, not a sailor. I'd completed Airborne school over the summer during ROTC. Made time for the Ranger leadership course during this, my first deployment, but despite my comfort on a board, certainly wasn't a SEAL. Hadn't endured their BUD/S training, conducted five miles away at WARCOM. Nor was I officially a Ranger, like those opposing us, not having been selected for the 75th Ranger Regiment by completing RASP.

My ROTC Instructor at Cal Poly San Luis Obispo choked up laughing when he read my first name. Thought I looked like a Sam: a cocky beanpole of a surface-to-air missile. Faked a crestfallen expression when I mumbled and conceded I couldn't play the harp, despite having "Harper" embroidered on my uniform's nametape.

To a surfer second lieutenant, freshly commissioned with a degree in electronics engineering, a job to devise a hydrofoil eSurfboard for the Pentagon sounded like the perfect deployment.

I played with dense lithium-ion batteries.

Wired them to a silent-running torpedo-shaped electric motor.

The motor spun a hand-polished aluminum propeller.

Whole assembly connected underwater to the end of a three meter carbon fiber cylinder.

The hydrofoil, a swept-back fluid dynamics wing, braced that pole about a third of the way up.

Ahead of me, the top of the shaft floated my prototype short-board above the waves. I cut through the water toward it.

I loved surfing and engineering, so why did I hate my work?

First Sgt. Keith Bishop, top NCO of the 75th Ranger Reconnaissance Company (RRC), despised ocean swimming. Especially in waves colder than a penguin's balls. Sure, Coronado Peninsula was surrounded by a bay, or a channel, or something, but when the Major gave him the option of staying dry or taking part in this tech demo, he'd opted to watch remotely with the SEALs in WARCOM's crisis center.

And then the red-headed-step-child of the Company, 1LT Schnier, looked at him with his Texan puppy eyes bigger than a tornado and begged him to come along with his OPFOR platoon. "It'll be fun! What? Salty old hound like you afraid of a little salty water?"

Bishop could only put on a brave face to take his medicine and respond, "Roger that, Lieutenant."

Decent head for tactics, but Schnier never seemed to think how hard-living and partying would get him that ranch he always talked about.

Now, Schnier and his platoon spread out evenly ahead of him, two Abrams tank-lengths apart, dispersed across the 650 meters of water between Coronado and Smuggler's Cove. A SEAL-sleek underwater propulsion device (UPD) pulled each Ranger along. Made them blaze through the water, wearing wetsuits, combat vests, and high-speed waterproof goggles.

Bishop splashed along behind his UPD. To the rear of the line of Rangers. Observed Schnier's platoon, as ordered. Shook his head. Got a cheekful of brine for his trouble. Coughed and spit it out. What was he doing here again?

How did all this playing in the water help him get his family moved to Korea?

No way even an underwater opponent could sneak past Schnier's ambush. They'd be the anvil in this scenario.

Schnier'd stationed a sniper team off Zuniga Point. Out front. The hammer; set to chase 2LT Harper and his HVT into this channel. Prevent retreat.

Just when his hard-working wife'd gotten the desert dust out of his sacred tan underwear, this trip'd fill his britches with wet ocean sand. She was gonna fetchin' kill him.

His Poppa never swam. The Commonwealth of Virginia's beach and swimming pool segregation policy saw to that. Whenever he asked to learn, Poppa gave his usual commentary on life, "That dog won't hunt."

Different for Bishop after he signed-up for the Army, but learning to keep his bulky muscles afloat almost lick'd him. He could drag behind a UPD, though.

Besides, he just had to watch, not fight. Schnier's platoon set up along the only path from the Pacific Ocean into the bay where the USS Midway lay at anchor. Schnier gonna tear this cocky engineer a new one, no matter how gussied up his highfalutin' improved UPD was.

Bishop almost felt sorry for Harper. When the SEALs wanted an evaluation against realistic opposition, the Major volunteered Schnier's platoon. Back from a combat deployment in the middle-east, on their way to South Korea to train some locals, playing in the water sounded like a nice break to the *other* Rangers.

Not for Bishop. Another wave smacked him in the face. A reminder he'd rather hang with the piddlin' WARCOM brass and SEAL leaders *evaluating* on dry land. Teeth-rattlin' missions like this are why lieutenants are the nemeses of senior NCOs.

Chapter Two:
I Get Around

I didn't detest the ocean and technology portions of my job. Just couldn't take the bureaucratic component. My boss, the Procurement and Supply Colonel, who insisted on "periodic perfect Pentagon paperwork plans properly prepared."

When I outlined this combat-drop test of my prototype, I'd analyzed the map. Looked for the narrowest part of the entrance from the Pacific into San Diego Bay. Found the gap between Smuggler's Cove and Zuniga Point.

A perfect ambush spot. Right next to Naval Base Point Loma on Coronado Peninsula.

If the 75th RRC platoon stationed a pair of Rangers in the water here at Point Loma, they'd get here before I returned to Michelle with the eSurfboards.

The Opposition Force (OPFOR) better choose the best ambush location, instead. Then we might have a fighting chance.

Life in the Army is full of little risks.

The buoyant surfboard and its torpedo-like propeller formed a sideways U-shape with the low-drag carbon fiber tube and wing in the middle. The eSurfboard's natural tendency when not in motion was to lay flat on top of the water.

Everything else hid in the depths below.

Their small parachute anchors combined with the motion of the waves. Dragged them conveniently toward the shore. My direction.

Wiggled my equipment through the rolling waves. Grabbed the rail of the closest board. Slid from the water onto the deck.

Tugged the harness line behind me; ensured my carbine came along.

Once aboard, released its chute to the mercy of the waves.

Michelle fluttered a hand at me. Bounced slowly up and down in the surf. Treaded water like a champ. Despite her lack of experience, no fear of the ocean there.

Pulled my wireless Bluetooth hand controller from a breast pocket. Pushed the power button.

Two green LEDs on the controller lit up. Showed both motors active.

Designating this board as primary, I put the secondary into 5-meter follow-mode. I'd loaded an expert system into the board's waterproof miniaturized computer. It'd track the relative position of both boards. Adjust the speed and direction of its propeller. Stay as close to exactly five meters away as possible.

Sometimes, I love modern technology.

I balanced on my knees. Used the speed-trigger on the hand controller to accelerate. Leaned a bit left to aim for Michelle.

Ten seconds later, I guided the secondary next to her. Released the trigger to stop both.

Activated my waterproof bone conduction earpiece. Grinned. "Attention all intelligence officers. I'll be your sunset cruise director this evening, please board at the promenade deck."

Slender, and relatively young for her level of responsibility within the CIA, Michelle also spent her teens in San Diego. We lettered in Track and Field together at Fayelyn High School. Her Track, me Field, mostly jumping.

No way she ever beat me, even in practice. Might come close at long enough distances, but not in a sprint.

Small chested, long legs, built for distance running, but not muscular enough for sprinting, while I placed at the CIF Championships in the 100 meter dash and the Triple Jump.

More of a beach bunny than a surfer, she tentatively climbed up on the secondary board. Put into practice what I'd taught her in an hour-long familiarization session yesterday. Sat up. Laughed as she balanced.

Flipped her hair around. Flung water at me.

Tapped her own earpiece to switch on its microphone. "Exotic *and* fun. Water landings aren't nearly as rough as hitting dirt."

How'd she convince the Agency to let her join my demonstration mission? Her knowledge of at least one key participant gave her a leg up, but that didn't usually cut much weight with the bureaucracy. "Did you call in a favor, just to support me?"

"Always willing to help an old friend, but there's more to it than that. Long story. Let's save it for the celebration later." She grinned. "Assuming you win this."

I shifted closer to the center of balance on my board. "Ready? Final boarding call."

She had a spare hand controller tucked away, just in case, but our plan was for her board to continue to follow mine and mimic its movements through the water.

A hydrofoil, a wing-shaped curve, extended underwater from the central shaft of each board.

The only thing she controlled with her body was how far to lean forward or back. Tilted the hydrofoil forward or back.

The speed of the board, the hydrofoil's angle as it cut through the water, combined to set the height of the board above the waves. Its steerable electric propeller determined direction.

Michelle got up out of the ocean. Leaned forward on her knees. Displayed a thumbs-up. Gripped the board's side rails in anticipation. "Let's go."

Departure time.

The Ranger defenders expected us, but I wanted the OPFOR to locate us on our terms, not theirs.

Fast is smooth. I eased the trigger back on the wireless controller.

Our boards made headway against the water.

Centered my thumping heart with a deep breath. In one continuous motion I stood and balanced. Left-foot forward.

Triggered more power.

The board reached closer to half speed, 15 mph.

Shifted weight toward my back foot.

My hydrofoil's underwater wing pushed against the water. Lifted the board gradually a foot into the air. Held it up via the shaft. "Now flying."

Michelle's eSurfboard faithfully followed mine, five meters back.

Her knuckles on the side rails turned white. Didn't have the experience to stand up in this bumpy surf.

Began to fall behind me. Board in the water. Too much drag.

Sat back a little. Shifted her weight onto her knees and heels. Ascended. "Hell yeah!"

We cruised through the waves. Only the torpedo motor and propeller encountered hydro-resistance.

Without boards, tactical equipment, and body masses dragging in the water, we could move 50% faster than the latest underwater propulsion device (UPD) designed for Frogmen.

The OPFOR outnumbered us. They could wait hidden underwater, but we enjoyed a definite speed advantage.

Twenty-five inches above the water, I leaned left and then right to cutback. Ran my board perpendicular along the swells.

Picked up even more speed.

The sunset to our right would shine into the eyes of any coastal defenders.

Michelle's board followed mine. We flew down the Point Loma coast above the waves. Crest-hopped at 30 mph.

Any faster and we'd both bounce off. My wetsuit actually dried out in the wind.

Tapping a button, I fired up "Surfin' USA" in our ears. Nothing like the Beach Boys to get your motor running.

Michelle cocked her head. "What's that?"

It wasn't in the specs. My boss might tank my next fitness review if he found out before my tour of duty ended, but I'd programmed an extra feature into the earpieces. When no other sound was transmitted, they acted as miniature mp3 players.

I grinned. "Just a little music to keep things chill."

We swept along to the rhythm. Cruised over the water.

Became the king of the waves. Stretched my arms out wide. "Yeah!"

Even if my plan didn't work, this was still the most fun I'd had all year.

Two minutes later, we passed the end of Point Loma. Cruised

the ocean due west of the opening into San Diego Bay.

Tidal flows out of the Bay shifted the current. Pushed us away from land.

I course corrected back.

San Diego Bay forms a crescent shape to the north and east of Coronado Peninsula. Over centuries, the ocean shaped Coronado into a curved war club. The thin 250 meter wide handle at the south end connected to the mainland.

The only open channel into the Bay rounded off the two mile wide northern head of the war club.

Opposite the middle of the thickest portion was our objective on the other side of the Bay. A permanently docked aircraft carrier turned into a Museum exhibit.

The USS Midway.

The Midway closed to the public at 5pm. A perfect stand-in for one of the real carriers in the Bay, without the naval disruption their use in an exercise would cause.

From Zuniga Point, a rocky breakwater extended over a mile out as a spike from the war club's head. The only way into the Bay via water.

Our defenders would surely guard that passage.

No amount of extra speed would avail us if we rode right into their blazing guns.

I-MILES sensors on our shoulders, chests, and boards would register any hit from the laser designator on their weapons.

That'd wipe out the exercise. Send me back to run a recycled project. Waste a year of my combat engineering platoon's time. Kill the impending potential promotion to 1LT I was about to reach the requisite Time-In-Grade for.

We must evade the enemy to achieve my plans for the next couple of years.

All true, but really, I needed to prove to myself that a foster kid surfer could succeed as a military engineer.

Damp ocean spray in my face and the watery reflections of the sunset off to my right tried to distract me.

Focus on the plan.

We'd cleared the Point. Any Rangers in the channel entrance threatened us.

I slowed us down. Shifted more left and right. Drew random length curves in the sea.

Continued to make southern progress. With the bounce of the waves, the changes in distance, any long-range sniper couldn't track us in his scope for long.

Staring into the sun wouldn't help.

They'd expect us to turn in at this point. Instead, I sped right past the channel mouth.

Something rose a few inches out of the water at Zuniga. A trio of Rangers in full tactical scuba and weapons. Ahead and to our left.

Their rifle cartridges banged at us.

Michelle instinctively ducked at the noise. Wobbled on her board. "Sam! Aren't they a little close?"

Flashes of laser light crossed the ocean spray. Announced a sniper. He created a stable shooting platform from the breakwater's black rocks.

Unmoved by wind and wave.

The other two defenders pushed individual sleek black UPDs into the water. Grabbed the controls. Sped off on an intercept course between us and Coronado.

They'd want to funnel us closer to their firepower. Herd us back to the channel ambush.

Probably anticipated a shooting gallery once we entered the channel. Setting up that classic naval strategy, *Crossing-the-T*.

No such luck. Didn't even bother to unsling my long gun in response.

On a less stable platform, buoyed up and down by the ocean waves, I wouldn't hit anything not right in front of me.

Have you ever tried to aim while bouncing up and down in the water at high speed?

"Don't worry, all part of the plan."

Out-Of-Position, I called their strategy.

The deflection angle from the sniper increased, so I straightened out more. Increased our speed.

The Rangers in pursuit couldn't hope to keep up.

We outpaced them. Flew above the waves. Curved around them. Closer to Coronado

The pair wallowed through the surf. Turned this into a stern chase. Clawed in and out of the ocean. Lost distance.

They had to stay near the surface, lest they lose sight of us. They *knew* we had to turn back to the channel entrance at some point. Then they could either intercept us again, or if we evaded, push us into the ambush surely waiting at the narrowest part of the northern channel into the Bay.

Surprise occurs in the mind of your enemy. I switched the music in our ears to play "I Get Around."

Three miles past the channel entrance to the top of the stick part of Coronado is Gator Beach, where the tadpoles in BUD/S roll around in the sand. Just 300 meters wide. Tight next to the Naval Amphibious Base (NAB).

Five minutes later, we hit Gator Beach's shallow sand.

I powered off the eSurfboards with my controller. We each grabbed one out of the water.

A combined 55 pounds of equipment, mostly batteries built into the board, wasn't ideal for me to carry across the sand, but I could easily do the third of a klick across the peninsula.

Hopefully, the SEAL referees wouldn't hold it against us that we ran on their sacred sand right past WARCOM.

Michelle kept up with her own 25 pound load. Carried just the weight of the eSurfboard. Held it in her right hand. Gripped the torpedo tube motor in her left so it stayed balanced.

Her Aqua-shoes slapped the sand past a white wooden life guard tower. Pounded the concrete sidewalk behind me.

We fast-walked along Avenida Lunar. Fenced in WARCOM parking lot on one side. Fifteen-story beach condos on the other.

Our waddle down the street probably looked ridiculous to the couples here to enjoy the sunset, but the *mission* was going well.

Half a block later, Avenida Lunar ended in a T-intersection. Silver Strand Way, a four lane California-style divided highway.

Checked both ways for traffic. Started to cross Silver Strand. Got hung up on the concrete center divider.

Waited for a waddle-sized gap in the speeding cars.

Waddled for the other side!

Crossed a saltwater washed parking lot. Powered down the Glorietta Launching Ramp. It created just the right depth to enter the Bay.

A Petty Officer in dress uniform gaped at us from the deck of an open motorboat tied to a floating pier on the right. A Captain's gig. You'd think he'd be used to odd goings-on near WARCOM.

I pictured the pair of Rangers behind us, pulling their 90 pound UPDs ashore in a fury of practiced motion. Realizing that to chase us, they'd have to haul a lot more weight.

Their fastest solution would be to carry one UPD at a time together.

Right now, they must be radioing their teammates hiding from us in the northern channel. Their teammates who waited in the perfect ambush position, now on the *other* side of the USS Midway from us.

They were all slower than us. Now they had farther to travel.

Rangers who give up don't pass RASP, but these guys could move like Olympic athletes in their outdated gear and they *still* wouldn't catch us.

A car honked back on Silver Strand Way. Our pursuit's turn to play Frogger.

Time to depart. I slid into San Diego Bay. Home once again.

My powered-off board rode steady on the water, protected from the ocean waves by Coronado. The Bay contained a bit of tidal power, but the surface only rippled compared to the rough ocean we'd left behind.

Michelle floated in behind me.

We knelt and balanced on the eSurfboards.

Limbs clear of propellers, I hit the power button on my controller to fire up the electric motors again.

Nothing happened. Sometimes, I hate modern technology.

The sniper team Schnier'd stuck at the end of Zuniga Point reported over the tactical radio feeding Bishop's headset, "Contact, two o'clock. 500 meters. Harper plus HVT. Movin' fast."

They put up a ruckus, firing their I-MILES gear, so Bishop knew where to squint into the sun to find 'em.

Made out Harper and his surf-momma as they skedaddled above the waves on some weird contraptions. Bishop'd never let his teenage stepdaughters wear a tiny wetsuit like that. Wouldn't fit. They'all took after their Samoan mother.

Harper looked happy cruisin' the waves, for someone fixin' to get whupped by Army Rangers. Too afeared, though. He'd already veered off-course. Angled away from the only channel into the bay.

"Pursue." Schnier ordered in response.

Their sniper kept firing. His two teammates dove into the water behind their UPDs. Chased after Harper. Vanished from view. "They're running. We'll cut 'em off."

Schnier popped his red mop of hair up out of the water a few meters away. Looked at Bishop and grinned, "Harper's all hat and no cattle. They'll herd 'em around, doncha worry."

"Not worryin'. Just observin'."

Schnier nodded. Turned back to prepare for the upcoming battle.

A few moments later, their radios crackled again, "Harper's beached. Left the water."

Left the water? Bishop couldn't recall anything in the agreed rules which required the teams to stay in the water. Could Harper get to the Midway that way?

Schnier frowned. "Keep after him."

"In pursuit." The chasing Ranger team grunted and gasped. Must've left their mics active. "Leaving one UPD behind."

Bishop laughed. Coughed. Spit out more water. Turned his UPD toward Coronado.

Schnier's whole platoon was stuck here in the channel. Waiting in ambush for someone who'd never intended to come this way.

Schnier spun through the water right beside him. "Dad gum it! Harper might could make it."

Three of his men trailed behind their own UPDs.

Bishop agreed with Schnier's military assessment.

Schnier and his men pulled ahead.

Bishop's UPD must not be as fast. Had nothin' to do with his muscles, nor swimmin' ability.

The four of them reached a pile of rocks leaving the water. Not even a beach.

Schnier and his trio rolled their UPDs up onto the rocks. "Two men per."

Slung his rifle. Demonstrated. Grabbed one side of his now above-water propulsion device.

Trailing behind, Bishop crashed his UPD into a square boulder. Left it there. Crawled out of the water.

Dry land!

Schnier shook his head. "You gonna help?"

"Just here to observe." Bishop stood. From the added height, a road paralleled the shore. Not too far away, maybe thirty meters.

The only sign of life a yellow pickup truck parked next to a weird Navy building built into a dirt berm. *Miguel's Handyman Services* and a local phone number on its side.

In pairs, Schnier and his three rangers carried two UPDs.

Bishop trailed along behind them. What was Schnier's plan? Couldn't hope to walk across the miles to where Coronado hit the bay again.

Schnier found Miguel on the other side of his work vehicle. A stocky Hispanic man, but with Bishop's darker skin tone. "We need your truck."

Miguel's accent sounded south of the border, "My truck? No way."

Schnier explained something in Spanish. Miguel shook his head. Their voices rose. Schnier won.

At least, Schnier and his men loaded two of the UPDs onto the truck's roof rack, designed for construction materials.

Miguel strapped them down. Pointed a pair of fingers at the ripped upholstery in his cab. "Dos."

Schnier gestured for one of his men to climb in.

Got in after him. Closed the door. "Pier K."

Miguel took the driver's seat. Fired up the engine. "Kah muelle." *K dock.*

Bishop put his hands on the rim of Schnier's open window, "No ride for Top?"

"You're just observin', right? Vehicle only transports combat forces."

Bishop sighed. A first lieutenant on his first tour with the rangers, bless his heart, outranked a first sergeant. Despite the first sergeant's decades more seniority.

He lifted his hands from the door. "Send the truck back for us."

Schnier yelled into the wind as they drove away, "We'll get 'em, come hell or high water."

Bishop walked after them with Schnier's other soldier, a lowly spec-4. Sand ground at every joint inside his shorts.

Dagnabbit, that truck better come back.

Chapter Three:
You Don' t Know What I' ve Got

I pounded on the side of the controller. Shook the water off the case. Tried the button again.

Still nothing. Whiskey Tango Foxtrot.

Technology blows.

Instead of relying on the guys from the Agency who do secure classified transport to ensure no damage, I should've double-checked everything myself before we got on the Navy whirlybird.

Stupid.

No way we could swim to the USS Midway. Not fast enough to evade the Rangers about to catch up to us.

We'd made it to land. Coronado Bridge crossed the bay a mile away. Its tall concrete curve connected the fattest part of the peninsula to downtown San Diego.

Maybe we run the rest of the way? Steal that Petty Officer's boat?

I shrugged at Michelle. "Doesn't work. Feel like a run?"

With the right equipment, I could override the electronics in a boat. Back in high school, I'd done that enough with cars around here.

"Even if we made it on foot, you'd fail your real mission."

She was right. If we ditched the eSurfboards because they malfunctioned, even if we beat the Rangers to the USS Midway, the observers would rightfully fail the test run anyway.

The Midway wasn't the objective. Just the criteria to prove my eSurfboard was better in many circumstances than the existing Spec Ops waterborne options.

"Pretty soon a pair of pissed off Rangers will come over the crest of that boat ramp and shoot us. Any ideas?"

Could use a good idea right about now, otherwise my whole tech test would be a failure.

I'd never make the 1LT promotion list.

Michelle pulled the spare controller out of her wetsuit's breast pocket. "Try this?"

Duh! I leaned over. Snagged it out of her hand. Pushed the power button.

Beautiful emerald lights. The power was on again. "I could kiss you!"

"Easy, dude. You gave it to me in case of an emergency, remember?"

I tapped at her controller. Designated my board again as the leader. Put her secondary board into 5-meter follow-mode. "Gotta go now."

She knelt. Held on.

I stood. Pulled the accelerator.

We flew across the bay, steady as rocks above its more level water.

No longer bounced up and down by ocean swells, Michelle stood up on her board. "More fun this way!"

Crack! Crack! Blanks behind us at the boat ramp.

No lasers found their targets.

Well away from the pursuit, I didn't look back.

We flew in formation under Coronado bridge. Six-foot one-inch tall, standing on a board two feet above the water, I had plenty of clearance under the bridge girders while I dodged between a pair of the concrete pilings holding it up.

She pointed at a coast-guard-orange buoy. It bobbed on the other side of the bridge. "Isn't that a speed limit sign?"

Technically, we should travel a lot slower. "That's for civilian boats, not for uh, military vehicles. Ignore it."

We waved at the line of bare-masted sailboats anchored for protection in the bay. Cut between them and the Coronado Skatepark on the peninsula's inner coast.

When I skated there as a kid, pretty sure I didn't expect to see myself as an adult speed past at 30 mph two-feet above the bay.

The path of our boards bent along the curvature of the peninsula as it widened. We rounded a corner.

Pedestrians strolled with babies. Trailed pairs of dogs on leashes. Stared and pointed at us standing above the water. No visible means of propulsion.

Past the corner park, we had a straight shot diagonally across the bay to the USS Midway.

Four-acres of flight deck. As tall as a twenty-story building. Just another mile of open water to go.

No way our opponents' slower propulsion devices could catch us from either direction. I changed the music to play "Little Deuce Coupe" in our earpieces.

Time to relax.

At Pier K, ahead on the left, just before an active aircraft carrier in port, two Rangers unloaded UPDs from a yellow pickup truck. Only half a mile from the Midway. Could easily beat us there.

Occasionally, I forget Ranger dudes aren't newbs.

I pointed at the new Rangers for Michelle's benefit. "When the dudes behind us radioed to the ambushers where we'd gone, two of them must've hitched a ride across the island rather than swim around it."

"That sucks. Was a good plan."

"Maybe not good enough."

"I'm sorry, Sam."

Not ready to give up yet.

"Those sea walls protecting the carrier will slow them down. No need to panic quite yet. May still make it. After all, they don't know what we've got."

Pulled tight on the accelerator trigger. Maybe I could ease another smidgen of performance out of our batteries and motors in these calm conditions.

At least go down trying.

The Rangers worked as a team. Tossed their UPDs over the sea walls one at a time. Helped each other scramble over.

Guess they'd done it before the other direction. Must get lots of practice infiltrating fortifications.

They moved to an interception course to meet us just before the Midway's prow. A rope ladder wavered as if to invite us from the bay up to the netting above.

They'd arrive before we did.

I held us on a steady course. Straight through the tidal flow.

They swooped in a curve to the side. Released their UPDs. Treaded water.

No way to get around them, so I unslung my M4.

The two OPFOR readied their similar carbines for our arrival. No range advantage based on weapon-type in this engagement.

This time, however, I had more of the fixed platform advantage. Even in just the tidal motion of the Bay, they couldn't help but bounce up and down a bit.

Have you ever tried to aim while bobbing up and down in the water? We were still far out of their effective range with that level of interference.

I held the controller with my left hand. Supported the foregrip of my carbine with them. Selected semi-auto with my right hand, which took my weapon off safe.

Finger straight outside the trigger guard. I targeted the closest Ranger.

Focused through the scope. Relaxed.

Took a slow breath. The sight's reticle crossed my target. I pressed the trigger straight back.

Two blank cartridges cracked in my ears as I double-tapped the closest Ranger.

The I-MILES laser instantly shot out. Popped him center mass. Lit him up.

He raised his weapon horizontally as a casualty.

The second Ranger desperately sprayed his own blank rounds and laser beams at us.

Not even close.

With my rifle tucked into my shoulder, a steady seven feet above the surface of the bay, I reset my aim. Nailed his halo of helmet sensors.

Two down. Game over.

I selected SAFE. Slung my long gun.

We surfed past the pair, each dead in the water. Rippled them with our wake. The closest was a red-headed 1LT.

I shrugged as we passed him. "Sorry, Bro."

He shook his fist at us, but I bet his heart wasn't really in it.

Michelle gave them a delighted smile and a princess wave of her hand. Beating the pretend bad guys is fun.

A few seconds later, I released the accelerator.

A rope ladder dangled from the net below the prow. We coasted into it. "Thank you for enjoying our sunset flying cruise. Please board the carrier at the flight deck."

She giggled. I fought desperately to hide a grin. Might make 1LT after all.

Michelle's adrenaline from her impersonation of an HVT eventually wore off; left her hollow. Now her real work began. Was she up to persuading Sam to transform his life plans?

She wanted independence. Freedom from the career bureaucrats in Langley, but she had to go along to get ahead for now.

Back at WARCOM, she chose a shoulderless tie-dye sarong and black sandals to get out of her mostly air-dried wetsuit.

The others must preserve some semblance of their military uniforms, but she was under no such restriction.

She preferred a smooth, silky, flowing feel, which emphasized all the right assets to improve her social interactions with the local soldiers and sailors.

While Sam and the defeated Rangers talked through their endless post-battle analysis with the SEAL observers, she excused herself to use a private video conference room in the base's Sensitive Compartmented Information Facility (SCIF).

Had her own report to make.

Locking the conference room door behind her, she activated the in-use light outside.

Settled into an oversized black and gray conference room chair in front of a video teleconference screen. Stared into a pair of microphones and a camera.

Nothing but the best government procured equipment for

Special Operations Command (SOCOM).

Wire mesh built into the walls created a Faraday cage. Prevented any electronic leaks.

Two-inched of acoustic material on each wall dampened sounds. Prevented any audible leaks. As a bonus, no echos.

Her heart pounded in the dead silence.

She typed a CIA IP address into the telepresence system's tablet computer. From the DOD's secure network, she could reach the CIA's comm-net.

Bee-boo-bah-beep.

The Korea Mission Center's SCIF near the nation's capital appeared on the screen. The Assistant Director for Korea, Edward Metcalf, leaned forward in his chair.

She ignored his hulking athletic build. Back channels claimed he used it to make others underestimate his organizational savvy.

Neck-length tight dreads didn't fit with his Burberry pinstriped cashmere suit.

He didn't bother to fake a smile, but his deep bass voice created a sense of warmth anyway, "How's my favorite Berkeley non-diversity hire?"

Three hours later in the Eastern Time Zone, he could've just had her email a report. Clearly found this call more important than he'd be willing to let on.

Maybe the clothes she'd chosen earlier weren't the best choice. Wasn't usually this self-conscious.

"Evening, sir. Mission went according to plan. My little bit of sabotage passed unnoticed."

Sam's power controller wasn't as unreliable as he thought, but what he didn't know wouldn't hurt him. He'd just chalk it up to a random component failure.

The CIA's technical branch was every bit as good as the Pentagon's. Even better when it came to micro-electronics surgery.

The room's telepresence system used its stereo microphones to locate her and zoom the main camera at her face.

He nodded. "The target's reaction?"

"Convinced I saved his demonstration and his career.

Perfectly positioned for the next phase."

"Assuming that's true, I look forward to your work under the Chief of Station in Seoul as the new military attaché. It'll do his Yale ass good to have an up-and-comer push him. Maybe he can get back to DC and not waste away in Southeast Asia."

Assuming that's true? Metcalf graduated from Harvard and never resisted an opportunity to flaunt his pedigree.

Insecure men could be useful, but they *so* annoyed her at times. "It's a sure thing, sir."

"Better be. I've groomed a local protege in Seoul. Interested to see how you two stack up against each other, especially if we need to fill the Chief's shoes. First you need to earn your own ticket on Korean Air."

He made a throat-cutting gesture to an aide off-screen. The video conference session ended.

She hoped she'd sounded more confident than she felt. Her boss's boss, like most people, looked out for himself.

Wouldn't trust him even if he claimed to be her friend, but if she could align his interests with hers, she'd take advantage of this opportunity.

After all, she fully intended to be the youngest CIA Station Chief in Agency history. She'd bow and scrape to D.C. as required to run her own Station. To no longer be forced to kowtow to some local halfwit.

Michelle wiped the last call record from the telepresence tablet. Her instructors at The Farm taught her to never leave loose ends lying around.

A SEAL bonfire on Gator Beach is more like an attempt to repopulate the stars with embers. The SEAL observers built it from a tepee of telephone-pole sized logs once we'd completed our post-exercise banter. To get their tactical gloves on my eSurfboards for their own future use, they rolled out the fish tacos.

Good intelligence.

Sun long gone, the moon hung low over the water; provided just enough light to spot infiltrators from the ocean.

Previous occupants abandoned a weathered rowboat

upturned in the sand, so I guess they weren't worried about serious theft.

The bonfire threw shadows behind the wooden lifeguard shack, another obvious approach. At least the base and the street had security lights on.

For a beach next to a top secret amphibious facility, we weren't actually that secure.

On the other side of a tall dune and a privacy fence WARCOM built a nice grassy picnic area, but I guess they'd prepped for the mission aftermath and knew I'd prefer to hang out at the beach.

SEALs prepare well. Trust and rely on each other. Felt like a family who welcomed distant in-laws to dinner.

Nice to hang out with them and the Rangers, if only for one night. That's the kind of team I'd love to join.

Once I finished saving off the collected data, there was nothing for me to worry about until I returned to my platoon with the test results. Then, I'd need to finish a pile of reports about this trip.

Without as much to do, the Rangers reached the party ahead of me. Appeared from the burnt aluminum and dark glass in the fire they'd already tossed back a few.

That hot-headed 1LT Schnier, who led the Ranger defenders, loudly pointed me out as I arrived, "There's the smug hombre what swam over the land. Thought this was 'posed to be an underwater test."

We won, so I shrugged. No need to make more waves.

"One of this board's advantages is its lighter weight and better balance. Just a little demonstration of those enhancements."

"That board y'all rode must be hot stuff if it let a Big Army fella like you slide past a platoon of Rangers."

Ignoring his implications, I went for modesty. "Well-designed."

"Where'd ya learn to infiltrate places like that?" 1SG Bishop, the 75th RRC's wickedly wise top NCO, asked.

A nice enough dude. Not like my background was a secret.

I pointed across the bay to San Diego, "Snuck in and out of group homes and foster care around those hills. Used to surf with some of the SEALs. Ever roll with Jocko? Dude's a real bruiser. Owns a local MMA gym."

Schnier shook his head at the name. No recognition. "Explains a lot. Still might coulda had ya."

He pulled foil-wrapped Mahi Mahi grilled with brown sugar and pineapple out of the fire. Set it on an unburnt log. Blew on his fingers.

"Least the SEALs know how to throw a shindig. Gotta remember this stuff for barbecues on the ranch once I get my twenty in."

Credit where credit is due. "Where'd you dudes learn to hitchhike like that?"

"Anyone who wears a tan beret knows to improvise when faced with an enemy in a faster ride."

He shrugged, "Raised in the Republic o'Texas, so I spoke his language. Besides, government contractor on a Navy base? Couldn't say no. Welcome to Cali, right?"

"Only tourists call it that." I wandered to find some food.

Michelle arrived fashionably late.

Regulations stuck the rest of us in a semblance of uniform, but she'd changed from her wetsuit into some kind of translucent sarong wrap thing. Pretty sure I heard a few low whistles from the back of the crowd, but she wisely ignored them, or at least accepted them as her due.

Once the tale swapping, carbonated beverages, and Mahi Mahi tacos ran out, Michelle pulled me aside to chat alone. I had a gift for her, anyway, so was happy to comply.

We sat opposite each other on a pair of the telephone-pole sized logs the SEALs ran into the surf with to train.

She was officially an accountant with the CIA. If a government employee tells you they're a web developer with the CIA, they probably are. The accountants mostly aren't, even if their degree is in accounting and not in political science, like Michelle.

Who ever heard of a government accountant fresh from a poly sci degree?

Political analyst? Operations Officer, even?

But accountant?

Michelle leaned forward. Her sarong dipped toward the sand, her face hidden and revealed as the firelight danced across it.

"How do you like your current deployment?"

"After today? Better all the time."

"It's up soon, right? Do you plan another round with the engineers or to look for a different position?"

"They can use me and I get to build a lot of toys to play with."

She smiled. "At some point, if you want a real career as an Army Officer, get promoted to higher ranks, you need different types of experience, right?"

Where was this heading?

"Yeah, need a little time in command of a combat unit, to work on a joint operations staff, that kind of thing. Why?"

She pressed her finger briefly against her lips. "Don't tell anyone, but I have a new job I'm starting; sort of with the Army, sort of with the State Department. Military Attaché in the Seoul Embassy. Officially, I'll help manage the defense procurement contracts with suppliers located in Korea. Sort of an accounting job.

"When I talked to the people giving my interviews, I heard about another open position available, is all. Might interest you, with your promotion."

A CIA accountant. *Right.* Well, maybe her idea could get me out from under my paperwork Colonel. Sticking with the wrong leader sucks.

"What's the job? Designing stuff for use in Korea or to get built there? 'Cause I've worked hard to get my current engineering platoon to a level of competence I'm pretty proud of. I don't want to throw all that effort away."

"You already passed Ranger training, right? Things are heating up in Korea.

"The 75th Regimental Special Troops Battalion plans to send an MI platoon to support the RRC at Camp Kim. Support Major Williams, Schnier, and the others.

"The current MI platoon leader will be promoted to Captain and transferred back to a Regular Army company in a few months. I work with people who know people in Military Intelligence. With their recommendation, you'd be a sure thing.

"Apply to lead the platoon, get good experience in a two-year deployment, and we work together over there."

She practically bounced off her seat. "Awesome, right?"

"Slow down, there. Graduating from Ranger School just means I get a Ranger Tab to wear on my shoulder and maybe a few points in my promotion packet. Doesn't mean I have all the quals to join the 75th Ranger Regiment.

"Military Intelligence? You know what an oxymoron is, right? Besides, I don't want to owe anybody anything to get ahead."

Maybe she joked, but she sure looked serious all of a sudden. "Sam, why'd you join the Army in the first place?"

Women play dirty. Why'd she brought that up?

She knew today was the 20th anniversary. "Don't remind me. What happened to my parents shouldn't happen to anyone, that's all. Besides, I heard the Army was one big happy family, even if like a group home you usually get assigned your new siblings instead of choosing them."

"Trust me, this is an opportunity to choose your path. You can protect a lot more families leading a special operations platoon in Korea, technically at war with the DPRK across the DMZ, than you ever will playing with your toys in an engineering lab, even a military engineering lab."

For a lady who'd graduated from Berkeley in political science, she made a lot of sense. I considered it for a minute.

Did she understand the paperwork required for an officer to switch his MOS? A change away from engineering for sure, but intelligence work?

Maybe they'd let me do fieldwork, infiltrate places, as well.

A Ranger and a SEAL grabbed a log together and tossed it on the bonfire.

A shadow from the flare-up crossed her face. "It's the smart thing to do."

I pressed my chin into my palm. Pondered for another minute. "Perhaps."

The firelight flickered onto her face again. She slipped her finger into the corner of her mouth. Smiled at me. "And we'll have fun in Seoul."

There were obstacles. "They don't take Second Lieutenants as platoon leaders in the Regiment, so I'll have to get my promotion by then, plus get through RASP 2. That's no joke."

I waved around at the beach near WARCOM. "It's like BUD/S, but you test for the Rangers instead of the SEALs. All these Ranger dudes have been through it."

"You already have a TOP SECRET clearance for your current job. Could probably teach the Combat Water Survival Test. I know you can run, unless you stopped after high school. Maybe you need more ruck hikes after this desk job, but you'll pass.

"If you fail, what's the worst that happens, you go back to your current assignment, right?"

I nodded. "But also probably get stuck for a while after that. No more preferred assignment choices if I wipe out that way. Drop me to the bottom of the promotion list for Captain; force me to start over. Not many pass RASP. It's a big risk." I sighed. "I'll consider it."

She put her hands on her slender hips. Frowned. More cute than intimidating. "Do more than that. I want to see you in Seoul. Need a friend out there. It's a big assignment. Need your support. You going to leave me alone with those Rangers?"

Shook my head, more at her ploy than in real disagreement.

"Have I ever steered you wrong? I mean, I came up with that backup controller today, didn't I? Right now you're sort of playing with house money, in terms of your career."

I maybe owed her one. I'd have thought of the backup controller, eventually. Maybe even before the dudes chasing us arrived.

Time to stall so I could think it over. "Speaking of owing you."

I reached into a cargo pocket. Pulled out a large, flat jewelry box.

My heartbeat accelerated. "Here."

Her eyes widened, but she took the velvet box. Opened it to reveal the striated shell necklace I'd made for her.

Black and white alternated in the shells, like yin and yang, good and evil. She picked it up, dangled the clacking shells in front of the fire reflected in her eyes, and examined their curved patterns.

Smiled and pressed it against her chest. "Beautiful."

Don't know why I worried. "Collected them from low tide while we prepped for this acceptance test. It's to say thanks for you arranging to come play my HVT to escort. Otherwise, I would've been stuck with some engineering dude who can't jump nor swim."

"Oh, Sam. You're impossible. I can't take this. Not if you won't come to Korea."

Korea. A big risk, but life on another continent might be fun. A Ranger Major had to be a better boss than a Pentagon Colonel, right?

At least they have advanced technology there. I'd already gambled on my friend using my skills once today and won the jackpot.

Half of Ranger candidates pass RASP and qualify to join the 75th Regiment. I've never finished in the bottom half of anything in my life, except maybe when they handed out family histories. I wouldn't fail now.

At least I could trust Michelle to look after me in Seoul.

Argh! "Fine, I'll come, I'll come. With you on board, I can snag any wave they toss at me."

Maybe. If I pass the Ranger Assessment and Selection Program. Less paperwork to do at Fort Benning, anyway.

"Put it on already!"

She jumped up and gave me a bear hug. I didn't think the necklace was *that* great.

Ranger Selection and then Korea, here I come.

PART TWO

RED TEAM

Chapter Four:
The Unexamined Life

Just a normal day at work in Special Operations Command - Korea, right? The North Korean People's Army were all tucked away safely on their side of the DMZ.

SOCKOR, pronounced sock-core, assigned my Military Intelligence platoon half of an ancient red brick building, topped with a Japanese-style roof leftover from World War II, in Camp Kim. I leaned back in my utilitarian office chair.

Logistics had stuffed my desk into a coyote tan cubicle. Matched my Ranger boots and beret. Don't ask me how the Army pulled that one off.

Officially, Michelle was a military attaché with the American Embassy in Seoul, but her real duties were an open secret in the Special Operations community.

She wore her State-Department-chic outfit, adding an over-engineered shell necklace and sensible black shoes to hike the subway. Must have a meeting at the embassy later.

No glasses today; probably wearing contacts.

She draped one black-skirted thigh on the edge of my desk. Leaned against the tan cubicle partition.

I poked the hosiery keeping her otherwise exposed knee warm. "Make yourself at home."

"Su casa es mi casa."

"That's not exactly how it's supposed to work."

We chatted while waiting for my platoon sergeant to arrive for our usual Friday morning intelligence update. I'd hopefully get back to studying the disassembled electronics on my desk later, after they both left.

Michelle played with the necklace I'd given her in San Diego, letting each shell rattle against the next one like a diamondback snake.

"When will you get to surf?"

Not that I'd admit it to her, but in the month I'd worked here, sometimes I wished I hadn't let Michelle talk me into this two-year tour of duty away from the Big Army.

Change is tough.

"Unless I want to illegally surf a river tidal bore in China, or wait for a typhoon to hit, my wave-riding days are over for a while."

Not sure this change was worth the pain.

"Yellow Sea isn't so far."

"Could ride some storm surge there, but the waves would take me north across the international border into North Korea. That's a no-go.

"Nope, Seoul is my self-imposed punishment detail."

She flashed me a bright smile. "Seoul isn't so bad. I'm here. We just need to hang out more after work.

"The Agency gives me an expense account so I can spend it, after all."

I shook my head, "Dense cities away from the ocean are places for me to visit sparingly, not live in. Too many people equals too many potential threats. The crowded sight-lines make situational awareness impossible in peacetime."

"Don't tell me you'd rather be in Seoul during a firefight?"

"Don't want anyone hurt, but in an urban battle you can keep friendlies segregated. Perform reconnaissance by fire everywhere else."

I grinned. "For some reason, the Army prefers Rangers avoid those destructive tactics within *friendly* cities, especially when not actually fighting anyone.

"Rules of Engagement suck, dude."

She let go of her necklace. "Well, I love the city. All the people, the exotic food, the checkerboard of lights on the night skyline."

"Kimchi? Ten million people, spread across forever?

"Drives me crazy. No good escape routes. Those glass skyscrapers will collapse in a heap of dust and broken concrete if North Korea ever opens up with all the artillery they've pointed across the DMZ.

"Overkill, if you ask me."

"You must love Kim and Yongsan, then."

Camp Kim is part of the 630 acre Garrison Yongsan, aka *Dragon Mountain*. Stuck like a target in the center of Seoul, it's within one of the few depopulated areas downtown.

"There's a thousand sniper perches overlooking every part of the city, including Yongsan's perimeter walls. Not exactly the safest location for a military base."

Michelle just shook her head.

"That nearby double-hill with a stiletto tower on top is about the only nearby open space. Mostly they cram people into those block-sized multi-story apartment buildings."

I mock shuddered.

She leaned back. "Hey, I live up in one of those apartment buildings, which you'd know, if you ever bothered to visit me in the month since you've been here.

"It's not so bad."

"Probably better than the BOQ at the air base."

She winked. "You'll have to show me sometime."

Women.

Sergeant First Class (SFC) Lee Dong-geon walked up, distracted by the most recent reports on his issue phone. He wore the South Korean black-and-green digital equivalent of my own camouflage uniform.

Michelle straightened up at his approach. Glanced at a pretend watch on her wrist.

Wasn't like him to be late.

The Korean Central Intelligence Agency (KCIA) embedded Lee as my platoon's senior NCO. Nice to have help from a local, but naturally he and Michelle rarely saw eye-to-eye.

She was almost six inches taller than Lee, so she mostly admired his thick black hair from above. That's an issue I encountered in most of my dealings with the locals; they tended to be much-shorter-than-tall-Americans. I deliberately *sat* at my desk for our morning briefings.

I blanked my face. Didn't pay to take sides between them. "Let's get started."

As usual, Michelle had the latest skinny from the Korea Mission Center in D.C.

With half a world of time zone differences, thirteen hours apart, our stateside counterparts worked their daytime while we slept. We worked while they slept.

Intelligence frequently got lost in temporal translation.

"Sam, Lee, the most critical issue is from the Air Force's Cybersecurity Center. They report a massive increase in hacking attempts against the ROK's top secret metallurgical lab."

Lee shook his head at us, "That's unconfirmed intelligence. Wouldn't put too much credence in it, sir."

He liked to read the raw reports and form his own opinions, which sometimes contradicted the summaries the CIA sent us.

As part of our work attached to the Ranger Reconnaissance Company (RRC) to support the South Koreans, my MI platoon filed a preliminary report about the lab two days ago. We found eight critical and high vulnerabilities, plus dozens of less serious issues with their security.

Not good.

Michelle tugged on her shell necklace. "It's not unconfirmed that distributed network traffic maxed out the lab's inbound links. The traffic's source shifted as fast as the Cyber guys could squash it, but the DPRK is the obvious originator.

"Who else would care?"

"Scuttlebutt says the lab's ROK Army security guards aren't happy about our report." Lee sighed, "Respect and embarrassment are more important in Korea than in America. We've made them look incompetent. The network attack could be a misguided attempt to show us up."

Lee tutored me daily on Korean language skills, but he seemed happiest when he explained cultural issues.

For example, Koreans write names the opposite of Americans. Their family name is first, followed by a two-part given name. The first given name can be shared by everyone of the same generation in the family. The second is that individual's specific name.

So Lee, his very common family name, plus Dong, his shared generational name, plus Geon. Sergeant Lee Dong-geon.

To complicate names, Koreans habitually referred to people using a relationship title, like Uncle, Mother, or Teacher.

Took serious work to decode who a Korean was talking about, but I liked the formal informality of it all.

"Well, if the shoe fits . . . Fortunately, our report didn't find any vulnerabilities from the network side. The lab isolates top secret data on a separate network. In fact, it's too isolated.

"They need to improve their off-site backup plans.

"Really, the lab's security needs to worry about physical access to the facility. Lee, what's the most serious vulnerability in our report?"

"The retinal scanner. Protects the heart of the lab, the experiments, where the scientists work and keep their data. Unless you pass the mantrap with the retinal scanner, you can't get past the routine administrative areas."

I nodded, now that he mentioned it, I recalled the theoretical article we'd based our analysis on.

"Then I'll prove that vulnerability out today."

Michelle shook her head. "Shouldn't we wait to get lab security's feedback on your preliminary report? I hate to say it, but Lee is right, you need to show them you're part of the team."

"We should prove the worst vulnerability exists *before* one of the locals calls it unconfirmed speculation and ignores it.

"The glass door into the gym SOCKOR just built has the same retinal scanner. If I crack that, it proves we're right."

Major Williams, the commanding officer of the RRC, my current boss, authorized me to test the weaknesses listed in our most recent report.

At least, he didn't say no to my emailed request when I submitted the report, which I took as authorization.

Lee messaged me and Michelle the link to our report from his phone. "Do you want me and an analyst to assist?"

A convenient excuse to work outside, get away from my desk, wasn't an opportunity I'd miss.

"Thanks for the offer, but no need for the whole Red Team. It's just one door. It'll look less unusual to the operators who work out in the fitness center if I go alone. Just need an RFID scanner/transmitter. I can take care of the rest."

Michelle leaned forward. "The CIA has one in the Embassy. Our facilities are vulnerable if the retinal scanner isn't secure."

She laughed. "That'd embarrass a few people. I'll let you borrow it, if I can watch and write up my own report."

I'd been here a month and she and I hadn't had a good opportunity to connect. Of course she could come along.

I stayed casual, "Sure, won't take long. If you take the subway to your office to pick up the scanner, we can do lunch at the Officer's Club afterward."

"Sounds like a date."

Paperwork always takes longer than expected, especially when you're single and new to town with a hot date planned. Or at least, some semblance thereof, with our ancient history.

Call it a working relationship for now.

After signing off on a million forms, I had Lee snap a set of infrared photos of my eye using my military issue phone camera. Printed the closeups at actual size, plus a few two-percent larger and smaller.

During ROTC our instructors drilled into us the necessity of contingency planning.

Our building opened up onto one of Camp Kim's internal streets, cleaved out of Seoul by an Army-green block wall topped by concertina wire.

To comply with a base design pattern stored in the Pentagon somewhere, a baseball field hibernated across the street; its brown grass maintained in razor-sharp rows by the local cadre.

I'd read in Seoul Survivor that the Spouses Club scheduled weekend tournaments when it was warmer, but otherwise SOCKOR mostly used the outfield as an ad-hoc soccer pitch.

No point in shipping a personal vehicle from base to base, but the gym was within easy walking distance. Michelle would meet me there for our *date*.

The iced-up sidewalk conspired against my desire to be on

time. Leaning forward to preserve my balance, I strode out.

Rapidly advanced on the objective.

Today was my best opportunity for a little fun since San Diego. Like everything else before suffering past RASP, that seemed a lifetime ago.

Michelle must've pulled plenty of strings to get me into Korea this fast, but I guess the 75th Regimental Special Troops Battalion (RSTB) really wanted a new MI platoon leader with a technical engineering background.

My tan Ranger beret didn't protect my ears and neck from the cold. Frozen rain rattled down at me like long-range machine-gun fire, bullets spent by the distance, but with a bit of sting remaining.

Should've brought more gear than just my uniform coat and issue cargo pants.

Numbness crept into my hands. Maybe I could find a gap in the weather for my attempt.

I dodged from building to building. Sought cover from the hailstorm under their ample eaves.

Toughened by decades of coal soot, most of Camp Kim's red brick buildings suffered beneath steep Japanese roofs.

Nuking Hiroshima and Nagasaki ultimately liberated Korea. Ended the Japanese occupation the older locals eternally refuse to forgive.

After America smashed the Empire of the Rising Sun, the Koreans assigned us Japan's leftover buildings.

Recently, the Army has sprouted some newer buildings, like the gym just ahead; a sparkling diamond buried in red charcoal.

Who spends thousands of dollars to secure a glass door into an exercise room full of Special Joes with a retinal scanner, anyway?

The Army, that's who.

Specifically, SOCKOR, determined to keep the nearby Big Army riffraff out of Camp Kim's new exercise facilities.

Sure, they built the floor to ceiling windows and the door from tempered glass, but that's nothing a rock or an elbow wouldn't solve, if anyone *actually* tried to break in.

Erection of the fitness center had nothing to do with the

SOCKOR Commander wanting a finer gym than the grunts used in the rest of Yongsan.

Nope, not at all.

I blew on my hands to recover some feeling. Fast walking kept the rest of me warm.

Rangers and Green Beanies in PT gear dripped sweat together inside the palace. Black issue shorts and sweatshirts emblazoned with "75 RANGER STB" in imitation of our normal shoulder scroll distinguished the good guys from the rest.

The hum of treadmill motors and the thump of running shoes kept time with their miles.

Oh, don't get me wrong, there'd be a chance to ruck run on the chilly streets later, but for individual workouts, most of the Spec Ops dawn patrol avoided numbing their hands and feet in the brisk wind.

A repetitive clacking sounded behind me. Light steps crunched across the parking lot. Both just sharp enough to hear over the clank of weights inside the gym. I looked back.

Michelle carried her purse and the RFID antenna I'd asked to borrow.

Her necklace clanged in time with every other step. Does the Agency still teach stealth in The Farm these days?

My fault, I guess.

"Here." She handed me the antenna. Nodded toward the glass. "We're on stage. This better work."

Half the dudes on the other side of the gym's glass front wall didn't bother to disguise their stares. The other half were either oblivious or just better at covert surveillance.

Likely wondered what I was doing with a handful of electronics and our cute CIA liaison officer.

Didn't need people distractions and *certainly* didn't need to worry about how the operators in our company judged my actions.

A radio frequency identification card (RFID) reader set into the wall, about the size and shape of a playing card, secured the fitness center's entrance. I cloned my valid access card using Michelle's portable scanner/transmitter connected via USB cable to my ruggedized military issue smartphone.

Sending my RFID signal would trigger the bulbous retinal scanner at chest height.

Shoulder height for most operators, who ran a little on the tall side, but I'm even a little taller than most.

Either way, the South Korean contractors who'd installed the retinal scanner next to the glass door were likely shorter than anyone who would ever actually use it.

The gym's retinal scanner is the same model used in the lab and countless other protected facilities around the world.

Was also made by the lowest qualified bidder. Built to a spec sheet created by a bureaucrat who didn't understand the technology.

I swiped the RFID transmitter's antenna across the embedded reader. That sent my ID. Triggered an eyeball check.

The access LED turned yellow. Ready to go.

I pressed the life-size infrared photo of my eye up to the optical sensor.

The access light glared red, mocking my inability to pass the glass door's security.

Wipe out.

The scanner looked for an infrared image of the specific eyeball associated with the RFID number transmitted. Sounds foolproof, right? Well, to this fool it'd be epic to prove it wasn't.

Leaning over holding my phone and the RFID transmitter in the air for the next half-hour was a good way to lose situational awareness. Not to mention gain a stiff neck and back.

I knelt on the frigid concrete sidewalk. Let my equipment rest on the ground until needed.

Fist-sized whitewashed rocks, spaced with military regularity, like pre-positioned glass-smashing ammo, edged the walkway; the only visible remains of an unlucky grunt's punishment detail.

"Why didn't my eyeball photo do the trick? Should be a perfect size and infrared pattern match for my actual eye."

The ruby red LED said I was sinking fast.

"How would I know? You're supposed to be the techie around here." Michelle was always lots of help in these situations.

"No worries." Yet. "Just the first try."

I shifted on the rough concrete. Adjusted which knee froze faster.

Swiped across the door's reader. Transmitted the cloned RFID signal again.

Inhale and hold. Yellow light.

Were there size and scale distortions from the way the infrared camera in the scanner worked? I switched to a slightly larger eyeball photo. Presented it instead.

Red light. I exhaled. Another wipe out.

Michelle pressed up against the Ranger Tab and Scroll on the left shoulder of my camouflage jacket. The jasmine and citrus shampoo from her amber brown hair arrived in a wave.

She swayed over me. Stared at the photos I'd taken. At the retinal scanner. "How much longer? Will it work?"

Getting this right was sketchy enough without olfactory interruptions. "Give me a minute. We'll see."

I dug my fingernails into my palms. Why didn't this work?

Took a deliberate breath. Triggered the badge reader.

Yellow ready light.

Held up a smaller photo for my third attempt.

Another red LED stared at me in my real eye.

No pressure, but definitely a flaw in my technique.

The retinal scanner's little plastic protective dome contained a tiny infrared camera. That recorded blood vessels in the eye.

A camera just like the one on my phone.

Only one camera lens. Not stereo vision. A flat photo should look just the same as an eye to it, shouldn't it?

Breathe in. Breathe out. Forget all that. Focus.

Shook my head. "Gimme some space."

Michelle swayed a little, but didn't break contact.

Wanted to know if the issue retinal scanners were vulnerable almost as much as I did. Tens of millions of South Koreans would be vulnerable if the North Korean dictatorship got the lab's research.

"Try again."

Queen of tact. Already knew to try again. Muttered a phrase in Spanish I'd learned while working in a warehouse in response. Focused on getting the photo placement just right.

Felt her breathing slowdown in synchronicity with mine. Put her out of my mind.

Swipe. Yellow light.

Next size eyeball photo up.

Red light.

Maybe I should've perfected this by myself. Without an audience.

Kneeling here goofy-footed wouldn't endear me to 1LT Schnier, leader of the Ranger platoon working out in the gym. The platoon we'd evaded in San Diego.

A former West Point linebacker, built for long ruck hikes over uneven terrain, he watched us from a pullup bar just inside the door. The lack of sweat in his abbreviated ginger hair showed how little effort he put into his slow chin-ups.

Party dude.

Nor would it endear me to First Sergeant Bishop, the RRC's black NCO.

Bishop way too casually sat on a weight bench. He'd slowly mopped his brow with a puke green towel this whole time. His rest between sets never lasted anywhere near that long.

Company's momma bear.

My MI platoon's tasking to analyze sensitive installations for SOCKOR took me out of the direct chain of command for the shooters. We mostly fed them information.

Typical localism led to inevitable friction between the support analysts in my platoon and the Ranger operators.

Bringing Michelle to a gym full of soldiers was perhaps a mistake. I didn't totally fit in, so I guess my desire to finally impress someone with what I could do got the better of me.

Lunch at the *O Club* was a great idea, wasn't it? The red access light above the scanner indicated otherwise.

I hoped the operators enjoyed the show, because it was about to end, one way or another.

Only two more photo sizes to try.

After four failures to unlock the electromagnets holding the door shut, I worried about my technique. After all, I'd only read about it. Never actually done it.

That's why I needed to test it. In front of Michelle. And the RRC's shooters. Brilliant decision making, 1LT Harper.

The longer I fiddled with the door, the longer they all stared at me. Wondered about my actions.

Last thing I needed was negative attention from the officers and noncoms I'd failed to impress in my first month here. I shivered from my knees to my shoulders.

Why wasn't Michelle wearing an overcoat? Maybe she just didn't expect to be out here this long. "Sorry this is so slow."

Felt Michelle shake a little through my coat shoulder. "You've always been pretty slow compared to me."

"Wow. Thanks."

She chuckled.

Maybe the first, actual size photo I'd tried was right. Just needed to be shaped more like an actual eyeball to match what the scanner expected.

"Loan me one of your contact lenses."

She'd known me long enough not to make me explain why. "Here's an extra."

Rooted around her purse. Came up with a pair of small plastic circular containers, marked "L" and "R".

Swiped across the RFID reader. Yellow light.

Positioned the original photo of my eye.

Delicately removed a contact from her case with my fingertip.

Lined up the image with the damp contact lens. Double and triple-checked it. Ensured it stayed in a tiny half-bubble shape.

Ideally, it'd mimic the curvature of a real eyeball.

Held the photo and lens in front of the retinal scanner.

The access LED turned a solid green.

After an eternal split second, the door unlocked with a thunk. Success!

Heart racing, I stood. Flung open the glass door.

Maybe a little too hard. Nothing broke *this time*, though.

The clank of steel bars slamming onto posts and weights rattling against spring collars halted. We became the center of attention.

Now we were putting on a show.

Let them rubberneck.

I gave Michelle my best Korean head tilt. Swept my arm with a flourish. Pointed her toward the open doorway.

She giggled. Took a step forward.

Paused for me to gather my equipment off the ground.

"Hey El-Tee, whatcha messing with?" I recognized Bishop's growl from the gym.

His question didn't bother me. With almost 25 years as a noncom and the razor-wire scar on his cheek to prove it, he'd earned the right to be a little casual in garrison.

Besides, everyone not a total grom knew to stay on the senior NCO's good side. If the commanding officer is a father figure, his top sergeant is the mother of the Company. Mopping up non-existent sweat from under his chin, he just spoke aloud the question most of the dudes in the gym thought.

I grinned. "Just a security test, Bishop."

Pretty boy Schnier stopped his slow-motion chin-ups. Stared at Michelle.

His practiced voice cut through the rest of the chatter, "Babe, if you want a real Ranger to show you a few things instead of that Techno Ranger, come on over here."

My jaw stiffened. Not cool, dude.

Michelle reacted before I could compose a reply.

Stepped through the doorway. Tilted her head back. Flung her right hand up to her forehead, palm facing Schnier. "Yes! Please! Take me NOW, you big strong man!"

She paused long enough in her fake southern belle pose for the laughter to start among the other soldiers.

"Will you SAVE me from my loneliness?"

Michelle struck her pose for another heartbeat before she put her mock salute down and transformed her face into a glare.

Schnier frowned. "Look, lady . . ."

Michelle giggled again. "I'd look, but they don't make a powerful enough microscope for you to show me anything of yours. Besides, I'm not always a lady. Ask Sam."

I already didn't fit in. As my guest, Michelle was charming and diplomatic. I groaned involuntarily.

Now, if I'd been thinking straight, I'd have just let Michelle continue to take him down a few more pegs. I mean, her nickname was 'The Bruiser' after all. She was used to popping all the big egos around Camp Kim.

Instead, fresh off the adrenaline rush of success from my bypass of the retinal scanner, I couldn't help myself. "What do you mean by 'Real Ranger' and 'Techno Ranger', Lieutenant?"

"Everyone knows there's us shooters and nerds like your platoon, Harper. No offense, you desk geeks can be useful too, sitting behind the lines as the butt-of-the-spear. Filing reports while the real Rangers go out as the sharp tip." Schnier inflated his chest and grinned.

Dealing with bullies wasn't new to me.

Growing up, frequently they were older and bigger kids in the system. Occasionally they were temporary guardians whose own lives weren't under control.

As a line officer, Schnier might be in tight with the other Rangers around Camp Kim, but he didn't impress me.

Amped, I gestured toward the gym's unarmed combat mats, laid out ready for a fight.

"Really, dude? Let's see what you've got."

Chapter Five:
Top Babysitter

Doctor Yang Hyo-jin's breakthrough nuclear detector was just beyond her grasp. She scribbled green mathematical symbols as her hands flew across the three portable whiteboards stuffed into her private office.

So close.

The final design for a more practical conversion material to detect radiological materials using neutrons while eliminating the false positives from normal background gamma rays was there, if she could just bring it into her conscious thoughts.

Hyo-jin tucked the thin dry-erase marker into the breast pocket of her white lab coat next to three others.

Red, green, blue, black. A complete set.

Now she just needed a complete theory.

She stuck her hands into her coat's spacious side pockets. Technically, the elongated coat protected her conservative skirt and long-sleeved blouse from chemical stains and other minor damage, but really it was a symbol of her work and authority.

The lab's Director of Advanced Metallurgy, she'd worked hard on the volleyball court in University to earn her coat. Unlike some of her subordinates, she preferred wearing it outside the lab's testing and fabrication areas.

She stared at the board and reviewed each equation in turn. Had she missed a term? A connection between ideas to improve the materials involved?

Maybe she should check the experimental data in her computer again.

Thankfully, her office was isolated enough from the rest of the lab to allow for plenty of privacy.

Part of a hallway of offices for the other scientists, its location tucked behind the top secret fabrication and testing labs meant few people who didn't actually work on a research team had access authorization.

Promoted six months ago, she'd insisted on soft, padded walls. Their gray mesh material sucked up sound.

She used her polished steel desk and laptop computer only when she had to.

Preferred to stand or pace. To think and to write on a series of smart whiteboards for notes.

A push of a button saved the contents of the boards into the lab's data storage.

Hyo-jin did the work, but she wasn't in love with materials science. She could take or leave the chilled or boiling metal she worked with.

She believed radioactivity a critical concept, but not the core of what genuinely interested her.

Differential equations left her cold unless they solved one of her thermogenic passions.

Raw theoretical physics, energy surging, solids reacting to the world around them, teasing apart the mysteries of reality. Those were the narcotics she partied with.

Once in a mental state of flow, Hyo-jin could focus precisely for hours on a problem; make incredible progress as long as no one interrupted her.

So of course Captain Rhee Yun-seok chose this moment of concentration to burst through her doorway in full Army uniform, the top of his short black hair bouncing.

Why, in this massive lab and warehouse complex, did he choose to intrude on her little corner?

He should stay in the security offices, where he belonged. Leave the scientists alone.

Rhee gave her a perfunctory and disrespectful bow. Skipped over the small talk which builds relationships.

"It's been decided at the highest levels. We must remove administrative access on the computers from you and the scientists in your section. I will personally see the access removed."

Another one of his tirades? "This is why you interrupt my work?" Hyo-jin asked, "To deal with your bureaucratic nonsense?"

"Merely thought you'd want to be informed of the change in procedures, as it affects your team. With the American security report, the entire lab's funding may be in jeopardy."

A traditional Korean officer, stuck at Captain's rank far beyond the usual promotion timeline, Rhee clearly considered whatever he was doing at any given moment to be more important than anything a mere girl might be doing.

As usual, he exaggerated his importance.

"Without my work, the lab's funds are wasted. Do you know anything about the improved detectors we're creating? The advanced applications, both military and civilian, these materials will enable?"

She pointed at the whiteboard she'd just written on, "If I can solve this last problem, it will unlock the next generation Miniature Nuclear Detection System. My administrative assistant in the front office will deal with your paperwork."

Hyo-jin didn't have time for Rhee's dominance games today. She was so close. He just needed to go away. Perhaps she could recapture her mental state.

Rhee looked up at her. Pretended to pick lint off the shoulders of his uniform. "Your Olympic gold medal may have gotten you this job, but you may not rely on your assistant to take care of these critical responsibilities. As Director of Security for the lab, I am required by policy to inform you of security changes which affect the scientists. What you do with the information is not my concern."

Hyo-jin's ten inches of height advantage rendered his intimidation attempts ridiculous. "While I remain in charge of my department, you'll handle these administrative matters with my assistant."

She purposely flipped her long black ponytail around abruptly as she turned her head away from the interruption and returned to stare at her previous writing.

Rhee dodged back to avoid the ponytail whip. Turned away with a stomp. Muttered, "After I meet with the Americans, we'll see how long that remains the situation."

Empty threats, trying to have the last word.

She deliberately ignored his words. They were supposed to be on the same team.

The slam of her office door told her she could finally return to work.

Perhaps she'd stay late tonight. Get more work done without a horde of interlopers to break her concentration.

When Rhee behaved like this, Hyo-jin felt the urge to spike a volleyball into his face. Perhaps she should keep one in her office.

She briefly considered filing a complaint to his military superiors outside the lab about his disrespectful attitude, but not for long enough to further interrupt her flow of ideas onto the whiteboards.

Who cared about the American security report?

She was a scientist, not a soldier.

First Sgt. Keith Bishop's job babysitting junior officers never ended.

It shouldn't take a black sergeant from Virginny to talk sense into a pair of what were officially gentlemen. The last thing he wanted to do in the middle of his daily workout was referee a testosterone-fueled dispute over that doggone CIA woman.

What was she doing here in his gym, anyway?

Dagnabbit, why'd Harper have to bring her over here to cause such a ruckus?

Usually at most during workouts he'd have to remind a Ranger to keep his t-shirt tucked in, or correct their lifting form so they didn't hurt themselves.

Lieutenants would be the death of him.

Rangers recruit high scorers on the Army's Aptitude test and the RRC had even higher standards than the Regiment as a whole, but they must make exceptions for lieutenants.

Maybe he could keep 'em from making fools of themselves in

front of the two-dozen Ranger operators now distracted from their PT to bet on the fight.

Bishop could hear the odds running heavily against Harper. At least Schnier and Harper planned to settle this in the ring, rather than in a Soju bar downing rice liquor bombs, the way the locals preferred.

Not a real ring, of course.

A padded black combatatives mat overlaid the wooden floor of a basketball court at the back of the gym.

"Own It" was stenciled on the olive green block wall beyond, a reminder to take personal responsibility for your actions. If only the officers would listen a little more.

No stands for spectators, just safely enough away from the now quiet weight racks and benches to not bash a participant's head into a barbell.

Bishop scanned the gym. Recently abandoned treadmills and VersaClimbers, designed for cardio, looked out the glass panes which covered the front. Next a line of artificial green turf simulated part of a field with sleds, battle ropes, tractor tires, and other heavy objects for Rangers to struggle with.

They trained to be anti-fragile, able to carry heavy loads unknown distances. Push themselves mentally far past the point where their bodies ached to give up.

In the corner, an ice bath aided recovery. Maybe he could come up with an excuse to dunk Schnier and Harper's heads into it.

Free weights occupied the back. Closest to the rear wall rested the mat; a large yellow circle marked out the arena for unarmed combat bouts.

He'd spent more time than he wanted crushed into that mat's padding, the strips of plastic fiber in the cover pressed against his face. Bishop much preferred to be the crusher, rather than the crushee.

After he'd trained soldiers for years, that's how it usually went.

He rubbed his chin. That's how it went, except for his few combatatives program bouts with Schnier. Those ended poorly.

Kid grew up literally taking bulls by the horns.

Schnier, dressed in a regulation black t-shirt tucked the proper distance into his matching PT shorts, threw a few air boxing punches to warm up along one side of the mat. Stood bowlegged, as if he'd ridden too many horses for his legs to ever straighten again.

He joked with the Rangers under his command. Appeared totally unconcerned about the fight with Harper. Probably saw this as a way to get a little back for losing in San Diego.

Schnier was an overall good soldier, and a fine operator, but one day, probably before he ever retired to his ranch, that boastful mouth would write a check his egotistical body couldn't cash.

Short term thinkin'.

Today weren't likely to be that day. Harper's level of technical competence was only matched by his naive inability to fit in.

Bishop figured he struggled with that in regular life, too. Certainly wasn't used to Ranger culture yet, not after a few classes and tests at Fort Benning and just 30 days in-country. He'd hoped to ease him and his Red Team nerds into the company a little more gently than this.

No, Schnier would demolish Harper, so Bishop considered it his duty to ensure he was at least fit for duty at the end of it all. His tougher mission was to heal the breach between the high-speed operators in the line platoons and the support staff who did much of the day-to-day work.

The parts focused on coordination with and improving the warfighting ability of the Republic of Korea (ROK).

Would this fight help that relationship? Physical conflict could bring combatants together in newfound mutual respect, but often it just tore the team apart.

Maybe if Harper could at least hold his own for part of a round or two.

Harper stood on the other side of the circle in the mat. Still wore his baggy OCP trousers, but he'd stripped down to a tan t-shirt.

His uniform jacket and tan beret hung on the end of a weight set next to his MI issue phone and whatever that contraption was he'd used outside the door.

He stood with muscles relaxed, a dumb surfer from Southern California. Buzzed dishwater hair, all six foot one inches of lean nerdy machine. Oh, Harper was built like a typical RASP 2 graduate, with running and rucking muscles, but nothing like Schnier.

Harper was more like a toddler Ranger at this point, stubborn, always asking why and getting into trouble whenever Bishop turned his back.

Schnier hunched on his side of the mat. Flexed his shoulders at Harper. "Let's get some." Schnier slapped his green plastic mouth guard between his teeth and grinned across the ring.

Bishop rubbed the scar on his cheek.

It took way too much work to raise up real officers from lieutenants and they came dumber every two-year duty cycle. Schnier's lack of confidence in his own abilities made him too much of a braggart. He didn't need to talk about his skills; he had enough to demonstrate instead.

The CIA brunette, Michelle, leaned over to Sam and advised in a whisper loud enough for the entire gym to hear, "Don't be stupid, Sam. This isn't worth it."

At least she had a brain, if the tact and diplomacy of a revenuer amongst the stills.

Bishop walked over to where Harper waited in the other corner of the training pad. "She's not wrong. This is stupid, sir. Lieutenant Schnier is the base unarmed combat champion. Even the green beanies don't mess with him without a weapon. Be lucky if you stay uninjured. Doubt you'll even get a point from him."

Harper thought for a second, but obviously not long enough. "Schnier insulted the whole support team. Not just me. My men. Supposed to just laugh along with him?"

"Sure this is about your men, sir?" Bishop glanced over at Michelle, fiddlin' with her crazy necklace. "You're supposed to fight alongside the operators, not against them."

Harper gestured across the makeshift fighting ring, where Schnier ran his hand through his buzzed red hair, "Tell him that."

Puma take 'em, nobody could restrain dumb lieutenants.

Bishop shook his head. "Try not to hurt yourself, the paperwork will finish us all off."

He walked across the mat. Split the distance between the two combatants.

Spectators pulled out their personal phones to record. Just what they needed, a dumbbell to post the fight online.

"All right, gentleman," Bishop said, "A brief reminder of the rules."

Legally, these idiots were officers and gentlemen. Bishop needed to remind himself of that continually, lest he really go off on them and set a bad example for the men who stared in anticipation from around the ring. Instead, he gave them his standard spiel about allowed blows and holds to prevent permanent injuries.

Finally, he concluded his explanations with "The winner will be the first to two out of three falls. We'll disregard draws."

He paused for breath. Checked both lunatic officers held a guard position. "Ready... fight!"

Harper rushed in at Schnier, as if to catch him by surprise.

Schnier didn't keep his distance, but stepped forward with perfect timing.

Jammed a right palm into Harper's left shoulder. Spun him sideways.

Harper used that momentum. Stabbed toward Schnier's eyes with a left thumb hook. Would've been an illegal disabling blow, but he stopped mid-swing and frowned.

Schnier completed his move. Stepped to the right. Slipped his left arm between Harper's left elbow and body.

With a knee in Harper's back and his right arm around his neck, Schnier controlled Harper. Forced him down to the mat to a soundtrack of cheers and taunts from Schnier's supporters.

Inevitable.

Took three more seconds of raw muscle and squirming to compete the pin.

"First round to Lieutenant Schnier." Bishop waved the over-testosteroned officers away. "Back to your sides."

Schnier took a quick sip of water.

Bishop stalked over to Harper and Michelle. "Saw you pull

that eye jab."

"Sorry." Harper caught his breath. "Not used to ring fights. No need to worry. Won't break the rules. Instincts just wrong."

Michelle handed Harper an olive green towel. Stared at Bishop. "At least we know he has an impartial referee, with all the time you spend over here giving advice and talking up Schnier."

This CIA officer was definitely not destined for the diplomatic circuit. Bishop could see why they made her a military attaché as her official cover.

"Bishop's a Mormon." Harper wiped the sweat off his face. "Doesn't even drink coffee. Doubt he'll cheat for one of us."

"Don't worry, Ma'am. A junior lieutenant is gonna get me killed one day. Try not to get too attached to any of 'em in advance, begging your pardon, sir."

"Totally. Let's get on with this. He won't get me goofy footed like that again."

"Look." Bishop put his hands up. "As an impartial observer, the next round will go a lot like the first one. You never had a chance.

"Why not throw in the towel before one of you gets hurt, the Major gets involved, and I have to do all sorts of paperwork for him to sign and send up the chain of command?"

Harper slowly shook his head. Stared at the floor. "If I give up, that's worse than if I try and lose."

Bishop stomped over to Schnier, who sat on a stool and sipped water in a slow rhythm, one squirt at a time from a green bottle. "You've made your point, lieutenant. He can't take you on the mat. Why not call it a day and quit while you're ahead, before someone gets hurt?"

Schnier looked up at him. "You mean before Harper gets hurt, right?"

Surrounded by stubborn morons with rank. "Forget I said anything, sir."

Harper and Schnier stepped up to opposite edges of the marked yellow circle. Stared each other down.

Bishop walked back to a point halfway between them. Waved at the two combatants to get in place with their guard up for the second round. "Ready."

Harper looked wary, but prepared.

Schnier stood bowlegged opposite him, one hand on an imaginary belt buckle. His gaze scanned the crowd.

"Fight!"

Harper shuffled toward the center of the mat. Used the balls of his feet to step. Circled in a spiral so as not to approach straight on.

Schnier moved in an opposite circle. Kept only a few feet from the edge. Studied Harper's footwork.

When he reached the edge of Schnier's punching range, Harper dropped. Swept his right leg out.

An attempt to nail Schnier behind the left ankle.

Schnier took a half step back like he teaching a clinic. Laughed. "Need upper body contact to trip that-a-way."

Harper continued his momentum across the mat. Rolled over. Extended his left leg even farther. Smashed it into Schnier's left ankle.

Caught flat-footed and watching, Schnier's weight distribution was all wrong. Tried to pull his left leg while his center of gravity was over it.

That didn't work at all. Instead, he landed on his side with a loud thud.

Harper took advantage. Wrapped the crook of his right elbow like a snake around Schnier's neck. Created leverage with his left arm and Schnier's leg.

Schnier refused to tap out right away.

Bishop called it as soon as it was clear he couldn't progress toward escape from the hold. "Second round to Lieutenant Harper. One and One."

Lucky point for Harper, with Schnier overconfident, but maybe that'd be enough to earn him a little respect from Schnier's watching operators. "Back to your sides."

This time, the sounds of Schnier's supporters rumbled to fill the gym.

Harper reached his area, the side of his t-shirt dark with sweat. Grunted a few words to Michelle. Grabbed a water bottle from her.

"One more round." She put her hands on her hips. "This was your idea. Don't be a loser, or I'll go see what Schnier's doing for lunch."

"Don't worry. I've got this. Underestimates me."

Bishop wasn't sure Schnier's mistake would last into the third round, but only one way to find out. "Ready."

Harper and Schnier crouched and raised their fists into the guard position for the third time.

Sergeant Lee, one of Harper's Red Team analysts on loan from the KCIA, entered the gym. Wore the uniform of the day, so not here to work out. A bad sign.

He spotted the commotion in the ring. Stopped near the weight benches to watch. Arrived just in time to see his leader battle Schnier.

"Fight!"

They circled as they approached. Schnier crowded forward. Reached behind Harper's head. Pulled his upper body down to meet Schnier's knee thrust into his chest.

Air rushed out of Harper in a low grunt.

Had to hurt. Wouldn't be long now.

Harper's right fist became curled knuckles. He turned it into a stiff blade on the way to jab it into Schnier's throat.

Bishop stepped toward the combatants, ready to stop the fight. By force if necessary; if Harper's disabling blow landed.

Windpipes were strictly off-limits. Too much risk of permanent injury.

At the last split second, Harper diverted his hand. Wrapped it around the back of Schnier's neck. Pulled Schnier's head down. Lifted his own head.

Jammed it into Schnier's chin.

Despite Harper's grip on the back of his neck, Schnier's head snapped backward. A bead of sweat flew into the air above him.

Bishop tried not to wince, glad the combatants wore mouth guards.

A long "Oh . . ." released from the spectators.

Somehow, Schnier recovered enough to hook his right leg around Harper's left calf. Shoved Harper with two stiff-arms.

Harper went down hard. Led with his shoulder blades. Tried

to kick his right leg into Schnier's groin as he fell.

Failed to connect. Hit his opponent's muscular thigh instead. Harper's back slammed into the mat.

The thud echoed across the gym.

Schnier pounced. Pressed Harper's legs into the air with one arm. Forced the rest of his body into the mat.

With Harper's shoulder blades pressed into the mat and his body under Schnier's control, he had no choice but to slap the mat with his flat palm to tap out.

Bishop stepped over for a closer look. Ensured neither combatant required first aid. "That's two out of three to Lieutenant Schnier."

Not a surprise ending. No serious damage, though.

Schnier's supporters chattered like a passel of chipmunks discussing their nuts, even the ones who paid off bets against Harper at low odds.

Harper recovered on his back in the middle of the mat. "Let your plans be dark and impenetrable as night, and when you move, fall like a thunderbolt."

Bishop smiled as he recognized the quote. Harper couldn't be that damaged, if he tossed around bad jokes. "Who wishes to fight must first count the cost."

The young lieutenant wasn't the only one who could quote Sun Tzu's Art of War.

Schnier stood. Reached out his hand to help Harper up.

A brief pause. Harper accepted the offer.

After Schnier heaved him up, the red-headed officer winked at Michelle, standing nearby. "So, how's about that lunch I heard you mention? Ten minutes to shower and I'm ready for you."

Michelle let out a long breath. "Maybe another day."

She turned away from Schnier to follow Harper as he walked past her to the weight benches.

The crowd surrounded Schnier to pat him on the back. Congratulate him on his victory.

At least there wouldn't be any paperwork from the Major on this one.

Bishop decided to follow the loser. Do what he could to smooth things over.

Schnier wouldn't miss him in the victory party.

Harper picked up his tan beret and uniform coat from the end of the weight set. Shoulders slumped, he didn't look like he wanted to talk to anyone.

Sergeant Lee took a tentative step forward, "Lieutenant?"

Harper stiffened his shoulders. Squeezed a smile onto his face as he recognized his subordinate. "Yes, sergeant?"

"The CO wants to see you in his office right away, sir. Didn't say why."

Harper's face shuffled into blank neutrality. "Be right there."

On a Friday afternoon, an unscheduled command appearance for Harper in front of the CO wasn't good news. Maybe a problem with his first report?

The CO occasionally advanced their Ranger Reconnaissance Company and its attached MI platoon into trouble his 1SGT had to retrograde them out of.

Bishop decided to cut his own workout short and return to his desk in front of Major William's office. He'd figure out what was going on.

A sergeant's job babysitting officers is never done.

Chapter Six:
Dangerous Carpets

DPRK Deputy Defense Minister Meon Lon-chun didn't intend to destroy Korea today. He just wanted to silence the tanks outside his office for a moment.

He pushed his navy blue phone handset harder into his ear, but lost half the Reconnaissance General Bureau (RGB) Major's words. Outside his temporary office near the main base road, a line of tank engines rumbled.

Their treads clanked in the frozen mud of the main base road. Overrode every other word on the phone.

Still, he understood the essence of the message.

The Defense Ministry's elite hackers failed in their attempt to remotely gather the data needed to copy the Soviet weapon. Instead, he must dispatch Kwon's team into Seoul today, before the enemy lab remediated their remaining vulnerabilities.

He grunted an acknowledgment. Slammed the handset onto its cradle; one of five colored phones built into the sleek red-stained teak of his desk.

Meon picked up the white phone.

Blue for RGB intelligence. Green for the General Staff. Black for the Ministry of People's Security.

Most importantly, red. His special line to the Supreme Leader's office.

White was the only line connected locally; it terminated at his receptionist's desk inside this People's Army base just north of the DMZ holding back the Imperialists.

The activated line triggered an immediate response from his

secretary. "Yes, general?"

Interesting that she called him by his military title. Forced by circumstances to leave most of his mistresses in Pyongyang, he'd recently spotted her in his Special Operation Force's Peony Brigade and promoted her to intimate secretary.

Meon found her appropriately grateful for his attention.

Rising from within the Worker's Party, he preferred his governmental title. Of course, everyone on base knew exactly who he was, an essential survival skill in the People's Army.

"Get Lieutenant Kwon Chol into my office immediately."

He hung up, which rattled the *other* phones in their cradles.

A tanker chose that moment to rev his diesel engine. Right outside his lone window.

He needed an office farther from the base's dirt roads. The rules of the Juche society he'd been born into forced him to endure certain aggravations.

After all, man is the master of everything and decides everything. Only one man in the true Korea ruled as master of all, and it wasn't Meon, although he survived perilously close to the metaphorical Phoenix Throne.

Meon jabbed his fingers into his temples like they were acupuncture needles. Cursed the day the Defense Minister assigned him here.

His temporary office came equipped with concrete floors and bare walls, plus an intense portrait of Supreme Leader.

He'd had a bit of his own memorabilia, his custom desk, and his three-wheeled leather chair delivered from Pyongyang. Might as well be a little comfortable while stuck down south.

Now, he worried about their potential deterioration from the condensation put out by the steam radiator in the corner. Wood and leather were so sensitive to humidity levels in the air.

He missed his regular office at headquarters where, as one of the Party elite, he possessed one of the most advanced climate control systems in the country.

He sighed. Another few weeks and he'd complete his work here. Return to Pyongyang triumphant, with his furniture intact.

Or not at all.

Maybe an herbal infusion would help his headache.

Meon yanked open his right-hand desk drawer. Shook the telephones again.

The dozen dark brown plastic dropper bottles standing in the drawer wobbled and then lined up for his inspection like soldiers on parade for Supreme Leader. Ginseng, green tea extract, citrus oil.

All useless.

Chamomile?

Angelica extract perhaps, if he wanted to just knock himself out for the day. What happened to his peppermint oil?

If the conscript cleaning woman had touched his essential oils again, he'd have her shot out of a signal cannon.

Incompetent uniformed buffoons!

If Colonel Jong-rin's tanks didn't stop driving past his office in the middle of Friday afternoon, maybe he'd make an example of the cleaning woman anyway.

The Supreme Guard tankers should test their pokpung-ho tanks out in the fields until after Meon went home for the day. Last time he'd challenged them on their laziness in returning early, the Supreme Guard colonel used the excuse of Dear Leader's directive to save fuel.

Too bad the Supreme Guard were out of the Ministry's direct chain of command. One day soon, they'd need a favor from Meon. If not, he'd manufacture their need. Then they'd see the consequences of their lack of respect.

Watching them suffer would almost make the headaches from their tanks worth it.

The radiator in the corner popped. Hissed a white fog. A metal cap fragment rocketed through the air. Embedded into the thatched ceiling.

A steady stream of steam followed. Expanded into a billowing cloud formation. His office turned instantly humid.

He clapped his hands over his ears to block out the sound.

A poor omen.

If he didn't need to ensure everything went perfectly, he'd leave this place today. Even the radiator disrespected him.

The base could always burn wood or coal in the boiler, so there was plenty of steam available, despite the fuel shortage. He needed to revisit the policy of promoting all the competent men into special units.

Perhaps if he left a few to manage logistically important posts like steam room maintenance for the base's offices, he wouldn't boil to death. Probably one of the useless three-year conscripts.

Someone's cousin, given a cushy rear echelon job to collect a favor.

Meon lowered his hands. Searched his drawer one more time. Still no peppermint oil.

The white phone jangled in its cradle. He picked it up. Assumed the best, "Send in Kwon!" before he hung up.

Seconds later, Lieutenant Kwon Chol slid open his heavy wooden office door as if it were paper. Stepped inside. Closed it behind him.

Brought himself to attention. Rendered a respectful salute. "Reporting as ordered, Deputy Minister."

Meon gave him a half wave. Got straight to the point. "The lab mission is a go. In fact, it's now urgent. I've moved the timing up. Your team will depart immediately."

Kwon gulped.

"Immediately, sir? We planned for next week."

Naive puppy. "Don't tell me what I already know. What have you been doing? Why isn't your team ready to go?"

"Sir? I've been reviewing the mission with my team. We can of course depart as soon as ordered, if we need to move up the mission timeline. I'll finish briefing my team en route. May I ask why the sudden urgency, general?"

Meon took a long breath. Rubbed his temples.

"I shouldn't take my headache out on you. We'll start again. Relax, we can speak as adopted relatives."

Kwon's stiffness vanished from the shoulders down. "Yes, Uncle."

Better to give good news first.

"Supreme Leader personally emphasized the importance of this mission. Gaining this information is key to our plan to finally unify Korea again.

"I promised him by name you would be successful at the imperialist lab. Quite an honor for you; the opportunity to impress him yourself."

He'd known Kwon's family from before he was born. Even allowed them to keep the extra cooking grain ration each week after the boy's brother was killed.

Still, Meon detected a certain wariness in Kwon's face whenever he spoke to him.

Kwon smiled. "Thank you, gracious Uncle. I'm delighted to serve in any way I'm able."

Despite calling him Uncle when permitted familiarity, Meon supposed Kwon still thought of him as the powerful village political officer of his childhood.

The price of authority in the true Korea.

Meon glanced at the red phone on his desk. The Great Successor took a personal interest in anything bearing on their one opportunity for parity with the Imperialists, nuclear weapons.

"New intelligence has revealed the lab plans to tighten up security. Our agent inside the lab is stalling matters, but if we don't move today, we must rethink the entire mission, and then only after we discover what changes they make. Our best opportunity is for your team to go now, before any changes, while we can use the same plan."

"Thank you for your confidence, Uncle. My team is ready to go. I will never let you and Supreme Leader down." Kwon thrust out his chest.

Meon frowned at his cockiness. "This is your first time across the DMZ. Do not allow imperialist temptations to make you a fool."

Kwon patted his uniform's left breast pocket, where Meon knew he kept a photo of his dead older brother and sister-in-law. "We've lost enough to the enemy. The Imperialists have nothing to offer to force me to betray my family."

"Remember that and I'll have full confidence in your team. You know what happened to my predecessor who led the special projects office."

Strapped across the mouth of an anti-aircraft cannon just before it was fired.

"There is no need to stress how important this mission is, but the matter is urgent."

Kwon bowed his head slightly. "We will achieve a great victory!"

Meon paused for a moment to look Kwon over. Thin, but wiry with muscle from years of calisthenics and marches. He studiously ignored the steam in the air while a thin sheen formed on his broad forehead. His dark hair demonstrated his purity as a Korean.

Overall, an excellent specimen of the People's Special Operation Force, and even better, personally loyal to Meon.

"Don't forget your ancestors, but our glorious system is your family now. Don't forget that, either. You won't want for anything as long as you have me to call upon."

"I'm grateful for your patronage, general. I wouldn't be in my splendid position without your advice and interventions, especially after my family died."

Meon nodded. Grateful and respectful.

"Lieutenant, your team will resolutely foil the aggression and intervention of the dominationists. It's essential for peace that we can show weapons parity."

Kwon's back and shoulder muscles tightened up. He stared up at the antique Tommy Gun which Meon had taken from a prisoner and hung on his office wall.

"We will implement the behests of our great leaders, sir!"

After plenty of repetition, they both knew the latest comforting slogans from the Ministry.

"See that you do. On your way out, tell the Officer of the Day to shoot the boiler mechanic responsible for my office. Also, have my receptionist send a clerk to requisition earplugs."

Kwon sucked in a deep breath. "Are you sure you want the boiler fixed that way, Deputy Minister?"

Meon rested his chin on his thumb and first two fingers, elbow on his desk. He deliberately ignored the possibility Kwon questioned his orders. His protégé wasn't that stupid.

"I've reconsidered. Have the guards throw him alive into the steam furnace instead. That will be more suitable. Fuel for the fire."

"Alive?"

"A better lesson for his replacement. Supreme Leader ordered us to conserve ammunition. Don't forget the earplugs."

Kwon's eyes pointed at the exit door. "I'll need to hurry to get my team started toward the tunnel under the DMZ."

Meon always had to do everything himself to ensure it was done properly.

"I'll take care of the mechanic and the earplugs. Nothing can stand in the way of landing this blow against the Imperialists.

"Now, go!"

Like a middle school principal, no one wants the commanding officer to call you in. Sure, I *might* be here to receive congratulations on completing my initial primary tasking, except I hadn't had time to file an addendum about the success I'd had bypassing the retinal scanner at the gym.

After losing to Schnier, that victory felt like a massive wave I'd ridden as a teenage surfer, fun while it lasted, but a long time ago. Since arriving in Seoul, I'd had limited exposure to Major Williams, but I didn't believe the CO spent a lot of time congratulating lieutenants on doing their job.

He couldn't have already heard about the fight, could he?

I tried to rub the bruise out of my shoulder where Schnier had slammed me into the mat.

They'd headquartered our unit in a group of one-story red brick buildings surrounded by uniformly carved hedges, spiteful and comatose for the winter. I think the Japanese either used them for warehouses or stables.

Camp Kim had seen better days, inside and out.

In the SOCKOR hierarchy, and everything established via bureaucracy in the Army was a hierarchy, the ancient Special Mission Units formed from the Budweiser Frogmen and the Green Beanie Snake Eaters believed themselves above the rest.

As part of the 75th Ranger Regiment, more fashionably late to Special Operations Command, the Ranger Reconnaissance Company (RRC) ranked below the other "Special" groups, except maybe the flyboys who drove the trucks out at the Air Base.

SOCKOR had stuck my temporarily attached MI platoon in another building. In the RRC main HQ, our CO had the only private office.

Squeezed into the corner near the major's office door was a ratty red leather sofa next to a beat-up coffee table with a glass top.

Waiting for the major to call me in to report as ordered, I sat on the sofa and tried hard to think about anything else.

Like waiting for the dentist. I picked up an old copy of *Stars and Stripes Korea* advertising Namsan Seoul Tower as the premier romantic attraction.

A spiked tower on top of an unpopulated double-hill, the observation deck 500 meters above the city was open until midnight to view the cityscape at night. The tower was close enough to be visible from anywhere on base.

Great place to take a date, if I ever got one in Seoul.

After Michelle watched me attempt to defend her honor and then fail miserably, I wasn't sure any romantic towers were in my near future. At least this meeting gave me an excuse to skip out on our now awkward lunch plans.

I stared past the rest of the pages of the magazine without really seeing them.

The remaining area outside the CO's office was stuffed with light oak panel desks, all with the requisite glass top to protect the finish from Rangers who cared more about their hot beverages than the company's furniture budget.

Army issue maps and plaques dotted the walls. On each desk rested a chunky milspec laptop, monitor, keyboard and mouse.

All that glass and electronics would create plenty of shrapnel if a terrorist detonated a bomb nearby.

Bishop's desk was closest to the major's door.

Besides the obligatory picture of his wife and kids, on his desk rested a small walnut stained plaque, the back smooth from those passing by rubbing it for luck, *There are no dangerous weapons; there are only dangerous men. - Heinlein* engraved into it.

With my Red Team, my desk, and the other support analysts in another building, I held no territory in HQ.

Instead, I sat rigidly on the front of the sofa. Ignored the clatter of sergeants and clerks who waited to get away from the base on a Friday.

Why did I fight Schnier? Losing wasn't going to impress the shooters in the RRC.

Schnier was good. I knew that.

Even Bishop didn't think I'd have a chance to win, and he'd seen us all train. I know I could've done better in a real fight, like those I'd grown up with. Wasn't used to the restrictions of a formal match.

My strengths are adapting to the environment, using what's available against my opponent, out-thinking my opponent, not following rules.

I rubbed my forehead, knuckles white.

Who was I kidding? Even with all my training, I'm still like one of those college freshmen from UC San Diego.

They'd show up late Saturday morning on the beach, carrying a brand-new surfboard without a coat of wax. I'd never been in a real fight to the death with the Army.

My military training was good, but mostly theoretical.

Sure, I'd learned to hold my own against bigger foster kids and even bigger drunken foster parents growing up, but a trained enemy who wanted to kill you was different.

Had no business fighting Schnier.

Should've tried to make friends with the operators. Figured out what they needed. Made sure they had it; not tried to impress them with my martial prowess.

Bishop slipped in through the front door to the office space, back in the uniform of the day. He wore his tan beret cooler than anyone else in the company. I watched as he chatted with the staff on a ricochet course toward me.

To the casual observer, he just made small talk, but I could tell by the way every new conversation led him in my direction that he hunted bigger prey.

Obviously, the humiliation at the gym wasn't enough; he wanted to talk about it even more. Good thing I wasn't already stressing about my imminent wipe out in front of the Commanding Officer.

Bishop sat on the edge of the desk closest to the CO's door.

"Lieutenant Harper. Good to see you're healthy, sir."

"Yeah, you tried to warn me. Lesson learned."

"What lesson would that be, sir?"

Dude, no need to rub it in. "To listen when your first sergeant suggests your current course of action may not be ideal."

Bishop blew out a huge breath. "Always knew you were one of the smart ones, El-Tee. May live through this yet."

At least I hadn't turned the senior NCO in the company against me by a refusal to listen to him. Now I just needed to figure out how I'd impress the shooters in the RRC. Or at least, let them know I could contribute to the mission.

Michelle was probably a lost cause for now. I'd known her long enough to believe this wasn't the end, but it certainly wasn't a way out of the friend zone with her, either.

Bishop was usually tuned into the local private news network. "Any idea what the CO wants with me?"

He pulled a bottle of his famous Cherry 7-UP out of a desk drawer. Popped the cap on the edge of his desk. "Not my position to say, sir. Maybe you should've taken a shower. Too late now, I suppose. A little extra formality when you report won't hurt, though."

I ran my fingers through my buzzed hair, then around my neck and across my chin, rubbing off dried sweat from the gym.

Bishop wasn't going to razz me about being worried enough to ask an NCO to comment on the doings of officers? I knew he'd talked to the rest of the HQ crew on his way in, so he must have *some* idea. Not a good sign.

Bishop took a sip. His desk phone rang. He turned away to answer the call.

I looked around the room. The other staff NCOs casually pretended I didn't exist.

At times like these, I didn't feel particularly wanted around the 75th RRC. The shooters didn't wear glasses. Instead, tended to walk around as if muscles and swagger determined the hierarchy of life.

Despite a more wiry appearance from years of cross-country running and track & field in high school and college, I was a Ranger. Beyond just the tab on my uniform from Ranger School,

I'd earned my scroll leading my MI platoon on detached duty with the RRC.

After his brief phone conversation, Bishop turned back to me. "The major will see you now."

I tossed down the copy of *Stars and Stripes Korea* I hadn't read a page from. Stood. Tucked my tan beret under my arm. Gave the back of Bishop's plaque a quick rub. Rapped once on the major's door.

"Enter."

I pushed open the office door. Long breath. Time to face the cold waves.

Bishop made a brushing motion toward the doorway. Head held straight, I marched in.

Halted two steps from the front of the CO's desk. Stood at rigid attention. Saluted with a crisp forearm motion. "Sir, Lieutenant Harper reports. Rangers lead the way!"

The CO leaned back in his office chair and waved vaguely in the direction of his upper body. "All the way. At ease, Lieutenant."

I completed my salute. Took up a position closer to parade rest.

Stared at the wall above his head.

My peripheral vision picked up an ROK daewi, equivalent to our rank of captain. He perched on a metal folding chair. Back rigid.

We hadn't met, but I recognized him as the leader of the security unit assigned to protect the research facility. The lab we'd just submitted a report criticizing the security of.

Bad news travels fast.

Major Williams didn't let me get on the board before he tossed me to the sharks. "One of our esteemed allies, Captain Rhee Yun-seok, is here to provide feedback on your vulnerability report."

Rhee stood, back straight. Clasped his arms behind him. Leaned forward, his forehead inches from my shoulder.

I was at least a foot taller than Rhee. Fixed my face in a firm line. Tried to look intimidated.

He circled me like a buzzard. "Hop'ung. That for your

libelous report. Not worthy of use as toilet paper. You do not show our true capabilities. You do not consider the completed retraining. You ignore the technology upgrades our scientists performed."

I lifted my chin. Did I really have to stand here and listen to this? "Sir, that's all covered in the report. For example, the upgrades from the lab's scientists violate the security principle of separation of duties. Allowing the scientists administrative access to the security systems to upgrade them violates risk management principles."

"Do not interrupt, Lieutenant Harper. You are new to our country. You know nothing of our culture, of our history. You are ignorant of how our advanced technology works.

"Ignorant of the trust we place in our science staff.

"No, each copy of this report must be burned and the task of analyzing security at the lab reassigned to another officer. One who will pay the proper respect."

All that work to prove the retinal scanner vulnerability? They weren't even going to let me defend my security analysis?

I appealed to the CO, "Major, surely you've read my report yourself. Even a single compromised guard at the lab can simply open the loading dock and bypass all the security measures in the front office.

"The lab doesn't even schedule tests of their data backup systems.

"If you'll allow me to lead my Red Team to infiltrate the lab, I believe I can establish the vulnerabilities outlined in the report exist, sir."

Major Williams glanced down at his laptop screen. "Request denied, Harper. We're here to work *with* our Korean allies, not insult them. This is their country, after all."

Knew it'd be on the edge of insubordination, but had to try one more time.

"Sir, I know I'm new to the ROK, but I intended no insult. I've already successfully validated one of the vulnerabilities in my report. If you'll just allow me . . ."

Williams held up his hand like a stop sign. "I've allowed you enough already. I'll have Bishop remove your report from the system. You're to be relieved of any further duties with this command.

"Present yourself to the Company Clerk first thing Monday morning, with bags packed. He'll have orders for your return to Benning.

"Dismissed."

Relieved? That's a career killer! "But, sir, my analysis is accurate."

William's nostrils flared. "You have a lot to learn about teamwork and about our host country. Dismissed, I said."

I clenched my jaw. "Yes, sir." There was no way to fight it.

Total wipe out.

Rhee gave a crisp nod, apparently satisfied.

This proved I didn't fit into the RRC. So much for the Army as my new family.

With no career and no way to impress anyone further, I turned precisely on my heel with my tiny bit of remaining pride and marched away.

Chapter Seven:
Peripheral Intelligence

Jin-sun's Mother despised the barbarian half-breed, Toby Howell. He always spoke so presumptuously to her, for one so young, as if he were her equal, or even her superior.

Instead, he appeared barely a decade older than her son, Kwon Jin-sun.

The American Embassy's disrespectful staff had forced her to suffer through thirty minutes of waiting outside.

Once she'd finally satisfied the office workers that she had an appointment with Officer Howell, a junior clerk had led her into a small office with a large interior window that overlooked their immigration directorate's cubicles.

No outside window to provide a view of even the parking lot, let alone the nearby museum grounds, so Toby wasn't an important man.

The young refugee officer lazed behind his dull metal desk. He wore a charcoal workday suit, but his Korean black hair and American complexion would be in more harmony with a gray suit.

Something light, similar in tone to the walls of the cubicles outside. His tie was not at all suitable for a government official, garishly bright blue silk.

Americans. No harmony with nature, but what could you expect from a person whose mother married a foreign soldier and fled Korea after the war?

The office itself was worse.

Harsh black-bordered frames on the wall. Steel floor cabinets stacked with bureaucracy-filled cardboard boxes on top. A white laptop computer with a grimy keyboard.

No earth, except for the thick dust on desk and shelves. No water. Not even a single plant.

The industrial carpet had an odd black and tan flecked pattern to it. Probably to hide dirt so they didn't need to vacuum.

They obviously didn't think much of her, to bring her into this office.

Experience taught her how difficult it was to fit into a new culture, especially when forced. At least Officer Howell wasn't of Japanese descent. That would've been the ultimate insult.

Jin-sun's Mother would endure what she must to acquire their refugee visas and thus assure her son's success at an American university. After an incredible amount of work, which she'd ensured he invested, her son had applied to and been admitted by Harvard Business School's MBA program, conditional on a difficult to get visa.

Her son would need his Mother to continue to drive him forward. Unable to accompany him if he only obtained a student visa, she'd hatched a plan to get them refugee status. This was possible because she'd fled from the North to the South.

He was a good son, even a brilliant son, who learned quickly, but could be impulsive at times. She'd taken care of that. His GMAT and his English test scores, required for admission, were flawless.

He'd grown up without a Father, with no other close relatives in reach besides her. That was already enough of a disadvantage. She wouldn't let a little humiliation in front of this American half-blood block a better life for Jin-sun.

Her only son would become part of the world's global elite in business.

Jin-sun's Mother put her arms close to her waist. Pressed her red chima skirt closer to her hidden baji pants. Bowed to the seated refugee officer.

She wasn't so old that she could no longer bend at the waist.

Besides, her woven ramie cloth hanbok was designed to flow for comfort. The four foot deep blue ribbon tied in a wide knot the center of her jeogori jacket fell forward and almost touched the ground.

Just a nod in return from Officer Howell. The usual foreign rudeness. "Please, sit down."

She flipped her chima forward a little and settled into a modern metal chair in front of his desk.

Thin cold steel. Typical.

Looked up at the consul. Kept a hopeful expression on her face.

Hiding her feelings from officials came as second nature. There are skills you don't lose.

He shuffled thick papers into a folder. "I'm recording this interview so I don't have to slow you down to take notes while we talk. I'll get it transcribed later."

Flipped a black rocker switch built into the desk, then intoned formally, "Toby Howell, interviewing Yeo Min-jung about refugee visas for her and her natural child, Kwon Jin-sun."

She nodded as if she cared about his process. She just wanted to get her son to America. She'd undergo another dozen interviews if it would make that happen. "Happy to be recorded by machine."

"I'm sorry about your husband. Really, it would help the application for a refugee exception if you'd start at the beginning and tell in detail about how you came from the North to the South.

"Not many North Koreans end up traveling to the United States. Less than a hundred each year, in fact."

"Of course. Strange to think we escaped from our own country. Now I try to do it again. We married for several years, but just moved from husband's parents' farmhouse into apartment in town. On top floor near stairs. Usually had at least part of roof to ourselves.

"Party Secretary lived below us. Too lazy to climb two extra flight of stairs. Barely made it up stoop of own apartment."

"Is this all relevant? We're really just looking for why you crossed the border."

"You said start at beginning. This beginning." She took pride in her careful English to the half-American. He wouldn't be able to look down on her.

He sighed. "Go on."

Living on the other side of the border, he didn't realize about not having to live with her husband's parents and his baby brother in a one room farmhouse.

"The small apartments new. Radiator in bedroom even work, not just stove in kitchen, but wallpaper pasted the month before fell off walls in small chunks. Bad glue. Was downstairs to help Party Committee Secretary rehang his wallpaper while husband rested between shifts at yoke factory.

"He trained as mechanical engineer. Was promoted to department supervisor, which when the Party Secretary assigned us apartment."

"I'm sorry, yoke factory?"

"Yes, for oxen. They pull plows and wagons. Otherwise, people must pull for themselves. Government loaned yokes out to farmers in rotation when time to plant or harvest.

"No one think to use valuable machinery for such a purpose, like they do here in South."

"And your husband grew up on his parent's farm, so he understood how these yokes worked, huh?"

"Spent most of his time taking care of equipment they used to produce yokes, but did once suggest how could use less wood making yoke, but would remain strong enough to pull proper loads. Party studied if improvements work or not when we left.

"Of course, once we left, they throw away as fruit of traitor. Odd to think of other people thinking of us as traitor. Didn't think of ourselves that way.

"Just wanted to survive. Have child."

"I think we're off track again."

"After came back from re-papering Party Secretary's apartment, brought extra scraps. Thought husband be happy, but instead seemed upset.

"Tried to act normal, but could tell by way he huff as he sat. How turned away to sleep that night. Something upset him. Tried to explain needed to stay on good terms with Party Secretary, especially after promotion, but that didn't seem problem."

"What was his name?"

"Husband?"

"The Party Secretary."

"Secretary Meon Lon-chun."

Officer Howell seemed to find that important. Actually scribbled notes rather than just relying on the recording. "Go on."

"Next morning, on weekend, I helped him get dressed. Ready for day in volunteer labor battalion.

"Husband admitted he found my radio, between mattress and wall where hidden. Learned guitar in school. Told him I missed guitar. Liked music on radio from South.

"That our first fight after marriage. Out on farm, radio been fine, but he thought too risky where we lived.

"Suppose now, must admit he right in our fight, even if didn't lead only to bad. Life balanced that way.

"Wish he here for me apologize. Don't think I ever did, for fight."

Officer Howell looked toward the door. These half-breeds had no ability to concentrate on important matters.

"Shouldn't have told husband. If had listened to neighbor, might been fine."

"Told him what?"

Officer Howell's brain was impenetrable. Did she really need to spell it out?

She felt her cheeks heat up at the memory.

"Didn't need to worry about radio being found. Party Secretary gave radio last time forced himself on me.

"Gift to justify actions."

For once, Michelle wasn't going to spend her Friday evening diplomatically gulping rice soju and belting out karaoke with the local State Department losers.

Instead, she'd left work early.

Returned to the low-rise apartment the CIA comp'd her. The Station Chief probably listed it as a safe house on the books. Towed his local mistress up here before Michelle'd moved in.

His loss.

She planned to relax and forget about work completely, but even living on the sixth floor, she still unlocked more deadbolts than most.

Professional paranoia.

Kicked off her flats. Sat back in her balcony's deck furniture, the bare horizontal wooden slats pressing into her shoulders. Stretching her feet up onto the blue steel railing overlooking Seoul, she didn't worry about her pencil skirt.

A little cold never bothered her. Besides, she wore thick enough stockings.

With no one around, she could afford to let go a little.

Drop her everyday pretenses.

She tuned out the K-pop which blasted from a nearby apartment. Ignored the mix of pickled cabbage kimchee and winter sewage rising on the updrafts.

At least the cool breeze took her wrinkled neighbor's weird floral vaping fumes away.

Even with official cover as a defense attaché and the attendant diplomatic immunity, she'd never become used to always having to put up a front. Wondering who might watch her with ill intent.

Ensuring she made just the right amount of eye contact, but not too much.

Especially in Korea, where no one considered it rude to stare at obvious foreigners in public.

She sighed.

How was she supposed to know who paid too much attention to her when both the locals and the soldiers she liaised with constantly ogled her?

When even taking the subway subjected her to constant physical contact with handsy Korean pretty-boys?

Easy to pass intelligence off covertly in the thick crowds, but otherwise a field officer's nightmare location.

At least sitting on her apartment balcony, only her neighbors could see her. They didn't come outside except to tend their balcony of herbs during the day.

Safe here, she'd be able to watch dusk overcome the skyline, leaving random apartment building window lights and gleaming office buildings reflecting the setting sun.

Seeing the lit spiked tower rise above Namsan mountain. Could finally get away from work for a while.

So of course, her mobile phone rang. She glanced at the phone's screen, but the number was blank. The symbol indicated a secure call. Encrypted.

She did the time zone math in her head. Late afternoon here in Korea, a Langley resident was calling her in the middle of the night there.

A bad sign.

She dropped her feet to the harsh balcony floor. "Seoul."

CIA Assistant Director Edward Metcalf's deep bass voice echoed in her head, "With your promotion to uncovered control, we're looking for faster results."

She'd only met him once in person, during a meet and greet before she flew out. Her immediate boss, the Chief of Station here, reported to him back in Langley. This was the first time he'd called her directly since their video conversation in San Diego.

"I have two potential resources on the hook. One gives me access to the Ranger's technical and intelligence side. The other to details of their combat mission planning and after action reviews. They're at odds right now, so I can play them against each other."

She really did have the start of two good relationships going. Was even a little attracted to both men, albeit for different reasons. Not exactly a tough duty, despite her potentially conflicting loyalties. Anyway, Sam should look out himself.

He was just being dumb, otherwise.

"The clock is ticking. The enemy's pieces are moving. Your competition has a new high-level source in the DPRK government. Very promising.

"You need to be more aggressive on this. Track down if the Rangers have any plans on the other side of the DMZ which could impact our efforts."

A good relationship with power in Washington would certainly help Michelle become the youngest Chief of Station anyone had ever heard of. She needed to demonstrate her value to his team.

With this personal interest in her work, she had to deliver.

She quenched her natural rebellion. "My source has access to that. I could use additional details on a local. Captain Rhee Yun-seok, ROK Army, assigned to head one of their security details."

Information exchange with Washington was potentially a two-way street.

"Run it our way. The desired crisis is larger than your mission. You just need to guide them in the right direction at the right times. Don't make us regret choosing you."

She crossed her legs. "I'll make sure you have no regrets, afterward."

"Remember, the easiest way to figure out a puzzle is to start with the whole picture and then cut it into pieces. *Then* solve it.

"No need to reveal we created the puzzle in order to be seen to solve it. If this goes down as planned, we all look great for picking up the pieces. If not, you'll be finding the pieces of your career for decades."

Michelle's phone clicked loudly as the secure line disconnected. Suddenly, it was freezing out here.

She shuddered, no longer relaxed.

Her Agency career was now a throw of the dice. Win or lose, interesting times lay ahead.

Chapter Eight:
Embrace the Suck

Lieutenant Kwon Chol careened down the muddy hill on his pack. Slid past Sergeant Stro and the other five special forces sergeants on their team. Ran up against a burnt-out stump at the bottom.

Looked back. Waved and laughed.

Showed his men he was physically intact, even if his dignity took a brief hit.

He opened his mouth to suck in some of the chilly rain. No reason to waste it on the production of additional treacherous mud north of the DMZ.

Already plenty for everyone to share.

They'd hiked from their drop-off point at the Kaesong Industrial Area along the mud paths leading toward the clandestine tunnel entrance. Despite the wet cold, his team hummed with excitement.

Real soldiers despised barracks duty. Professionals wanted to take the fight to the enemy. Preferred a mission to almost anything.

Besides, the food in the South was better. While preparing, Stro told Kwon stories of the street food. How they indulged each time they went South. The meat, especially. Not that they were there to eat, and certainly not to drink while on duty.

At least he'd escaped arranging for that boiler mechanic's demise.

He frowned. Kwon could be stealthy when required, but preferred a clean kill. Rather look into the face of his enemy.

Not that he'd ever actually killed anyone before. Despite their unending war with the ROK, begun decades before his birth, he'd never even seen the enemy in person. His team was vastly more experienced, especially Stro, second in command and their unarmed combat specialist.

He told bizarre stories about his kills, but from the glint in his eyes, the relish in his tone, Kwon could tell Stro enjoyed the visceral slaughter he described.

Not Kwon. He accepted it as part of their job; as something he'd have to do, but just wanted a normal career. An orderly life.

Even a regular family back.

The other five sergeants were also long time sniper reconnaissance brigade. Ready to infiltrate enemy positions.

One pair were demolition specialists. Another pair trained as backup medics. The odd man out carried the heavy weapons and doubled as a communications specialist; he possessed the least useful training for this stealth operation.

Between the six men of Team Goshawk, they'd completed dozens of missions south of the DMZ.

Stro was built similar to Kwon, both a couple of inches taller than average in the DPRK, so about 5'7". Dark hair, muscular runner's build from years of calisthenics and marches in the Army.

With better food than most under the oppression of America's attempts to cut off their country from world trade, their team could afford to hone themselves into a deadly blade poised at the throat of the dominationists.

Level 10,000 guys for sure. All with the right attitude.

Kwon's men, slower, but more sure-footed down the hillside, reached his prone position. Stro offered him an arm up. Failed to hide a grin.

He'd need better acting skills on the other side of the DMZ, pretending to be the enemy.

They spread out and continued their march into history.

Kwon joined the People's Special Operation Force three months ago. Team Goshawk's previous lieutenant received a medal for unspecified Services to the People.

Promoted to Captain, he now led a company of the Supreme

Guard in Pyongyang, responsible for protecting his country's only Marshal, Dear Respected, the Great Successor, Chairman of the Worker's Party.

Kwon aspired to follow his predecessor's career example.

Perhaps if this mission went extremely well. After all, Uncle said he already had Supreme Leader's attention, and they hadn't even crossed under the DMZ yet.

Felt traitorous to wear the ROK Army's black and green camouflage uniforms with red, white and blue yin-yang patches, but their disguise would make Kwon's team almost invisible in Seoul, just another group of soldiers going about their business.

No need to look in the big black duffel bags.

Up ahead, along these shallow ridges covered in scrub brush, the border guards had buried a camouflaged observation post. If the Imperialists noticed it at all, they'd assume it's placement was to observe the DMZ.

The four soldiers in the post were actually tasked with guarding a hidden tunnel entrance. Conscripts carefully excavated the tunnel over the years, digging it just large enough for a standard 200-liter drum of chemical weapons to pass through horizontally, should the need arise.

They could've driven along the DMZ road to an even closer position, but then observers from the South might wonder about the unscheduled truck traffic. Might watch carefully when they stopped to disembark.

No, better to hike in, even if they had to follow a narrow mud trail. They were used to long marches with a ruck full of equipment.

For Kwon, this was his first true independent command. In addition to their standard tactical radios, they'd been issued a pre-paid mobile phone purchased in the South.

Their orders were to observe radio silence until they reached Seoul. Could hide communications amongst the many radio point sources within a large city. Every other mobile phone would mask their own transmissions.

Right now, he was in charge and on his own, with only his elite team to support him until they reached the other side of the DMZ.

Ruck marching four klicks from truck to tunnel mouth was like laying down and eating rice cake for Team Goshawk.

Kwon paused as he spotted the observation post.

Designed to blend into the top of the ridge, it'd been built from concrete and covered in dirt and scrub brush. Only a dark horizontal slit for visibility faced south.

A less-well disguised rusty steel door faced down the north side of the ridge, opposite the DMZ. The border guards hid the tunnel mouth to prevent detection from both observers across the DMZ and overhead satellites and aerial reconnaissance.

After picking his way through the frozen mud to the observation post, Kwon motioned Stro forward to join him.

Stro slung his K2 rifle. Grasped the U-shaped steel door handle with both hands. Yanked it open.

The door's hinges protested their rusty state. The open doorway exposed the inside of the bunker to what little sunlight filtered through the dreary clouds.

Two border guards jumped to their feet.

Kwon noted their positions on the floor. No way to watch the DMZ from there. Likely asleep. The Party selected border guards for their loyalty to their families, not for their effectiveness.

Kwon's team possessed both.

Still, the guards reacted fast when prompted. Kwon's team could only have shot them a few times each before the two guards aimed their newer Type 88-1 assault rifles. They even thought to unfold the side stock on their rifles as they stood and exited the bunker to confront Kwon in the small clearing outside.

Clearly boiler mechanic material.

Kwon held his Pyongyang resident identification card and the typewritten sheet containing his orders out like a knife.

Only a select and trusted few could boast regular access to the capital, Pyongyang. Kwon's prized residency card should ensure immediate respect.

Stro took a position to the guards' side.

The more senior guard, wearing the wide and narrow bands of a sergeant on his uniform tabs, seemed relieved for Kwon to present documents rather than a demand for surrender. What, did he take their ROKA uniforms seriously, as if a patrol from the South had appeared here on the other side of the DMZ?

"We're here to use the tunnel, sergeant. Please review my orders."

Politely, the sergeant nodded. Took the documents. Read them over.

No one saluted near the DMZ, except during formal ceremonies.

Kwon's remaining men casually took up positions which kept them below the top of the ridgeline, but allowed them to surround the two guards in a wide semi-circle.

Well trained.

The sergeant handed Kwon his Pyongyang resident card back. "Thank you, sir. No one advised us of your planned arrival. Will your team be staying with us in the post here for the full week?"

Great, he'd encountered a boiler mechanic trainee. Had to be able to read to pass the sergeant's examination, but bribery or connections wasn't unheard of. "What week? We're to use the tunnel immediately to cross to the South."

"Sir, respectfully, your orders state your team is to traverse under the DMZ in a week, not today." He pointed at the date in the document. "Perhaps there has been confusion in your mission timing?"

"There wasn't time for revised orders."

The two border guards stood there like stumps, unwilling to talk back to a superior office when not absolutely required.

Truthfully, Kwon hadn't even considered that with the change in plans he'd need to get revised orders typed up and signed. He'd only been in command of the team for 90 days, not nearly long enough to learn the required bureaucracy for his new position.

"Supreme Leader has deemed our mission critical. We leave now."

"Sir, I'm afraid I can't allow your team to pass through the tunnel without proper documentation. Our standing order is that anyone not authorized who attempts to cross the DMZ is to be shot.

"You may of course wait here for my superior when the relief truck comes past, or return and have your orders updated with today's date."

The sergeant left unspoken how border guards and their families were punished if they allowed anyone unauthorized to cross the DMZ.

Kwon knew the guard's predicament. He'd normally even sympathize a little, but that same punishment would await him and perhaps his whole team if he failed to even begin their mission.

"Call your headquarters. Ask them to connect you to Deputy Defense Minister General Meon Lon-chun. We're here now at his personal direct order to me. You can see he signed my paperwork."

"I'm sorry, sir, but the field telephones in this area haven't been functional for the last three days. Something to do with this nasty weather, I'm told. Our only method of communication is via flare gun in case of an invasion. Otherwise, we wait for our relief cycle to pass on our report."

Stalemate.

Kwon looked at Stro to see if he had any suggestions.

Stro glanced at the rest of the team surrounding the two guards, then gave Kwon a wink.

Kwon nodded to Stro. "I'm sorry as well."

With that, four members of his team stepped forward in unison and each grabbed a guard's arm. The other two stood warily by, ready to intervene if the guards fought back.

"What? You can't do this!"

Kwon reached out and took their rifles from unresisting hands.

"We have a mission to complete. I'm sure it won't reflect poorly on you, but we'll need to leave you bound until your relief arrives. We'll leave you a copy of our orders to show your superior.

"He can inquire with the Deputy Minister, who will clear everything up for you."

His team made quick work of securing the guards within their bunker with four of the tactical vinylon ratcheting cable ties they all carried. Light-weight, but they'd last long enough restraining the guard's legs and arms that it wouldn't matter.

They'd be through the tunnel quickly enough.

The tunnel opened just to the side of and three meters lower than the guard post door on the backside of the ridge.

Icicles stabbed down from the edge.

Looking at the outside it could've been a small animal cave, but Kwon remembered from the maps he'd reviewed that it reached much farther than a den, all the way to the other side of the DMZ.

He bent over. Inspected the tunnel's internals. About the diameter of a large outdoor trash can.

Just inside the entrance a pair of wooden tracks held wheeled wooden carts. Each cart attached to the next with strong vinylon rope. The final cart's rope connected through a pulley hanging from the concrete ceiling. Each cart rested on four small polyurethane wheels with a groove to fit loosely around the wooden rails.

Crude, but effective.

The concrete portion of the ceiling ended before the line of five carts did. Gave way to more natural materials.

No large amounts of metal were allowed a permanent place in the tunnel. The Imperialists could find many things with their almost magical instruments for peering into the ground, but organic material within a small tunnel was the most difficult for them to sense. Ground penetrating radar might be able to detect them, but not this deep, and not from a distance.

Kwon checked his Moranbong wristwatch. Good Korean steel. Removed his pack from his back. Brushed off the mud.

Removed a black duffel from the pack.

Their packs would stay behind. He pulled black fingerless gloves and a chrome miner's light out of the duffel. The small LED light attached to a flexible band, which he slid around his forehead. Drew the gloves over his hands.

He'd once again lead the team from the front. Lying on his back on the closest cart, he clipped his duffel to his belt to keep it on his waist and chest.

Used his legs to slide on his back to the lead cart in the line.

The others copied his example, transporting their tactical gear, weapons, and explosives, with Stro in place on the final cart. They all shuffled around a bit, listening to the creaking of the wooden cart joints, until comfortable.

Resting on his back, Kwon gripped the other strand of vinylon rope suspended overhead, both hands reaching forward into the darkness. "Goshawk One set. Count off." His team was named after their national bird, the true hawk.

"Three set."

"Four set."

"Five set."

"Six set."

"Seven set."

"Two set. All prepared, sir." Stro added.

"Let's go." With that, Kwon pulled with his right hand.

As each hand reached the duffel on his waist, he began pulling with the other. Like an easy rope climb, but horizontal instead of vertical.

With seven strong soldiers pulling, the carts quickly reached a speed they could physically maintain for hours with little effort. Kwon intended to give the team a break every twenty minutes.

No reason to arrive worn out.

First, one klick to the turn. They'd built the gradual turn to line the tunnel up with the restored Gyeongui railway line. Following the line would confuse any seismic sensors, just as the construction to restore the only railway connection between the true Korea and the South provided cover to build the tunnel they sped through.

Four klicks under the railway to cross the DMZ and reach Dorasan metro station.

Kwon's gloved hands picked up a slimy coating of mud from the rope. It passed through periodic pulleys to keep it off the ground.

With only darkness beyond the short reach of his light, the hum of the wheels and the earthen ceiling sliding rapidly past were the best indicators of their continued speed.

Kwon found it odd Defense Minister Meon focused so much on temptation during their last meeting. Did Meon believe his team weak?

Then why did he choose them to infiltrate Seoul? Kwon took a moment during the rhythm of pulling to tap his breast pocket for luck.

In the end, it was the Imperialists' fault his team was in this tunnel.

Kwon tilted his head back even farther. Caught the flow of earthy tunnel air across his face.

The slight damp helped to wake up. He needed to focus, but he kept just pointing the light up ahead, hoping to see the end of the mud slurping at the darkness.

Time to *Achieve a Great Victory* and *Smash the American Bastards*, as posters regularly reminded them in their barracks.

Sliding through this tunnel in the dark was too much like death; kilometers of nothingness. Not enough to think about. Just the eternal sameness of earth propped up by periodic flashes of wooden supports.

The supports held the ceiling above and the rope below. At least underground was slightly warmer than above.

Kwon reviewed their planning in his head. Anything to keep his mind occupied. "Always advance straight ahead, following the Party!"

At the end of this tunnel following the railway, his team would leave the wooden carts.

There would be a left turn into a 50 meter tunnel. Long crawl to an abandoned greenhouse, 400 meters from Dorasan Peace Park.

Well south of the DMZ.

Team Goshawk would stage out of the paddy-field farm with the greenhouses.

A farm prepared as this tunnel was, thanks to the foresight of the Stout Fighters in the Korean People's Internal Security Forces. Unlike the older kilometers of larger tunnels built with cement, suitable for infiltrating entire battalions in a long stream of men and trucks.

Instead, the Security Forces switched to smaller tunnels.

Just large enough to fit special forces teams and their equipment, the better to infiltrate and prepare the South for eventual unification.

The Imperialist's blood money couldn't purchase equipment to detect these smaller tunnels.

Staged and armed, his elite commandos would travel by borrowed military truck through Seoul to the lab. The truck would blend in with the other traffic near the DMZ.

Once at the lab, he would lead his team to "Resolutely foil the aggression and intervention of the dominationists!"

After more than a decade spent memorizing orders and official slogans, Kwon derived great comfort and focus from remembering Minister Meon's exact inspiring words.

For now, it was enough to be reborn from the end of the tunnel.

The sword of the dictatorship of the proletariat was coming.

There was nothing the Imperialist Bastards at the South's top secret metallurgical lab could do to stop them.

I was tombstoning my mental board. Sinking into the depths. Getting relieved of duty is a total bummer.

At a time like this, most dudes would call their parents for advice. Mine'd vanished from my life in an explosion when I was seven, leaving me to mature in the Southern California foster care system, keeping one eye open anytime I napped. A legion of guardians and bunkmates, and no family at all.

The Rangers didn't understand; I'd learned early to only rely on myself.

Headed home to pack.

Not in the mood to talk to anyone from my unit, I skipped the normal exit.

Cut through Hotel Elle. Entered from the Camp Kim side.

Most employees of populous businesses ignore people they don't know, so it's easy enough to take advantage of a service entrance or back hallway here or there. This time the only one who even looked at me as I sidestepped past the hotel's ginormous washing machines was a housekeeper.

She hopped up and down on her toes trying to reach a big bottle of bleach someone had stuck on top of the machines.

About a foot taller, I just grabbed it down for her and nodded in passing.

No big deal.

That worked to cut through the hotel laundry areas. Letting the commercial door bang behind me, I stalked through the winter air.

Entered the subway from a long gray concrete walkway.

Technically the wrong direction, but that put me right on the train platform, without crossing icy streets and having to inhale diesel bus smoke mixed with kimchi's sour garlic and fish odor, ever-present in the Seoul air.

The Metropolitan Subway system is clean enough, even on a crowded Friday afternoon.

Namyeong Station is a high slanted roof projecting over faux marble floors, with wide steps and tubular steel handrails everywhere. Modern Gangnam-style.

Doubt the couple of cameras at each end of the platform aimed along rows of silver aluminum doors would provide any useful evidence in the event of a pick pocketing, let alone a more serious incident like a terror attack.

Unlike the open tracks back home, those lined up doors prevented the masses of dark-suited Korean workers from pushing each other onto the tracks before a train arrived to catch them.

During an emergency *someone* would surely push one of the big red call buttons stashed at intervals next to the fire extinguishers and flashlights.

It's a testament to the locals' basic law-abiding nature the Metropolitan Police doesn't get a false alarm and a stolen flashlight every half hour.

My train for home arrived. The row of double-doors opened. A rush of air and people unloaded.

Edged my way around the crowd. Stepped aboard.

Row after row of billboards flanked each group of seats in the train car. The billboard pairs alternated between advertising a slim young woman wearing a black silk dress under a casino logo with a different-yet-same model extolling the benefits of the plastic surgery South Korea is famous for.

Both industries attract wealthy Chinese. None of it attracted me right now.

Despite the crowded train, I scored a spot between billboards on a blue plastic bench seat paralleling the track.

As usual, the short Koreans surrounding the tall foreign devil shrunk back as I arrived, behaving as if I carried an infectious disease of violence.

My uniform probably didn't help their perceptions.

Our train passed into the darkness under the Han river. Banked twice.

An ancient Korean lady minced her way on wearing what must be her most formal and traditional outfit. Looked like she was an opera star.

She looked around the train car, but couldn't locate any empty seats besides the space everyone was giving the dangerous foreign devil.

Stared at me for a moment. Sighed. Grabbed onto a pole as the train started up again.

Not wanting to be rude, I stood and gestured toward the now open bench.

The Korean lady shook her head, as if the seat had been contaminated by my presence.

I took another step into the aisle. Pointed again. She finally decided there was enough of a buffer between us and perched on the edge of the bench farthest from me.

Tempted to sit back down next to her, but decided I could just stand for a few minutes.

Didn't fit in anywhere.

After a few brief sets of exhaling and inhaling passengers later, we crawled into Suseo Station.

Almost home.

I crossed two streets to the turnstile at Seoul Air Base, nicknamed K-16 during the Korean War.

My fingers began to numb from the cold, just walking outside for a few minutes. Rubbed my hands together and blew on them. Half-checked my non-existent pistol holster.

Always need to be prepared, but officers on base aren't authorized sidearms.

I'd never heard of anyone relieved of duty for standards in the Rangers where it didn't kill their career. Getting relieved was the Army's equivalent of being fired for cause, except they expected you to stick around to count spoons for the mess hall in Iceland until you finally quit.

Even if you turned out to be right later, being relieved meant your superiors thought you couldn't cut it. A nice way of letting you earn out your pension without hope of future responsibility.

Not in the Rangers, nor even back to a job as a platoon leader in the Big Army.

I've lost more families than anyone I know. It's less painful to bail out than to get trashed by your fake parents.

The Major just trashed me.

The Korean Army PFC outside the K-16 pedestrian turnstile wore a high visibility yellow coat over his uniform. Saluting being against his standing orders, he merely gave a Korean half-bow version of a head tilt, "Lieutenant Harper", eyes forward, staring at my nametape.

More security theater, as anyone in uniform with a fingerprint made from super glue and a cloned RFID badge to trigger the turnstile could walk right onto the base, only civilians got additional security scrutiny.

I trudged over to my Bachelor Officer Quarters (BOQ) apartment in building 900. 54 company grade officers, lieutenants and captains, each got 650 square feet in the vertical tan tower. That gave us a combined kitchen/living/dining room with a separate bedroom and bathroom.

Not sure what they made the thin flooring from, just that it was a speckled black, tan and white, designed to hide dirt. All the rooms tastefully furnished in light oak particle board, with a piece of bonus foam on top of the bed's mattress.

South Korea's equivalent of Ikea must've gotten an Army contract to furnish it all.

That sounds bad. The living room's puke green couch and armchair, complete with shiny raised floral patterns, really was horrible, but compared to the sergeants without families stashed two at a time into only 220 square feet of shared space elsewhere in the building, officers had it relatively good.

Not great compared to the guys with approval for off-base private apartments, but at least if we had to get the Republic of Korea Air Force's (ROKAF) 15th Special Missions Wing or our own 2nd Aviation Regiment to give us a ride into battle, they conveniently located their Sikorsky UH-60 Black Hawks within walking distance.

Definitely hearing distance at night as well.

The flyboys for SOCKOR were good guys. I'd arranged with one to bring a prototype eSurfboard with me to Korea. It cluttered up my limited closet space, but I'd stuck a local tide chart on the fridge with magnets. Planned to see if I could get out to the southern coast, or maybe Jeju Island to surf if I ever manage more than a weekend pass for leave.

Now I wouldn't be here long enough to even *see* the ocean.

Reeling from the reality of being relieved, I tossed a duffel on the bed and started packing. Grabbed extra uniforms and civvies from behind the sliding closet doors. Chucked them on the bed.

Dismissing my analysis without even verifying it? Had the CO even read it? Was he that afraid of upsetting our hosts?

Wasn't our mission to provide training and analysis to the ROK forces so they could improve? Did Captain Rhee have political pull somewhere I'd missed?

Stopping when I ran out of closet contents, I stared out my bedroom window at K-16's parallel runways. The heating unit hanging embedded in the wall's top kicked on. Its noise competed with a landing Black Hawk helicopter.

Embrace the suck.

OK, so fire me for doing a bad job on the analysis, but I knew it was accurate. Didn't the scientists in that lab deserve to have at least one person looking out for them? Making sure security vulnerabilities got remediated?

Fixing things which could get them killed?

I moved to the tiny bathroom. Decided to leave the cheap Korean tea tree shampoo I'd purchased. Those bottles always spilled in transit, even if you put them in a plastic bag.

What if someone stole their work?

Years of effort to stay ahead of our joint enemies lost. Even if they considered the scientists expendable, why didn't anyone care about their work?

Care enough to send in a red team to take advantage of my reported vulnerabilities and prove if they existed or not.

How can I fight my company commander?

Not to mention the military bureaucracy and Rhee Yun-seok's now-apparent political connections? This just wasn't a wave I could ride.

Not even the most hardcore can surf a tsunami.

Not thinking straight, I knocked over my shampoo bottle. Splattered the bathroom floor with glops of thick green liquid. The room filled with the smell of peppermint and eucalyptus.

Screw this.

What was I doing? The CO didn't say I had to pack tonight, just to report with my bags Monday morning for new orders.

Until then, I was still technically assigned to the 75th RRC, with the task to improve security for the lab. After my reception from the locals, whoever they gave that task to next would just gloss over any issues.

I dumped the contents of my packed duffel bag out onto the bed.

The uniform of the day would work well to blend in at a military-run lab, as much as a non-Korean can in Seoul. Slipped my wallet, the contact lens case I'd forgotten to return, and my smartphone into pockets.

Plenty of fun tools on my phone to get the job done.

My Gerber multi-tool might come in handy, so I slid it into a cargo pocket. I paused for a second. Stared at my bed.

Did I need anything else? Knowing I'd be walking outside, I grabbed my small black folding umbrella, just in case the frozen gods of the sky turned their back on me once more.

Needed to borrow the CIA's RFID reader/transmitter from Michelle again.

Time to get back up on the board.

With a little more equipment, I'd be my own red team and prove my lab analysis was true. Could call Michelle on the way.

Surely she'd help me out, just like old times.

What could Major Williams do, relieve me of duty for taking things into my own hands?

Chapter Nine:
Risky Business

Lieutenant Kwon Chol felt a little guilty at being glad the hackers back in Pyongyang couldn't get the lab's data by traversing the American's network, but not enough to dampen his high spirits at finally leading a mission to strike a blow against the Imperialists.

He tossed his black duffel bag into the cab of the Kia KM450 all-terrain military truck. Climbed up into the passenger seat.

Their Security Forces contact in Seoul had left the truck for his team at the rice farm. In this vehicle, near the DMZ and even within the connected city, they'd be invisible, just another Southern Army vehicle in olive and brown camouflage, hauling a random cargo underneath a military green canvas top.

Sergeant Stro, also dressed in a black and green enemy uniform, took his place behind the steering wheel.

The truck bed thumped as his other five soldiers folded down the integrated wooden slat cargo fencing in the back to form troop seats. They stowed the rest of their equipment in the bed.

Stro pushed a button on the dash. The diesel engine roared to life.

He released the brake to edge forward. Drove away from the greenhouse containing their tunnel back across the DMZ. Bounced along the hard-packed dirt road leading to the railroad tracks.

Smooth ride, for a military vehicle.

The Imperialists of the South were clever, but when his team arrived at the lab, they'd demonstrate mere material shrewdness didn't compare to the unconquerable will of the true Korean People.

Turning left to parallel the tracks, Stro deftly brought them up to 70 kph on the straightaway. A little fast for a dirt road, but the giant truck tires and suspension could take it.

Kwon spent his childhood on a farm.

He understood how much work and wealth the rice paddies they passed represented. Despite being carved out of the surrounding forest, there were enough fields in this half kilometer stretch to feed an entire village.

In winter, they lay flooded with water, probably pumped from the nearby river.

Just before reaching the river, Stro turned left onto a gray asphalt road which had crossed the railway tracks at grade. The road curved back away from the river.

Another 500 meters and they passed the entrance to Camp Greaves, a giant military sign advertising the "DMZ Experience", where civilians could stay in a barracks converted to a youth hostel and go on tours of bunkers from the war.

Stro fell in behind a bright red and white tourist bus, taking the wealthy home from touring the DMZ, where they could stare at the potential destruction prepared in their name.

Whoever heard of having fun touring a military installation, the remains of a war, weapons poised to resume the killing?

Had they no shame?

Did they glory in the destruction visited on the North by the dominationists? "Surely these tourists are the most callous of our enemy."

Stro gave him the look of an experienced sergeant straddled with an idiot lieutenant. Kwon knew it well from his early days in the Regular Army, before Meon selected him to lead a Special Forces platoon.

"Yes, sir. Wait until we get into the city, on the other side of the river. You'll see what I mean."

Kwon felt his cheeks glow. Reminded that while this was his first trip into the South, Stro had plenty of experience.

How should he respond to embarrassment by a subordinate?

Best to remain silent and observe, gaining experience during their trip.

Kwon nodded to Stro.

It's not as if he had anything to do until they reached their objective, the lab. Stro had driven the streets of Seoul before.

Kwon could rely on him.

They drove past a children's school. Reached a junction of three paved roads. They joined into one wide highway with three lanes in each direction.

Must be a major military route. Gave the name "Unification Road" sinister connotations.

No doubt unification by force.

Stro turned their truck on to the highway behind the bus.

Sedans immediately surrounded them, weaving in and out of traffic to gain an advantage over their relatively sluggish truck. Such a fine highway, with poles supporting street-lamps every 15 meters and a steel center divider.

Must be a meeting of high-ranking government officials nearby, to have dozens of newer vehicles around.

Red brake lights ahead. Cars stopped at an inspection booth.

"That checkpoint ahead, any problem?"

"We have the necessary permits and identification."

Stro lifted a clipboard from next to his seat.

"Easy for our specialists to forge, as long as no one checks against their central databases. Won't need them, though. That's a toll booth, not a security measure. As a government vehicle, we don't even need to pay."

Pulling up to the checkpoint, Stro rolled his window down.

The guard, in a dark blue uniform with a highly reflective yellow overcoat, saw an obvious military vehicle and waved them on.

"Easy enough," Kwon said. "At least we don't have to pay to use the roads. Any more like that?"

"This highway will take us all the way into Seoul. No more stops."

Kwon nodded, fascinated as they crossed the 500 meter wide Imjin River on a massive four-lane highway bridge.

The South even had light poles staggered on both sides of the bridge. Knowing the history of the early conflict between North and South, surely their Army would have explosives in place to destroy this fine bridge in the event of an invasion.

Such a waste.

With the wicked grin of a young boy about to get away with something, Stro pushed the accelerator pedal to the floor. Their truck accelerated to its top speed of 100 kph, matching the speed limit.

Kwon rarely traveled so quickly.

Still, the private cars streamed past them on the left, each traveling at least 40 kph faster.

After another 45 minutes of highway travel, they reached the outskirts of Seoul itself.

The left-most lane became lined with blue, designating it for the matching blue government buses only. As the other two lanes narrowed, fifteen, twenty story buildings began to appear on the side of the highway.

Seoul already matched Pyongyang in size and they were only at the outskirts. Stro slowed the truck to 60 kph to keep pace with the surrounding traffic and the lower speed limit. "Almost there."

Shops everywhere, lining both sides of the street.

Intellectually, Kwon knew Seoul was more populated than anywhere in the North, therefore they must have large buildings, but he'd never seen so many places to buy different products.

And signs. Signs blazing light in every direction. Must be an important commerce district.

The area even had its own four garage fire station. That made sense, as there were so many cars everywhere. Not just cars, but motorbikes and scooters weaving in and out of the traffic, filling into the gaps whenever they reached a red stoplight.

In Pyongyang, everything was red and white. Here, a riot of colors assaulted his senses.

The Imperialists must gather all the wealth of the South to this place; otherwise, how could they afford all the goods he saw displayed for purchase?

All the hefty men and women strolling down the concrete sidewalks, wearing puffy winter coats and gloves, browsing racks of merchandise outside open door shops.

Did all the people in Seoul gorge themselves on the fat of the surrounding countryside?

Must be sick inside.

He smelled a cart with a blue and white umbrella before they reached it in the thick traffic.

Stro caught him staring at the man handing out corn tortillas filled with beef and kimchi. "No time for that type of pleasure right now. Will taste better once we get our fill of the other sort. After the mission."

Kwon nodded. "Of course."

Passing a metro subway station, Stro turned onto a side street. Drove around a curve between three-story businesses. The line of cars and minivans ahead of their truck stopped.

The vehicles didn't move for minutes.

Kwon didn't have much experience with non-military vehicles, but he'd never had to wait in a car before. Was there a military parade ahead that they hadn't briefed his team on?

The light in the sky began to fade.

Street-lights popped on, competing with neon shop windows. Dusk approached, "We need to reach the lab on time or we'll waste our agent's preparations." Kwon unbuckled the straps holding him into his seat. "I'll go find out why the traffic stopped."

Stro shook his head, but didn't argue.

Maybe wandering around alone in the enemy capital wasn't such a great idea? "I'll keep within sight of the truck. Be prepared to move if I can find us a way around this."

Kwon opened his passenger door. Stepped down to the concrete curb defining the edge of a wide sidewalk.

A burly man in black jeans and a puffy navy jacket detoured around Kwon on the sidewalk.

Kwon stared as he watched the sole of the man's shoes light up in a row of purple LEDs with each step. Gold chains rattled around his neck, one exhibiting a giant dollar sign.

The South's elite displayed their wealth brazenly.

This man should instead be ashamed. Even though the powerful in the North possessed a few human flaws, trying to do good for their families while surviving the Dominionists in this difficult world, at least they didn't exhibit this crass commercialism.

How could these people stand it? The American Imperialists obviously corrupted them decades ago.

Kwon followed the burly man's shoes through the crowd, taking advantage of his wake to clear a path for him.

At the next intersection a police officer in a dark blue overcoat with high visibility yellow wrists and ankles stood in the middle of the street. A two-door Hyundai luxury sedan had embedded it's crushed front bumper into the driver-side door of a similar car.

That explained the backup and the people standing around watching. The local pedestrians probably took pleasure in seeing the mighty car drivers with their own private vehicles brought low.

He looked back to gauge his distance from the truck. Stro peered forward at him from behind the wheel.

Too many cars stopped.

No room in the street to go forward.

The police officer in the intersection wasn't even directing traffic around the collision. One driver stood outside his vehicle, but the other just waved her hand from her window for attention; the setting sun reflected off a diamond ring on her third finger.

Trapped in her seat by the other car bending the frame inward around her.

The disrespect and inefficiency in the South!

These civilians surely didn't think they could interfere with a military unit? Maybe they didn't see the truck Stro drove.

Kwon stepped forward into the intersection. "Here. You." He pointed at the police officer talking to the woman stuck in the car, "We have military business. Clear these cars out of the way."

The police officer tucked his radio microphone onto its black plastic hook on his wide utility belt, next to a .38-caliber revolver. "I've called for a tow truck and the fire department. We'll have you out of here soon, ma'am. You're sure you're all right? You may be in shock and not feeling an injury yet. Can you move all of your arms and legs?"

Someone tapped Kwon on the shoulder.

He spun around into a crouch.

Another policeman confronted him. "Who are you?" The policeman made brushing motions with his hands towards the curb. "Unless you can help, stay back. We have an accident to investigate."

Kwon pointed back at the truck. "My platoon is on a critical and time sensitive mission. You must let us past."

"Identification?"

Why wasn't this policeman intimidated at dealing with a member of the military?

Wait, this was the South. Kwon felt his cheeks redden.

He hadn't fully considered the potential difference in cultures. What if this man was of a higher status in this situation, despite being a lowly police officer?

Kwon gave a respectful nod, hoping to cover any previous indiscretion. "Our paperwork is in the truck."

The police officer curtly returned his acknowledgment and pointed back to the curb. "Don't have time for this. Go wait with the others."

Kwon nodded. This place confused him. Better to retreat.

Couldn't get into an argument with the police in the enemy's capital. He walked back toward the truck along the curb, avoiding the crowd on the sidewalk.

The setting winter sun shone into his eyes. Not much more until dusk.

He'd really wanted to arrive early and have time to recon the target first.

Reaching the truck, Kwon noticed the other side of the road was mostly clear of traffic. Of course, the accident would stop vehicles traveling the other way as well.

He walked around the front of the truck to the driver's side. Only one stopped silver sedan to the left of the truck blocked them in, preventing a U-turn.

Kwon knocked on the window of the silver sedan.

Startled, the old man inside rolled it down. "Excuse me sir, but

I must ask you to turn your car around here and travel the other way. This is the only method of freeing up my truck to do the same."

"But . . . that's illegal in the middle of the block."

He pointed at the rank tabs on his uniform shoulder. "It's fine. This is an exception. The traffic is stopped and this is an emergency military matter."

The old man nodded, clearly impressed. "I'm going."

Kwon stepped to the back of the silver car as it pulled farther into the street, turning around to head the other way. He blocked off the car behind it, standing at the bumper to ensure the space remained unoccupied.

A piercing police whistle warbled from the intersection with the crash.

Apparently this wasn't strictly legal, even in this situation.

Kwon gestured urgently for Stro to take advantage of the space he'd created.

The gears crunched as Stro downshifted. He cranked the giant truck tires around and got turned facing the sun instead.

Hopefully the police officers, staring into the sun, wouldn't be able to capture any identifying information about the truck which made an illegal turn-around half a block away.

Kwon ran around the front of the truck.

Climbed into the passenger's seat. "Go." Buckled himself in as the truck lurched forward.

Stro gunned the accelerator, swerving around the slowly driving old man whose silver car was the only obstacle ahead of them. "I have an alternate route we can use."

"I'm counting on it. No going back there now." He patted his breast pocket. Wouldn't embarrass his family further.

He'd mentally record these new sights and sounds and leave analysis for after they hit the lab.

Maintaining situational awareness requires either absolute focus on external events or at least remembering to pay attention to your surroundings.

A flight of Black Hawks or a VIP's private jet might've taken off at K-16 while I strode from my BOQ apartment to the Air Base gate to leave, but I didn't hear more than the low engine rumble in the background.

Somehow, I made it through the air base's exit turnstile. Walked back to Suseo subway station.

Oblivious to the sights and sounds of Seoul around me.

Pretty sure I swiped my green T-card to enter the station. Gate wouldn't have opened if I forgot.

There's a sense of being in the zone. A complete absorption. Perfect focus on the task at hand.

At first, I only achieved that feeling while surfing.

Complex patterns flowed for me. Could see the point off the beach where each set of waves from the ocean combined with their reflections from shore produced the perfect place to wait.

Analyzed. Observed the shaped water.

Predicted when the next big wave must arrive.

Anticipated the coming break-point. Paddled furiously to hit it.

Stood to catch the thrust of the breaking wave against my surfboard. Achieved perfect balance on the wave's face.

Maintained harmony.

Couldn't lose momentum from shooting too far ahead. Wouldn't tumble to the ocean floor via the rushing barrel of chaos crashing down on me. Strung together moments of terror and majesty.

Awesome.

Learned to recognize that level of concentration. Encourage it in myself.

Dropped into the flow while escaping mundane life. Read. Lived in another universe of mental worlds.

Then focused competing in high school track and field.

Attacked by an older foster brother or three? Massive fight-or-flight adrenaline rush. Stayed calm and rational.

Excluded everything else from my mind.

Visualized the relationships between technical concepts in college.

Felt the exact moment to press the trigger of my rifle. Break the perfect shot.

Needed that pinpoint focus now. Needed to figure out how to crack a top secret materials lab by myself.

Prove the truth.

Break in without my Red Team members. No fallout could splash on them.

Gain illicit entrance. No help from the operators in the rest of the company. Schnier wouldn't understand.

On my own.

But not without resources.

Knew our report on the lab by heart. Worked on it for the last thirty days.

Seen ID badge pictures of the staff. Reviewed the guard schedules. Studied their procedures.

Read the technical manuals and security bulletins for their security systems. Analyzed tons of background information which didn't make it into the report.

Monitored their security.

An idea formed. I blinked. Sat on the crowded metro train at Suseo.

Ignored the Koreans ostensibly ignoring me.

South Koreans work long hours. A cultural thing, to be seen late at work.

Captain Rhee, the security chief who'd been so offended by my report, went out for dinner every evening. Checked back in at shift change to ensure the security team properly handed everything off to the night crew.

The same time the cleaning crew and the night shift of the administrative side of the lab arrived for work. After, he went for drinks with his cronies or to his home to sleep.

His expensive eating habits would be my entrée into the lab. Just needed to re-borrow a piece of CIA equipment first.

I could ride this wave.

Bluetooth earbud in place, I pressed Michelle's contact on my mobile phone. Her Facebook photo, automatically imported into my contacts list, displayed on the screen.

No headshot, just a postcardy snapshot of a forlorn coastline, thick storm clouds at sunset over a rocky promontory.

Clearly not wanting anyone to connect her name and image in

any online databases. Facial recognition was everywhere these days.

"Michelle? It's Sam."

"Howzit going?"

"Been better. I'll explain later. Hate to put you on the spot, but can I borrow the Agency's portable RFID scanner again?" Could build one, but just shopping for the parts in an electronics store with my limited language skills would take more time than I had.

"Sure, Sam. Stop by and pick it up first thing Monday morning?"

"Thanks, dude. Assuming you're at your embassy office right now, can I just stop by instead? Only about twenty minutes away. It's urgent."

"Relaxing at home instead of haunting the office. Guess I can meet you there. Scanner's in my desk. In trouble?"

"Not as much as I'm likely to be in before the night is over. Does the Agency still run flights out of the country for refugees? You may need to save me a spot for later."

"What?"

"I'm kidding. Mostly." I considered how to explain. Maybe later. "See you in a few."

Chapter Ten:
Spiking Paperwork

Doctor Yang Hyo-jin romped around to relive her volleyball career. She preferred the lab's offices between shifts, with no administrators around.

A ten-foot wide walkway through the admin spaces connected the main lobby to the mantrap guarding her team's cavernous experimental lab space and science offices.

In this Olympic gym-sized cubicle farm, those who could neither theorize nor engineer solutions slaved away on either side of the walkway.

Hyo-jin glided between cubicles.

Her lab coat flowed through the air with the speed of an Olympian goddess.

An itsy break room and three generous conference rooms overflowed one side of the bureaucratic space. Windows for more privileged denizens lined the opposite edge.

Everyone else made do with the potted Areca Palms and Chinese Evergreens scattered around, slowly turning carbon dioxide into oxygen.

The main security office controlled the lobby turnstiles; the guards only additional territory a camera room standing watch over the loading dock on the far side of the lab and warehouse zones.

She used her height and reach to shuffle paperwork directly over partition walls and onto the desks of the powers-that-be she owed forms and reports to.

The government wouldn't pay for the people and experiments

she valued without the requisitions, signed purchase orders, justifications, and grant progress reports she littered the office with.

Wise in the way of the bureaucracy, she'd finished her paperwork earlier, but if she'd made her offerings to officialdom before the staff went home, she'd have had to stop, enter each cubicle, bow politely, make small talk, inquire after relatives, and then explain to each person one at a time what the papers contained, repeated a dozen times.

Waste of an entire day.

This way, as long as no one stayed late, and who besides obsessive scientists stayed late on a Friday night, she just cruised down the aisles, delivering each stack of paper as a spike over the net.

The main security office door popped open.

Rhee Yun-seok stalked backwards into the hallway near the turnstile. Faced the guards on duty inside the office. Issued a rat-a-tat-tat of instructions to his subordinates.

Not what she needed right now.

Hyo-jin ducked into the break room before Rhee looked around the office area.

No time for another confrontation.

She wanted to make a few copies in here, anyway. She placed a stack of papers onto the combination scanner/printer/copier's auto-feed. Punched the buttons to make duplicates.

Plenty of time for him to clear out of the building while she waited for the photocopies, then she could head back via the mantrap and through the experimental area to her office without further interruption.

Staying late at work involved many hazards.

Was I crazy to attempt to infiltrate a top secret lab by myself? Lieutenant-walking-career-destruction?

I fought the after-work crowds. Smoothly evaded the ankle-biters. Changed subway lines at Wangsimni station's indoor mall.

Icy weather flooded the subway with people to dodge. I

observed their patterns.

Traffic is like the flow of a wave.

Rode fifteen minutes to Gwanghwamun station. The central government and business district of Seoul.

Half a block south of the US Embassy.

Train slowed. I texted Michelle. "Almost there. Meet me outside with the scanner."

She'd head home again after we met, so I didn't want to waste time with embassy security.

Departed the station. Headed north.

A twenty-five foot bronze statue of ancient King Sejong on his throne reflected the dying sunlight.

Demonstrators set up rows of chairs in the plaza across the street from the embassy.

The King raised a frozen benevolent hand to bless visitors, but one of his legs was as large as a normal Korean man. Pretty sure he wasn't built to original scale.

What did I have to lose?

Streets surrounded the embassy building on three sides: east, south and west. The remaining north side bordered the National Museum of Modern History.

If I had to break into the embassy to appropriate the RFID scanner, how would I get in? The embassy building's security precautions made it stand out like a shark fin from its neighbors.

They embedded three feet of Y-shaped anti-climb steel fencing in the top of each ten foot block wall. That controlled the inside edge of each sidewalk and the north side toward the museum.

Cameras hung every fifteen feet along the wall. Security officers watched the streets.

More than sufficient basic security to keep unruly foreigners out of the complex.

Williams could court martial me, instead of just relieving me. In taking initiative to fulfill my platoon's mission, I wasn't sure I'd technically be doing anything wrong.

My orders were clear, but vague enough a JAG prosecutor would have to argue I violated the spirit of them, not the letter of them.

In the western plaza, a line of not-exactly-protesters waved

American and ROK blue-red ying-yang flags. Held up signs like "We Go Together", supportive of the ROK-US Alliance.

Unusually positive for a typical American embassy.

Walked up the wider western road. Stepped through a pedestrian gap in a line of three foot planter boxes at the curb.

Planters designed to keep a truck attack away from the main embassy wall. Didn't even bother planting flowers in them.

That side also had a double vehicle gate. Allowed legitimate traffic to flow in and out.

Contained the employee entrance, which wouldn't permit me.

Mirrors hanging over the gates gave security a view of the roof of any vehicle waiting to enter or exit.

The eastern street contained short portable trailers blocking the way. They turned the sidewalk between them and the wall into a tunnel.

The south side, a narrower street, coincidentally had police buses parked along the road's edge to block vehicle access. The only gap between buses was the pedestrian entrance. The portion of the wall reserved for walk-in visitors.

The parked buses were no accident.

Whoever planned security for the embassy was ready to keep anyone with a car bomb well away from the building itself.

In the end, a military court would need to conclude that excessively doing my job before I officially departed was against the Uniform Code of Military Justice (UCMJ).

As long I didn't cause any major damage, or hurt anyone, I didn't see how a panel of officers would justify that verdict. Most likely, they'd be satisfied to drum me out of the Army with a less than satisfactory discharge for my aggro moves.

At the pedestrian entrance Seoul Metro Police officers in black and neon yellow uniform coats required proper identification. Queried visit purposes.

More police officers stood or paced every 20 feet around the perimeter. Bored, yet professional.

Additional polite police patrolled the opposite sides of the surrounding streets.

If an attacker made it past the exterior wall and into the courtyard, steel security screens protected the bottom two floors.

Overkill for a peaceful city like Seoul, but I couldn't fault the security design.

Vertical three foot concrete pillars protected the walk-in entrance from vehicle attacks. A green glass dome kept rain off the waiting crowd.

The embassy's American flag flapped in the winter wind atop a 40' pole in the courtyard. Scattered external climate control units illustrated the hierarchy. No heat nor AC for your office showed less pull.

Antennas and satellite dishes dominated the roof-line eight stories up. Peeked above edge railing designed to prevent falling deaths, accidental or otherwise.

As long as Michelle loaned me the CIA's RFID scanner, I wouldn't have to break in to borrow it.

If I did, it'd be from the sky. A flat roof surrounded by walls doesn't protect you from above.

But then, I'm more paranoid than anyone else I know about physical security. I looked for potential vulnerabilities everywhere, especially noticing places vulnerable to car bombs.

A car bomb killed my parents.

Shortly, I planned to use my security analysis to infiltrate a military lab for real, rather than just help defend it. Was that justified? Would I stand condemned? Used my family legacy in the attack?

If I didn't prove the lab vulnerable, an enemy might take advantage of their problems. Problems we could've fixed if I'd followed through on my plans tonight.

Other families might die. More collateral damage.

As a United States Army officer, I owed a duty to those families.

I'd be responsible for whatever happened because I chose to prove my platoon's report was correct. Couldn't blame the foolishness of Captain Rhee or Major Williams for my decision.

Across the street, Michelle waited for me outside the embassy employee entrance. I couldn't help comparing her slender beauty to the Korean demonstrators surrounding me.

She lit up as I walked past the rows of chairs, probably happy to see a familiar face in the sea of Koreans.

I stopped just to stare. To capture this moment in my mind. After this weekend I might not be in Korea for long.

Might not see Michelle for a while.

Stepped back. Created the perfect framing. Kicked the side of a chair someone had set up behind me.

Tripped.

Collapsed across three wooden folding chairs. Knocked them over like bowling pins. Scattered destruction in a circle around me.

Ruined the friendly demonstrators' work.

They probably thought a uniformed giant had invaded. I wanted to crawl up into a ball and somehow roll away unnoticed.

Michelle ran across the street, ignoring stopped traffic, to see if I was okay.

Mostly just my ego was bruised. I stood and brushed water and ice off.

Volunteers in long sleeve blue shirts under puffy jackets surrounded me. Wouldn't let me fix the chairs I'd knocked asunder.

Insisted I leave immediately.

At least their peace and reunification organization wouldn't be out of business anytime soon.

Knowing when to advance in a retrograde manner, I fled with Michelle.

Wasn't sure what else to do, but pretend it hadn't happened. "Taking the subway home? We can walk back and talk on the way."

"Sure." She patted her black leather purse, as if to check for something. "Let's go."

We walked toward Gwanghwamun station. The wide plaza stretching from King Sejong's statue to the subway entrance split the road in half.

I pushed the pace through the thickening crowd. Dodged furry boots and flying scarf ends.

Michelle kept up.

Wasn't currently pouring from the sky, so everyone had their space-sucking umbrellas tucked away. Michelle had long enough legs and the track running muscle memory to go quickly when she needed to.

Helped to anticipate and navigate that we could both see above everyone else's heads.

We reached a clearer stretch of the walkway near a line of dormant fountains embedded in the concrete ground. A statue of an admiral wore what looked like Samurai armor. I guess nobody wanted to take the risk of the water turning on in the cold.

I extended my arm. "I can carry the scanner."

She didn't hand it over right away. "What do you need it for, anyway? You sounded rushed before."

After the chair incident, I didn't really want to get into my dressing down from the CO.

"Probably better you don't know much. Then you can't catch any heat if this goes wrong."

"Nothing illegal?"

"Of course not, but bureaucratically a few people won't be happy."

She wrinkled up her forehead for a moment as we walked. "You don't need trouble either."

"Michelle, this is important."

She went silent for a full thirty seconds. Highly unusual.

Sighed. Handed over the scanner and its USB cable. "Hope you know what you're doing. You know you can talk to me. Really wish you would."

"Better for you to have deniability on this one."

Didn't seem to believe me, because she went quiet for another minute as we dodged around a strip of hibernating grass.

"Sounds like a throw of the dice. You have your Red Team involved?"

"Not this time."

"Use your team. You're a nice guy, Sam, but you take too much responsibility on yourself. Go out on too many limbs. They get cut off sometimes, you know?" She smiled. "I can't always be there to get you on the next plane out of town."

"Sometimes you have to just get things done yourself and if a tree falls in the woods, a tree falls in the woods. Maybe nobody but the lumberjacks will notice."

"Are you okay?"

I wondered if the skit reference was deliberate. With a grin, I gave her a sing-songy "I work all night and I sleep all day."

She laughed. "At least you don't wear women's clothing, like those Brits."

We walked down steps into the subway station. Stood staring at each other between wide white pillars halfway between the two platforms designated for the opposite directions we needed to travel.

Korean architecture involved lots of rounded edges, especially where the ceiling met the subway walls. Both sets of glass safety doors were closed, no trains visible on the far side.

The locals nearby gave the American giants a clear circle.

Maybe it was just me. I put on my serious face again. "You should at least know Captain Rhee from the lab lodged an official protest about my report. You'll hear the scuttlebutt on the private news network about how Major Williams responded, but it wasn't pretty."

She cocked her head. "He stood up for you?"

I shook mine. "Not exactly. More stood me up in front of the firing squad."

"Ouch."

"Exactly. Gotta bail. Have someone to catch up with, but won't damage your baby." Tucked the scanner/transmitter into a cargo pocket.

My subway train arrived.

"Sam, we've developed a high-level source in the DPRK government. Don't know all the details, but it'll probably turn into something. Something soon, on the north side of the DMZ.

"So don't get yourself kicked out of the country. Don't want to miss out on this one."

The glass safety doors opened. A sea of demonstration attendees in matching shirts and puffy coats crowded out from the train cars. Normally I'd drag more details out of her, but had no time for this.

"Let me get through tonight, first."

"Don't take too many risks. Do the smart thing."

"Always."

"No, you usually do things in a smart way, but you also tend to do the principled, stubborn thing, which is occasionally the dumb thing."

Okay, she maybe had me pegged, there. I just shook my head before hustling away.

She blew me a kiss as I looked back from the train window.

Odd. Probably a sarcastic send-off for my non-response. I waved. No hard feelings.

Carrying the right tools, the lab infiltration would work out just fine.

What could possibly go wrong?

All the neon hurt Kwon's eyes. Didn't the South need these resources for all the cars he'd seen?

Storefront signs lit up central Seoul.

Towering office skyscrapers rose behind the storefronts; windows lit up despite the hour growing later.

Surely this wealthy city's inhabitants must keep the rest of the South dirt poor, stealing all their energy and other resources well beyond those due to central government officials.

Twenty more minutes of Stro's driving through the crowded streets of Seoul and they arrived at a loading dock off an alley.

The rear entrance to their target; an enormous secret facility, like a giant warehouse, taking up most of a city block. A sheltered alcove led between the bumper-high dock and the wide steel back door.

Stro backed their truck up to the loading dock. Pushed the engine shut off button. The diesel pistons rumbled to a halt.

Kwon opened his door.

As planned, four of the five soldiers in the back jumped down. Set up a casual perimeter watch, just some Army guys taking a smoke break.

The fifth, his communications sergeant, carried a black duffel bag from the rear up to the passenger door. He held up a mobile phone, issued for use in Seoul. "Shall I transmit the next checkpoint, sir?"

Pleasant to work with competent soldiers, unlike those in his last platoon, conscripts he could tell just wanted to finish their duty and get back to their regular life.

Now his team was the elite of the North Korean People's Army. Easy to trust. "Proceed, then pass out the radios."

His com sergeant pushed send twice, transmitting prepared text messages to two numbers.

Their Security Forces contact would forward their milestone check-in message to Deputy Minister Meon and pass back any changed orders. The second message confirmed their arrival to their lab contact. That message would trigger a sequence of events to get them into the lab.

Kwon nodded to Stro. "Let's go."

Stro hopped out of the cab on the driver's side. Organized the other men with quick, curt, commands.

Had them don their plate carriers. Equip them with reloads, grenades, and their other tactical gear. Personally, Kwon preferred a mag panel, placing a row of pistol reloads in front of his chest for a little extra protection.

Body armor could only be bullet-*resistant*.

The two demolition experts also double-checked each of their prepped blocks of explosives. They'd waste no time inside.

Kwon took a radio and earpiece from the com sergeant. Attached the radio to his belt. Inserted the earpiece.

The sergeant passed out similar devices to the rest of the men.

After seeing the men sorted out, Stro ordered a pair to guard the rear entrance to the lab, thick steel embedded into the concrete block outer wall.

For this mission, Goshawk team would operate in pairs; his com sergeant sticking with Stro, each of the demo guys paired with a sniper. Kwon by himself had the easiest and most important role of all.

Get the data they needed to turn the tables on the Imperialists.

With everyone else loaded up, Stro and Kwon began their own transformations into soldiers ready for combat. Kwon strapped a pistol holster to his leg. He'd do without the K2 rifle everyone else carried. No reason to develop tunnel vision.

If they needed him to carry a rifle, they'd already blown the mission.

The others stacked up into positions on either side of the lab door. Allowed space for the door to open outward.

If they'd traveled fully tactical, Kwon's team would've stood out from regular soldiers around town, but that didn't matter now.

Just a little longer until his team could act openly and land their blow on the Imperialists.

Kwon slid a tactical vest over his head. Tightened the waist strap. Snapped his mag panel into place. Double-checked the magazine in his Baek Du San clone of the CZ 75 semi-automatic pistol.

He'd join them in a moment.

A careless soldier eventually became a dead soldier.

Chapter Eleven:
It's All Fun and Games ...

My biggest worry was getting close to Rhee.

I rode in artificial isolation on the subway train. Leaned back against a vertical advertisement for a casino, ignoring the girl in it.

My uniform wasn't uncommon around the lab. Plenty of soldiers hung around because US and Korean joint forces ran the place, but my height and other features wouldn't blend into the crowds on the nearby streets.

Rhee didn't exactly walk around with his head on a swivel.

More the type to decide all foreigners looked the same. To not bother to really look at their facial characteristics.

On the other hand, he'd seen me earlier in the day, so if he got a good glance at my mug in person, he'd recognize me pretty quickly. It did say Harper across the nametape right there on my uniform jacket, pretty much eye-level for a Korean.

If he bothered to look.

A man of Rhee's nature didn't pay close attention to his inferiors. A captain outranked a lieutenant in anyone's army.

My train stopped.

I followed the thinner inbound crowds out and up an escalator onto the street. The storefronts lining the ground floors of each building lit the wide concrete walkway with their flickering neon signs.

Tried to combine a huddle with a slouch. Reduce my height to fit in better. Inconsistent lighting, the type to create lots of shadows on the street, helped.

Good thing I wasn't a real spy. Wasn't any good at this spy game.

At least I'd be able to see Rhee over the heads of any others in a typical crowd. Needed to remember to duck if he looked toward me.

The signs in English advertised familiar stores and brands as I wandered down the sidewalk.

Could've been back in the Gaslamp Quarter of San Diego, except the background chatter of the crowds wasn't in English. Most of the shops had Korea's Hangul lettering below their English signs.

Also, San Diego never dropped below 50 degrees in the evening, even in the winter. A curious mix of the familiar and the strange.

Icy rain fell; rattled off the buildings and sidewalk.

Shouldn't think about the lousy weather, so different from where I'd grown up.

Made being here worse.

Why did I try so hard to stay again? Oh, that's right, duty to the people my team protected, responsibility for my platoon, mostly sheer stubbornness to prove myself right.

Unfolded my umbrella to defend against the onslaught.

Made it across the street from the lab complex.

A predominantly gray split-face block building, like a big warehouse taking up most of the block. A street corner asphalt parking lot on one side, service alley on the other. They'd set the thirty feet tall lab physically apart from the neighbors.

No billboards revealed its secret purpose.

Just thick tree trunks and boulders around the street-side perimeter. Set close enough together in the landscaping a car bomb couldn't pass between them.

The only windows faced the protected parking lot.

In the alley a half-dozen Korean soldiers waited at the loading dock near one of the local Army trucks.

Probably there for a pick-up or delivery.

Wasn't planning to use the loading dock entrance, anyway. The mantrap at the back door provides a shorter path into the secure lab zones, but it doesn't get enough foot traffic to hide in.

I walked over to a Paris Baguette café across from the lab's main entrance.

They mostly got a breakfast and lunch crowd. Relied on the local workers for repeat customers.

Fresh out of the oven, the warm yeast smell made my stomach growl. No reason I couldn't fill up and warm up at the same time.

Yellow, red, and white frosted pastries beckoned from the glassed-in shelves. Too much pure sugar there.

Asked the attendant for a hot chocolate. A black and white cartoon Korean cat face surrounded the outside of the cup she handed me.

Dark bitterness would help keep me alert while watching.

Folded up my umbrella.

Settled into an open table near the pop-out glass bay windows.

Set my back to a wall opposite the entrance so I could see down the street in both directions.

Watched for Rhee's return from dinner.

The portable RFID reader/transmitter I'd borrowed from Michelle was a small electronics board inside a sun block tube-sized hard plastic case. Really just a smart antenna to send and receive 13.45 MHz signals, the frequency used for security cards. You could get a cheap commercial-off-the-shelf (COTS) version from China for a couple hundred bucks online.

CIA probably paid a few thousand for this one.

While waiting, I pulled the reader and mini-USB cable out of my cargo pocket. Ran the cable inside my uniform jacket and out the sleeve to my right hand.

Connected the cable to the reader and pushed them both up into my right sleeve a couple of inches, so they were no longer visible. Threaded the other end from my waist out through my left sleeve and into my smartphone.

Made sure I could load the correct software. That my phone properly detected the reader.

Set the reader/transmitter app to run in the background, hunting RFID signals.

Pulled up the camera app. Set it for night mode, which turned off the infrared filter.

Tucked the phone into my left sleeve.

Now I was ready for Rhee.

Reviewed the interior lab layout in my mind. Main entrance foyer facing the street. Security turnstile inside used smart badges.

That process had to be fast, or else the lines of people entering and exiting would quickly bog down.

Primary security office next door, with guards watching the camera systems. Each badge swiped in the turnstile popped a photo up on a guard's computer screen so they could glance out and confirm the picture on file matched a real person passing through the turnstiles.

Administrative area beyond that.

Cubicles and conference rooms, printers, computers, phones, nothing exotic.

Farther on, they secured the entrance into the giant lab facility itself by not only confirming the RFID holder had the proper permission, but also validating them with an iris scanner inside the mantrap.

To prevent tailgating into the lab, a motion sensor enforced the rule that only one person at a time could pass through the mantrap. If the sensor detected additional movement, the entrance locked.

The only way out was forward.

If an intruder failed the iris scan, the mantrap kept them in the little room until security released them.

Once within that mantrap, I'd either catch my wave or get worked by it.

No way to bail.

The back of the lab zones held a secondary security room. Used to monitor the cameras in the lab and control the rear mantrap.

Every building must have emergency exits.

Rather than make the scientists and engineers walk all the way around after a fire drill, security would pass them through the rear mantrap next to the loading dock.

However, without a guard in one of the security offices

triggering an unlock of the rear mantrap, that entrance didn't normally admit anyone from the outside.

The back door wasn't an option for me. Too many cameras for a mostly deserted area.

To anyone who watched the security monitors, a single person would attract attention I couldn't afford.

Better to stay with the more populated main entrance.

This mission called for an individual to blend in with the crowds, not a highly visible team raiding the place.

Needed to be more realistic in my planning.

Couldn't count on my opponent to be a moron, even if he usually was one. If Rhee recognized me, my career was over.

Army facilities like the lab would remain vulnerable to our enemies.

How would I ensure he didn't spot me?

Needed to get the reader in my sleeve within a few feet of his card to be sure of triggering the RFID tag inside and acquiring the right number to play back later.

The wind shifted directions. Icy rain splattered against the shop's glass window.

I looked at my umbrella. Smiled.

Suddenly, the Korean winter weather was perfect.

Just in time, too. Rhee staggered up the sidewalk toward the lab.

Probably coming back from dinner.

Dropped a green 10K Won bill on the table to cover my drink. Stepped through the exit.

Opened my umbrella.

Pointed horizontally into the sleet, if I stooped a little to disguise my height, my umbrella made a fine piece of mobile concealment.

Positioned it to hide my face.

Rhee swayed casually up the sidewalk.

About 15 feet away now. No doubt he'd indulged in a little Soju with his meal. He'd have to pass the café before crossing the street to the lab's entrance.

I sauntered back out on the sidewalk.

Kept my umbrella between us.

Slid my smartphone out from my sleeve.

Turned the master volume all the way off. No need for clicking sounds at this point.

Just another city denizen mesmerized by his phone.

Timed Rhee's approach in the windows behind me.

Lifted my phone as he closed in.

Still set to the mode which captured infrared as well as visible light, I held the built-in camera lens just under the edge of my umbrella, as if I looked at directions or something equally innocuous.

Zoomed in on his face. Held the camera icon down. Took a batch of quick photos.

Of the twenty photos before my phone had to stop and dump them to physical storage, hopefully at least one would contain a good view of his eyes.

Rhee halted just past me. So did my heart.

Had he spotted me?

Rather than recognizing me, he pulled out his own phone.

Glanced at a text.

Must've been important, because now he walked rapidly.

A man with more purpose than just checking on the night shift of guards.

I fell in a few feet behind him while he crossed the street.

Stepped with a slouched lean, umbrella facing forward, as if I fought the weather.

Brought up the app on my phone controlling the RFID reader/transmitter.

Verified it remained ready.

Only a few seconds to capture the right data.

Shifted my umbrella to my left hand, my phone jutting out at an angle as I held both of them together.

Merged in with the foot traffic lining up for the main entrance.

Got right behind Rhee.

He didn't even look around. Stood and tapped his foot in the short line.

The other Koreans waiting to enter were dressed as cleaning crew, in light blue janitorial uniforms. Their access cards hung around their necks from black lanyards.

Slid as close as I dared to Rhee.

Fortunately, the standards of personal space in crowded Seoul are tight, so he wasn't likely to consider a stranger edging up behind him as unusual.

Reached out with my right wrist next to his right side. Triggered the RFID reader software with my left.

Nothing.

Tried again. This time right wrist next to left pocket.

Bingo!

The RFID antennae next to my wrist triggered his card by simulating any other RFID reader. Recorded the number from his access card in return.

In a normal RFID system, the reader would take his card's ID number and compare it against a stored list to determine what access he was entitled to.

In my system, it recorded the number to prepare for the next step.

Rhee strode into the foyer. Stayed in line for the turnstile just inside.

This next step was the riskiest part.

Had to count on Rhee not looking back.

Closed my umbrella. Tucked it under my arm.

No excuse to keep it open inside the small foyer, protected from the weather.

Staying behind him, I took a white credit card out of my wallet. Indistinguishable at a distance from the lab's ID cards.

Rhee stepped through the turnstile.

Swiped his card near the sensor.

In the main security room, a guard saw the photo from his badge appear on his screen. Confirmed that yep, the guy in the photo, who happened to be his boss, just walked through the turnstiles.

Following less than a foot behind, I stepped through the turnstile.

Swiped my credit card across the RFID reader with my right hand.

Really, I triggered the app on my phone. The transmitter in my right sleeve sent the card number I'd recorded moments earlier.

The security system received Rhee's badge number again. Again, his photo popped up on a guard's computer.

Had a few things going for me.

First, a card being read multiple times in a short period is normal.

The RFID reader triggers anywhere from one to three feet away. Doesn't know when you take your hand away. Just knows that it's been getting a particular code and now it isn't.

So usually, no one worries too much about duplicates, one right after another.

For proximity sensors, accidental double-swiping is common.

Second, they designed this setup for speed around shift change timings. More than one guard got the picture pop-ups on their screen.

If two different guards saw Rhee's photo, they'd independently see him walking out of the turnstile ahead of me and confirm they knew him.

They didn't watch the turnstiles; they watched their monitors with the habit of glancing up to check the face in the pop-up was present to ensure the wrong person wasn't using someone's badge. If they notice a person whose face didn't show up on their own screen, a different guard probably got that person's picture to check.

Habits and routine can be deadly.

Third, when you see your security boss coming through the doorway, you don't wonder if someone cloned his RFID card.

You naturally start wondering if you look busy enough, if you remembered to file that paperwork he wanted, and so on. The last thing on your mind is that he's a security risk.

Human nature.

The turnstile indicator light turned a beautiful green in response to Rhee's valid card number. I pushed through and entered the less secure administrative portion of the building.

Rhee turned toward the door marked "Security Office" in English and Hangul characters.

According to the blueprints I'd seen, his desk shared a room where the guards sat and watched the security feeds and the turnstile.

Headed into the hallway. Toward the administrative area.

Almost all the regular staff had departed, leaving cleaning folks to take over.

I walked with a purposeful stride, trying to look as if I was on my way somewhere and couldn't be interrupted. As long as you look like you belong, most people won't challenge you, or even notice your presence.

Drop ceilings. Short cubicles. Rolling office chairs.

Plenty of places to hide, not much cover from bullets. Tended to penetrate office partitions and walls.

Most of the administrative space was too open and airy.

Our tax dollars at work.

Just as soon they hadn't sprung for the glass-walled conference rooms. Needed a place I could stop and conceal myself.

Still had to bypass the mantrap to get into the lab itself.

With the place mostly deserted by its regular workers, the guards watching the monitors showing the administrative area would eventually wonder who I was.

Had a few free minutes while they greeted Rhee and talked about whatever they usually did when he arrived to check on their shift, but that would only last so long.

Needed to enlarge and print an eyeball photo to fool the retinal scanner.

Also needed a distraction, to ensure a guard wasn't staring at the security camera monitor which happened to show me using something besides my eye on that same scanner.

Time to go borrow a little office equipment before a guard noticed me and wondered who I was.

Kwon gripped two sets of old bricks with his frozen fingers.

Peered around the building's corner.

Watched the service alley. Leaned against the outer edge of an alcove for the loading dock.

The alcove behind him led to the steel door of the cargo mantrap entrance. He didn't want his tactical gear to be obvious from the nearby major road.

Stacked up tactically, three on each side of the door, assault rifles pointed forward, but away from each other, the rest of Team Goshawk prepared to enter and execute their individual tasks.

Inside the covered alcove, they'd be invisible from the street.

The shifting breeze chilled his fingers on the bricks. The freezing rain stopped, at least temporarily, but the city noise level remained suppressed by the weather.

He'd hear any intruders in the alley long before they saw him.

Standing next to Stro along the right-hand side of the door, the com sergeant's mobile phone vibrated.

He looked at the number. Answered. "Ready."

Hung up. Gripped his rifle tighter.

The prearranged communication reassured both sides everything was ready.

Clunk.

In response to an internal override, the magnetic bolts holding the door withdrew into the metal door frame.

Stro, leading the stack on the hinge-side of the door, reached out to the steel handle.

Pulled it open.

Kwon moved to behind his last man. "Execute."

This was the most dangerous part of the mission. All seven of his team would be inside the mantrap simultaneously.

If this was an ambush, if the enemy caught them in there, they might as well surrender.

Sometimes there is no choice but to trust others to do their part.

The left-hand stack moved through the doorway. Into the small room.

Stro exhaled and led his stack in behind.

Kwon followed, head on a swivel.

Pistol in hand. His trigger finger and the barrel pointed at the floor.

The room was designed to move cargo in and out of the facility. Fully equipped in bulky vests carrying armor and munitions, the seven of them took up space for ten regular men.

Even with rifles pointed at the wire mesh ceiling, they pressed against each other and the walls. The imperialists had constructed the floor and walls from a thin sheet of steel.

If an enemy fired at them, ricochets became a real danger.

A matching wide steel door to the one they'd entered via was set into the opposite wall.

That door wouldn't open unless the outer door was closed. Even then, after checking the mantrap camera, a guard on the inside had to push a button to electronically unlock it.

This entrance was really only used for scheduled deliveries and fire drills. Both required the approval of the lab's internal security guards for entrance.

Kwon pulled the door closed behind his team.

Ker-chunk. The outer door locked.

The traitor held their lives in his hands.

Chapter Twelve:
... Until Someone Gets Hurt

To prove my platoon's report correct and break into the most secure section of the lab, I needed a high quality color laser printer and to not be disturbed for a few minutes.

Scanning the office area, I strode out between the cubicles. A combo photocopier dominated the corner of a break room.

The crowded break room contained a steel sink embedded in a counter, a cheap microwave, an automatic paper towel wall unit, a stainless steel refrigerator, and a bottleless water dispenser on the floor next to the copier.

A four seat table on the other side and a small drain in the tile floor didn't look like they saw much use.

Most importantly, actual walls and a thin door divided the room from the rest of the office space.

Closed the door behind me.

No one took breaks in Seoul. Hopefully no one would choose late on a Friday night to prove that particular reputation wrong.

Besides, I heard they passed a law against staying late at work.

They'd purchased the deluxe model of scanner/printer/copier, with all the bells and whistles. Only the best and most expensive for the government lab.

Away from suspicious eyes, I unplugged the RFID scanner/transmitter from my USB cable. Tugged my phone to pull the cable out of my left sleeve.

Flipped through the high-resolution photos of Rhee stored on my phone. Selected the one with the best view of his eyes.

With night mode on, the photo included the infrared details of the blood vessels in his iris.

After cropping the best photo, I enlarged it to life size. By itself, that wouldn't fool the iris scanner, but it was a start.

Using my trusty USB cable, plugged my phone into the printer long enough to get a full color high quality print. His life-sized ugly mug was beautiful on the page.

Might pull this off alone after all.

Set the RFID transmitter up again.

Now I needed to figure out a distraction for the guards.

Once I entered the lab's main mantrap, I'd no longer be just another figure walking down a hallway for a few seconds before the guard's next camera view flickered onto the screen. Instead, I'd be alone in a room with a camera dedicated to watching who came and went.

Could sort of fake putting my face next to the retinal scanner while trying to use Rhee's face with a contact lens on it, but anyone who paid much attention would spot my unusual behavior and lock the room down.

That way led to disaster.

Instead, needed the guards talking about an unusual event with each other in the security office. Maybe even a few of them responding to an issue in the building.

No longer watching their bank of monitors.

Checked the kitchen portion of the break room. An issue with the fridge, perhaps?

Could probably rig the compressor to start smoking. Even start a fire in the microwave.

Didn't want a fire alarm, though.

The mantrap would lock down for incoming people. Security would expect everyone to exit the building.

That's the opposite direction from where I wanted to go. It'd make me stand out even more like a shark in the bay.

Maybe clog the sink and turn on the water?

That'd overflow pretty quickly. Turned on the water for a moment to test the flow speed.

A flood would work, but I wanted more water than that.

Inspected the water dispenser next to the copier. Had an independent flexible water line from the wall.

A second source would create a reasonable deluge, especially when combined with the sink flow as a base.

The water dispenser had faucets for hot and cold, one with a red plastic lever and a second in blue. Any movement up or down of each released water from the internal reservoir.

Just needed to figure out a timer.

The multi-function copier had a finisher tray, where if you had it staple and collate your copies, they'd land on the tray as it moved down to make room for the next set.

That would be enough.

Put the sink's drain plug into the drain. Grabbed a handful of paper towels from the wall unit.

Dampened them.

Unscrewed the floor drain's catch basin with my multi-tool.

Bunched the damp paper towels up. Pushed them into the little floor drain. Replaced the catch basin.

Should clog it nicely.

For good measure, I stuffed a few into the overflow hole in the top of the sink's side.

No way out for water but over the lip.

With a little muscling it around and a bit of leverage rocking it side-to-side, I turned the water cooler and moved it over a few inches. Swung the plastic lever for both faucets around so they extended out from the base.

Now they poked out under the edge of the copier's finisher tray.

Pulled half a dozen sheets of blank paper out of the copier. Set them into the document feeder.

Programmed the machine to collate and staple 99 copies.

With the clunking of rollers and gears, it dutifully began spitting out the result, moving the tray down about a quarter of an inch each time.

Each copy took two seconds, so the finisher tray should press down those little blue and red levers within a couple of minutes.

At that point, my wave of distraction would be coming.

Turned on the water at the sink.

The timing wouldn't be exact, but the basin would also fill up within a minute or so and then overflow onto the counter and the floor.

With the floor drain plugged, wouldn't take long before the water began to seep out into the hallway. I'd close the door to restrict the flow into the hallway and let the water build up.

No cameras in the break room.

With luck, I'd have an inch or more of water on the floor before anyone noticed the carpet outside turning dark.

Time for me to go before my tan combat boots got soaked.

Despite my love of the ocean, I was a Ranger, not a SEAL.

Clunk.

The steel door in front of Kwon's Goshawk Team unlocked.

Kwon let out the breath he'd unwisely been holding.

Deputy Minister Meon's inside man came through for them. At least there were still a few people loyal to the true Korea in the South.

Stro looked at him for orders.

Kwon pointed forward with his off-hand.

Stro pulled open the door from the cargo mantrap leading into the lab. The team crowded back against each other to give the door room to swing open.

"Go."

The mantrap exited into a wide concrete-floored space.

The first three of his men stacked up. Moved forward and left to secure cover and create open fields of fire around the perimeter beyond the mantrap exit.

Kwon knew from their informant that the metallurgical lab space was arranged into four zones, delineated by colored markings on the floors and walls.

Their mantrap exit opened into the red zone.

Inside the red zone, the security office in the corner on the right and the data center to the left were their immediate targets for control.

Past the steel data center door outlined in red, a hallway marked in blue represented the beginning of the lab's science offices and their secure conference room.

With their forward and left-flank covered, Stro led the other two soldiers toward the auxiliary security office to the right of the mantrap exit.

Before following, Kwon scanned the area for people or movement.

His job right now was to maintain overall situational awareness so he could adjust the team's orders in response to the unexpected.

The rest of the space they stood in opened up into a cavernous warehouse area. Marked on the floor as the brown zone.

Mostly for storage, long three-meter-wide aisles provided access to floor-to-ceiling pallet-wide metal racking used for storage of materials and unused equipment.

Only a glimpse of the wide-open area on the other side of the warehouse, marked in orange to show where the scientists ran their experiments, was visible from here.

The first two men who'd left the mantrap spread out forward.

Took positions behind the closest racks where they could cover the aisles into the brown zone.

The third hustled to the beginning of the blue zone hallway.

Used the block wall corner near the data center door to cover the hallway.

Just as they'd rehearsed.

Nodding in satisfaction, Kwon followed Stro and the two men he led.

Their inside man should have turned off the red zone security cameras when he unlocked the mantrap door. After being allowed to exit the cargo mantrap, Kwon had no reason not to trust he'd succeeded.

Kwon would deal with the data center later in the mission.

A matter of priorities.

For now, it was enough to know they wouldn't have any unexpected surprises while taking care of the security guard.

As the only armed individual besides Goshawk Team on this side of the orange zone personnel mantrap, neutralizing the threat of the lone guard was their priority.

Before the guard noticed he was no longer getting a camera feed on his monitors from the rest of red zone.

Stro reached the closed security office door. Took position along the block wall, opposite the door's hinges.

The next man behind him went to the wall on the other side of the door.

The final soldier, his com sergeant, stacked up behind Stro.

Kwon took one last glance around to make sure everything remained under control. Stacked up behind the com sergeant. Tapped him on the shoulder.

He in turn tapped Stro.

Stro slung his rifle over his shoulder. Slid his left sleeve up his arm.

Revealed a stubby wooden dowel wrapped in thin steel wire and attached to a thick black wristband.

Grabbed the dowel with his right hand. Dropped his left arm to quickly unwrap his Spetsnaz-inspired garrote.

A one meter loop spun free between a hole carved out of the center of the dowel and his wristband.

He stretched the wire taut. Nodded to the demolitions specialist on the other side of the door.

That soldier reached out and pounded on the security room door.

Grabbed its U-shaped steel handle.

As soon as the door began to open, he yanked it as wide as possible.

With the unexpected door movement, a South Korean soldier in black and green digital camouflage uniform stumbled through the doorway, caught off balance.

Stro flung his garrote wire around the enemy's neck.

Slid in behind him.

Crossed his wrists as he turned to face away from the guard.

Levered him into the air on his back.

The guard's hands tore at the wire around his neck. His mouth hung open, but he couldn't produce any sound beyond a weak gurgle.

His cheeks bulged and flushed.

Kicked out his legs. Caught the demo specialist in the face with a boot.

That'd leave a bruise later.

The com sergeant moved in behind Stro and the struggling guard. Scouted around the corner into the security office.

"Clear."

Stro panted. Excitement gleamed in his eyes. Hauled on the garrote. Muscles bulged with the effort. Kept the Dominionist guard flailing on his back.

Kwon couldn't not stare at the guard.

In his panic, the guard didn't even think to reach for his holstered sidearm.

Poor training. No one on Kwon's team would be caught like that.

The skin around the guard's lips transformed from pale white to light blue. Losing oxygen and consciousness fast.

Death wouldn't wait long.

Chapter Thirteen:
Lots of Eyeballs

Tried to look like I belonged.

Strode down the tan carpeted walkways laid out between cubicles in the lab's administrative offices.

Only another minute or so until the flood spilled out under the closed break room door.

Wanted to be well away from the area before then.

Clutching the eyeball printout I'd made in the air between finger and thumb, I nodded to a short Korean man in a janitor's sky blue uniform. Dodged past his cleaning cart and out into the main aisle leading from the entrance turnstile to the personnel mantrap.

Needed to be across the office when my distraction hit.

Copier and sink timers ticked away in the back of my head. Not so loud that I didn't notice the janitor deciding this would be a good time to clean the break room.

Sped up my walk even faster.

Wasn't even pretending to have a purpose. Really did have somewhere I needed to be soon, if I wasn't going to get caught short of my objective.

A gush behind me.

Glanced back.

The janitor stood outside the now open break room door.

Water flowed from the doorway. Formed a growing puddle.

A two inch wave reflected off his scuffed white shoes. Created reflective eddies in the expanding pool of water as it overwhelmed the nearby carpet.

The thin tan floors around the cubicles closest to the break room became chestnut-under-lacquer as the flood's irregular edge advanced into the rest of the office.

Excellent.

Now I just needed the janitor to call security, rather than deciding to resolve the issue himself. Surely with that much water he'd assume there was a leak of some sort, which he needed the building's authorities to fix.

Creative destruction took talent.

I reached the end of the main hallway. A solid security door with an orange sign, "Lab – Authorized Personnel Only", and an RFID scanner built into the wall barred any further progress.

Put my hand on a nearby cubical wall for a second. Bent over to adjust my shoelace.

Looked back again as I bent over. The janitor spoke on the cubicle phone closest to the break room door.

Perfect.

Like most government employees, he wasn't about to try and deal with a problem which was securely not-his-job.

He'd likely be willing to mop the place up afterward, maybe even ride an extra set of waves and get a few fans to speed up the drying process, but fixing leaks wasn't in a janitor's job description. That was plumber, or at least handyman, work.

An entirely different department, which only security could summon in an emergency.

Right on cue, the main security door opened.

Two guards rushed toward the janitor.

Had at least three minutes of all eyes in the security room on him while they avoided the water, interrogated him, and then distracted the boss by asking what to do next.

Finished my fake shoe tying.

Reached out my right hand. Swiped my transmitted clone of Rhee's RFID card across the reader.

Clunk.

The outer mantrap door unlocked.

I slipped inside.

This was where I was most vulnerable.

Hoped the guard in the other security office, the one near the larger loading dock mantrap, was just as distracted.

He had the whole lab area to watch, so I wasn't too worried.

The orange experiment zone by itself was huge. The warehouse section almost as large.

The blue zone with the scientist's offices contained lots of little rooms to check camera angles within.

While the red zone was small, it was also important.

The odds of not being on camera for the rear guard were well in my favor.

Inside the personnel mantrap was another solid security door, protected by yet another playing card-sized RFID reader in the wall, but also with my nemesis from the fitness center above that, the same model retinal scanner.

I let the outer door close behind me.

Ker-chunk.

The outer door locked.

If I didn't fool the retinal scanner, I wasn't going either direction.

The doors looked kick-proof. Walls and ceiling each contained a steel mesh.

A camera in the upper corner of the far wall sent a live feed to the security room monitors.

I'd be stuck in this five foot square room until one of the security guards came to investigate and let me out.

A phone on the wall with a dedicated line to the security office facilitated that process, but I wasn't exactly looking forward to that call.

Careful not to drop it, I removed a contact lens from the case in my cargo pocket. Pressed it up against the printout of Rhee's eye.

No time like the present.

Iris scanners are really just cameras. They take an infrared picture of your eye, simplify the lines in the image, and then compare a mathematical representation of that picture to what's stored in the database.

Someone's eye is never at the exact same distance and angle to the camera, so there's a lot of slack in the system.

What it's looking for is the relationships and angles between the structures of your eye.

As long as those boil down to the right mathematical range for what's stored in the security database for the associated RFID card, you're allowed to pass.

I swiped my right sleeve against the inner RFID reader. The light on the retinal scanner turned yellow.

Used my left hand to push the printout and contact lens in front of the scanner.

It had to recognize that as Rhee's eye.

Ruby red may have been the color of Dorothy's slippers, but the now glaring light on the retinal scanner didn't spell escape to me.

Couldn't spend much time on this.

Every second a random guard might happen to look at the live security camera footage.

This could work. I'd done it already. Well, after half a dozen tries.

Hope remained.

The problem with biometrics is you're constantly showing your password to the world around you. If a biometric measurement is compromised, you can't swap out your eyes, nor fingers, for new ones.

Had Rhee's eye, just needed to use it properly.

Maybe I'd been too hasty, not lining the contact and the photo up in a direct line with the camera in the retinal scanner.

Took a deep breath.

Focus.

Exhaled deliberately.

Transmitted Rhee's RFID number from my wrist to the reader in the wall again.

Yellow light.

One more try.

Took a moment to use both hands to line the contact lens up.

Double-checked it.

Slid it directly in front of the scanner's camera lens.

Emerald city, dude!

The inner mantrap door unlocked with a clunk. Dorothy wouldn't escape this time, but I would. The seafoam green of the deep ocean is my favorite color, anyway.

Right now it stood for freedom.

Who needs a whole red team of infiltrators, anyway?

I pushed the inner door open.

The slight overpressure outside the mantrap forced in a rush of air. Smelled like smoke from melting solder.

Always loved electronics lab in school.

The top secret orange zone, where the scientists and engineers ran their metallurgical experiments, welcomed me like an old friend.

Needed to find a distinctive object to prove I'd been here. An object Major Williams couldn't ignore.

Otherwise, if I showed up at Company HQ claiming I'd successfully infiltrated the facility, I doubted anyone'd listen long enough to get Rhee to turn over the security footage proving the lab was vulnerable.

No, he might be tempted to just make any evidence disappear.

Time for my personal scavenger hunt.

Kwon unclipped the RFID badge from the enemy guard's motionless chest.

With the lone guard in this area down, Kwon was ready to split his team for maximum efficiency.

Stro tucked the guard's sidearm into his bag.

Grabbed the guard's feet and hauled him back into the auxiliary security office. There, he'd be safely out of the way from casual discovery.

Their inside man would cover for any missed check-ins while Goshawk Team worked.

The guard was just a cog in the capitalist system, enforcing the will of his masters on the oppressed.

For a moment, Kwon entertained the thought he might have a family.

That was the sort of weak thinking Meon had warned against. Kwon rubbed his left breast pocket, feeling the edge of the photograph inside.

The Imperialists murdered without reason.

He refused to sympathize with one of their soldiers. He'd lead his men to decisive victory.

No weakness.

"Stro, you two move into position to cover the primary personnel mantrap in the orange zone. Any armed resistance should come from there." Kwon pointed at the com sergeant, indicating he should accompany Stro.

Stro nodded, "Roger that."

He left the security door open a crack in case their inside contact couldn't monitor the security cameras for them and they needed to return. He and the com specialist headed toward the forklift aisles in the brown warehouse zone, hustling to reach the orange zone on the other side.

Kwon didn't need the reminder of their limited time ticking away.

Already had a mental drop-dead time noted whenever he checked his Moranbong wristwatch. Plenty of tasks to accomplish.

Clicked his radio microphone live with a thumb. "Two and three have forward defense. Four and six, follow and clear the orange zone, then set your charges." Goshawk Four, the sniper of the pair, would be best at room clearing, while the demo specialist would take the lead on the explosives.

His radio crackled with their acknowledgments.

"Five and seven, clear the warehouse aisles, grab anything worth hauling back with us, then set your brown zone charges. I'll begin on the data center. Let you know if I need a forklift later."

He'd saved the most important target, the red zone room containing all the scientist's records and information, for himself.

A good team can accomplish multiple tasks at once.

The rest of the small unit he commanded hustled forward to complete their assigned duties. The real prize here was the electronic data.

According to their contact, the lab didn't have good off-site backups.

Everything else they'd planned would slow the enemy down,

but if his team could capture the enemy's top secret records and bring them home, they'd set the Imperialists back years on their research while ultimately pushing the true Korea's research efforts forward by decades.

The dead guard's badge would grant Kwon entry into the data center. Time to achieve a great victory for Supreme Leader!

Chapter Fourteen:
Scientists and Saviors

What could I carry out to prove I'd been here in the top secret section of the lab?

Something small, yet unique.

In the wide-open orange zone to the right, the scientists ran their metallurgical experiments.

Cordoned temporary spaces off not using walls, but by forming virtual hallways from bright yellow lines painted on the concrete floor.

If you stayed outside those lines, you weren't going to hurt, or be hurt by, the bubbling and popping experiments.

Tables with commercial kitchen-sized pans of molten metal, giant rolling presses, plus the occasional industrial-sized beaker setup dotted the area.

Plenty of ways for someone to get hurt.

The orange zone likely held plenty of distinctive items, but they were probably either too dangerous, too large, or too secret to go wandering out with.

They used the second warehouse-sized zone on the left for storage.

The brown zone's floor to ceiling pallet racks contained old experiments, unused equipment, boarded up crates, cardboard boxes, glass bottles with acidic liquids, and sealed plastic buckets of raw materials.

Brown zone was a possibility, if I could find an object distinctive enough, yet non-secret. Perhaps one of the electric forklifts had the lab's logo on it.

Be a pain to drive through downtown Seoul, though.

Behind the orange zone, a smaller blue zone branched off a hallway with connections to individual offices and conference rooms for the scientists, keeping the secret information partitioned from the purely administrative office workers.

Blue zone was promising.

I bet a scientist's office held a personal item that they'd miss, but wasn't secret in and of itself. A one of a kind object, like a plaque or a diploma hanging on a wall.

At the other end of the blue zone hallway, toward the back of the building and bordering the brown zone with the loading dock, there were smaller rooms containing the data center, the backup security office and the rear mantrap.

That was the red zone.

Unless he was dealing with the soldiers on the loading dock I'd seen in the alley earlier, the lab area's lone guard would sit in that office watching the security cameras.

To keep him from catching me, I'd need to avoid the red zone until it was time to leave.

Voices sounded from the warehouse aisles in the brown zone.

Time to get moving.

I snuck down one of the outside yellow-striped hallways in the orange zone, careful not to disturb the dangerous experimental areas.

Ducked when necessary to stay out of sight.

Even in the open hallway, well away from the marked off areas, could feel the heat of molten metal in a few of the experiments.

Wasn't looking to interrupt their sizzle. Just wanted to get over to the blue zone.

Raid the offices.

Unlike the cubicled administrative staff, the scientists worked in offices with actual doors and walls.

Apparently they occasionally needed to concentrate, rather than just be seen at work.

As I walked down the blue-marked hallway, I cracked open each door. Inspected one office after another.

Looked for my distinctive proof.

Maybe a unique, yet portable sculpture an engineer created out of a failed experiment.

I should be so lucky.

In the distance, heard those same voices from the warehouse area move into the orange zone.

Needed to hurry, before they either caught up to me or pushed me into the red zone.

First four offices were a bust. These scientists showed no personality at all.

The fifth office I peered into wasn't empty.

Inside, a tall, slender Korean woman's mouth gaped open. Fumbled with the green dry-erase marker in her hand. Stared right at me in the doorway.

Long arms and skinny legs poked out of a fluffy office skirt and blouse. Wore her white lab coat loosely over it all like a soldier displaying her rank.

In the hopes she didn't get a good look at me through the sliver of open door, I tried my best Korean Engrish accent, "So sorry. Wrong room."

Gently closed the door and backed away from it.

She pushed the door open right in front of me.

No luck.

Apparently, more observant than most.

Why couldn't I have run into an absent-minded type?

"Who are you?" She pointed her thin green marker at me. "You're not part of the lab team."

Wow! Closer up, I could tell this Korean woman was almost as tall as I was, approaching six foot. Her chest jutted forward accusingly as she jabbed the marker at me.

Time for a bit of social engineering subtlety.

I pressed my finger vertically into my lips. Spoke softly, "Surprise security inspection, Ma'am."

"I'm the lab director. They'd have notified me if there was an inspection planned."

It'd worked, a little. She'd softened her own tones back to normal in response to my almost whisper.

"Then it wouldn't be a surprise. Look, as a manager, I'm sure you know there's a law limiting the work hours of government employees, but I like you. You seem like a sensible woman. Don't want to get you into trouble for being here this late at the end of the work week, so if you'll return to your office, I'll just pretend I didn't see you and get on with my inspection duties."

"Really? I'm not stupid. Anyway, I have a critical duties exception to work extra time." Her voice rose again.

She peered closer at the nametape on my chest, "Lieutenant Harper, eh? Show me your security pass. This entire area is classified top secret. Foreigners, even soldiers, don't work here without an escort or a pass, and I sign off on enough paperwork every month to know I haven't seen your face on a recent application."

Maybe I should have gone with a janitor disguise today, rather than wearing my uniform, complete with my name for all to see. This scientist was entirely too observant.

Knew when I was too beat down by the waves to recover. "I really am a military intelligence security analyst with the U.S. Army. I'd appreciate it if you'd just look the other way, but if you insist, we can walk down to the security room in the red zone and the guard there will be able to verify my identity with Captain Rhee Yun-seok or the administration at Camp Kim."

"Is this another of Rhee's power games? Let's go, then."

I nodded in acquiescence.

She was the first Korean woman I'd seen to even come close to my height. Most barely managed five feet.

And she appeared to have no love for Rhee, even better. Despite getting worked by her suspicions, I felt amped.

After all, I made it into the lab. She'd be my proof.

She marched me down the blue zone hallway, a naughty boy to the principal's office.

Been there before.

"If you don't mind my asking, Ma'am, what's your name?"

"Doctor Yang Hyo-jin. I run the carbon fiber program."

Tried to start over. "Nice to meet you, Doctor. I'm Lieutenant Sam Harper."

"I know what you're thinking. Why is she so tall? It's what everyone wants to ask me, so get it over with."

"Actually, I was wondering how a woman as young as you

came to be in charge of a major research program at a lab like this. Already know why you're tall."

"Really? Why?"

"Mostly genetics plus sufficient nutrition, Doc." I paused, but she didn't laugh. "Actually, been reviewing the files on everyone who works here for a month. Didn't recognize your face, but recognize your name. Don't mean that I memorized everyone's name and background, but your past on the South Korean National Volleyball team stuck in my mind. The London Olympic Games, wasn't it?"

"Yes. And to answer your other question, I played for years for Hyundai Engineering's professional team. In the process went to school for material sciences and eventually ended up here."

The office hallway turned left.

Could see the red zone ahead. "Having a national hero on the staff here probably didn't hurt."

"Oh, I don't know anyone around here cares that much."

I grinned. "Well, you certainly stand out."

We reached the end of the blue zone hallway, where the data center door marked the beginning of the red zone. I faintly smelled a horrible sickly sweet scent. Not one I liked. I hoped security had found a dead dog or cat or something.

"Doctor, I think you should stay here."

"What? Certainly not. I'm taking you to security. It's right over there."

I ignored her. Stepped lightly past the mantrap. Edged over to the backup security room.

The door was just a little open, but the smell reeked.

She held her nose. Followed behind me.

I pulled open the door just enough to look inside. Instantly focused.

The guard lay sideways on the floor, pushed up against his chair, face pale blue, eyes bulging.

No RFID badge. No sidearm. Cause of death obvious, extreme strangulation.

"Get me plastic bags."

"What?"

"Plastic bags. You must use plastic trash bags around here. A janitor's closet, something nearby. Packing tape, too, if you can find it. Just get them, but don't go far. The guard's dead. You don't want to see this."

Of course, she pushed past me and peered through the doorway herself.

Tendons stood out on her neck, pulsing rapidly. She began shaking, so she jammed her hands into her armpits, hugging her own chest. Not asking more questions, she turned to go and find bags and tape.

At least she hadn't accused me of killing him.

Guess she figured I wouldn't have calmly walked over here with her if I had.

I instinctively faced away from the body. Held a deep breath.

Wasn't going to think about the source of the smell.

Whoever killed the guard might still be in the lab.

My pulse pumped harder.

Needed to take off on this new wave before I got raked over by it.

Turned back into the office.

Stepped over the body of the guard.

Transmitted Rhee's RFID code. Unlocked the functions of the security console.

The red zone cameras weren't working for some reason, but scanning the camera feeds covering the other three lab zones, I found dangerous visitors within seconds.

Six men in black and green digital camouflage uniforms worked the area in three teams of two.

One pair guarded the primary mantrap I'd used, shoulder weapons aimed toward the door.

A second pair moved through the orange zone, leapfrogging each other around the yellow-painted lines using standard room clearing techniques.

The third pair worked together, loading a heavy-looking steel box covered in international warning symbols on a forklift.

They all carried K2 assault rifles, a locally produced cross between an M16A1 and an AR-15.

Almost.

These K2's had shiny black plastic where the real item from Daewoo Precision Industries used dull gunmetal. They were also missing the standard ROK Army rail with PVS-11K red dot sight.

Despite the uniforms, these soldiers weren't South Korean.

No, they were North Korean Special Forces.

My personal red team exercise had transformed itself into a deadly infiltration, with everyone's lives now in danger.

My first instinct was to set off an alarm and call the cavalry.

But who was the cavalry?

Couldn't *wait* to explain to Major Williams about how I'd broken into the ROK's top secret metallurgy lab and just *happened* to find North Korean commandos in it, proving my point about how easy the place could be infiltrated. I'm *sure* he'd be in the mood to listen carefully. After all, he'd *never* jump to conclusions or take the side of the locals.

What a Charlie Foxtrot of a situation.

Could wait and observe. Gather more info on what they did. Gain a little breathing space.

However, inaction was unlikely to improve the situation.

Was already on the crest of this wave, whether or not I wanted to ride it.

Had a feeling if I waited long enough, the pair of soldiers clearing the orange zone would move on to the blue zone and then back here to the red zone to complete their sweep of the lab areas.

Once they arrived here, they'd spit me and my new scientist friend into the washing machine.

If I'd planned this heist, at that point they'd help the pair working the warehouse contents in brown zone move out via the mantrap at the rear of the building.

Presumably that's how they'd entered in the first place.

That truck parked in the alley near the loading dock!

Likely their escape route.

Once the others cleared the area, the pair guarding the front door would rapidly exfiltrate and they'd all drive away.

Great.

My only explanation of how and why I was even here was an

unauthorized security penetration test.

If we were all caught in here, or worse, if these guys got away, there's no way Rhee would believe I wasn't in on it somehow.

Hell, I wouldn't believe me under these circumstances.

Getting relieved was now the least of my worries. At this rate, I might need that secret Agency flight out of the country.

My only hope was to call Rhee and throw myself on his mercy.

At least if I set off the alarms and reported the bad guys, with a national hero of a witness to that fact, I could probably avoid time in the brig. As long as they caught the North Koreans, we could save face and minimize the damage all around.

Maybe just a court-martial for insubordination and a dishonorable discharge.

Lofty goals, I know.

Chapter Fifteen:
Irish Car Bombs

Schnier *was* sort of Irishly cute, in a brash and annoying way. Maybe Michelle could squeeze his muscles and coo approvingly.

After watching Sam walk away at the subway station, she hadn't felt like just going home again.

The way he'd ignored her gesture at the end, she figured he must still be upset about his loss to Schnier, not to mention whatever was going on with his lab report.

Besides, after her call with the big boss in DC, she had work to do. Needed to find out if Schnier's platoon would be making any trips soon which might screw up anything related to their new high-level source across the DMZ.

So she'd called Schnier and casually invited him to meet her for drinks at Route 66 American Bar, a hole in the wall identified by garish red and blue lettering on a luminous white sign only two blocks from the edge of Yongsan Garrison.

The whole area catered to U.S. GIs, cheap Korean goods competing with familiar restaurants like Subway, Outback, KFC, all mixed together and ready to part soldiers from their pay.

That's not to say the locals didn't still outnumber those from the States, but unlike most of the city, you could count on seeing at least a few familiar faces.

The bar was upstairs, above a money exchange, set back from the street in a little pedestrian cul-de-sac.

Could sit on the patio and watch the nightlife, but she shivered at the idea.

Instead, she climbed up the exterior staircase. Pushed her way through the main entrance. The crowded scene inside created all the warmth she needed.

Michelle looked around for any rowdy Rangers.

Most groups inside gathered around beat up wooden tables oriented toward the bar, periodically sending messengers to the long-haired gods of the tap to provide liquid sustenance.

A pair of hand-written chalkboard signs tilted out above the bar advertised "66 BOMB SHOTS" and "Long Teas".

Rows of empty wine glasses and a brass bell attached beneath an antique metal "Route US 66" highway sign hung from the top of the bar.

Michelle giggled as she read the drink specials, "Tic Tac Agua, Irish Car Bomb, Hand Grenade, Drone Strike".

A drink for everyone.

The manager must've served enough soldiers to gain more than a passing familiarity with Army military gallows humor.

For the right money, apparently you can fake a foreign culture.

Army culture confused Michelle less than Korean society, at least.

Two rows of mixed patrons, half of them American, the other half Korean, pushed up against the bar.

No Schnier over there.

"Fake Love" by the Bangtan Boys pounded from the opposite corner, but Schnier wouldn't be by the K-pop karaoke machine, at least not this early in the night.

She dodged through the crowd to gain a different perspective.

Spotted his buzzed red hair above the crowd.

He scribbled his name on a wall covered from the waist up with black chalkboard paint. The chalkboard area surrounded a pair of dartboards filled with writing in ever-expanding circles from the targets, so much so that a few people had just written their own messages in a different color chalk over the previous layer, creating a drunken archaeological dig.

A cheap plastic red skull and crossed daggers hung beneath one target, oddly out of place. The same spot under the second dartboard was empty, lonely, and missing out.

Schnier finished his illegible name with a flourish. Dropped the thick chunk of chalk into a scraped-up wooden box provided for that purpose.

He stood bowlegged in jeans tucked into cowboy boots. Wore his best Hawaiian shirt open over a black tank-top.

An enormous silver and gold belt buckle declared him a bareback bronc champion.

He'd obviously taken care with his appearance after receiving her call.

Good, he'd been anxious to meet her. Worried to not look his best. This would be easier than she'd thought.

Michelle smiled and danced over to him.

He grinned at her arrival, his complexion already ruddy between scattered freckles.

She ran a hand across his herculean biceps appreciatively.

Leaned in close.

He'd assume that was so she didn't need to shout. "Wasn't sure you'd be able to make it on short notice. Your platoon has been busy recently."

Schnier nodded a greeting, almost a Korean style bow. "A Ranger's work ain't nevah done, Ma'am. If-in the men run out of thangs ta do, we can always come up with new stuff for 'em. Not that there ain't always some fun around here, with the DPRK just across the DMZ."

She wanted him in the habit of confiding little details about his work to her. That way it wouldn't seem strange if she had a specific piece of information she needed to know.

After all, she was the local military attaché.

He also saw her as the CIA liaison to his unit. Understood she had a high clearance and thus shouldn't be suspicious if she talked shop occasionally. "I heard Sam had a run-in about his team's report."

She began by passing a bit of juicy gossip to him, even if it was info he'd already known, so he felt like he needed to volunteer more information to top it in response.

"Yes, ma'am. Bishop asked us all to lay off a him. I reckon he'll be gone next week, anyway. Let's not talk about the geek squad. Ah'd rather hear about you. Where ya from?"

Gone?

Sam's run-in with the CO must've been more serious than she thought. Maybe that's why he'd been so distracted when he walked away. She'd have to call him later and drag the full story out of him.

Right now, she needed to find out Schnier's schedule. Kept her hand on his upper arm. "Oh, Berkeley as a kid, then we moved to San Diego. Went back to Berkeley for school. Stayed with an aunt. How 'bout you?" She tried to subtly match his accent, make him even more comfortable. Was from Podunk east Texas. Former football linebacker, a Texas A&M Aggie.

She'd read his military file and his background checks.

"Oh, my family has a ranch in the Lone Star State, ma'am. We're all built bigger there, if you know what I mean." He flexed his arm a little under her hand.

Wow. This guy laid it on thick. Did that actually work?

Maybe on a blonde college coed with too much to drink and unable to see past his Ranger status and his admittedly thick shoulders. "Oh, you don't want to know what I know." She giggled. "I want to know what *your* plans are. Going to be busy next week?"

She felt Schnier's muscles shift. He reached out a massive paw. Tapped the shoulder of a passing barmaid.

Ordered a Drone Strike in fluent Korean, then paused, "What do you want?"

Annoyed at the inopportune interruption, Michele forced a giggle and fiddled with her shell necklace.

This required more casual flirting. "Oh, I'll take an Irish Car Bomb."

He grinned and added her drink to his order.

The waitress moved on through the crowd. He turned back to her.

Leaned in so she could hear. "Like ah said, Rangers always keep busy. Volunteered just for all the experiences while I'm still young." He glanced around the room. "Maybe someday I'll show you my ranch." Paused. "Play darts? Gimme a game."

Michelle sighed. Schnier conveyed an infuriating lack of detail in his responses.

She pulled a trio of darts from the target above the red skull as her answer to his question.

This might take longer than she'd first thought.

I watched the movements of the People's Army soldiers on the stack of security feed monitors.

Sitting down would mean moving the dead guard's body, so I stood inside the tiny room.

None of the bad guys roamed near Doctor Yang Hyo-jin. On a blue zone hallway monitor, she returned from a janitorial closet across from the data center entrance.

Walked past the loading dock mantrap door, long steps, legs churning, lab coat flapping behind her.

Seconds later, she arrived with rolls of black plastic trash bags and silver duct tape.

After using the first one to retch in, she helped me wrap the body inside two others. We sealed them together with tape.

This place needed a better ventilation system.

Grabbing the dead guard's legs through the plastic, I twisted him around. Dragged the body outside the security office.

The bags would help with the smell, as well as preserve most forensic evidence.

I showed her the North Koreans on the displays. Summarized their movement pattern for her. "I'll call the primary security office. When they've checked out the truck out back and are ready to hit both mantraps at the same time, we'll go out the emergency exit next to the rear mantrap. Watch the fireworks from safely across the street."

She nodded, not ready to speak yet.

Instead, she stared at the monitors. Watched the North Koreans move from the orange zone to the blue and begin clearing offices.

Not much time left now.

I rang up the primary security office on the console's land-line phone. Could see a guard answer via one of the security cameras. "Captain Rhee Yun-seok, please."

"Who is calling?"

"Lieutenant Sam Harper, 75th RRC."

"One moment."

On the monitor, the senior Sergeant of the Guard held his hand over the phone. Called Rhee over.

At first he tried to explain, then he just handed him the phone.

"Harper? How did you get this number? Not more of your tricks, I hope."

"No, sir. I'm inside the facility. Calling you from the other security room. The one which monitors the lab spaces and the emergency exits."

"What! How did you get in there?" He paused to fume, then shouted into the phone, "I'll call your CO. Have you thrown out of Korea immediately."

The last thing I needed was another argument with the locals. "Let's discuss that later. The important thing is that if you'll switch over to viewing the inside of the lab, you'll see six North Korean operatives have infiltrated the facility."

He paused again. Deep thinker. "Are you sure they are from the North?"

"Can't be 100%, but I'm sure enough to call you and ask you to get your men in here to bail me out. Also have one of your scientists here with me."

"Thank you for your call. I shall hang up and arrange for a rescue. Stay there."

He ended the call without waiting for a response. Guess he didn't feel the need for a lot of heavy coordination.

We watched Rhee on the security monitor.

Rather than alerting the guards he was with, Rhee stepped away from them. Unlocked his cell phone. Dialed a number.

Spoke urgently. Jabbed his finger at the floor.

Without audio, it was difficult to tell what he said, but he certainly appeared emphatic.

On a different monitor, one of the North Koreans guarding the personnel mantrap door also spoke on a mobile phone.

I tapped Yang on the shoulder. Pointed at the second conversation. "Can you read lips?" She shrugged and began watching them both with me.

The enemy soldier and Rhee hung up at the same time. The two North Korean soldiers chatted for a moment and then turned and headed away from the primary mantrap.

Yang spoke aloud my thought, "They're working together."

I rubbed the back of my neck. "No kidding." From her file, she was single with no kids, no one to leave behind her, but I didn't want my new favorite scientist to become collateral damage for these dudes.

The head of security for the lab just betrayed us all.

Shouldn't be surprised.

Bitter experience has taught me you can't always trust people who're supposed to be on your side.

Two minutes tops to do something about Rhee *and* the enemy soldiers.

Chapter Sixteen:
Help! I Need Somebody

Blinking light overload. Kwon stood in the data center between two rows of racks full of servers, network devices, and storage. He'd never seen so many computer-like things in one place.

He'd passed the land navigation course using the stars at night with no problem, but this was like seeing the constellations in an unfamiliar hemisphere. There must be a pattern to the colored LEDs, but they baffled his unfamiliar eyes.

Maybe similar to the equipment the elite hacking teams in Pyongyang used?

He'd memorized instructions on how to figure out what to take. They even showed his team pictures of how storage device hard drive trays appeared. After that, he hadn't expected overloaded confusion.

A tangle of colored plastic cables ran everywhere, even blocking access to a few pieces of equipment.

And the fans. Whirring fans blew hot air out of each device.

He pushed his tactical radio earplugs in tighter to block out a bit of the white noise.

Start small.

He began at the top right of the racks.

Carefully scanned, row by row.

Pushed cables out of the way as needed for a better look.

Found a rack of metal shelves. Each held fourteen of the shiny gray hard drive trays set vertically.

A pair of LEDs blinked rapidly on each.

He exhaled deliberately. Must be the information storage.

His radio crackled to life. "Goshawk two to one." The data center's metal racks interfered a bit with the electronic signal, but he could understand Stro well enough.

"Goshawk one. I've located the package. Status?"

"Word from our contact is we have an unarmed soldier, apparently a kind of technical officer, and a scientist in the auxiliary security room. They've reported us to him, but that's contained, as long as we contain them."

Kwon minutely shook his head. "Don't scatter ashes on cooked rice. Take care of it."

Working together as a team requires figuring out how to do your part. With this data center puzzle in front of him, Kwon didn't have time to babysit a group of experienced noncoms.

"Roger. Four and Six, continue your sweep of orange, then flank via blue. Five and seven, finish setting your charges. We'll join you in three at most so we can move on the Imperialists. Keep your eyes open."

Four clicks answered Stro's updated orders to the men. Kwon'd been right to rely on the experienced sergeant. "Also, seven, find me a forklift on your way. It'll be faster to transport our target that way."

He analyzed the room.

Officers weren't expected to do menial labor, but these were exigent circumstances.

Could at least begin the job of hauling and stacking just inside the door into the data center. A pair of finger-tight thumbscrews held each shelf into the rack.

He pulled off a glove to get a better grip.

Unscrewed the highest shelf.

Rather than attempt to manage each storage drive individually, he'd just take a shelf full of drives at a time. Collective solutions were the best.

After his team converged on and destroyed the two Dominationists, they could move the shelves full of data out to the truck quickly enough.

I pulled another pair of trash bags off the roll Doctor Yang Hyo-jin brought from the janitor's closet. Tucked it over the camera hanging from the ceiling of the backup security center.

Now we had a little privacy.

Rhee must be actively keeping his men in the primary security office from monitoring the cameras in the lab portion of the building, but no point in taking more risks than required.

Doctor Yang sat heavily on the dead guard's rolling chair. Probably needed a minute to deal with recent events.

I've heard home is where they have to take you in, even after you've screwed up.

Mostly didn't have much of a home, myself, but I was willing to give the theory a try.

Would take time for them to arrive, but I was ready for reinforcements.

Hit three on my speed dial to call Bishop's issue mobile phone. Luckily, he was the after hours Duty Sergeant this week, required to be available on call to summon the rest of the Company in case of an alert.

I needed a Ranger who could make things happen.

"75th RRC, Sergeant Bishop."

He sounded bored. I could fix that.

"This is Lieutenant Harper. I authenticate Whiskey, Tango, Foxtrot, one-three."

My pre-arranged emergency code. Just stoked to talk to a friendly at this point in the evening.

"What can I do for you, sir?"

Knowing I was on my way out Monday morning, he probably wondered why I called in an emergency after hours.

"Top, need you to roundup a few operators in full tactical gear with live ammo and get them over to the metallurgical lab immediately. Inform Major Williams. North Korean spec ops infiltrated the lab. Captain Rhee Yun-seok, head of lab security, is actively working with them."

"North Koreans, Lieutenant?"

"Get firepower over here ASAP. Can either arrest the Captain or arrest me once you arrive. Also, call the Seoul police. Have them cordon off a two-block radius around the lab. We'll need ambulances and the coroner's van. Probably MPs as well. Understood?"

"Sir, is this a prank, sir? Because I have to say, sir, a lieutenant who has gone out by the numbers can still be in even more trouble before his departure, sir."

"The dead ROK guard at my feet and six NKPA I'm watching on the security monitors here are no joke, sergeant. Have to go. Text me when the cavalry arrives, my phone is on silent. Confirm."

"Roger that. Six Tangos plus Rhee, police cordon, ambulances, coroner, and MPs. Wilco. Your funeral, sir."

"Hope not. Harper out." No more time to waste, I disconnected the call.

Let him have Lee GPS locate my issue phone if the CO wanted verification of my location.

Bishop could command attention from the bureaucracy when he desired, but even if he expedited the red tape, it'd take Military Police and Rangers time just to drive here through the crowded city streets.

Maybe the metro police would arrive outside sooner, but I didn't expect them to actually break into a secure government facility, especially with the dude officially in charge of security refusing entry.

Rhee'd have plenty of time to use his authority to make his escape and then slip across the DMZ to the North.

"Stay here for now." I told Doctor Yang.

Was now in giving orders mode. No time for Korean politeness.

"Will the Army come soon?"

Too many questions. Must be worried. With good cause.

I shook my head. "Maybe twenty, thirty minutes. Until then, we're on our own. Need more supplies, whatever I can scrounge. You'll be fine here." I pointed at the enemy soldiers on the monitors. "Keep an eye on them. I'll be back well before they can arrive."

Sliding outside the security office, I stepped around the sealed body. The smell began to clear as the local air mixed with the far larger volume of air in the adjoining brown zone warehouse.

Glancing down the nearby palletized aisles, I confirmed what I'd seen in the security monitors.

No enemy in sight.

Still, not much time until we had unwelcome visitors.

I slung another black bag over the lone camera in the red zone loading dock area.

Ran to the janitor's closet.

The data center door near the blue zone hallway was closed.

Inside the closet, I found industrial sized cleaning supplies, plus a push broom, mop, and wheeled mop bucket. Light aluminum formed the broom and mop handles.

Despite looking exactly like every other set of warehouse cleaning supplies I'd ever seen, this stuff was probably all custom ordered for government facilities via an exclusive procurement contract.

Grabbed a heavy ten gallon plastic container of bleach. Dropped it still capped into the bucket for transport.

Bleach always comes in handy.

Unscrewed the mop handle to take with me. Left the mop head on the closet floor.

Rolling the mop bucket along the corridor outside, I stared at the emergency exit door next to the loading dock mantrap.

It would be so easy to just grab the doctor and head out the emergency exit. Get ourselves lost in a crowded shop until the police arrived.

Even jump on the subway to go home and re-pack my things, letting the proper authorities sort it all out.

But then where was the proof Rhee was involved?

A few ambiguous actions on security cameras he controlled and could erase or edit at will?

The dead body of a guard and the missing materials and technology from the metallurgical lab?

He could explain all that.

In fact, I bet Rhee was already working on his story.

About how crazy American Lieutenant Harper, the guy with an unreasonable grudge against him, broke into his lab to frame him. Stole the materials, killed a guard when he was caught and took a scientist as a hostage, who unfortunately became a heroic martyr to the cause.

All very plausible if the security system only showed me following Rhee into the lab. I broke in, then disabled the camera feeds somehow, losing most of the rest of the footage.

I'd go to Leavenworth on a murder rap, he'd get off scot-free.

The enemy would achieve everything they'd planned.

Not tonight.

Time to drop in on the uninvited.

Michelle formed a pyramid on their table with her third overturned Irish Car Bomb glass.

She'd let Schnier win two out of three games of darts, keeping just enough pressure on to not make it obvious she had no intentions of defeating him.

Now, settled into a cozy table in the corner away from the deafening K-pop, with a few drinks under their belts, she was sure his tongue would loosen.

She kicked off her shoes and prepared to create an accidental encounter.

So of course, his mobile phone rang. "You don't have to answer that, do you? We just started to relax."

Schnier shrugged. "Sorry. Issue phone. Duty calls." He grinned. "Sometimes, literal-like."

Michelle frowned. At this rate, she'd never see a promotion. Couldn't even squeeze useful info out of a horny drunken soldier.

"75th RRC, Lieutenant Schnier." Stiffened up a little just to answer the phone.

She focused her hearing, but couldn't quite make out what whoever it was on the other end of the call was saying.

"Roger." He slurred his words a little. "Call the rest of my platoon. Meet at the base fer outfittin'."

The voice on the phone grew louder, but more distorted. She'd make him feel guilty for the interruption of their date and hopefully Schnier would tell her what this was all about.

"No, I'm fine. For this job, at least, or will be by the time we're ready. Call the platoon."

The voice on the phone said something about Sergeant Lee, police, ambulance, coroner.

Whatever it was, it sounded deadly.

Her internal priorities shifted to finding out more on this situation.

"Good. Relay to the CO I agree. Should keep this mess inside the Company. Deal with the uppity sumbitch ourselves. ETA 10 to the equipment bays."

He disconnected the call.

"Who was that?"

Gazing toward the ceiling rather than at her, where his eyes had remained focused all night long, Schnier's attention was a million miles away. "Oh, just Bishop. Unexpected alert. Sorry, gotta go."

She needed to recover at least a little recognition from him.

Michelle put her elbow on the table and slid the tip of her finger into her mouth to exaggerate her frown. "You're just going to leave me here, all alone?"

He stalled for a second, grasping for an answer out of his thick head, then she could see a light bulb go off in his expression. "Well, you're cleared, an' all this is about yer best buddy. You could come. See us in a little action. Maybe see your techno Ranger buddy's expression when I show up with my platoon, all armed-up, to grab him."

She reached down and slid her shoes back on under the table. "I'm all yours."

Maybe she could text the Agency about this when Schnier was distracted with getting his men organized.

What had Sam gotten himself into this time?

Chapter Seventeen:
It All Comes Falling Down

How would Doctor Yang Hyo-jin handle recent events? I took a deep breath. Could I rely on her?

Made a semi-futile attempt to slow my own heartbeat.

I'd left my commandeered cleaning materials outside the auxiliary security office door.

Staring at the video screens, I pointed at the pairs of enemy soldiers in brown, orange, and now blue zone. "Doctor, those men on the screens are hunting us right now. We must stop them before they find us, but I can't do it alone. Need you to keep an eye on the security monitors here. Let me know what they're doing. Where they're going. Understand?"

She nodded somewhat convincingly. I hoped she'd come through under pressure. Was all I had at the moment.

Her life was on the line as well.

I put my Bluetooth earbud in. Used the desk phone to call my mobile number. After connecting the call, I handed her the desk phone's handset.

Now we had communications.

"Bolt the door behind me. Don't let anyone not in a police or an American Army uniform in."

Didn't think that'd hold any sort of serious attempt for more than a moment, but it may make her feel better about sitting in that little room and staring at the monitors.

Less likely to think about the dead body bagged out on the floor.

Stepping outside, I removed the bleach container from on top of the mop bucket.

Unlocked the rear mantrap by transmitting the captain's RFID number.

Shoved the mop bucket into it.

Closed the door.

The mantrap's internal sensors would detect someone already present and not let anyone else enter. When the bucket never exited, an alarm should show up on the primary security console.

Hopefully, the alert would distract Rhee with explaining to his men why they shouldn't investigate it.

Couldn't all be corrupt.

The ten gallon bleach container was too heavy to carry stealthily around with me, so I parked it next to the mantrap door.

Grasped the mop handle at shoulder width in the middle. Gave it an experimental swing to check the balance.

Headed for the warehouse section.

Need to take care of the enemy pair in brown zone before the pair coming through blue zone reached the Doctor.

If I made enough noise there, the other teams would head that way, ideally coming from the other direction.

Doc told me exactly where the pair went in brown zone.

Kept me updated on the progress of the other two teams.

I'd worked in a warehouse connected to a rail yard and a highway as a teen. Seen my fair share of accidents.

Loaded merchandise on trucks for a regional shipper.

Okay, I'd usually messed with the computerized pick and pack system in the warehouse, not having to do too much loading.

Still had all the safety lectures memorized, though.

Mostly they involved momentum, pallet angles and not ever, upon pain of firing, overloading the rack supports.

After sneaking into brown zone, I crouched between stacks of black and red chemical barrels on pallets in the three-meter aisles.

Decent cover.

They'd been moved off the shelves, blocking this aisle to

forklift traffic.

In fact, they had North Korean bricks of C-4 taped to them, wired for remote detonation.

Maybe this wasn't the ideal location to hide.

No anti-tamper devices were present, so I eased the detonators out of each brick.

Now they'd just make a little bang if triggered, instead of a big one.

Bags of powdered materials and glass containers full of acidic liquids stretched floor to ceiling, held up by pallet shelves resting on thin steel racks.

A sign on the end of the closest rack read in English and Hangul, "*Never climb on racks during or after assembly. Storage racks are not designed to be stepped on or climbed on. A slip or fall may result in serious injury.*"

That's what I needed, serious injuries. "Doctor, can you find me a forklift in this place? In a location not near them?"

"Uh... sure, one moment." A pause while she scanned the brown zone security monitors, "Turn right at the next opening, then left to the end. You'll find one in an open area where the aisles meet."

"Thanks."

I followed her directions, trying to keep my voice to a minimum.

At the end, an electric forklift.

Perfect.

First safety rule: always have an audible warning on a fast-moving, quiet vehicle. I found the speaker and yanked the wire away from it.

No beeping sound to warn the bad guys when I moved around.

Fortunately, the warehouse workers left the little plastic-looking key in it, so I just climbed aboard and experimented a bit with the controls.

Like riding a bike.

Now that I had wheels, I moved faster.

Headed toward the enemy team.

According to my reconnaissance asset, they shuffled

materials, with some sort of scientific name which I ignored, toward the loading dock.

That filled their arms with non-weapons.

"Doctor, do you see that forty foot long aisle of warehouse racks full of heavy glass bottles and powdered metal? I need you to tell me when they reach the other end of that."

That aisle was the heaviest section I'd seen. Weight was important.

"Third aisle in?"

"That's the one."

Each vertical structural column on the pallet racking had a 6-inch wide, 42-inch tall lime green column protector. The protectors were made of high-density polyethylene. Held in pairs to the column with reflective straps.

Safety first.

Flipping open a knife on my multi-tool, I slit the straps. Put the column protectors to the side.

They were designed to thwart accidents.

This wouldn't be an accident.

I picked up a solid looking empty pallet with the forks.

Tilted the forks and pallet up a bit.

Set up in the forklift with a slightly angled straightaway facing the heavy section of floor-to-ceiling materials.

With that angle, I was out of sight of the aisle itself, but had a direct run to the end of it.

Considered the potential for collateral damage.

The Doctor and I were the only friendlies in the lab zones. She was safely locked into the security office.

Was confident I could avoid my planned disaster.

The bad guys marked themselves as targets as soon as they killed the security guard.

Everything else was just material goods. Expensive, but not as costly as the loss of life these dudes would cause with stunts like that C-4.

No, just needed to wait for her signal and then execute.

"Now! They're there now!"

One-one-thousand. Two—one-thousand.

Gave the DPRK special ops pair time to reach the middle of

the warehouse aisle.

Floored the electric accelerator. Battery-powered motors. Excellent acceleration.

Charged forward.

Crossed the entrance. Three-meter aisle.

Expected them there. Too late to stop my momentum.

Entered their field of view for a split second.

Good reflexes.

Dropped their small boxes. Grabbed at shoulder straps.

Much too late.

Drove the pallet into the front corner of the rack.

The support for this end.

Smack.

Momentum carried me up and forward. Rear-end cleared the seat by six inches.

Everything slowed.

Focus on the closest 24 foot stack of pallet rack shelving.

Each shelf four feet tall. Eight feet wide. Two full pallets supported on each level.

The tons of powdered metal bags above the now bent support collapsed it.

The column no longer resisted weight.

Powdered metal rained down.

Poured across the aisle.

Torn bags floated after the flood.

The falling mass pushed the pallet on my forks down.

Shoved my forklift away from the shelving.

Lifted rear wheels off the ground.

I slammed the steering column lever.

Forklift into reverse. Forks angled down.

Dropped the impacting pallet.

Please slide freely off the front!

My rear wheels bounced. Spun. Gripped the concrete floor.

Managed to retreat a few crucial meters.

At least three shelved warehouse pallets crushed the pallet I'd left behind.

Another nine pallets worth of materials hit. Slid off to the sides.

Created a wider and wider mountain of destruction.

The remaining contents splashed into the columns holding up the next rack.

Into the two racks across the aisle.

More pedal!

As fast as the forklift could reverse. As far as the warehouse allowed.

The enemy spec ops pair unslung their rifles.

Adjoining supports collapsed.

Couldn't resist the push of sideways spreading masses.

Not and hold the weight above.

Their collapse added three-times as much powdered metal and glass bottles to the growing 12 foot mountain of destruction.

Metal powders flowed well enough, but as glass bottles of chemicals shattered, the spilled liquid lubricated everything.

Sped up the horizontal spread.

Two enemy soldiers raised their rifles.

Took aim.

The carnage reached them.

Swept them off their feet.

The pattern continued. A giant erector set of dominoes.

Materials flowed in waves from the top of the collapsing pallet racking.

Followed the paths of least resistance.

Piled up in the aisle.

Spread sideways into the next vertical supports.

Knocked those over.

"Wow."

Understatement in my earpiece from the Doc, watching the camera feed.

Ruin first spread to the other end of the row of racks I'd originally hit.

The racks across the aisle weren't far behind.

The enemy pair vanished as the surrounding racks collapsed. Covered them with metal powder, pellets, and glass shards.

A pause.

Everything hung in the balance.

Two 40-foot long aisles containing ten 24-foot racks crumpled;

the enemy between them.

Then the wreckage got out of hand.

The wave of materials reflected off the back wall of this section of the warehouse.

Spread out a little farther.

Far enough to impact the supports of the next aisle over.

That aisle collapsed from back to front.

I spun the wheel.

Fled farther.

Backed my forklift into the loading dock area of the red zone.

From right to left, one, two, three, four, five, six aisles of floor-to-ceiling pallet racking toppled in turn.

Destruction flowed with a roar like the ocean.

Concrete floors turned bottles into shards. Barrels burst open or rolled into nearby supports. Pulverized bags filled the air with shiny metallic particles.

Noise might attract a little attention.

Pieces of broken pallet stuck out here and there from the 40-foot long, 100-foot wide, mountain of rubble.

Destruction filled the space where six rows of racks had been.

I wiped my forehead. Glad I'd made it back to the loading dock area.

Outside brown zone.

The dust cloud caught up to me.

Turned my sleeve into an impromptu air filter, but choked and hacked anyway.

"Hope the Army doesn't make me pay for this mess." Cough. "Lieutenants don't make much."

"You've set back our research by at least six months, just to clean up and get new supplies. Wasn't there a less destructive way to stop them?" Her singsong accent in my Bluetooth earbud sounded lovely, even if her sentiments bore tinges of out of control collateral damage.

War is destruction.

I set my jaw.

Tried to estimate where the enemy soldiers lay under the wreckage.

Leaving the forklift, I grabbed the mop handle.

Clambered over the spilled goods to the spot the pair of spec ops soldiers disappeared into.

Scrambled to stay on top of bent frames and the shredded pallet planks, not sure if I'd sink into the rest nor what Frankenstein mix the random acidic liquids and powdered metals would create together.

"I'm mostly winging it here, Doc. Let me concentrate on checking if they're still a threat."

Pulled aside shredded bags and shifting collapsed boxes to search. Took a minute to locate the enemy.

Dead.

At least unconscious.

Buried under shards of glass and powdered rubble.

Found an open angle. Jabbed them each with the mop handle.

No movement.

No longer a danger.

Maybe I deserved to feel more triumphant, like a beating of battle drums, while standing victorious over my fallen enemies, but the only pounding I felt were the pulses of adrenaline hammering my ears.

These guys never had a chance, but better them than me lying under all that rubble.

Couldn't dig down to reach their rifles, slung partway over their arms, without slicing myself open on the glass.

Most likely ruined anyway.

Doc cheered. "Nice work, Lieutenant."

Must be watching my progress on the cameras. "Don't celebrate *too* early, still four more out there."

A Ranger's work is never done.

Even over the white noise of the data center's fans, Kwon heard rolling thunder from outside the room.

Came from the much larger warehouse space. Sounded like the whole place collapsed in on itself.

Did one of his men's explosive charges detonate prematurely?

Took two tries to click his radio microphone on. "This is one. Report."

His own transmission stepped on Stro's, "... and seven, report. Repeat, observe major collapse in brown zone. Five, seven, report."

Nothing but whirring fans for several endless moments.

What happened to his men?

Why didn't they respond?

Maybe splitting up the team hadn't been the best idea.

After an eternal wait, an answer, "Four and six. We also heard it. Currently clearing blue zone offices. Empty so far." Wrong pair.

Whatever the issue, it was with five and seven in the brown zone. The others were fine.

"Four, six, return to orange zone. Regroup with two and three. Locate the others. Skip the nonessentials. Accelerate the timeframe."

"Four, ack."

"Two, ack."

With his team back on track, Kwon looked at the almost completed pile of storage drive shelves stacked near the steel data center door.

What could he do to quicken the pace of his own efforts?

One last shelf, then he'd go hunting for a forklift to carry it all.

Even if this collapse delayed his team's departure, he'd complete the most critical goal of their mission himself.

A junior officer's work is never done.

Chapter Eighteen:
Survival Training

I careened around a corner into red zone, rear wheels sliding at the edge of control.

Floored the electric forklift again. Its motors whined with effort.

With brown zone cut-off by the collapsed aisles, needed to get over to blue zone to ensure the Doc didn't have to deal with any unwelcome visitors.

The last thing I wanted was the only witness to this mess who might actually be on my side getting herself killed.

Besides, I kind of liked her attitude.

Not to mention she was the only local who I didn't have to stare down at the top of her head.

"Lieutenant, the pair in blue zone turned back. They're talking on radios and moving toward the other pair. I think they'll meet up in orange zone. You can't reach them separately. You'll have to confront both pairs at once."

I skidded to a stop near the cargo mantrap in red zone. The security office door remained closed.

Good.

Really didn't want any collateral human damage from my choice to stay behind and repel the invaders. Putting a stop to that sort of thing, not doing paperwork, was why I'd joined the Army in the first place.

Lifted the giant bleach container onto the forks. Maybe my ROTC junior year course in *Nuclear, Biochemical, and Chemical Warfare* would come in handy.

More than the *Law of War* course did, preferably.

I'd need to drive more carefully now that I had cargo again. "How close is the pair in blue zone to reaching orange zone?"

"Almost to the end of the hallway."

Really didn't want to turn the corner and see them at the other end of a long hallway. Rifle fights at a distance go notoriously poorly for the dude without a rifle. "Please tell me when they clear that last hallway into orange zone."

Drove across the open concrete of red zone.

Passed the data center door, then into the blue zone hallway.

Paused for a moment just before the hallway's right turn.

Waited for word from the Doc.

The forklift wasn't really intended for the people parts of the lab.

Barely fit into this hallway. Definitely wouldn't fit around the corner.

Too bad.

I squeezed past it. Ducked down next to the bleach container.

Waited, concealed by the turn.

"They're into orange zone, almost to the others. Don't believe they can see the hallway entrance anymore."

Didn't sound very confident, but life in the Rangers is not without its little risks. "Thanks. That's helpful."

Heaved the container of bleach onto my shoulder like a longboard.

Turned the hallway corner.

Took both arms to keep the bleach awkwardly balanced there, but was thankful for the intense ruck training I'd survived in RASP. Thirty days gave muscles time to heal, but not enough to lose their tone, especially with daily workouts in the diamond palace.

Scanned past the office door. Toward the end of the hallway.

No one waiting to shoot me.

So far, so good.

"Four of them are together. Examining the wrecked aisles. Maybe looking for a way through."

"Doctor, need you to find me a large experiment. Something with a lot of molten metal."

"Oh, but you'll ruin our work. Months of effort, gone!"

"Better that than those four ruin us. Also, is there a large fan nearby?"

Quelling her protests, I lugged the bleach down to the other end of the hallway.

Took a quick look in both directions.

No enemy forces in sight.

Just a maze of yellow lines, experiments, and stacks of equipment to navigate.

Luckily, I had a native guide with eyes in the sky whispering in my earpiece.

Set down the bleach. Followed her directions.

Peeked around each corner.

Stayed low. Kept out of sight. No noise.

Acquired an industrial extension cord. Pocketed a roll of duct tape. Moved a big box fan.

Slid the bleach over to a furnace table with pans of liquid roasting metal.

Components gathered, I plugged the box fan in. Pointed it across pans of bubbling metal, aimed to cover a short aisle just past a turn, with the other edges blocked by tall stacks of equipment and materials.

Coiled the extension cord.

Tossed it up to uncoil in a loop over a steel girder.

Tied the dangling end to the handle of the ten gallon container of bleach.

With a little jiggering, I worked them over to a spot above the pans of molten metal.

Even from a few feet away, the heat toasted my hands and face.

The radiating heat would've been pretty nice, if I'd just come in from the cold outside, but my recent physical exertions already had my blood boiling.

"They've given up getting through. Coming back toward blue zone."

"Almost ready. Let me know when they'll turn the corner in front of me."

Knelt behind the fan. Held the end of the extension cord to

keep the container in the air.

This better work. No time to test.

The metal furnace sat next to the quickest path from brown zone back to blue zone, so I only needed a little luck.

The aisle I hoped they'd take would lead them around the corner.

Right past the experiment.

If they used a different route, the Doc could warn me, but they'd likely get past me and into the blue zone, where I'd have to figure out how to take them out from behind.

We'd cross that bridge only if we came to it.

Two escape routes from my position.

Another aisle behind me led toward the personnel mantrap and the administrative offices.

A gap between a steel table and a filing cabinet interrupted the stacks of equipment on my right flank. That connected up with the aisle to blue zone in front of the experiment.

Bet they kept the detailed records of the experiment I was about to ruin in that filing cabinet.

"Close to the turn."

Switched the fan on full blast.

The air passing over the molten pans would cool them a little, but not enough to matter, not in the seconds left.

The first two DPRK spec ops soldiers leap-frogged around the corner.

I released the extension cord.

The bottom of the plastic container evaporated into black smoke.

Released bleach boiled with a sizzle, causing it to flash into vapor form.

The cloud of gas expanded.

Smelled garlic, so I turned and sprinted away.

Ducked around the metal cabinet for cover.

The thump of K2 semi-auto rounds. Cabinet shook from the impacts.

Good reaction time for the front two, but a prepared individual can beat a team.

I scooted away. Stayed out of sight below the tops of the

scientific equipment.

Needed time to let things work.

After a few seconds, I heard coughing and anguished speech.

Army crawled back.

Glanced around the bottom corner of the stainless steel lab table. Ready to duck back or overturn it for cover if they spotted me.

Thick clouds of yellow-green gas surrounded the two leading soldiers.

The two men farther away had also turned the corner. Breathed in the gas's edge.

The pure mustard gas worked.

After blowing it into their faces, the breeze generated by the fan began dispersing the clouds. Spread the vaporized bleach into lower doses diffused across the rest of the open area.

The two soldiers closest to the fan and furnace dropped their weapons to the floor, scattered and forgotten.

One soldier bent over. Attempted to retch as he rubbed his eyes.

The other spun in a slow circle. Coughed. Clawed at his throat.

With the gas in their lungs, neither would breathe well for a while.

One of two soldiers farther from my makeshift trap rested on his belly next to his rifle, coughing. Reached back and pulled a canteen off his belt.

The other leaned against an electric crane, eyes watering, tearing his eyelids apart. Swung his elbows for his surroundings, alert for dangers he couldn't see.

The garlicky mustard smell faded as fast as the fan scattered the fumes.

I circled around the aisle leading toward blue zone.

Approached the group from behind.

Might have a small permanent loss of lung capacity, but they'd recover basic functions soon enough.

Walked on the outside edges of my boots to minimize the noise.

Approached behind the one I'd seen on the phone with Rhee

earlier.

Easy target, bending over to retch.

Almost reached the furnace table covered in molten metal.

Side-kicked him in the back of the knees.

His legs and waist folded forward.

Grabbed his arms. Pulled them behind his back. Used upward elbow pressure to force him the rest of the way to the ground.

Ripped pieces of tape with my teeth. Secured his wrists and ankles behind his back.

Picked up his imitation K2.

Checked the selector and magazine.

Ready to fire.

One of the farther soldiers, the one already on his belly, recovered enough from coughing to grab up his rifle and blast in my direction.

I'd spent too much time dealing with the closest soldier.

Despite apparently missing much of the gas by hitting the floor quickly when it first appeared, he still couldn't aim well through watery eyes, at least by spec op standards.

One of his rounds slapped me across the top of my left shoulder.

Searing pain.

Like someone laid a red-hot poker across my shoulder.

Focus.

Life-saving tasks only.

I returned the favor, with interest. Aim unaffected by chlorine gas, my two rounds impacted him in the face.

Tight grouping.

The most immediate threat dealt with, shock settled in.

All I could do to collapse to the floor.

Roll over under the furnace table.

Watch my two remaining enemies attempt to recover.

My back baked from the furnace's residual heat above me.

Wouldn't survive staying here very long.

Kwon peeked out of the data center room door.

No one in sight.

He fully opened the steel door.

Stepped into the deserted hallway.

His team better be all right, but they were level 10,000 guys with experience south of the DMZ. Could take care of themselves.

Right now he needed to do his part.

Get the pile of storage drive shelves stacked inside the data center door out to the truck.

He spotted an electric forklift parked at the end of the blue zone hallway.

Perfect!

Hustling down the hall toward the forklift, he tried Stro on the radio. "One to Two. Status?"

Only static in response.

Kwon shrugged. Maybe the metal in the lab equipment and the walls blocked their transmissions.

Reaching the forklift, he found the key ready to go.

Did one of his men leave it parked here for him?

Either way, he had no time to lose.

No room in the hallway to turn around, either.

He switched on the forklift. Shifted it into reverse. Looked over his shoulder.

Drove backwards.

Returned to red zone and the data center doorway.

Funny, no beeping noise, unlike the forklifts in the North.

Nice driving skills, though. Only scraped the walls twice.

With the forks situated in front of the data center door, he tried again. "Repeat. One to Two. Status?"

This time, a faint signal, "Abort. Get out ... can. ... follow."

Stro and the other men must've run into resistance from the locals. Their unfaithful contact better not have turned traitor on them! "Confirmed. One departing. Remainder of Goshawk to follow A-SAP."

Focus on the mission.

If he succeeded, the others would be fine.

He'd get the truck loaded. By then they'd surely be ready to depart.

Might even make it back to help load.

Kwon muscled one shelf of drives over to prop the data center door open.

He'd grab that one last.

Lugged each set of storage drives out. Stacked them flat on top of the forks.

The forks were tilted up about 10 degrees, so gravity kept the shelves nicely in place against the backrest.

He stacked the last metal shelf. Let the door bang shut.

The rear wheels definitely felt lighter, the forklift's counterweight just barely enough to keep the forks from pulling the whole machine forward.

He'd drive carefully.

Slowly backed up until he was safely in the red zone open area.

Turned in a slow curve.

Stopped to face the emergency exit and the cargo mantrap.

Leaving the forklift behind, he stepped out and swiped the badge he'd taken from the dead guard across the RFID reader for the mantrap.

It blinked red. Must be malfunctioning or something.

Checked his surroundings.

The security office door was closed!

Outside, a bundle taped up in black garbage bags.

Someone had been here. Might even still be in the security office.

Couldn't let them cut him off. Not when he was so close to mission accomplished!

Kwon hopped back into the forklift.

Leaned back in the seat.

Kept the weight distributed to the rear.

Only one try.

He pressed down the accelerator.

Pointed the forks at the emergency exit.

The forklift moved forward.

Picked up speed.

He'd reached a slow walking pace, so he eased off. Kept the pace level.

Lined up carefully with the exit.

The second to the top shelf in the stack of drives hit the waist-level crossbar.

Unlocked the door.

Triggered the emergency alarm. A siren whooped.

The door burst outward.

If the crash in brown zone hadn't disturbed the rest of the lab's guard force, the emergency exit alarm would alert them something was going on.

The forklift cleared the doorway. Made it out to the loading dock with his cargo intact!

Kwon pumped his fist into the air once.

Which unbalanced the forklift a little. Caused it to curve to the side on the wet pavement. Caused the shelves, not tied down with anything, to slide to the side, starting at the top.

He grabbed the wheel with both hands.

Course-corrected in the opposite direction until the forklift and its load mostly straightened out again. Braked to a stop.

Scanned his surroundings.

No one had seen his minor embarrassment.

No time to celebrate early, that's for sure.

The crack of several pairs of shots echoed from inside.

Must be his men defeating the enemy. They'd be here any minute; he'd be ready to leave when they were.

Kwon took cautious aim at the back of the truck, already open against the loading dock.

Drove right up to it, front wheels barely short of the concrete cliff, drive shelves suspended by forks over the truck bed. Gripping the hydraulic lever with a minimum of force, he lowered the forks almost to the bed.

In the warm server exhaust of the data center, he'd forgotten how cold it was out here.

Frozen pebbles rained from the sky.

Climbed out of the forklift.

Clambered through the side of the truck bed. Flipped up the rear seats designed for people.

Had more precious cargo to carry now.

He unloaded the shelves into the truck bed as fast as his groaning muscles allowed.

Backed the forklift off.

Closed the tailgate.

Got in the driver's seat.

Removed his tactical vest. Tossed it down between the seats in the cab.

Started the big diesel engine with a roar.

The whooping alarm from the emergency exit annoyed him. Reminded him Goshawk was exposed.

No sign of his men.

Well, Stro said they'd follow as soon as they could. His priority remained the data in those drives. His uncle always said the needs of the many outweighed the needs of the few.

He put the truck into drive. Pulled away down the alley. They'd have to find their own way.

Turning right from the alley on to the main road took him past the entrance to the parking lot and the lab's front door.

Men in American uniforms gathered around the security checkpoint just inside. Argued with one of the local guards.

After a moment of debate, they pointed rifles at the guard, who responded by falling back in surrender of whatever point they'd been arguing.

Barely made it out in time. Nothing he could have done for the others.

Besides, they had all the experience on the team. He was the new one to the South.

Unable to connect back together, it was every man for himself.

The street outside the lab should have at least some traffic, but the police had stripped it bare.

A block ahead, a group of police lined the edges of the road; little white cars with blue stripes and blinking red and blue light bars shooting colored rays through the snow.

Pedestrians on the wide sidewalk held their arms under their puffy-coat armpits behind a makeshift barricade of neon yellow tape with black lettering.

The tape stretched between the building shutter and the light pole next to the street's curb.

He aimed for an opening between police cars.

An officer stepped up to the driver's side as he arrived at the blockade.

He waved a clipboard of paperwork at them.

Ignored the whistles to stop.

Apparently, it and his South Korean military uniform alleviated their fears.

The whistling subsided. No police pursued.

Sleet turned into a thick snow, heavy in the air, sticking to everything.

No further word from Stro.

Kwon wasn't sure exactly where he was going.

Left the shopping area. Entered a residential district.

Virtually brand new mansions everywhere. This area diverged in style from the five story block-sized apartment buildings.

Must be where the super-elite lived, each family in their own massive thousand-square-foot estate.

Driving past a playground, he watched a little girl wearing a cartoon panda on her coat, couldn't have been more than six, rolling up snow into a ball.

Icicles drooped from the bare branches of the nearby trees.

For some reason, Kwon couldn't get the image of the guard's last breath out of his mind.

He shoved his boot into the brake pedal.

The truck slid to a halt in the snow and ice.

He shifted into park.

Opened the truck door.

Leaned over just in time to projectile vomit out onto the cold street.

The back of his throat burned from the residue of stomach acid.

Gathering fresh snow off the truck's hood, he melted it in his throat. Took the immediate pain away. Wiped his face with the back of his hand.

Felt a little better.

The little panda girl raced across the snow to stand next to the road. Pointed at his truck. Military vehicles weren't common in the residential areas of Seoul.

Another mistake.

For strict operational security, he should do something about the child as a potential witness who might go running to tell her parents what she'd seen.

Kwon could've had a niece like her if South Korean border guards hadn't murdered his brother and his brother's wife.

Instead, he chose to just wave innocently and shift the truck back into drive.

At least he had the data. The guard didn't die in vain.

Stro and the others might still make it, but either way they weren't sacrifices for a failed mission.

As long as Kwon delivered the knowledge in the back of the truck, their offerings were worth it.

Chapter Nineteen: Getting Fresh

The initial scorch of pain in my shoulder vanished under a new burst of adrenalin.

I half-slid, half-crawled backward. Farther under the furnace table.

The air entering my lungs got hotter.

My shoulder might hurt like hell once the adrenalin wore off, but for the moment, I needed to function.

Two down, two more to go.

"Lieutenant? There's another one I haven't seen before. He drove the forklift back this way, but with the cameras out in red zone, I can't see what he's doing now."

Okay, two down, *three* more to go.

Nothing to do for Doc Yang without resolving my local shark control problem. "Stay there. Keep the door bolted. Odds are, he'll ignore you."

I hoped.

This whole situation had rapidly escalated out of control. Thinking about that third guy loose in the red zone with the Doc was like watching a friend drown out in the ocean while a wave pushes you toward shore.

Fear of failure to protect those you care about, failure to take care of your responsibilities, can be good if it helps you focus in the moment, but also bad if it distracts you from what you need to do to survive or succeed.

Were my enemies afraid for other people, or only for themselves?

Maybe they could focus more, or perhaps it makes them less reckless, less willing to take the risks required to outfight your opponent.

The lack of hesitation necessary to win.

Maybe if I was a better soldier, I wouldn't need to gamble to win. Maybe I'd be able to plan it all out ahead of time and watch things fall into place like dominoes.

Wishful thinking.

The kind of distraction that would get me killed during a fight.

Ancient military wisdom: *No battle plan survives contact with the enemy.*

I bet everyone feels alternately helpless and all-powerful during *every* battle.

The soldier who'd been spinning in circles probably felt helpless as he knelt on the lab floor.

He still wasn't getting enough oxygen to threaten me.

No need to take him out.

The other, who'd been farther from the cloud of chlorine gas, hunched intelligently behind the electric crane, only the edge of a pant leg showing.

Didn't have a decent shot at him, so I crawled backward until I could rise into a crouch out of sight behind the furnace.

Backed up, eyes laser-focused forward. Knocked over a trio of short steel bars with a clatter.

No matter.

I flanked farther to the right.

Took quick steps around tall shelving for finished specimens of twisted metal, presumably the end result of whatever process the experiment tortured molten metal with.

He leaned around the crane's body from a kneeling firing position, rifle barrel searching for me with his reddened, but apparently clear-enough eyes.

Too late.

I rested my barrel on the end of the shelf to stabilize it. No longer trusted my left arm to support a rifle.

Aimed center mass. Prepped the trigger.

Pressed twice to break the shots.

The first bullet shattered his bent left arm at the elbow where it protected his chest.

Fired from his flank, he didn't see it coming; just slumped over to scream in pain.

The second bullet clipped the bolt carrier of his home grown K2 rifle. Gouged off metal before it ricocheted into the air.

Someone will find that stuck in the ceiling one day.

My earpiece made noise, but I was too focused to listen.

Not wanting to remain in one position for too long, I lifted my rifle off the shelf.

Turned back the way I'd come.

A barely visible wire caught on my rifle's barrel as I lifted it.

The wire's swooping momentum yanked the whole rifle toward my face.

Instinctively ducked.

Spun away to face my attacker.

Left my rifle to bob in the air.

It weighed down the garrote he sought my life with.

Couldn't afford to fall behind in the observe–orient–decide–act loop.

The last remaining soldier, the one whose lungs I'd assumed were most affected, had recovered enough to sneak up behind me.

He growled.

Released the wooden dowel in his right hand.

That freed up his right arm, but his tangled garrote stubbornly refused to release my rifle. It sagged to the ground.

Dragged down his left wrist.

The tangle gave me time to re-orient.

To decide. To act. To attack.

Form my right hand into a blade. Jab it at his windpipe.

Maybe I could make whatever breathing difficulties he had even worse.

No oxygen, no muscles, no strength, no fight.

He dodged back on his heels. Tried to grab my right wrist with his unencumbered right hand.

Quick reflexes.

Two hands are better than one.

I grabbed his wrist with my other hand, thumb on top.

Stepped back to create a little space.

Locked his wrist back. Twisted it clockwise.

Took another step back.

Forced his body to follow my arm down where it met my snap kick to his head.

That had to hurt.

Apparently not enough.

He grasped the barrel of my rifle entangled in his garrote with his previously useless left hand.

Used it as a club.

Pounded the stock against the outside of my right knee.

Ouch.

Knee aching, I remembered the pile of steel bars I'd literally stumbled over before.

Backed up toward the furnace table. Sought with my heels.

Pulled him after me using his wrist.

He lurched forward.

My heel kicked a steel rod.

I plucked it up with my free hand.

He swung the K2 rifle at me.

Diverted it with the steel rod. The rebound lined up the rod's tip with the plate carrier protecting his chest.

Thrusting the steel pole upward, I shafted him through the throat.

Finally put him down for good.

"Lieutenant? That last soldier put equipment on a truck at the loading dock and drove away."

I sighed. Slumped down a little, adrenalin wearing off. "The police cordon should stop him." If they'd set it up as I requested. "Any other threats I should know about?"

"Captain Rhee Yun-seok just entered the orange zone from the primary mantrap. A dozen men with him."

So, rather than running, Rhee decided to bluff it out. I guess having those dudes to back him up made that a decent option for him.

Did he know that I knew he was working with the North Koreans?

Perhaps a little Sicilian blood?

Was he coming to kill me, or just to blame me?

Did he know the DPRK spec ops team were mostly dead or disabled, or were they supposed to be gone by now and he was about to officially discover the technology theft?

"Doctor, I'd appreciate your company as quickly as possible. Don't suppose you know anything about gunshot wounds?"

"No, Lieutenant. Not that kind of doctor. Worst I've seen is a sprained knee in a volleyball game."

"Never mind, just come and see if you can talk these guys into not shooting me. Wait for you here."

Glancing at my phone, I noted the absence of a text message from the 75th RRC announcing their imminent arrival.

No help there.

Took a deep breath. Stood in the aisle between downed enemies.

One of these guys must have a bandage. Maybe even a few ampoules of morphine.

Preferred a strong local anesthetic for gunshot wounds, but beggars can't be choosers.

Especially when the dude whose plans I'd just ruined came for a chat and brought a dozen of his closest armed subordinates.

No doubt his lesson to the boiler technicians would keep them efficient for months.

Deputy Defense Minister Meon Lon-chun sipped his fresh cup of chamomile tea. Still a little hot.

At least he'd gotten the steam radiator repaired.

His black phone, connected to the Ministry of People's Security, clamored for his attention.

He set his cup to cool on a plastic coaster on top of his desk.

Picked up the handset.

"Minister Meon."

"Sir, we have a transmission from Lieutenant Kwon."

"About damn time."

"Kwon reports he's still in Seoul, but he's secured the data."

"Excellent. How soon until his team can exfiltrate back across the DMZ?"

"He reports he's been separated from the rest of his team. No word on the radio. May be evading capture."

That incompetent. He lost his team?

Knew he shouldn't have trusted a junior lieutenant with such an important responsibility.

Stro and the rest of the team were accomplished enough he thought it'd be a good experience for him. Having a loyal unit in the special forces was always a bonus.

Perhaps he could salvage something.

Maybe they could call the mission a success, having retrieved the data and done irreparable harm to their imperialist enemies at the same time.

"Relay to Kwon to get the data here via the tunnel as fast as possible. The others will have to fend for themselves."

"Understood, sir. We'll pass on your orders."

Meon dropped the handset back into its cradle. Leaned back in his executive-style chair.

Should he pass on the status to headquarters? No, they might blame him for losing the team. The data wasn't back yet, so he couldn't rely on that to shield himself.

What if his communications relay in the Ministry of People's Security also kept others informed?

Would they turn on him, jealous of his position?

Desiring to see him brought down? His lips tasted chalky.

Meon reviewed the status of his most bitter rivals. Perhaps.

He should prepare for the worst.

But how?

He sipped his chamomile tea and forced himself to relax. It came to him.

He'd send for a new special forces sniper team. One with an experienced leader.

Between the new team and Kwon, after bringing the data back, they could activate the fallback phase of his plan.

Then if he required a quick way out, he'd have incredible leverage on the Southern Imperialists to make whatever he needed occur.

He made a note to send orders to have the Soviet weapon delivered from the research facility to the base here. Would take a few days for safe transportation.

He shrugged.

If destruction happened to Seoul in the execution of his plan, so much the better.

The spec op soldier I'd shot in the elbow sure complained a lot in Korean.

I taped his ankles and knees together, then his mouth, careful to keep his nasal passages clear. A quick search turned up a basic first aid kit with a simple twist tourniquet.

Tied it around his bicep, secured about two inches above the wound to cut off blood flow to his elbow. Wrote the current time on his bandage.

He'd stay put leaning up against a metal cabinet until the ambulance I'd ordered Bishop to request arrived.

His kit held two ampoules of morphine. My left shoulder stabbed me with pain every time I moved it, so I split the vials between us with two quick jabs. Me first.

Blood seeped through my shirt and coat. My right knee ached from the fight.

I picked up one of the K2 rifles, ensured it was safe. Used it as a makeshift crutch to take the pressure off my knee.

Two taped up prisoners, two dead intruders. A baker's dozen ROK guards on the way, with Judas Rhee leading the twelve others.

Yang or Bishop better arrive soon enough to keep them off me.

Rhee's men moved quietly.

Trained to US Army standards, routinely sharing soldiers and coordinated exercises, the ROK's military was no joke.

Only heard the first two pairs just before they rounded the furnace, the electric crane, and the other equipment enclosing the open experimental area I'd set my trap in.

My uniform coat half off, shirt pulled aside, I applied a bandage to my shoulder while Rhee and his men set up around me.

In no hurry to engage them.

In fact, I was lucky. The bullet carved a three-inch rounded valley across the top of my shoulder. A deep graze, mostly caught skin.

I filled the wound from an anti-biotic tube and then taped a clean bandage over to keep it in place.

Rhee stood in the aisle, ten meters away.

His dozen guards spread out on all sides, including around the corner behind me.

Now that we'd reached a confrontation, I'm not sure he knew what to do, what with the enemy soldiers scattered around. He'd need to put on a show for his men.

I needed time, so I casually put my tan undershirt in place.

Shrugged my uniform coat back on my left side.

Fumbled with the zipper.

"What are you doing in my lab with these unknown soldiers, Lieutenant Harper?"

Did he intend to bluff? "Don't let the uniforms fool you. These are North Korean special operators. Sent to infiltrate the lab."

"Nonsense. I was there when Major Williams relieved you this afternoon. I assume these are a few of your buddies? Maybe local contacts you made with your MI platoon? Out to vandalize the lab in a sad attempt to prove your point? My men will take you all into custody."

"I doubt that. We're at an impasse."

"You moron." He pointed at my crutch. "You can barely stand. Any of my men could take you in this condition."

Maybe my confusion bluff technique would worker better on Rhee than it had on Yang.

"Assumptions are the second most well-known blunder in history." I tried to ignore the fact that I was technically currently engaged in a land war in Asia. "Right now, members of the Seoul Metro Police Agency are cordoning off the area. The 75th RRC and the military police are on their way. They'll be here momentarily to take you into custody. You can't escape, Captain. It's time to make a deal. Start explaining to your men why you've been working for the North Koreans."

"You will show respect, Lieutenant! I don't need escape. If you try to evade my men, you'll be shot and it will be so sad. However, I thank you for the warning."

I started playing to his men, hoping to make him a little paranoid. "You think I came here alone? Doctor Yang Hyo-jin is well aware of your activities. That little scene earlier at Camp Kim? Just a trick to convince you not to warn your buddies. You're done, Captain. Just haven't heard the bars clang shut, yet."

Most of his men looked at him with puzzled expressions. Standing next to Rhee, his platoon's Sergeant First Class (SFC) looked thoughtful, as if the pieces of a puzzle snapped together in his mind.

"The Lieutenant is correct." Doctor Yang said, stepping into the aisle behind Rhee and his men, "I watched as Captain Rhee spoke with these invaders from the North."

"This is a setup! You and Doctor Yang conspired to frame me. You are the ones working with the North Koreans. We barely arrived here in time to stop your escape with critical technology."

"What motive would we have? I've only been in Korea for a month and the Doctor is a national hero already."

"More motive than I have. I've lived my entire life in South Korea. All of my family were born here. We are so patriotic, I was beaten as a child, made to show my respect to the Korean President, even when he had no respect for his people. But you and the Doctor? A hero who no longer receives the recognition she feels she deserves? You Americans in your arrogance have decided to use this as an excuse to take over the research facilities run by South Korea. Doctor Yang will become the puppet head of the lab under your control."

He was *fan*tastic at this inventing-motives-for-his-opponents game. My phone vibrated quietly with a text message. That reminded me.

Too bad Rhee was worse than even I was at spy games.

Doctor Yang Hyo-jin wasn't finished, "It won't work, Captain. The prisoners will tell everything about you and this technology theft."

I seriously doubted a People's Army Spec Op soldier would

ever say anything not calculated to convert the listener to worship of Supreme Leader, but it was a nice thought.

Schnier's platoon from the 75th RRC finally arrived, plus Bishop, Lee, Michelle and Major Williams.

Seeing Michelle, I wondered how she'd gotten roped in. Hope they didn't blame her for lending me the CIA's RFID reader.

The Rangers wore full tactical gear. Obviously, they'd stopped at the armory on the way over.

Schnier's platoon took up positions next to Rhee's men, casually guarding them while leaving to plausible deniability the idea they merely stood there to provide support.

Wouldn't want to embarrass the locals.

I turned to face Major Williams. Dropped my makeshift crutch. Gave a morphine-sloppy salute, "Sir, Lieutenant Harper reports. Rangers lead the way!" I frowned. "I've made a bit of a mess."

Rhee lost no time, "He certainly has. Major, your *relieved* Lieutenant not only led these men in here, but destroyed half the warehouse, including many valuable and scarce materials, vital to our efforts."

So he *had* been watching events in his office on the available security cameras. Probably hoping they'd take care of me for him.

"Sir, these prisoners and KIA are the North Korean infiltrators I told First Sergeant Bishop about. Rhee let them into the facility, where they killed one of his guards before attempting to sabotage the lab. Doctor Yang saw it all on video."

Captain Rhee likely deleted the security footage before bringing his men in here, so no need to get into exactly how the brown zone racks of materials got destroyed.

Major Williams wore his uniform, but looked like he'd been busy with one of his local counterparts drinking him under the table. "Lieutenant, the MPs on their way will take charge of the scene and begin a formal investigation."

Well, that didn't commit him to anything but following the bureaucracy.

Time for me to shoot the curl. "Sergeant, please secure this prisoner."

I gestured from Rhee's SFC to the mostly uninjured and taped up North Korean. The first prisoner I'd taken.

His SFC looked at Rhee, who nodded, so he came and reinforced the tape with zip ties.

Rhee seemed to share my opinion of the likelihood of the prisoner speaking for our benefit. He'd made no move to eliminate or release the prisoner, either of which would've proved to everyone he wasn't telling the truth.

"Sergeant, please reach into the prisoner's fatigue pocket and retrieve the mobile phone you'll find there. When you have it, dial the most recent number to call it."

He dialed.

The look of horror dawning on Rhee's face made the ringing from his pocket almost anti-climactic. At a brief word from Major Williams, Schnier had his men take Rhee into custody to await the MPs.

Hadn't totally dazzled my CO, but he was coming around, "Harper, I'm canceling your return to Benning. You're not off the hook, you stand relieved of your platoon command. Sergeant Lee will take charge there for now, but I need you here in Seoul for the investigation and court-martial, if it comes to that. Get patched up. I trust you can handle light duties in the meantime."

"Yes, sir."

Perhaps I could convince the Doc to go on a real date. I'd saved her life, after all, although she probably wasn't happy about the damage to her lab. If they docked my pay at all, I couldn't afford a date.

Hoped no one thought to wonder if my use of makeshift mustard gas was a war crimes violation. Besides, the fumes were already pretty much dispersed.

I sniffed the air. Only a slight garlic and onion scent remained. Maybe no one would notice.

PART THREE

BLUE TEAM

Chapter Twenty:
Keeping It Real

Most of the time hanging with Korean volleyball players doesn't end in shots fired, but after nearly dying, I needed a nap.

The Major left Bishop and Schnier with me and the late-arriving MPs to wrap things up and give statements.

MPs secured the prisoners, including Rhee. Carted them off to wherever they store captured enemy special forces the North will be sure to deny existed.

We stood around the lab area to discuss what happened, careful not to disturb the investigation scene cordoned off behind yellow tape.

Hyo-jin kept wanting to pick the experiment up and set it right, but the MPs stopped her.

Lee volunteered to coordinate with the local security team.

They were all ROK Army together, after all.

Actions of acceptance and betrayal reveal who is truly on your side. Almost all of my foster siblings failed that test regularly, deflecting consequences for their actions or blame for their transgressions toward anyone nearby.

Better to avoid official attention, but somehow I became the next center of unwanted scrutiny.

Innocently enough, my new friend Hyo-jin, the Doc, wasn't a medical doctor, but still wanted to see my shoulder to ensure I was okay. "You didn't do it right. Shouldn't put that dirty, smelly shirt back on after bandaging it. You'll get infected. Need to go to a hospital. Doesn't the American base have a hospital?"

Dude! "I filled the wound with antibiotics. Be fine until I can get it properly cleaned out. Besides, mostly missed anything important."

The gouge in my shoulder would leave a nice scar, though, even if it stayed uninfected. Was more concerned about my ability to stay on my feet.

My knee hurt, despite morphine making it tough to think straight.

Michelle came over, shell necklace clacking, to do her own reconnaissance in force.

She edged between Hyo-jin and me, without even a look at the Doc, who was actually taller than her. Stood there staring at me with her hands on her slender hips. "Sam Harper. How much trouble have you gotten yourself into now?"

Hyo-jin said something sharp in Korean under her breath as she stepped around Michelle, but I didn't catch it. "Who are you?"

I held up a hand to forestall Hyo-jin's question, "I'm fine, Michelle. Just a little gunshot wound and woozy from the morphine." Didn't mention the knee, but maybe I could sit on the edge of a nearby steel lab table, which would otherwise just hold up paperwork. "Doc, this is Michelle, an old friend from the American embassy."

Pain shooting in my knee, I took a deep breath. Leaned up against the table's edge. Took the weight off my knee. "Michelle, this is Doctor Yang Hyo-jin, lab administrator."

Hyo-jin stuck her hands in the wide pockets of her lab coat. "Scientist, thank you. I am the director of the metallurgical lab, but I lead the scientific efforts, not the paper ones."

Michelle turned. Looked her up and down. Mostly up. "Good to meet you. I've kept Sam out of trouble since he got kicked out of his third foster home."

More like *getting* me into trouble, but I wouldn't quibble. "Doctor Yang was tremendously helpful with taking care of the enemy soldiers. My angel in the sky. My singing voice in the clouds, watching over me and guiding my every action."

Hyo-jin flipped her pony-tail around like I was embarrassing her and she was upset at my description, but then paused and laughed. "The morphine is getting to you, lieutenant."

Michelle rolled her eyes. "I'm sure he's fine." She stared back at me. "You dodged my earlier question. What happened?"

"Is that an official inquiry? I'm not really in a condition to answer official inquiries, but I'm sure I'll think of something later."

"Oh, leave the poor man alone. You have no idea what he's gone through, stopping these men from blowing up my lab."

"Blow up the lab? They brought explosives?"

"My lab is extremely valuable. Destroying it would set back our research for years."

I tried to get a few words in, "How'd you end up here with the Rangers, anyway?"

Michelle looked around, craning her neck like she could see the demolished part of the warehouse area. "I happened to be near Lieutenant Schnier when the alert went out. Just trying to look out for you."

Sergeant Lee and the lab security SFC approached Schnier, Bishop, and Captain James D. Grant. Grant was a tall, gangly fellow. Pointed at things with his nose, like Ichabod Crane. Nice enough fella. Commanded the local MP detachment.

The officers didn't look happy about whatever he reported to them.

The SFC pointed at Yang. In response, they all turned and headed straight over to our friendly little group.

"Incoming," I muttered.

Michelle wasn't paying as much attention to our surroundings. "What?"

"Captain Grant," I said as they approached, "is going to be a bummer."

The two women turned away from me in time to provide a welcoming committee for the troops.

Hyo-jin squished her eyebrows together as they approached. Charmingly cute. "Sergeant?"

The SFC nodded to Hyo-jin. "Bad news, director. They've looted the data center; stolen the storage arrays."

Lee chimed in, "And I don't think the backups will work. That was in our report."

The report no one paid attention to.

Well, no one but Rhee. He probably read it pretty closely and passed the details on to the North.

My heart sunk into my stomach. Had I contributed even more to this disaster?

Hyo-jin put her left hand over her mouth in a half-fist and propped her elbow on her chest. She said nothing, but I was sure she remembered telling me about the extra enemy soldier.

Schnier smiled at Michelle. "Honey, we'll have to finish our date later. Sorting this stuff out will take all night, if not all week."

Michelle came because they were on a date? While I fought an enemy special forces team with only a civilian to help me?

On a date?

Bishop had his hands tucked together behind his back, standing at a relaxed mix of attention and at ease, uniform crisp, looking like he'd just gotten into the office on a normal day. "Lieutenant Harper, may we speak privately, sir?"

All the exhaustion hit me at once. "Sorry, I'll have to catch up with the rest of you in a while. Captain Grant, you'll have my statement later. I'll answer any questions, but right now I need a hospital bed. Top, if you'll drive me to the base hospital, we can talk on the way. Not so bad off I want to ride in an ambulance."

Grant gave Bishop a look that informed him of his responsibilities to monitor me until I answered the MP's questions, but otherwise they were content to let me go for now.

How much more trouble could I cause from a hospital bed?

The snow forced non-emergency traffic off the roads.

Kwon's driving wasn't perfect, but the all-terrain military truck's weight and tires churned slush into a twin-path of dirty ice.

Falling crystals lit up in hazy patterns from the signs for the shops he passed.

Would've been beautiful, if he hadn't just watched Stro strangle a man and then ran for his life.

With no one knowing his path, no one stopped him.

After consulting a map, Kwon found his way back across the river bridge and on to the side roads Stro drove in the other direction. He hoped Stro and his men were fine, but he didn't like not hearing from them.

Not knowing.

He was responsible for them. He'd led them on the mission.

Had the data, the mission successful, but kept playing back the limited briefing he'd given them repeatedly in his head.

What could they have done better?

The toughest burden ever was to lead this team and then leave them. Sometimes it's easier to tackle a mission on your own.

What might've made the difference?

Another week to plan, to train, to review the mission details, to analyze the lab's organization better?

May have helped, but Meon ordered them in a week early.

Meon had good reasons.

Kwon touched his jacket pocket with the photograph of his family. If his team was a sacrifice, he'd honor them. He knew how.

Complete the mission.

The truck slid a little once his tires turned off pavement and snow to instead churn mud and ice together, but it was only a short stretch to the rice farm near Dorasan Peace Park. Reaching the abandoned greenhouse, he turned and backed the truck up to the entrance.

Needed to be as close as possible to unload the drive shelves, because he was all alone. Without his team to use the wooden carts, he could load the drives on the carts instead, but he'd pull them back with only his own muscles.

Already been an exhausting day. He could leave the drives behind in the truck, then return with more manpower to haul them back.

No, couldn't risk the Dominionists recovering the data while he was away.

He considered if the border guards they'd tied up had been freed yet. Probably better if they hadn't, because that would mean their relief was coming soon.

Kwon would need the relief's truck to get the data back to

base. Wouldn't be hiking back out the way they'd hiked in with it all on his back.

Kwon's team had struck a blow against the Imperialists.

Now to finish the task.

The morphine hit hard. I felt a sudden urge to convince Bishop that he should really take up surfing.

He led me out to his blue minivan parked diagonally in front of the lab's main entrance. His bumper carried two stickers, *My Ranger is My Hero* written on the left and *Mormon Assault Vehicle* on the right.

Bishop hit a key-fob button. The doors unlocked. I picked a doll with oversized button eyes off the passenger seat and climbed in. "Nice ride. Not as nice as a surfboard, though."

"Sorry about the mess, sir. Borrowed it from my wife. Needed more seats and it's lower profile than a military vehicle in the city. Didn't know what kinda kerfuffle we all'd be walkin' into here. No time to stop at the motor-pool, anyway."

I yawned. Set the doll into the center console next to an empty Cherry 7-UP bottle. "Glad nothing happened to it."

"You and me both. The paperwork from the Army for replacing a POV if destroyed in combat within a non-combat-zone would probably be harder than just gettin' a part-time job to pay for another one."

I pulled out my phone and texted Lee, "Suggest you check KCIA traffic cam footage to track military truck."

Technically, he didn't currently work for me anymore, but unless he disagreed with my suggestions, didn't see him ignoring an officer who might be back in charge of his MI platoon again, especially if I kept to *suggestions*.

Bishop started his minivan. Cold air rushed out of the vents. "Take a minute to warm up."

A quick reply from Lee, "Metro police report seeing truck before and after lab incident. Tracking backward and forward from known sightings."

Bishop put his minivan into drive. Picked his way through the light snow covering the lot. "Yongsan Hospital?"

I wanted to close my eyes and pass out. "You can take me back to the BOQ. Just need rest. Shoulder'll be fine, but my knee is killing me, even with the morphine."

"Sure, sir? Believe the Major would want you to get checked out by a professional nut examiner. Need paperwork for your service record. Maybe even a purple heart, assumin' they don't court-martial you."

Had a point about the paperwork. "I defer to your extensive experience. Never been shot in the Army before. Guess there's more forms than when you just have a gang war."

"Ah wouldn't know, sir. Didn't exactly grow up in the hood. Poppa taught at VMI, Mama stayed home."

"More the barrio, for me. Least for a few years here and there, if I got a Latino foster family. You go to VMI?"

Why wasn't Bishop an officer?

"Long story. Had a scholarship, but after 9/11, enlisted right away. Rather work for a living, anyway."

A little later, but I also joined the Army to protect and get justice for people like my parents. People killed in a terrorist attack.

Gave us an experience in common.

Bishop would get to the point soon enough, but it was always more effective to gently ream out a soldier you had important things in common with. Still had at least one big difference, though. "I had lots of parents, and none at all."

Bishop rubbed the scar on his cheek. "Permission to speak freely, sir?"

I stared out the window. Watched the deserted icy sidewalks stream past. "Of course."

Might as well get it over with.

He took a breath. Paused, as if considering how to express his thoughts. "From what you all've told us about the lab incident, if you'd had a team with ya'll, done proper preparations, even just involved me, or Lee, or Schnier... They wouldn't have escaped with the data. Place might not be a disaster zone."

"Twenty-twenty hindsight, sure, but I didn't have that option. Had to ride this wave alone."

"Roger that. What I'm saying, sir, is perhaps in the future you might oughta consider involving more folks. Need a team to succeed as an individual. Sure you heard that enough in RASP."

"I'm supposed to lead the team. Responsible for my platoon's success, but sometimes I have to rely on myself. No offense, but I've always trusted myself to get things done."

"I get it, sir. I married into a pre-built family. Guy I replaced was a drunken, abusive loser. Useless as a screen door on a submarine. My two stepdaughters used to not want to even talk to me. Just stood there and stared, when they didn't run and hide. Said I wasn't their real dad."

He took another deep breath. "At first, was gone too much on deployment, didn't get to truly be around for a while. Had a tough time trusting me. Trusting anyone, really."

Would've been nice to have a stepfather like Bishop. A man to look up to. "Nothing wrong with my parents, except a tango's choice to bomb them. Their replacements just didn't live up to the same standards. A few kids get lucky in foster care, but not older boys. Not if they're the least bit stubborn."

"From what I see, you're like a mule. What I'm saying is, eventually, after a few years, the girls came around. They're fifteen and thirteen now. Few years ago on Father's Day, gave me the greatest gift ever. Got adoption certificates and legally changed their last name to Bishop. Now think if they'd known how it would end up from the start. How much sooner we could've been more of a family. Sure, part of that's my fault. Isn't an easy job on wives and kids."

Was Bishop worried about the DPRK escalation threatening his family? He lived in an off-base apartment with his wife and kids, much better than the limited on-base married housing. "What's your point?"

"You have a future in the Rangers. Eventually, you'll work better with the operators and others as a team, but it'll all be a lot easier for everyone if you burn through the learning curve. Rangers are your family now. Gotta accept 'em, that's all."

I shook my head. Easy for him to say. Guys in the Company listened to Bishop.

I'd just gotten relieved of duty and practically kicked out of the Company just for doing my job and turning in a report which accurately described how vulnerable the lab was.

Kicked out based on the complaints of a traitor. "I hear you, Bishop, and I'd like to work that out, but don't seem to be able to prove myself to the Major and the shooters like Schnier."

We arrived at Yongsan. Bishop handed his military ID over to the gate guard, "Schnier will come around, but you've got to show everyone you trust them, you rely on them, not just that they can rely on you."

Trust Schnier. The guy dating Michelle while I fought for my life.

Not Bishop's fault. Maybe he just didn't see the whole picture. Seemed genuine, at least. "Appreciate your advice. Could've caught the last guy if I'd been able to involve the team earlier. That's partially on me. I'll get it figured out. Is that everything, Top?"

After the quick security theater of passing a mirror on a stick under the minivan, the gate guard raised the metal barrier and waved us through.

"Almost to the base hospital, anyway. Think about it, that's all."

"I'm always up for continuous self-improvement, but right now I'll take a bed and a good nights sleep."

"Don't worry, I'm sure they'll come wake you up every few hours to give you medicine or something else as much fun as a rooster sparkin' a weasel."

"Good to know the military hospitals for gunshot wounds are just like the civilian ones."

Chapter Twenty-One: Rebels

Bishop's two girls won the genetic lottery compared to the local soccer talent. He loved to watch them give-n-go, running circles around the other kids.

He adjusted the picture frame on the corner of his desk with a photo of their team, his wife beaming as their coach.

This wasn't the first time he'd missed their soccer games for work. Stuck sitting at Company HQ making sure the required incident reports about Harper's mess last night were ready for Major Williams to sign and file later.

Done his best to maintain at least stability for his family. With tensions between North and South running high, he hoped his decision to move them to live near him in Seoul didn't come back to haunt them.

Have to make sure that didn't happen. His job as part of the military deterrent south of the DMZ wouldn't do itself, even if today it was mostly getting ahead of paperwork.

Lieutenant Schnier plopped onto the red leather sofa next to his desk and in front of the Major's door with a huff. "You believe Harper last night?"

Bishop frowned. Stalled for time by twisting the top off a bottle of Cherry 7-UP from his desk drawer. "Don't know what you mean, sir. Officer matters are above my pay grade."

"Gimme a break, Bishop. Just us here on Saturday mornin'. Loosen up."

Bishop leaned back in his office chair. "Yes, sir. Loosening up, lieutenant, sir." He smiled so Schnier would know he meant it as a joke. "The MI platoon's report about the lab being vulnerable was righteous. Harper got kinetic with a Spec Ops team by his lonesome. Sure, made a mess bigger than a green beanie's head for us to cleanup, but none of the good guys got killed and the taxpayers will cough up the money to help pay for the damage."

"So, you agree he's fixin' to be a hotshot loner who don't deserve to wear the scroll on his shoulder?"

Bishop interlaced his hands behind his head. "That what you think? And which part of you is doing the thinking, sir?"

"Doncha? Dumb luck he ran into those guys. Edjumacate me, oh wise one."

"Say we can get Harper singin' in the same choir as the rest of us. With his demonstrated capabilities, wouldn't you want him on our side?"

Schnier shrugged. "Sure, but that's the question, ain't it? Is he in our posse, or way out on his own, the lonesome cowpoke in the middle of nowhere?"

"Texans, always with the cowboys. The Army is the largest posse of them all. Kid has potential. Obviously capable of leading a team, or there's no way he could've passed RASP. Wouldn't hurt you to reach out and show a little appreciation to the MI guys once in a while. Might improve your platoon's intelligence."

Schnier laughed. "That's mean, Top."

"If the boot fits, sir."

Sergeant Lee banged open the door into the deserted Company HQ. Looked around. Made a beeline for Bishop's desk.

Bishop nodded toward the door. "Speaking of intelligence . . ."

Lee panted for two extra breaths once he arrived in front of Bishop's desk. "Found it!"

Schnier leaned forward on the sofa. "It?"

"The truck from last night. Metro Police spotted it near the scene of a traffic accident before the incident and while cordoning off the area afterward. Using the city's license plate trackers and traffic cam footage, traced it back from the first sighting and forward from the lab. The MPD cordon let the truck pass outside the lab, but some kid's parents complained to the police about it stopping at their neighborhood park. Thought it an unusual spot for the Army. Both routes converge on the same place, an old rice farm near the DMZ."

Bishop grinned. "Good work. Might be long gone by now, but I'll send the MPs over to secure the area."

The weekend might could hold a bit of excitement after all.

Jin-sun's Mother decided the half-breed Toby Howell must be an idiot, kept around to amuse the real embassy bureaucrats. He'd abruptly cut off their last meeting and insisted she return first thing Monday morning to tell her story again.

Government officials were petty and capricious everywhere.

She'd sat down again in the uncomfortable metal chair at his desk and repeated what she'd told him before, this time in front of the new woman listening in his dis-harmonic office. He called her the Military Attaché.

Some sort of army expert, she supposed, although what that had to do with her she didn't know. Definitely a western whore, though, that she was sure of. Jin-sun would *never* marry a woman like that.

She'd make sure of it.

The woman stood and leaned against the wall, listening. Her fabric textures were all wrong, mixing silk on top with cotton on the bottom. Tall shoes and tight clothing emphasized her long legs, small belly, and high breasts.

That's how Jin-sun's Mother knew she was a whore, whatever Toby Howell called her. No respectable woman would dress so provocatively at her place of employment.

And her jewelry, shells bouncing and clacking like a beach drum. Really! Every woman knew that only precious metals and gemstones were suitable for wearing as portable wealth.

Was she a Pacific island castaway, her wealth tied up in shells she'd found at low tide, which the locals used for currency?

Jin-sun's Mother shook her head, her own red chima skirt fluffed over baji pants were perhaps too formal for these two, but also modest. "No, husband didn't react well to news of how received black market radio. Knew it outside our reach, despite relative wealth in the North. Naïve at how things worked."

The new woman interrupted, "And this was Meon Lon-chun who raped you?"

Foreigners were all rude. No respect for their elders at all. Slow in the head, too. "Yes, what I already said. Was better sort. Felt bad enough after to give presents. Convinced we liked attention of government leader. Ran Party in village by himself. No one speak against him, but husband tried."

"Go on."

"I will, if you done interrupting."

The whore nodded, but said nothing further, not even to apologize for her disruption. What a mother will go through for her only child. "At first, husband intent on killing Party Secretary. Make it look like accident. Told him it no use. Even if wasn't caught, just appoint another. Behave same. Maybe worse. We spent enough time married together in farmhouse didn't matter."

"Didn't matter?"

"Month pregnant when moved into village apartment. Party Secretary's attentions not keep us from own child. Tire of me when condition clear.

"Husband determined go to factory manager. Complain. Manager high rank. Husband disagree with me. Say manager can speak to Party Secretary. Tell him leave worker family alone.

"Men like Party Secretary not like be told give up pleasure, but husband not listen. Say he valuable worker. Manager get credit for improvement to yoke making. Not want him unhappy at home.

"Yelled until red in face. Husband only settle down when he plan to complain to manager. Even then only after fed him last of rice wine. Quarter bottle we saved for baby celebration. Just as well. Never get to drink later, anyway.

"He right about manager, but husband wrong about Party Secretary reaction."

"Meon?"

"Yes. That night heard yelling downstairs. Never good. Factory manager tell Secretary Meon leave workers alone. Meon say he take care of problem. Brought manager upstairs to apartment."

"To apologize?"

Really? How ignorant of the North can this harlot be?

Party officials don't apologize to anyone not their superior in the Party. "To find radio. Brought manager as witness our apartment have forbidden thing. Send message who really in charge in village.

"Dumped stuff on floor. Pointed at radio. Told didn't deserve manager help. Were traitors bound for work camp. Work camps places people go die slow. If not pregnant, husband might kept calm. Attempted apologize. Offer gifts to Party Secretary."

"Instead?" Couldn't this whore just remain quiet and let her finish what happened?

Painful enough to recount the details without the constant disrespect.

"Hit him. Slug him in jaw. Knock him to floor. Factory manager throw hand over his face. Mumble. I need take charge. Grabbed husband hand. Run down stairs.

"Owe husband much. First person chose me as family after already know me."

She refused to cry in front of these Americans. "Fastest way leave village in Party Secretary's car. Only car in village, but not good idea to take."

"Why not?"

Wasn't it obvious? Dense foreigners. "Neither of us can drive. I never even ride before. Husband drove truck once in factory yard, but not exactly same. Because we have car, Meon not let us go easily. Commandeered truck from local Army post. Came after us.

"Village close to South. Chinese border easier. Ways there to cross river. No one shoot you if bribe guards. Not like DMZ.

"Meon caught up near border crossing. We stopped short, in clearing by old rice fields, to decide how to cross. Make plan. Husband always big plans. Now I plan for family.

"He came after us alone. Get help from border guards. Not want to lose respect of village by chase once husband knock him down and steal car.

"Big headlights appear behind us. Army truck pull into

clearing. Block us in. Knew instantly meant our death. Leapt from car. Ran across muddy fields in dark for border. Cross DMZ only hope.

"Meon follow on foot. Splash in the puddles. Shout. Shoot pistol. Ran back to truck. Sped past us down road. Reached DMZ before us. We hid there, near border. Found old ditch with scratchy bushes. Thought maybe wouldn't find us in dark.

"Patrol of border soldiers search along the DMZ with Meon. Spotlights too powerful for darkness we thought protect us. Instead of cloak by night, naked to rays. Ran again, straight across DMZ. Dodge and duck behind bushes and hills. Slid through little valleys. Jump creek beds.

"Escape foot race. Came close again at border. Husband ran behind, tell me faster."

"Obviously, you made it, Yeo Min-jung, or you wouldn't be here."

"Didn't catch me, but Meon shot husband in back. Last time saw body, lay face-down in mud. Meon stood over him. Held pistol pointed at him. Stop and make sure he die. Gave me enough time cross border. Soldiers from South kind to me, young muddy lady bawling like child who lost best toy.

"Gave birth to son seven months later. No living father, but has father's surname. Name him Kwon Jin-sun."

Chapter Twenty-Two:
Vampires

Michelle returned to her embassy office. Typed up a contact report on her meeting with that idiot Howell and the local woman. What was the Korean deal with referring to people by their relationships to someone else, anyway?

Bad enough couples here didn't adopt the same last name.

She sent an encrypted message to Metcalf in D.C. "Intelligence on Meon Lon-chun confirmed by credible source. Blackmail viable option." Attached her report.

Late at night on the east coast, but he replied quickly, "How will lab event affect plans? Why didn't we have advance notice?"

Ouch. Maybe she could do damage control. "Unexpected complication, but will work to our advantage. Partial failure puts additional pressure on Meon."

"Better be correct in your analysis."

Not like her career depended on it.

The bloodsuckers didn't get enough patients at a hospital designed for a war. Suffered for customers in relative peace time.

Made various disapproving comments on my shoulder self-treatment, then told me to stay 48 hours for observation in a sterile bedroom with curtains for walls.

Hyo-jin visited me twice.

The male nurses got annoyed when I called her Doc. Seemed

more angry about the damage to her lab the second time. Guess she'd gone back and looked at the mess in the daylight on Saturday.

Still smiled a lot at me, though.

The humorless military nurses confiscated my phone while I was in the hospital room. Some regulation or other.

Didn't see Lee, Bishop, nor Schnier.

Too busy, I guess.

The other guys in the hospital were mostly Spec 4s from the Big Army with too much time on their hands and too little natural caution. Never underestimate the destructive capabilities of a bored soldier.

Captain Grant stopped by to take my official initial statement, once I had a lucid period off mind-altering drugs. A tall, solidly built guy, ready to take down those bored soldiers if they got out of line, but a tough read. Apparently, nobody messes with the Special Investigators.

Wasn't sure if he approved of my actions, or was ready to have me taken out back and shot. He'd just nod and ask, "And then what happened?"

Sounded like one of the counselors they made me see every time they bounced me to a new foster home. Really wanted to ask him, "What could I have done differently?"

After his last question, he told me an Army CID investigator should be in touch later, so I could tell the whole story all over again. Maybe an investigator from the Koreans, as well.

They all have their own separate sets of paperwork, I guess.

Whenever the nurses left me alone, I played the events in the lab repeatedly in my mind.

What could I have done differently? Done to avoid so much damage?

Did I really have to take them out, or could I have just left with Hyo-jin and called in the professionals?

The Army trains every Ranger to handle close quarters combat, so wasn't I one of the professionals, just not assigned that way right now?

If the shot that grazed my shoulder flew six inches to the left, it would've caught the center of my throat and I wouldn't be here to obsess about it.

Needed to put the men I'd killed out of my mind. They'd been doing their best to kill me and destroy the lab.

Guess I assisted a little in that last part.

What could I have done differently? Nobody's perfect, but not much that I could think of, and I tried for days.

Didn't blame Hyo-jin for being mad at me.

At least, not much.

Still needed to figure out a way to make it up to her.

Times of tragedy become opportunities for loneliness and introspection. Like when I lost my parents. At least Hyo-jin survived.

Her life was a victory I could savor.

Major Williams visited me on Sunday.

I remained on his naughty list, but officially released by the medical staff for *light duties*.

Told me to come into HQ on Monday morning ready to do office work. Help clear up the mess I'd made.

All I could say was, "Roger that."

By the time I crashed back at the BOQ Sunday night, my knee had mostly stopped complaining and my shoulder was reduced to a dull roar.

The knee stiffened up on Monday.

Continued cold weather didn't help, nor did the iced up sidewalk to Suseo subway station. On thin ice, I walked with shorter steps than usual. Kept my center of gravity over my good leg.

Still made it to Camp Kim early to hang out near Bishop's desk and get the scoop on the progress they'd made.

Bishop looked fresh, even though he must've worked through the weekend. Guess being married has advantages over doing everything yourself.

"Major left a list. You get all the technical stuff. Lee needs help trying to figure out how to get the lab's data back. The lab and the spooks are each sending a representative over at 1430 to meet. Discuss what the strategic ramifications are of the DPRK having the lab's data. Guess which light-duty lieutenant our major has assigned to take charge of entertaining the civilians?"

"Sounds like I have my work cut-out for me. Get the lab's data back and then stop the North from taking advantage of the copy they stole. Got it."

"Lee tracked the truck that got away to a rice paddy near the Dorasan Peace Park. MPs found the truck parked in front of an old hothouse. Used a pulley and cart system to cross under the DMZ. Captain Grant posted a guard, but they'all won't come back that way again."

I shook my head. Amazing what people will do with virtually unlimited slave labor. "They'll close off the tunnel at the other end as soon as the guy who got away reports in. Might've done it already, unless they think we haven't discovered it yet."

"I know the MP sergeant tasked with the tunnel guard detail. I'll ask him to tell us if they hear anything from the other end." Bishop made a note.

Not allowed to *command* my MI platoon, I didn't go back to my desk.

Instead, pleading knee injury, I called Lee and asked him to bring over my laptop. Made myself at home in the lone conference room at HQ.

The scratchy coyote tan walls matched my boots, even if they contrasted with the beat up army green table made from metal.

Between the Company's colors and awards, a quote from the Ranger Creed hung on the wall, *Never shall I fail my comrades.*

The room had power, Ethernet and metal folding chairs, so it'd do as a temporary office. Plugged my phone into a miniature set of MP3 speakers.

Home sweet home.

Lee came by as soon as he could grab my ruggedized laptop from my desk and walk over. He'd somehow wrinkled his jacket. Probably been on base all weekend. "How's the shoulder?"

I flexed my left arm and winced. "Usable. What's going on with the lab's data backups?"

"Hardware problem with the tape drive heads. We flagged it in our report. They never tried to restore from their backups to see if they worked. To keep their stuff off the .mil network, they did their own backups locally. When the guys responsible checked after the theft, they discovered only the most recent incremental backup was readable. Only has the files which were changed that day, so it's mostly useless. Most recent full backup and the rest of the incremental backups might as well be garbage."

"Heard of that before. Magnetic heads on the tape drive get loose and drift over time. The alignment has to be consistent with what it was when they wrote the data to tape."

"So what can we do about it?"

"See if you can measure how much the heads drift for each new tape, then shift them back a little at a time to match up with the previous tapes. If you reverse the direction of drift for each tape they may get a full restore done. Somebody needs to get their government credit card and buy a bunch of drives and drive shelves to restore data back to, though."

Lee nodded. "Roger that. Should work. They make the hard drives in Seoul. Lab won't have to wait for shipping. I'll get 'em going on trying to re-calibrate the tape drive head."

"Sounds good. Hey, anything on unusual activity on the other side of the DMZ? Any visiting brass or a new unit?"

Lee shrugged. "I'll ask around."

"Whoever that spec ops unit was at the lab, somebody is running them from the other side of the DMZ. That's where they'll take the data. Be nice to have a few potential targets. Check on their chatter and their labs as well, see if there's been any unusual activity."

"Sure. Let you know if I have anything at our 1430 meeting."

My laptop beeped. Low on power.

I plugged it securely into the outlet set into the floor under the table.

Time to listen to a few tunes while I kept busy with paperwork explaining my actions. I set the MP3 speakers to shuffle play.

Looked forward to the change of pace when 1430 rolled around.

Chapter Twenty-Three:
Green-eyed Monsters

Lieutenant Kwon Chol slid open Meon's office door.

A stranger, another spec ops lieutenant, leaned up against Meon's desk, chatting with the minister.

Kwon stepped inside and closed the door behind him. Meon would want to maintain operational security.

At least the office was comfortable, rather than overbearingly humid. Must've fixed the steam radiator over the weekend.

A miracle by the notoriously inefficient service staff.

Kwon stiffened to attention. Saluted. "Reporting as ordered, Deputy Minister."

First time he'd seen Meon after his return through the tunnel. He'd collapsed in the mud after dragging the data storage across the DMZ on carts. Been just lucid enough to free the border guards, instruct them to wake him when their supervisor arrived in a truck for shift change, and then curl up and fall asleep.

Now, having filed a verbal report using the border guard supervisor's radio, he was more than a little worried how Meon would react to his mission results.

He'd gotten the data out, hadn't he? Surely, that would be enough.

Meon had let him rest and clean-up over the weekend, so he must not be in a rush to have him executed or sent to the camps.

Kwon trusted it would all work out for the best.

While Kwon held his salute, Meon actually stood up from behind his desk and rushed over to push his saluting arm down.

Meon leaned back holding both of Kwon's arms. Stared at him. "Kwon Chol! I'm so glad you made it out alive, unlike the rest of your team."

Kwon relaxed a little, "Is it confirmed? Are they all dead?"

"We have no word of the Imperialists taking any prisoners. It's as if the incident never happened. They are likely ashamed of their blood-thirstiness in killing true Koreans. No hope your team survived, I'm sorry."

Kwon hung his head. "They can't be gone. Were level 10,000 guys. The best. My family. I depended on them. I, I don't believe it. Not really."

"Hard to accept, but they are martyrs for the people." Meon paused and took a long breath. "Let me introduce you to your *new* family. Have you met Lieutenant Pahk Geon? With the loss of your team, I'm assigning you together for your next task."

No return to Pyongyang? No leave?

Must be an urgent mission.

Kwon looked over Pahk. Tall, probably 5'7". Thin, with sinewy muscles. Probably fine, but no Sergeant Stro. "No, we've never met before." Kwon gave a strictly minimally respectful head tilt. "No one can replace Goshawk team, though."

Pahk nodded back once, his chin about two inches higher than Kwon had held his, then looked Kwon directly in the eyes. "We're not here to replace them. I've lost men before. We're here to do a job. To maintain their legacy. To ensure their lives weren't wasted by their attempt to destroy the enemy's lab. I'm sure your assistance to my team will do much to further our mission."

Kwon leaned back at the intense stare.

Did they mean to replace him so easily? Replace his men?

He turned to Meon. "I'm sorry Uncle, my ears may have misheard. Will Lieutenant Pahk not be reporting to me? This has been my mission. My team made the ultimate sacrifice to complete it. I brought the required data back to you, personally dragged it under the DMZ. I'm most familiar with the required mission parameters, despite any seniority Lieutenant Pahk may have."

Meon hesitated, then nodded. "I trust you implicitly,

nephew." He faced Pahk. "Lieutenant, what are your thoughts on the matter?"

Pahk's eyes widened when he heard the minister refer to me as his nephew, even though we weren't truly blood relations. "I will defer to your wishes, General Meon, but Lieutenant Kwon isn't familiar with my men and has been through such a strain, I wouldn't want to throw him into a new command so soon after losing his last one."

Did this guy think his men were throwaway conscripts to be replaced, just like that?

That his hard-won experience could be replaced by the next team leader in line?

He had nerve!

Kwon settled his breathing. Stro would be proud of him for not taking the guy's head off, "Uncle, I mean, Minister Meon, of course you'll make the final decision of who you believe you can trust the most."

Trust was the ultimate requirement in the True Korea. Top that!

Meon sat back down at his desk, causing the colored phones to jangle on their hooks.

He nodded in agreement. "Pahk, you're familiar with your men and will continue to lead them, but Kwon raises good points. He'll be in overall charge of the mission. You'll report to him and place your team at his disposal. I'll communicate my orders through him. I expect that a fine, loyal officer like you will have no issues obeying them."

Pahk barely failed to control a frown before nodding to Meon respectfully. He'd obviously become soft, living in the People's Army as a member of the special forces, not needing to control his expressions as much. "As you command, sir."

"Good. Knew I could count on you two to work together harmoniously to advance Supreme Leader's plans against the Imperialists. Let me show you what we're doing with the data Kwon brought back and how your team fits in."

Kwon knew his team's sacrifice would be worth it.

"Bring On the Dancing Horses" by *Echo & the Bunnymen* poured forth from my portable MP3 speakers. Best song and group title combination ever.

1430 in the ugly conference room came faster than I'd expected.

Focusing on the paperwork spread across the side of the green table got my mind off my shoulder. I flexed it a little. Felt like the painkillers had kicked in.

No more shooting pains, anyway.

Sergeant Lee arrived before the others. Caught me typing to the synth-pop beat. "How come you always play that old crap, sir?"

I turned off the blasting music.

"Ancient pop is more complicated, but that's not why. Prefer upbeat music, but that's just my natural optimism, not why I love it. Can lose myself in a lyrical story, but better stories exist.

"Sung this music over and over through ruck marches, but that's not why I listen.

"No, none of that.

"My dad left me his CD collection. Used to sing along when he played them.

"When I listen to 'that old crap', he's back here with me. Barely remember my parents, but I had a family once.

"That's why I play oldies. My dad's music reminds me of him."

The lab's appointed representative arrived just in time to catch the end of my speech to Lee. Doctor Yang Hyo-jin.

Guess she appointed herself to come to the conference.

I involuntarily grinned at her arrival.

She tried not to smile back, but I think I infected her, because she finally couldn't resist.

We'd formed a kind of combat bond, working through danger in the lab together.

She half-nodded to Lee to show respect, then sat across from me. Tried to hide her smile by putting her head down and staring at her tablet.

Michelle clacked in last.

Took the folding chair at the head of the table, closest to the door, opposite Lee. "Thought this was an intelligence conference? To discuss the strategic options to minimize the data theft from the lab?"

Reserved, like always.

I put up a hand to slow her down before she really got going where I thought she might be going. "It is. Luckily, Doctor Yang could make time in her schedule to meet with us and outline the contents of the lab's data. Tell us how the North might benefit from it."

Michelle looked at Hyo-jin and cocked her head a little. "By all means, let Doctor Yang brief us on the threat caused by the traitor at her lab."

I sighed. This should be fun. "Doctor Yang?"

"Please, *you* may call me Hyo-jin." She tapped her tablet a few times. "I've sent the summary of captured data my team spent the weekend working up. You'll see the two most sensitive areas concern my research on nuclear detection materials and one of my scientist's data analyzing the materials used in tactical nuclear weapons. I believe these programs were the infiltrators' primary targets."

Michelle leaned forward. "Isn't it premature to render that judgment? We've just begun our review."

I took off my glasses and rubbed my eyes, then rubbed my forehead. "What specific threats does the North's knowledge of these two areas pose?"

"It's all in the notes I've sent you." She set her tablet down to speak from memory. "First, my detection research is what will ultimately enable us to prevent terrorists from smuggling tactical nuclear weapons into populated areas. It enables detection at much longer ranges than is currently possible. I hope you can see why the North would be interested in that, if only to protect their own weapons research from detection and destruction via a surprise attack."

Michelle jumped in, "And second, it's well known"—she stared at Hyo-jin—"in the intelligence community,"—she looked at me—"the DPRK has been working on converting a Soviet trashcan nuke. That would fall into both areas of concern,

I believe."

Hyo-jin's voice stayed unusually level. "Yes, the data will allow them to advance their research tremendously."

Replacing my glasses on my face, I tried again. "Which is the critical component? What can't they do without?"

"The reflector," Hyo-jin said. "It all keys around that. With the right reflector, the fissionable material will be amplified and can produce a weapon with yields of 20-250 kilotons, much like the American Mk-54 SADM the-"

"What she means is," Michelle said, "with an inferior reflector, they might manage a tenth of a kiloton, hardly enough to destroy a large building. Without a good reflector, they also must build each bomb with way more fissionable material, making them weigh too much to transport conveniently on a man's back or through one of their infiltration tunnels. It's really the reflector we need to focus on."

"I am perfectly capable of explaining what I mean to Lieutenant Harper. He and I communicated quite well together recently while defending our lab from North Korean special operatives. Operatives who I estimate probably attempted to steal enough materials and information on creating advanced alloys to enable them to design a new reflector. To produce hundreds of barrel-sized nuclear weapons based on the Soviet model they've got."

"I'm sure you and Sam have quite the cozy relationship, but we don't have all day to figure out how to stop them. Duplicating this bomb they've purchased threatens your whole country."

"Yes, my country. I am well aware of what is at stake, here. Perhaps we should appeal to Beijing to intervene with the DPRK government."

Michelle's eyes flashed. She took a breath and then slowly shook her head. "Beijing doesn't want to destabilize the DPRK."

I smiled. Adopted a cheerful tone, "I have the gist of the issue. To ensure North Korea doesn't start cloning this Soviet backpack bomb they've gotten an example of and using it against South Korea and the United States, not to mention selling it to the middle-east, infiltrating it into Europe, and generally giving the world a loose terrorist dream weapon, we just need to keep them from using the data they've stolen."

Deliberately, I turned away from the two women, "Sergeant, any thoughts?"

Lee didn't look like he wanted to jump in, but now everyone stared at him, wondering whose side he'd take, "Sir, the Soviets never had many of these things. They made them in a more primitive era. Kept 'em pretty tightly controlled. Decades ago, they knew as the only hostile nuclear power, they'd get the blame even if they smuggled one into an American port. Now?"

He thought for a second. "Now, if the North comes up with a mass producible advanced version, we can expect to lose at least Seoul, NY City, D.C., San Diego, Tel Aviv, Paris, London, Berlin... anywhere a tango has an interest in taking out; one with enough hard currency to pay the North Korean dictators, that is."

Michelle leaned back in her chair, as if the reality of the threat just hit her. Started playing with her shell necklace. "Realpolitik. The United States would have no choice but to lift sanctions and leave the Korean peninsula in exchange for controlled access to prevent sales or use of the weapons. The reunification of Korea under the DPRK."

She looked from Lee to Hyo-jin. "Your government would have to choose between surrender and massive loss of life followed by conquest."

Hyo-jin leaned forward. "Beijing has no interest in a unified and nuclear armed Korea on their border. We can appeal for their help via diplomatic channels."

Lee nodded. "You have the right idea, but Beijing isn't to be trusted until this goes much farther. By the time their bureaucracy acts, it will be too late. Fear paralyzes the Chinese Communists. Fear of Americans as much as of a hostile neighboring Korea. No, we need to act now, to intervene before they have time to develop a new reflector for the Soviet weapon and refine and mass produce their own. How long will that process take, Doctor?"

Hyo-jin stared at the ceiling and pondered. "Weeks, for sure, at least to understand the data they've stolen. Months, most likely, to get a prototype to test. Maybe as much as a year or two in building a factory to go to mass production. But once they disseminate the data to their scientists, that process will become inevitable. We need to find and destroy the data immediately."

"We have a new contact within the DPRK. Highly placed, with access to the military activities across the DMZ. I can reach out. Perhaps he'll make a deal."

Michelle smirked, like a cat ready to present a mouse. "That contact? This morning I came into possession of significant blackmail material which may make him much easier to persuade to our perspective. The sort of thing he won't want revealed, because the propaganda value would be huge. His superiors in the Party would execute him to save face. He'll know that. I'm sure we can come to an agreement."

Lee shook his head. "Appreciate your help with this, but negotiations are best done by a Korean, not a foreign woman. He won't trust you."

Not to mention, Michelle wasn't exactly renowned for her tactful negotiating skills. "You two can work that out between spies. If it pans out, great, but it can't be more than a backup plan. Not with what's on the line here. Michelle, need you to convince the CIA to arrange for the USS Michigan and an attached SEAL Delivery Vehicle. We need a physical penetration option."

Michelle stared at me. "Wouldn't a request be better coming from you? Covert missions submarines carrying SEALs are under the command of Special Operations Command - Korea. Last time I checked, the 75th RRC is still part of SOCKOR here in Camp Kim."

She wasn't thinking of our current strategic situation. "I'm not exactly the golden boy right now. They'll receive the request a lot better from your D.C. office than if it comes from a relieved lieutenant under the cloud of potential court martial."

"That'll take days to arrange. Can probably get an agreement in the next 24 hours, if at all, but the request may take up to 72 hours to wend its way through the Capital bureaucracy and over to the Navy to make the sub available."

"Then I suggest you get started right away. I want to go check out that tunnel they used to cross the DMZ. See if it could be useful. Maybe track the data a little farther. I'll call you later."

Michelle started to speak, then smashed her lips together.

She stood up. Kicked her metal folding chair backwards a few inches. "Sergeant Lee, come with me. I'll need to write up our proposed coordination with your port authorities for the sub. *Doctor* Yang, I suppose this concludes our meeting. We'll let you know if there is anything else we need from you about the data your lab failed to protect."

Hyo-jin frowned for a moment, speechless at what even I recognized as a dismissal. Then she leaned back in her chair and smiled.

Stretched her arms and legs out.

"I have a few more technical details contained within the data I want to discuss with someone who can actually understand them. Good luck with your paper pushing. I'll just relax here for a bit. You don't mind, do you Sam?"

"It's okay, Michelle. You and Lee go ahead. I'll be fine, here."

Michelle looked at her necklace for a moment. Gestured for Lee to follow and departed without another word, leaving me alone with Hyo-jin.

Limited window of opportunity.

To not be responsible for nuclear attacks, for massive civilian deaths, I needed to follow that data before the trail went cold.

Chapter Twenty-Four: Going for It

After that annoying CIA woman and her KCIA sidekick left, Doctor Yang Hyo-jin set her tablet back on the conference room table.

Had no intention of leaving just yet.

She had a read on the situation. Sam looked lost in thought.

She smiled at him to get his attention. "Plan to use the sub to infiltrate the North with a platoon of your soldiers?"

He shook his head. "Too slow. By the time the paperwork gets done, we'll have lost the data in North Korea."

Put his hand under his firm chin. "No, I must see if I can locate the stolen drives as soon as possible, before they're taken too far from the border. Or find whoever is in charge of the mission over there. Convince him to tell me where they're going."

Was he really contemplating going after the data on his own? She'd been impressed by the way he dealt with the intruders in the lab, even if he'd destroyed half the place, but he couldn't do everything by himself.

"You have a team here, on this base, right?"

"As Mother Bishop constantly reminds me, yeah."

"They seem supportive. I couldn't have won a gold medal without my volleyball teammates on the court with me. Without the support of Hyundai Engineering making sure we had what we needed. You can rely on your Ranger team."

She looked down at the ugly green table, afraid to stare at him anymore. "You can rely on me to support you."

"It's a good thing you didn't totally rely on Captain Rhee at the lab. Sometimes, people who should support you let you down. Have to start by relying on yourself."

"You've never let yourself down?"

He stopped, took his glasses off and rubbed his eyes.

"I'm sorry that dude got away with the data. Too busy with the other guys we knew about. Don't you think I know, that if I'd been relying on the other Rangers, had them there earlier, he wouldn't have gotten away?"

Her stomach dropped, she wanted to offer him a hug, but wasn't sure it'd be appropriate here, even though they were alone.

"Sam, no. That's . . . not what I meant."

He put his glasses back on. "This is all my fault. My responsibility. I'll figure it out."

She tried again. "My point is that your Rangers will help you. Just not that Michelle woman. She's trouble. I can tell. All she cares about is how she looks. About her career. I've seen her type before."

Why did she add that part?

How unprofessional and embarrassing! Every so often, she spoke without thinking first.

"Michelle? I've known her since high school. She's okay, although she's why I'm over here in the first place. Not her fault, though. You don't understand, anyway. Can't. You had a family."

She leaned forward and stared into his eyes. For once, she had to look up a little to do that.

"What do you mean? Try me."

"Lost my mom and dad when I was a kid. The child welfare people assigned me plenty of temporary parents. Foster brothers. Kids in group homes. Like I told Bishop. Had dozens of families, and none at all."

"Doesn't mean you can't rely on the other Rangers. They can be your new family."

"My new assigned family, you mean? Most of them are good guys, but I'm tired of trying to prove myself to them. Thought the Rangers might be different, but I know how it goes."

"You're capable of working with others. Relied on me to help you at the lab."

"That was a unique situation. Had no choice. No other way to track the enemy. Besides, you're different."

Different? Different good or different bad? "How?"

"I don't know... Just are. Smart and logical, even in a crisis. I'd choose you to be on my team *every* time, if I could."

"Thank you. I, think." Oops. She was staring. She blushed. Looked down at the table again. How western of her.

Such forwardness would horrify her mother. Hopefully, he hadn't noticed. "You seem so sure of yourself; of how you can't get along with the others. How does it go, lieutenant? Tell me."

"I'm the screw-up who's up for court-martial. The surfer dude who only fits in out on the waves. Still, I won't let it stop me. Wouldn't have stopped my dad from taking care of his responsibilities. Took a car bomb to do that. I won't be responsible for another kid losing his parents. Not if I can help it."

She snuck another look at him. "How are you going to do that? You're hurt."

He stood up and flexed his left shoulder, then his arm, "This? I'll be fine. Been hurt worse."

Sam walked around the conference table to stand next to her, then lifted the side of his uniform jacket and the shirt underneath. "See this scar?"

Pointed at a round hole in his waist, a darker red than the surrounding skin. "From a stingray. Usually they stab you in the foot, but I was body-surfing. This one got me in the side. Painful for hours until I found an old surfer who knew to put hot water on to break down the poisons."

He was close. And tall. She felt a little sorry for him. Maybe she would be his girlfriend. She didn't know anyone else tall enough; a girl had to be practical about these things.

"You were very smart about how to recover our missing data from backups at the lab, but I think you're stupid as well."

She poked at his stingray scar. "You have a poison left in you. One you can't see. Just like that stingray wound. It's hurting more than you realize. You need more hot water. We can work on it together."

Hyo-jin tilted forward in her chair, chin up. Leaned toward him.

Maybe he would bend down and kiss her.

Instead, he let his shirt drop back to cover his wound.

Turned away.

Stared at the ceiling, as if she no longer existed, "I'm in plenty of hot water already. Don't worry, I'll rely on other people to help, but some things I just need to get done myself. Cut through the paperwork. Find that data."

She picked up her tablet from the table. Doctor Yang decided she definitely would not fall for this guy. Not chase after him. He was too focused on his mission.

Anyway, she needed to focus on her own work.

And her mother would never approve of dating an American soldier.

Even if he'd saved her life.

Destroyed half her lab.

She stood up beside the ugly green table. "I'll be working on my detector. Tell me if you need anything."

Sam wouldn't do anything too stupid, would he?

I'd never been able to read women, but sensed I'd missed something with Hyo-jin.

She'd left pretty abruptly. What'd I say wrong?

Cute enough wahine, brilliant also, but the last thing I needed was to let someone else tear out my heart.

The Rangers I worked with were rough enough on a dude.

After Hyo-jin left the conference room, I filled out the chit I'd need for live ammo and sent it to the office printer. After it printed, I wandered over to Bishop's desk next to the ratty red couch.

The door to the COs office hung open, his chair empty, so I had a little time alone with Bishop.

Needed a favor to figure out where they'd taken the stolen data. Bishop had been around Seoul long enough to either owe or be owed by a noncom in just about every unit.

"Hey Top, you know the MPs they sent over to guard the

tunnel entrance?"

"Sure, El-Tee. What about them?"

"Do you have a contact there for me? Want to go over and check the tunnel out. See for myself how those tangos got our data across the DMZ."

He leaned back and rubbed the scar on his cheek. "CID will be all over that place like white on rice once they get the paperwork. Leave it to the professionals."

I fiddled with the quote plaque on his desk, "Said yourself the Major put me in charge of figuring out what to do about the missing data. Can't tell him I didn't even bother to go look myself."

"Sergeant in charge of the detail guarding our end of the tunnel owes me one. I'll make a call."

"Thanks, Top."

"With all due respect, sir, suggest you don't consider anything of a tactical nature in the future without going to Lieutenant Schnier to recruit a few shooters to tag along. I'm sure he'd be happy to help you out."

Must suspect I might do more than just check our end of the tunnel out.

Perceptive man, Sergeant Bishop.

Good thing that even when suspicious I was screwing up somehow, he was always willing to help an officer in need.

Just as long as he didn't add too much pressure. "I'll take that under advisement. Text me the details on that MP sergeant. Thanks again."

He nodded. "Roger."

Picked up his desk phone.

I figured if I requested help from Schnier, he'd just try to stop me.

After all, I was officially on light duty and wasn't exactly on the best terms with the shooters.

Walking toward the armory, I flexed my left arm.

With the painkillers, it seemed fine.

I stretched out my knee in the air and slid it forward a couple of times while holding my kneecap.

Still a little sore, but I'd be okay. I'd passed RASP, after all.

How hard could a little tunnel under the DMZ be?

Crossed Camp Kim to the Ammunition Supply Point (ASP) warehouse. They kept an empty 1,000 pound general purpose bomb out front on a concrete pedestal to mark their territory.

Gave the armorer from the 6th Ordnance Battalion running the ASP my chit to pull live equipment.

Wasn't worried, he was a spec-4 and I still had delegated authority on file for my platoon's ammo store to deal with emergencies, or our regular training schedule.

He handed over a full set of reloads and grenades to go on my plate carrier.

Wouldn't be caught out unarmed again by the bad guys.

My paperwork included a request for a dozen M86 Pursuit Deterrent Munitions (PDMs). Didn't weigh much, only a little over a pound each, but they'd come in handy if I needed to force pursuers on foot to tread cautiously.

Bishop texted me the name of the MP sergeant he'd notified I was coming.

Stopping by the company area, used for equipment prep, cleaning, and storage, I swung past my caged locker.

Grabbed my weapon, electronic toys, and other equipment of the non-explosive kind.

Stashed everything in my ruck, along with some green tape to secure it later for stealth.

Didn't want to walk around Seoul in full battle rattle, scaring the locals.

No, I'd be just another bored American soldier in uniform, taking the subway to the Dorasan Peace Park to play tourist, maybe go on a little hike across a nearby rice paddy farm.

Chapter Twenty-Five: Tunnel Rats

Kwon shook his head to clear it, but couldn't banish the idea something would set the device off and destroy them all. The truck suspension's random bounces as Pahk's senior sergeant drove it along the highway into the Kaeson Industrial area didn't help.

Pahk had squeezed into the middle of the bench seat filling the truck's cab.

Kwon rode by the window.

Pahk's other five men clung to life in the truck bed, held in by three horizontal wooden slats around the edges.

Kwon missed the softer ride of the truck he and Stro drove through Seoul.

He understood why Meon wanted the lab data moved to a secure location in Jiha Base. Too many people came and went from the main base, including rival departments and probably even Imperialist spies.

So they'd stacked the shelves of hard drives in the back, up against the cab.

Why did Meon also order Kwon and Pahk's team to transport the device strapped in the center of the truck bed to the base?

Away from the scientists who'd failed to duplicate it?

Their work stopped while Pahk's team stored the technology at Jiha.

Pahk's men obviously weren't happy.

They pressed up against the rim of the truck bed to avoid jostling, even touching, the round pack about the size of an oil barrel.

Clearly they knew it contained a tactical nuclear weapon, a so-called trashcan nuke, in reference to the small size.

Kwon thought the existence of the RA-115s only a rumor until they'd picked up the single device North Korea obtained from former Soviets.

The truck crossed a bridge over a small river. They entered Kaeson.

Pahk said something to his senior sergeant and pointed at a warehouse just off the highway to the right.

Kwon couldn't make out Pahk's words over the diesel engine's popping and clanging.

Could the apparatus actually detonate, or during their study, had the scientists disarmed it?

Surely they wouldn't give a live bomb to the protection of one special forces team with just an old military truck to haul it around?

They turned off the highway into the warehouse parking lot.

This warehouse received more than its share of military truck traffic. A careful observer might notice many trucks entered the warehouse, but none immediately returned.

In the Kaeson Industrial experiment, Dear Leader graciously gave peace a chance by allowing some foreign companies to pay his government for using North Korean labor. After their greed caused the experiment to fail, the People's Army posted signs to warn civilians who didn't live and work in Kaeson to stay out on penalty of death.

This close to the DMZ, there were no longer many non-soldiers around to observe much of anything.

They followed a truck, which hauled artillery rounds on wooden racks, into the warehouse itself.

A guard stood just inside the open warehouse doors. He checked their paperwork.

The warehouse contained two wide tunnels built at the end of a concrete truck ramp.

A pair of machine guns in identical sandbagged nests perched on the floor in each corner, simultaneously guarding the open sliding exterior doors and the tunnel mouths.

Rather than stopping to unload inside, Pahk's sergeant followed the ammo replenishment truck into the right-hand of the two tunnels.

If Kwon planned to obey his adopted Uncle's orders, he needed to work with Lieutenant Pahk. At least Kwon had been put in charge, although in the heat of battle he wondered how closely that nicety would be observed by Pahk's men.

He'd be forced to give his orders through Pahk, subject to the creative misinterpretation armies the world over suffered from through the ages.

They drove two more kilometers inside the concrete tunnel.

Walls flashed past with less than a meter of free space on each side.

Periodically, the left side of the tunnel opened up to the underground river the base was named after.

Carving through the mountain, the river's existence made turning this place into the ultimate fortified spot much simpler, even with virtually unlimited conscript labor.

Workers still had to be fed occasionally.

Besides, the water dripping from the ceiling crystallized a pattern of elegant stalactites and stalagmites, like a stone spider web. Too bad the road engineers sheered away the edges of the pre-existing caverns to flatten the floor.

War is hell when the life of the State is at stake.

The construction of Jiha base was no exception.

The guards allowed only incoming traffic via this tunnel. The other tunnel in the warehouse, paralleling the left side of the river, accommodated departing trucks.

The tunnels allowed for enough disguised traffic in both directions to keep the artillery battalion under the mountains supplied with everything they required.

Kwon couldn't think of a safer place to store the data and device until a special train arrived to ship them north.

An American Army Division couldn't fight its way into this mountain.

Jiha base was built to survive after raining death down on Seoul at the start of a war. Multiple nuclear warheads would be required to seriously affect it, let alone destroy the base.

They'd hold the data here until General Meon completed the proper travel arrangements.

The original schedule called for Kwon's team to transport the data to the IT specialists in Pyongyang later, but they were also originally scheduled to capture it a week later.

Original plans, contingency plans, extra plans, future plans; they all jumbled together.

Maybe he needed more sleep to recover from his trip south.

Either way, plans are modified by contact with the enemy.

Pahk's sergeant stopped the truck in an open cavern. He carefully turned in the limited space and backed up to a loading dock matching the height of the tailgate.

Kwon opened his door and jumped down.

Pahk followed.

Kwon got him started on their next steps. "Have your men secure something we can carry the weapon and the data on. Whatever kind of carts they use to transport artillery shells should work. They must be accustomed to delicate movements, or this base would've blown itself up years ago."

"I'll send someone to round up a few of the artillery battalion's conscript labor as well. They can drag that thing deeper into the mountain while my men pull security."

"I can see one of those skeletons falling in front of the cart, spilling the device, letting it go rolling down some tunnel. No, put a couple of men out front to clear the way, but we need trustworthy hands moving the cart. Besides, if we recruit help, they'll get curious why we want them to be so careful. No one but the battalion commander knows what we're bringing in. Keep it that way."

Pahk nodded his acquiescence. He'd been strangely subdued after the confrontation in Meon's office.

Maybe he was coming around.

As long as he continued to take orders, their team could make security around the weapon and data impregnable.

The locals wouldn't care about their team securing the drive shelves from the lab in their midst, but revealing the warhead to the artillerymen might cause panic. He'd need to decide on a proper code name for the weapon.

"I'll go ahead and inspect our new home."

With Pahk in charge of transporting the device through the cleared caverns, any mistakes or damaging drops would rebound on him.

He couldn't blame Kwon for his own shoddy work.

Kwon's lieutenant insignia and ID sufficed to get him to the Artillery Battalion HQ.

There, he sent a clerk to guide Pahk and team through the caverns. Recruited a facilities sergeant to take him to their new combination barracks and secret storage site.

Both men hunched over as the artillery sergeant led him down a winding tunnel.

They reached to a hollowed-out cavern about the size of a railroad car.

The sergeant gave him the rice-cup tour. "Unlike the artillery positions on the south side of the mountain overlooking the DMZ, this area doesn't open up to the outside, sir. Battalion's been using it for auxiliary shell storage. Cleared the shells out and installed those eight cots as requested."

"Good. Sanitary facilities?"

The underground river entered the far side of the cavern from the east before flowing westward. The sergeant pointed at some kind of wooden contraption build at the edge, "The CO had one of the engineers rig up a toilet for your men. There's a hook beside it so you can also rig a camp shower."

So no drinking out of the river.

No fires, either. Not enough ventilation. "We need an electric stove."

"Sorry, sir, used to eating our rations cold, so didn't think of that. I'll get something delivered. Anything else you need?"

"Can you get me some steel plates and hinges to block the entrance off with? Some steel netting for that river entrance? Need to physically secure the cavern from any possible intrusion point. I'm sure one of my men can weld, assuming you'll loan us the equipment."

"Can do, sir! The battalion commander made very clear the cooperation General Meon ordered."

Perfect.

Maybe he just needed a few days of easy garrison duty to clear his head and figure out how Meon's orders would lead to the reunification of North and South under their Supreme Commander.

That and win over Pahk and his team.

When they were done working, no one else would enter their vault.

Maybe he'd call it the Goshawk Bomb.

Goshawk Device?

The name bore further consideration.

The pentagon brass didn't name it the Ranger Reconnaissance Company for nothing.

Leaving the subway, I ruck marched across Dorasan Peace Park.

Besides South Korean tourists, the park held granite monuments and historically preserved razor wire fences overlooking the DMZ.

I strode through the crowds, out of place in uniform, a lone Ranger.

The adults were pleasant enough, but a little girl in a white jumpsuit, maybe five years old, pointed me out to her parents as if she'd never seen an occidental soldier before.

Virtually impossible; we wandered all over Seoul.

With the advent of dusk, the park closed soon, but it was less than half a klick from the park's edge to the greenhouse with the tunnel entrance, even hiking the long way around the hilly scrub-brush.

I whistled a marching tune as I advanced toward the rear of the MP jeep set to cover the dirt road into the farm.

Coming from around the rice paddies, I didn't want to startle anyone into shooting first and asking questions later.

I cleared my visit with the sergeant in charge of the guard detail. He handed me a Velcro chest patch with "DMZ Police" and an armband with "Military Police".

Apparently that made it legal under the Korean Armistice for me to carry weapons within the DMZ.

When I told him I might be awhile, checking out the inside of the tunnel, he warned me their orders precluded entering the tunnel itself.

If I ran into opposition, I'd be on my own.

The only reason he didn't call Captain Grant for clearance to let me in was whatever arrangement Bishop made with him. Probably told him a dumb 1LT wanted to play tourist.

He showed me the greenhouse with the truck the tangos used parked in front of it.

A broad metal hoop structure, the largest of three, it contained a concealed tunnel entrance, fitted to tight tolerances behind a stack of old irrigation equipment.

Seemed satisfied I took the dangers seriously when I pulled my plate carrier out of my ruck and began loading it up with grenades and ammo. Left one of his men in the greenhouse to watch me slap on a combat helmet and gear up.

Could sound the alarm if anything else came back through the tunnel.

I removed my MK18 from my ruck last. Loaded a magazine and slung it over my shoulder.

A Close Quarters Battle Rifle (CQBR), the MK18's barrel was four inches shorter than a normal M4A1 carbine. Would allow me to move much easier in tight spaces, like a tunnel, but I gave up a little long distance accuracy.

Confident I could still out-shoot a typical DPRK border guard with it, even at long ranges.

Not that I wanted the noise a gun battle in the DMZ would entail. That'd bring all sorts of unwanted company running, from both sides of the border.

Loaded down with equipment, I crawled into the enemy tunnel.

Lowered the Ground Panoramic Night Vision Goggle attached to my helmet. They not only amplified low-light conditions and overlaid thermal imaging, but outlined the edges of detected objects and allowed me to use my weapon scope as a targeting camera.

Each set cost the Regiment just under $70K, too.

The 75th RRC specializes in recon behind enemy lines; it's right there in the name.

That's why they let us play with the cool toys.

All I could see in the night vision was mud, covered by cold mud. Layered between muddy wooden rails. Underneath a rope and pulley system hanging from the short ceiling, the rope itself also covered by a thin layer of mud.

Did I mention the tunnel was muddy?

And definitely designed for Koreans. Couldn't even bend over and crouch inside. The height forced me to crawl.

In the mud.

I stopped to put my night vision and rifle back inside my ruck to protect the barrel and electronics from the environment. Hopefully, keep them usable on the other side.

Crawling through the tunnel, I focused like I was back in RASP, rucking sleep-deprived across rough hills.

Focused on anything but my screaming muscles.

Distracted my mind with daydreams about Michelle on a warm beach in San Diego; asking Hyo-jin out to one of those rooftop restaurants they have in Seoul.

Pretty soon I needed a cold shower. Don't worry, I got a continuous freezing shower.

Have you ever crawled a 5k?

In the icy muck?

Rather surf in the warm Pacific Ocean.

My gloves carried sludge.

I dragged my ruck behind me.

Eventually, my whole body oozed with frozen slime.

Couldn't get a good purchase with my hands and knees, but there wasn't much friction in the tunnel, either.

For once, height worked against me. I slid and wiggled my way up the tunnel.

Considered how I could improve my eSurfboard. How I might get it across the border. How to find the stolen data.

Anything to take my mind off the mud.

Any thought to prevent exhaustion from overcoming willpower.

Any focus beyond putting one arm and one knee in front of the other, over and over again through the dark.

Ignored the ache in my knee. The pain in my left shoulder.

Pushed it all to the outer edges of my mind, not allowing it to dominate my thoughts.

After forever, my numb fingers hit concrete.

Wanted to cheer, but couldn't muster the energy.

Besides, expected enemy sentries nearby. Surely they didn't leave their end of the tunnel unguarded?

Dragged my ruck forward a few inches at a time to move it close enough.

Removed my goggles and carbine.

The headset again turned the depths of night into day. Tunnel opened out onto a concrete pad with a line of wooden carts attached to the rails embedded in the mud.

Could see the outlines of a bunch of bushes and a hillside beyond.

I'd made it.

Now to figure out where I'd made it to.

Lying on my back to rest, I pulled out my issue smartphone. Pulled off my right glove and its coating of mud. Checked my location using GPS.

Definitely well into the DPRK side of the DMZ.

Typed up a quick email to Bishop and Lee, letting them know the coordinates of where the tunnel ended.

Didn't have the greatest connection back to cell towers on the other side of the DMZ, but was close enough the message would get through, probably as soon as I left the tunnel.

The ROK was happy to let mobile phones in the North access any cell tower they approached near enough to connect with. Any uncontrolled information entering the country was a threat to the dictatorship, not to the freer South.

The People's Army border guards used their privileged location to download and sell TV shows and movies not available in the North. Their customers did big business smuggling USB drives around the country for sale on the black market.

Considered taking a selfie of myself covered in mud at the end of the tunnel. Might ruin the camera, just by having my dirty image in it, let alone muddy paws on it.

On the bright side, people pay good money for exotic mud baths like this. Plus, I no longer needed to worry about icing my knee today.

What to do next?

Now that I'd reached the end of the tunnel, I didn't want to crawl back. I'm here, might as well just continue on and locate the data.

The Major tasked me to minimize the strategic damage from losing it.

Who was in a better position to accomplish that than I was right now? I'm sure that's what Major Williams intended. A one-soldier invasion of North Korea.

Search and destroy.

How much better to accomplish my mission than that?

Didn't have the option of bringing an assault team with me. They'd be too tough to hide, anyway, but I could take my friends' advice and ask Michelle and Lee to help out in my little infiltration.

I scraped up onto the concrete pad. Edged around the wooden carts.

Ran a tripwire across the tunnel entrance, ankle high.

Should ensure warning of unexpected visitors.

Scrunched backward into the tunnel. Laid on my back. Set my mental clock for thirty minutes.

Sleep is a soldier's best friend. Before I made any final life-altering decisions, I needed a friend.

Chapter Twenty-Six: Not Again!

I'd prefer to be fully fit before invading the North to locate the data and save a good chunk of the world from eventual nuclear destruction, but I only had two knees.

Woke with my head on my rucksack, hands numb, knee stiff from inactivity.

Lifted it up and down a few times in a futile attempt to loosen it up.

Wiggled my way past the parked wooden carts.

Slid across ten feet of concrete just inside the tunnel exit.

Dragged my pack behind me.

When I'd left the subway earlier, the south side of the DMZ lit up like a Christmas tree in winter, but the north side remained dark.

The DPRK didn't have the people and power to run electricity to many places, so they saved the lights for the tiny Joint Security Area (JSA) used for meetings between North and South and the empty village of Kijŏng-dong.

North Korea built Kijŏng-dong next to the DMZ in the 1950s to impress the South with how well the North lived.

Sucks when your fake, empty concrete houses are the nicest village in the country.

Even the nearby Kaeson Industrial used to be powered by the South as part of their trade agreements.

Along the rest of the 4 km wide DMZ, the North Korean People's Army stood guard in darkness. I counted on their lack of electricity and technology to survive.

Without it, this little jaunt would be suicide.

Tilted my night vision out of the way.

Took down the tripwire I'd set at the tunnel exit.

Slung my ruck.

The tunnel opened out from the side of a hill, so I couldn't make out anything beyond thorny scrub brush and a muddy slope.

Slid out and crawled a dozen feet down the hill on my belly, carbine ready.

A cross between a growl and a low whistle up the slope behind me.

I froze.

A beast in a cave?

Flipped through my memories of the known indigenous wildlife in the area. Specifically, anything dangerous the Yongsan welcoming committee warned us about hiking in the Korean hills.

Ruled out giant hornets and various snakes from the sound.

Wild boars?

Korea has a few deaths from boar maulings every year. Revenge for all the tender samgyupsal Koreans eat.

Maybe I should've stopped at a shop and brought some grilled pork belly in my ruck rather than just First Strike Rations (FSR).

A grunt and a growl.

Head on a silent swivel. Nothing in sight.

Another cave nearby used as a den?

Tough to tell in the night vision's restricted 97 degree field of view.

Do I go find it, or just leave it be and hope it leaves me alone?

Drew my combat knife.

Didn't want to shoot if I could help it. Gunfire would be sure to bring DPRK quick reaction forces directly to me.

Silence.

Couldn't let something stalk me. I'd go find the beast.

Face it in its lair.

I moved to face uphill.

Edged through the sandy soil on my belly.

Twenty feet closer to the crest.

Artificial lines. Concrete walls protruding from the dirt. Outlines of an observation bunker rear entrance, steel door closed.

Was the animal inside? Didn't make any sense.

Another grunt.

Definitely from within the bunker.

Not a wild boar.

Something even more dangerous if disturbed.

Rose to my feet. Slipped up the hill to the door.

No light from inside.

Tucked my knife away. Readied my rifle.

Didn't want a loud exchange, but in this situation, that might be out of my hands.

Pulled open the door.

Of course it creaked, alerting any residents to my entrance.

Two border guards lay on the floor, not even in a position to observe the DMZ through the slit on the other side of the bunker.

Glass bottles strewn around made clear where they spent their limited pay.

At least it wasn't just people on our side who let down their team.

One made a low-pitched whistling sound, like a buzz saw in heat.

Can't believe I mistook snoring for a wild animal.

Used to that background noise, the creak of the door didn't wake either one up.

I pulled a half-dozen double self-locking nylon tactical restraints out of my ruck. Disposable thick zip ties with two loops, one for each arm.

Could get a pack of ten online for $10, but the Army probably paid that much for each one, even in bulk.

Secured their ankles together first.

Didn't even wake them up.

Tiptoed around the bottles on the floor to where the guard's heads lay, thankful for night vision to guide my path.

They woke when flipped over.

I restrained their arms and wrists. Taped their mouths shut.

Could breathe through their noses for a while.

Cut the wires to their communications system. Broke open their flare gun.

Wouldn't warn anyone without a long walk first.

Neither spoke to protest or complain the whole time.

Just startled awake.

One shrugged when he was aware enough to realize what happened. The other lay there, eyes wide open and watching me, but not moving.

Model prisoners.

Almost like they'd done this before.

Kwon tugged with all his might.

His hand slipped. Almost made him fall into the cavern's river.

Setting his feet again, he put all his weight on the steel cable embedded into the wall.

Tugged with all his might.

Cable and anchor held.

This final cable was one of six Pahk's men used to stretch a braided steel net across the entrance of the river into the cavern. Now, nothing larger than a snake could enter that way.

The net would hold anyone who tried underwater.

Drown them.

He strode across the cavern floor to the new doorway.

The Artillery Battalion had plenty of two inch steel plate leftover from their own fortifications.

Pahk's men welded steel plates together. Attached them to concrete and rebar anchors set into the ceiling and floor. Added hinges to one panel.

Secured the new door with a pair of steel pins as bolts, only retractable from the inside.

Kwon ordered two spec ops soldiers to guard the tunnel outside.

Keep the curious away.

Half of the rest slept next to their weapons. The others on duty inside the now vault-like storage cavern played cards.

No one could reach the stack of disk drive shelves storing the data his team sacrificed their lives for.

Even more secure, he'd locked up the Goshawk device inside a separate makeshift safe of welded steel plates anchored into the floor.

Nothing to worry about. The data and device were safe.

A team which worked together succeeded together.

Hadn't seen any more border guards since I found that bunker. Could risk a tiny bit of noise.

Huddled with my back against the wind on the side of a hill, I checked my phone.

No messages, but plenty of signal from cell towers on the other side of the DMZ.

Turned on my Bluetooth earpiece. Called Lee. Woke him up, but didn't tell him exactly where I was in the middle of the night.

He might not approve.

"You were going to check on unusual activity, especially visitors, on the other side of the DMZ. Any info?"

"Right now?"

Lee usually provided first-rate team support. Sleepy, I guess.

"Yeah. Need the information immediately, *Sergeant* Lee."

His voice perked up. "Roger. No unusual activity observed, but KCIA has reports of three sets of visitors. The first is Deputy Defense Minister Meon Lon-chun. Had a temporary office setup at their main base a few weeks ago. Second is a peace delegation we've invited to a conference. Came in last Thursday. Third is a new spec ops team. Arrived via train over the weekend."

"Meon is a mean one. Weaseled his way into a succession of promotions by stabbing his superiors in the back. Wouldn't want him working for me; be afraid to turn around. Bet he's running the show over there. The new team are probably replacements for the ones from the lab. Dudes to guard the data until Meon can send it north securely, or maybe some new activity we won't expect. Bears checking out."

"Concur, sir."

I stretched out my knee.

Did a 360 of the area to ensure my continued solitude. "What about your new contact? He check out?"

"Too early to tell, sir. Not even sure we know his real name, yet. We're negotiating. Not only wants a way out of Korea for his trouble, but a lavish lifestyle. I'm confident we'll be able to work something out, eventually."

"If you do, let me know right away. Could use an inside source on the north side of the DMZ in the next few days."

"Roger that, sir."

"Meon's still at the main base?"

"As far as we can tell, sir. At least his car and driver hang out in their motor pool parking lot, judging by the satellite photos. A long, black Mercedes limo stands out over there."

"Great, thanks." Maybe I'd finish riding this wave after all. "Michelle may need access to my BOQ room when I'm not around to pick up some equipment. I'll send her your way, so you can clear her in."

"Roger that."

"Thanks, Lee. Appreciate your help."

"Anytime, sir."

I hung up and dialed Michelle.

She jumped right on me. "Where've you been? Partying with that lab chica?"

"No, haven't seen her since the conference. More important things to worry about, like getting the data back. What, are you jealous?"

Her voice settled down. "Don't be ridiculous. Just worried about you. Whatever you do, don't let them send you across the DMZ after that data. That'd be a suicide mission."

A little too late for that. "A tough one, for sure, but that's a bit morbid, even for you."

"Oh, it'll be tough, but that's not what I mean. Not exactly what I mean, I mean. Oh..."

"What *do* you mean?"

"I know you aren't the greatest at politics, but I have a degree in it. Even you should realize that after what you did at the lab, some people have it in for you. Maybe even your CO. The powers-that-be will want to sweep that mess under the rug without major embarrassment for the Army or the South Koreans. I'm sure if you stick it out, they'll let you off without charges. The last thing they want is more publicity from a high-profile court-martial."

I thought about her theory for a moment. "I can see that, but what does it have to do with crossing the DMZ?"

"If you don't make it back, they don't have to worry about a lab investigation. Ties up a big potential leak. You've already shown them you won't play ball and suppress inconvenient information, the way you went into the lab anyway."

Her voice softened, "Need to watch your back on this one."

That's a cheerful thought. "May be too late for that. Did you arrange for that covert sub?"

"Put in the request earlier. That's why I'm still awake. Should hear back from D.C. soon. Just waking up over there. They'll need to call the Pentagon, or at least the Navy. See if they have a team of SEALs they can shake loose. If we get them, you can just sit back in the office on light duty and let those guys go hunt the data from the sea, assuming we get a line on it."

"May be a little closer to getting a line on it than that. Took a little trip. Traced the tunnel back under the DMZ. I'm actually calling you from the North. Surprise!"

"You're what?"

I tried to sound meek. Not sure I succeeded. "In need of a little favor?"

"Wait, is Schnier with you?"

"Pretty sure he'd tell the Major, not come along. Bishop says I need to trust in other people more, though, which is why I called you."

"You can't keep doing this crazy... What do you need?"

"That sub, ideally full of operators for backup, would be a great start."

"Start?"

I smiled. "May have a plan. Will you put my eSurfboard on a plane? Got the prototype in my room at the BOQ. Contact Lee, he'll let you in."

"You either have a plan, or you don't. You can't *may* have a plan." Now she sounded wary, "A plane to where?"

"Uh, they fly crop-dusters out by the Ganghwa Peace Observatory. Right across the river from North Korea. Treaty permits unarmed agriculture planes to fly over the DMZ. The Army uses them to take long-range photos of river and train movements from a side angle to fill out sat pics."

"Okay?"

Dubious is better than wary.

"Get Lee to hang the eSurfboard from a GPS-guided parachute. They can fly quite a ways sideways if you drop 'em high enough. Include the spare controller, just in case. I'll send the coordinates for a spot across the border upstream in the river. If you can have it in the air starting the day after tomorrow, that'll work fine. Text you later the exact drop time. Might be on short notice."

"Sam, dropping a secret prototype into North Korea isn't exactly kosher. Sure that's not too much of a risk? What if the wrong people are waiting for it?"

"Just have to trust me. Ideally, I'll be waiting before they let it out of the plane." Took a deep breath. "Michelle, I need this and the sub. Even if my plan goes perfectly, they'll be my only ticket out of North Korea."

"Trust is a two-way street, but I'll get it done. Be careful."

"You know me!"

"That's why I said to be careful."

Chapter Twenty-Seven: Helper Ambushes

The stars and the city lights were a distraction. One Michelle couldn't afford.

She lay back on her balcony's wooden chaise lounge and closed her eyes. Should she go back inside her apartment, rather than talk to D.C. out here?

Theoretically, one of the sleeping neighbors might overhear a detail they shouldn't, but after her conversation with Sam, she didn't particularly want to follow the rules.

He never did.

She checked her phone for the time. Late enough in D.C., so she dialed.

The duty officer at the agency picked up. Didn't bother to verify her identity.

Who else would call from her encrypted mobile phone? "Please hold for the Assistant Director for Korea."

Edward Metcalf's powerful voice echoed across the satellite links, "You requested a covert mission sub and a dozen SEALs? Don't ask for much, do you?"

"My local contacts in the special operations community felt the request would be better received coming from our agency."

"They already knew all the SEALs in the region are tasked and there's no way they'll get their missions changed based on the speculative bullshit you're feeding me. Did you not already know that, or are you running your own game here? What's reality?"

How to put this politely? "Sir, we have some solid data points. The lab info is across the DMZ. We have two contacts on the other side, one American soldier I'm personally confident is reliable, the other a high-level DPRK official. I believe the risk is worth it to back our soldier up, even if we ultimately don't end up using the SEALs."

"Request denied. We don't expend political capital with the Navy just in case some Ranger gets caught short across the line. As far as I know, everything is now proceeding as planned, so what aren't you telling me?"

Michelle sucked in her breath.

Sam trusted her. He wasn't perfect, but if she ever needed him, he'd fight an Army to help her.

Wasn't he in Korea, changing his whole career path, under threat of court martial, because she'd asked him to come?

Taken advantage of him?

She held no illusions of herself. She knew how to work people to get ahead, but Sam wasn't like that. He was oblivious.

Naive.

Immune to social reality.

"Still there? What's wrong, can't think of a new lie that fits fast enough?"

Air escaped her in a rush. Her chest dropped and rattled her necklace.

She grabbed the yin-yang shells to silence it.

Sat up.

Strained for how to respond.

Nothing else she could do for Sam.

Metcalf obviously didn't want the CIA to provide any support.

To spend any political capital.

She should just go along. Keep her positive career prospects, even if it'd take her another decade to make Station Chief.

"Sir, there's nothing I haven't told you, except I'm willing to put my career on the line for this. Sending these SEALs is the most important thing they'll do all year."

Willing to put her career on the line?

Where did *that* come from?

"Your career is always on the line; so is mine."

He paused.

"Fine, I'll send your request to the Navy to borrow the USS Michigan. Just sitting in port doing nothing anyway. But it'll take too much to get the SEALs re-tasked. You'll have to scrounge up somebody else to staff your little stand-by relief mission. If you can't find a qualified spec ops team through your own contacts, we'll cancel the whole deal."

No SEALs? At least she had a sub. "Thank you, sir. I won't disappoint you."

"You already have, but I'll give you a little more rope before you hang."

What had she done? "It's all going to work out, sir."

Click.

She hoped, anyway.

If not, she might need to join Sam on that agency plane ride out of Seoul, assuming they both lived to reach the airport.

Stay off the paths. Stay off the peaks. Stay away from terrain choke-points.

Anywhere the scrub brush or hills tried to lead me, I needed to take the more difficult direction instead.

Not the time to get blowed up, as Bishop liked to say.

If the DPRK had more observation points, if they'd mined any land, if they guarded anywhere, it'd be in the places people naturally walked: along creeks, following animal paths, all the easy ways to traverse the hills.

Using their tunnel, I'd already bypassed the known mined and fenced areas closer to the border.

Much better to infiltrate alone and not draw any attention.

I shifted my ruck up a few inches. Tightened the belt strap. Move more of the weight from my aching shoulder to my waist.

One foot in front of the other. I'd get to their main base quickly enough.

Two klicks on flat ground, even with a full ruck, should only take me 20 minutes.

I flowed like water through bushes without disturbing their

outlines in the dark.

Slithered over hill peaks to not silhouette myself in the sparse moonlight.

Stopped every five minutes to reorient myself, making sure I continued in the right general direction.

Paused every minute.

Turned. Listened. Watched.

Strained senses for any sign of the enemy.

Willed my breath quiet to increase my hearing range.

Slipped in the mud more than once.

Bugs buzzed. The occasional field mouse scurried into a bush.

A hunting bat fluttered past my helmet; one of the sharks of the rodent world.

I tried to ignore the possibility of land mines. In the dark, even with night vision, would only discover one the hard way.

Surely they'd mine the trails people most likely followed?

The ones wide and flat enough to accept a tank or another vehicle.

After an hour ruck marching over uneven terrain, a string of lights emerged from the darkness.

The main base perimeter, complete with circles of razor wire topping chain-link fence punctuated by guard tower observation posts.

The spotlights in the guard towers were dark.

Shut off.

Needed to stay that way.

A hundred-meter outer security area circled the fence line.

The potholed highway from the Kaeson Industrial Area ended at the northern main gate.

A southern gate fed into a system of dirt and gravel roads covering this section of the DMZ.

Smaller sally ports, suitable only for foot traffic, pierced the east and west fences.

I hunched down just outside the cleared security area.

Once I left the relative safety of the brush, all it would take was one especially alert or especially bored guard to flip on his spotlight in one of the nearby towers and run it across the open space.

Then the machine guns would take over.

Oh, I could take out the spotlights with a bullet as fast as they could switch them on and point them at me, but one against the few thousand men and tanks they could mobilize sounded like a losing proposition.

Wasn't even carrying that many rounds for my carbine.

No, my plan involved my multi-tool. Just needed a little leverage to make it work.

Made out movement in the closest tower.

At least they didn't have night vision to guide them.

Strictly low tech, more used to guarding against fleeing conscripts. Probably spent most of their time watching inward, toward the base.

More entertaining than 100 meters of mud.

Time to move out.

I pushed one hand forward, checked the surface.

Damp dirt.

Moved forward on my left elbow and my right knee. With my belly taking some of the pressure, only sunk an inch into the mud.

Right elbow and left knee. Check the ground ahead.

Elbows and knees alternating. Repeat.

Didn't need a whole platoon of Rangers out here, bumbling around.

All it took was one soldier making a single mistake to get caught.

Doing fine by myself.

Crawled fifty meters.

Hand touched wood. Sphincter tightened involuntarily.

Froze. Focused.

Analyzed the situation.

A wipe-out here would be my last ride.

Land mine.

Something in the PMD series, old Soviet blast-type anti-personnel mines made from a wooden box with a hinged lid.

Push down the lid and a striker hits a detonator. Wooden box to avoid metal detectors.

Rain must've washed the thin layer of dirt off the lid.

Let's avoid that whole getting blowed up part.

The story of Bishop's cheek was a company legend, passed on whenever someone new joined up.

Major Williams, the RRC CO, was once 2LT Williams in the Big Army. First deployed as Bishop's brand-new platoon leader in Afghanistan.

On his first day in country, their platoon stumbled on a poppy field in a hidden valley amongst the rocky hills.

Bishop watched Williams wander over to a cleared dirt track bordering a poppy field.

Williams thought it was a road for harvesting the poppies.

In Bishop's experience, that'd be a minefield to keep anyone from stealing their cash crop, not where you'd want to walk.

So Bishop took off yelling.

Sprinted the couple of hundred meters of bushes and rocks between them.

Towards the end, he jumped over a razor wire fence to stop Williams.

Well, tried to jump. Actually tripped over a rock on the take-off and rammed his head into a concertina spiral of wicked metal barbs.

Earned his cheek scar.

Williams couldn't understand what Bishop was yelling about, but when he saw him tangled up, turned around and went back to help.

Turning back saved his life from the minefield.

To this day, Bishop swears a lieutenant will get him killed someday.

Land mines remind me of that story, except there was no sergeant here to stop me from getting blowed up. I'd have to do that on my own.

At least I wasn't risking anyone else's life.

Well, besides all that future collateral damage if I died here and didn't recover the data.

A Soviet PMD has to be pushed all the way down to trigger. I lifted my hand instead.

Where there is one mine, there is usually a whole mine field. A mine field I lay in the middle of.

Time to move even slower and hope no one in a tower paid attention.

I eased my knife out.

For once, the mud worked for me, creating less resistance to the blade as I pushed it into the ground diagonally ahead of me with each crawl.

Unless it rained or snowed pretty heavily in the next few hours, when the sun came up, my path across the cleared security area would be obvious in the mud.

That's assuming I made it away from here before the sun came up.

Only had three more hours.

Should be plenty of time.

Managed about a meter every twenty seconds.

Fifteen minutes of sheer terror, imagining another mine in front of me.

Actually only detoured around three.

Three was *way* too many. Rather dodge shark fins in the waves.

Laying next to the fence, I discovered a feature I hadn't seen from 100 meters away. A thick wire weaved in and out at waist height.

Electrified. Great.

Well, didn't really want to go over the fence, anyway. My recovering knee already felt the recent overuse.

Used the wire cutter on my multi-tool to grip one link at a time. Rubber coated handles.

Each link snapped as I put the full leverage of my arms on it.

Each time, I paused to listen for one of the tower guards alerting on the click.

Snip after snip, I carved up from the ground tall enough to slide under. Cut wide enough for my shoulders to clear the side.

Folded the chain up on itself.

Secured it with a zip tie.

Pushed my ruck through ahead of me.

Slid under on my back, looking at the stars.

Clipped the zip tie so the fence appeared undisturbed.

Returned to its previous shape.

Crept along the inside of the fence line until I found a building close enough to hide me in its shadow.

Without much electricity to waste, the interior of the base slept in darkness.

I darted from building to building.

Followed churned up mud until I located the motor pool parking lot by the simple expedient of looking for the largest collection of trucks and cars.

Among the beat up troop trucks and tiny blue Pyonghwa Chinese knock-offs, I mean re-branded passenger cars, there was only one black Mercedes limo, parked by itself.

High-ranking military officers drove the passenger cars.

The North limited the Mercedes limos to very high officials in the DPRK government.

They considered enlisted lucky if they rode in the back of a truck rather than walking everywhere.

I'd seen my share of vehicle security mechanisms when I was younger, but chauffeurs for North Korean officials don't need to lock their cars. Having the power of instant life or death over anyone who might dare to trespass is a sufficient deterrent against petty vandalism.

Opening the back door of the limo, I took off my pack and set it on the car's floor.

Removed a wireless motion sensor from my pack and stuck the unobtrusive monitor to the grill on the front of the hood. From that perspective, it covered the aisle anyone would use to approach.

Crawled into the back, which spread mud across the red leather upholstery.

Fed myself cinnamon zapplesauce and a peanut butter dessert bar from an FSR.

Downed two pain pills with a chocolate protein drink.

Set my alarm to vibrate just before dawn.

Hated to sleep on the job, but my shoulder hurt. Plenty of time for another nap before recovering the data.

Chapter Twenty-Eight:
Hot Wheels

Unlike just after she'd borne her son, Jin-sun's Mother had properly arranged this kitchen to fill their home with the nourishing energy of Feng Shui.

She dropped the cucumbers from the morning farmer's market on the kitchen table.

Her table's surface was made from a good Korean hardwood. The stove represented fire; the sink water.

The tile floor filled the kitchen with earth to offset the hanging copper pots.

She'd make her son his favorite Oi Sobagi Kimchi with the cucumbers later.

She pitched her voice to carry, "Jin-sun? We have little time!"

"In here, Mom."

Of course, in his bedroom. Always laying about. Bad Chi.

He could get out on his own. The hall right outside their fifth-floor apartment contained an elevator, after all.

She tapped on his open door as she walked into his room.

Jin-sun lay on his bed, back propped up with yellow silk pillows, laptop on a folding bed table above his legs, tapping away.

She gave him the look. "Why you always play video game?"

He stopped tapping. "Mom, I told you, it's not video games. This is important work."

She stepped forward and walked around his bed to look at his screen. Just a bunch of lines and half-formed anime pictures. "Look like video game to me."

"Yes, Mother. It's for my friend's video game, but I'm doing 3D design, not playing."

Was always video game.

He needed to go to Harvard Business School, like she planned. Get an important job. "Put that away. You haven't tried your new chair yet. I'll get it."

He sighed, but dutifully moved his laptop and table to the side.

Powerful arms.

She thought maybe he could have been an Olympic swimmer, if not for the infant botulism which made him sickly when he was young.

The doctors claimed botulism came from the honey mixed with juice she'd fed him while they were still poor, before she'd started her seamstress business. *She* blamed the lack of proper Chi in their old ground-floor apartment.

Stepping out to the kitchen, she sat in his new chair.

Used the little lever on the arm to drive it into his bedroom and park it next to his bed, "See, even I can drive this one. Experimental model. New, smoother drive thingy. Not all jerky like last one. All-terrain tires. Twice as fast as before."

She climbed out of the chair, but refused to help him get in. Some things, he needed to practice doing on his own.

His mother wouldn't always be there for him.

He didn't have a problem sliding over and dropping into the new chair, though.

Legs paralyzed since six months old, he had decades of practice with wheel chairs.

Buckled himself in.

"Good boy. Have early appointment at Embassy. They want to meet you, talk about visa to America. I'm sure they like you. Everyone like you."

Everyone did.

My phone alarm vibrated me awake.

I lay on my back. Clung to my carbine.

The red velvet ceiling helped me figure out I was muddying

up the minister's Mercedes limo and not resting on my bed in the BOQ.

Phone vibrated again. Glanced at it.

The motion detector on the hood sent an alarm.

The enemy cometh. Time to catch a new wave.

I leaned up. Peeked out the front windshield.

A man trudged toward me along the gravel path from the entrance gate of the motor pool. Wore a People's Army uniform and a black chauffeur's cap.

Just the driver I needed. Not only did Meon's chauffeur create a vulnerability for Meon, but he started work even earlier than I'd expected.

I opened the driver side rear door, away from the chauffeur.

Slipped out into a crouch.

Flipped the selector on my rifle to FIRE, just in case.

I'd be smoked if I had to use it.

Even suppressed, a rifle bullet is too loud to hide. At most, you can keep them from making your eardrums bleed.

Circled around and kept the limo between us.

He rounded the front of the limo. Stepped up to open the driver's door.

I reversed direction. Stepped out from behind the trunk, carbine aimed at his unarmored chest.

He reached for his pistol, but I shook my head.

Must've convinced him, because he left it alone. Slowly raised his hands instead.

Motioned for him to turn around.

He complied.

Once he could no longer see me, I stepped over and patted him down.

Removed the cartridges from his pistol, some North Korean POC, and the extra magazines from his pockets. "Get in."

Eyes wide, he perched on the front of the driver's seat.

At least he spoke some English. Probably a job requirement.

Meon likely got to attend international meetings occasionally.

I closed the driver's door.

Slipped into the rear where I could keep him covered without being seen by others. "Just want a short limo ride and to ask a few questions. If you mess that up, if you warn Minister Meon somehow, I'll have to shoot you both just to get away. Even if I only get one of you, if that one isn't you, I'm sure you can predict how they'll treat the guy who let the Deputy Defense Minister get shot."

His pupils expanded even more.

He nodded up and down, as if he was trying to pound in a nail with his chin. "I keep mouth shut."

Good, this guy would float with the tide. "Do that and everyone lives, plus we avoid an international incident."

"You not here. I understand."

"Exactly. Now let's talk about when and where you're supposed to pick up Meon and how that will go."

Compromising a target's defensive tactic, say, their bodyguard chauffeur, makes the enemy more, not less, vulnerable.

This kidnapping should be no problem at all.

Chapter Twenty-Nine:
Caught!

How should Michelle play this interview with Jin-sun and his mom?

She could give them what they wanted, visas to America, so there was no reason for them not to cooperate.

She sat on the edge of Toby Howell's desk in the embassy. Ignored Howell and played with her shell necklace. Went well with her black pencil skirt and stark white blouse. She'd dressed more formal than usual today, because she could tell the old Korean lady liked that.

Howell grunted as a light on his desk phone turned yellow. "They're here."

Michelle nodded. "Show them in, then make yourself disappear."

"Won't they wonder about that? I've been her case officer from the beginning. Only introduced you as an observer."

"You're not cleared for this entire conversation. I'm sure you can come up with an excuse."

He stepped out of the room for a minute.

Returned leading Kwon Jin-sun in a powered wheelchair followed by his mother, Yeo Min-jung, dressed as usual in her ancient Korean formal-wear.

She gave a precise bow at the waist. After a moment, her son added a mostly respectful head nod.

Michelle sighed and returned the nod to embarrass them.

This was just an interview, no need to dress for the opera.

Howell waited until the mom sat down and Jin-sun parked his

land cruiser next to her. "The ambassador has summoned me for a consultation this morning, but the attaché will fill in for today."

How stupid did someone need to be to think the ambassador needed a low-level refugee functionary like Howell to tell him anything? "Thank you, Officer Howell. I'll take it from here."

Michelle flipped on the recorder built into Howell's desk. "Need to ask Jin-sun a few things, but first I'd like to confirm your recollection of the village political officer you spoke about before. The one who killed your husband."

Jin-sun's Mother leaned forward in her chair. "Of course." She bit down on her lip, as if she had more to say, but held it back.

Michelle picked up a propaganda photograph showing Deputy Defense Minister Meon Lon-chun standing next to four other senior DPRK officials. Slid it across the desk. "Is the Meon you spoke of in this photo?"

They both leaned forward to look.

Mom nodded. Pointed at Meon. "That him. Look older, but same gae-sae-kki." She made a mewling sound and stopped talking. Rage? Sorrow? Mourning for her husband? All of them together?

"Sorry, I'm not familiar with that phrase."

Jin-sun patted his mother's arm. "They don't teach it in foreign schools. She means 'son-of-a-bitch'. Why do you care so much about him?"

No need to get into anything she wouldn't want leaking.

She smiled at the naïve young man. "Just part of our process, to verify as much of her story as we can. Her identification shows she knew Meon."

Nerds like this, still living with their mothers, were always putty in her hands.

He drove his chair to the edge of the desk. Leaned forward. "Cut the crap, lady. Mother may be a respected elder from the black hole across the border, but I grew up with access to a world of information"—he gestured at his useless legs—"and nothing to do but dig through it. I know exactly how these special visa interviews usually go. Coming back a third time to meet with someone connected with the defense industry isn't anything like normal. Who is this guy?"

He folded his arms over his chest.

His mom shushed him. "Excuse son's manners. Has spent little time in public."

Michelle tried again. "Certainly. Meon is a senior government official now, but the important part is that her story checks out. We also received confirmation from the guards who found her on this side of the border."

"I have people every day try to convince me they don't notice I'm sitting in a chair while they walk around. I know when someone is putting me on. You Americans clearly want something from us. Why are we really here?"

Okay, so perhaps not so naïve, nor easy to manage. She reached out and flicked off the desk recorder. Howell shouldn't hear the rest of this. "Very well. What I'm about to tell you is something you may not repeat to anyone, not even Officer Howell. If you do, we will prosecute you under both U.S. and Korean law."

Jin-sun nodded. "Now we're getting somewhere."

"Meon is a Deputy Defense Minister. Runs a good chunk of the DPRK People's Army and he's currently right across the border. A colleague of mine"—who she'd specifically not invited to this meeting, because she suspected Lee was her real competition for promotion to Station Chief as some kind of sop to the locals in the KCIA—"has exchanged messages with a source we believe to be him. He has certain valuable information we'd like to know. Having your mother's story to hold over his head, threaten his exposure, is likely to enable us to convince him to see things our way. Maybe even turn him into a permanent asset on the other side."

"So you want to use us, to get at Meon?"

"No, while I suspect your Mother wouldn't mind revenge, I want a trade. You get the visas, even an expedited path to U.S. citizenship if you desire. In return, you give us what we need to control him."

"Sounds a little too good to be true. What exactly will we need to do?"

"Oh, likely not much. Do media interviews if we need, that

sort of thing. Just the threat of introducing his victim, your mother, and her sympathetic son of the man he shot in the back, will be enough. The loss of face for the DPRK government would be enormous. They deal with public embarrassments in a final and speedy manner. Meon won't risk that."

"Now you're finally being straight with us."

Michelle hoped it all worked out that neatly. Usually didn't.

If I ever did this again, I needed to acquire a set of Ranger combat uniforms like the shooters wore off base. No names or ranks, just an American flag on one shoulder.

Before we picked up the minister, I made sure a little mud covered the Harper on my nametape.

Was fine shooting back at anyone shooting at me, but hoped not to add any foreign deaths to this little cross-border excursion.

No need for him to know my name for sure.

Didn't think the chauffeur paid that much attention, not with a carbine barrel staring at him.

The gate guards just opened up and waved the minister's car out onto the highway to the Kaesong Industrial Zone.

They'd no doubt seen the chauffeur leave to pick him up most mornings for at least two weeks now. Plenty of time to get used to the routine.

Officials, enlisted, and officers needing help severely outnumber infiltrators in a gate guard's experience, so they have a tendency over time to become more helpful than guarded. If they want to keep their cushy job at the gate, that is.

Hard labor in North Korea is a slow and painful death sentence.

We drove through Kaesong, past rows of deserted thin-walled warehouses and concrete factories, all built to some master plan which required them to be interchangeable cogs in a government commission's blueprints.

When their deal to supply semi-slave labor to companies from south of the DMZ broke down, the Dear Leader shipped the workers back to the interior to grow food.

Their centrally planned economy couldn't support a bunch of skilled factory workers without outsiders to pay the DPRK government for their time.

As I'd instructed, the chauffeur pulled up in front of Kaesong's only hotel.

A three-story beast which looked like a Japanese tea garden planted on a concrete Soviet main battle tank.

Turned on the audio recorder in my phone, just in case I heard something I could use later. Standard intelligence practice.

Never know when a timely recording may come in handy.

Meon waited in a pick-up lane out front. Tapped his foot and scowled at the car. Looked hot under his black wool coat.

I'd delayed the car's arrival by a few minutes. With no traffic on the roads, he'd expect a consistent arrival each morning.

I lay low behind the driver's seat, my rifle pointed at the door.

The chauffeur put the car in park. Jumped out and ran around the hood. With a courteous bow, opened the rear door for Meon.

"You're late!" Meon began to slide into the seat, but froze halfway. "Who are you?"

Aimed my short-barreled carbine directly at the center of his chest. "Get in and stay quiet, if you want to be a live deputy minister rather than a dead hero." Didn't look like the hero type to me.

Sure enough, his instinct for self-preservation won out.

Meon finished sitting down.

The chauffeur closed the door behind him.

I wasn't too worried about Meon having a weapon. Guys like him order other people to do their killing for them; they aren't prepared to do it themselves.

At this point, the chauffeur could've run for it.

There was little I could do to stop him and keep Meon under control, but I guess the idea of life after the Deputy Defense Minister in his charge was killed sufficiently scared him to continue to cooperate.

He got back into the driver's seat.

"Let's go. Just drive around the city while we chat back here."

Meon transitioned quickly to indignation. "What do you want? You must know who I am. There's no way you will get away with this."

"I'm taking a survey of the number of calories consumed per day by the local residents. Let's go."

The chauffeur paused for a second to see if Meon would countermand my order, then started driving figure-eights through the crumbling concrete jungle.

After what happened at the lab, I wanted to pound into the sand the guy who planned it all.

Instead, my hostage negotiation training kicked in. Needed to build a relationship of trust. Lock anger and frustration away. Create a bridge to coax him out on.

Could stay calm if it meant recovering the lab's data and preventing mass destruction.

I let the barrel drift a few inches toward the floor; less intimidating that way. "Must be tough, holding responsibility for the defense of an entire country in your hand. I wouldn't want to do it."

"Yet you do. Your actions here will have consequences."

"I agree. They will."

Taken aback by my easy agreement, but clearly suspicious. "Why have you taken me hostage?"

He peered out the windows of the limo. "I don't see a team with you. Surely your government hasn't sanctioned this action."

"Oh, I'm way out on a limb. Must be desperate yourself to avenge that team you sent into Seoul."

He paused. "What team?"

"Please. We have Rhee and the others captured. I'm sure you're aware we could parade them out in front of the media at any time."

He folded his arms. "I've spoken to representatives of the imperialist intelligence services about this matter. No need for you to invade to discuss it further."

Spoken to whom?

What is that all about?

Well, not what I'm here for, anyway. Better to save other topics for later. "You sound upset by this whole situation. That's understandable. I'm more interested in the drives full of data someone got away with. We tracked it across the DMZ to you."

"I doubt that."

"I'm sure it's tough to understand how we might get across the DMZ and gain information on this side, but as you can see, I'm here in the back of your car holding this handy carbine. That should at least indicate we have some capabilities on this side of the border. Obviously, I can't reveal our sources."

Mostly because I'm relying on guesswork rather than hard info. "How did this whole thing get so out of control, anyway?"

He tightened his grip on his upper arms. "Everything is under control."

We reached a bridge crossing a river on the highway around Kaesong.

I pointed the muzzle back in Meon's direction. "Really? Doesn't look so favorable to you from here. Where's the data? I can either have your driver drop me off after you fill me in, or we can drop your body off a bridge like this one. It's a simple choice."

Okay, so maybe my empathy with enemies still needs a little work.

Meon just sat there.

I moved my finger from the trigger guard to caress the curved piece of metal which barely resisted his death; moved slowly enough to ensure he noticed.

"Last opportunity. Convince me where the data is and you both go free. Otherwise..."

I aimed at his nose. He literally stared death in the face. I wasn't going back without that data. He had to know that.

Too many lives at stake, otherwise.

He nodded. "I'll tell you what you want to know."

I slid my finger back to the trigger guard as a gesture of good faith. "Go on."

"I don't mind telling you because it's secure inside Jiha Base. There's an entire Battalion of artillery guarding it. You'll never even get close."

Now we were making some progress. "An entire Battalion, eh? Then there's no harm in sharing where it's located."

I already knew, of course. Jiha is a major installation, which the joint forces to the south spotted under a nearby mountain years ago at the time the North dug it out and created new camouflaged caverns.

They used it to hide and protect the howitzers threatening nearby Seoul with destruction in the event of a war.

He pointed out the window at the river. "That river carved a path through"—he shifted in his seat and pointed farther left—"that mountain over there. The mountain contains Jiha base. We buried your precious data inside."

At least he was telling the truth about the location of the base.

"I'll need a map and details on how it's guarded."

He emitted a brisk laugh. "I don't concern myself with petty details. That's what I have subordinates for."

Best news I heard all day. I grinned. "Perfect. Instruct the driver to call the one in charge of guarding the data on the car's military radio."

His shoulders sunk. "Very well."

He nodded to the driver, who was watching us in his rear-view mirror. "Call Kwon."

The chauffeur spoke an objection. "We're almost out of petrol, Minister."

Didn't need them able to drive very far, anyway.

"Good." I checked the area for nosy neighbors. "Park in front of that boarded up auto mechanic's shop and turn off the engine, then make the call."

The chauffeur turned on the speaker-phone connected to their military radio network. He requested Kwon, the lieutenant in charge of their defenses.

Used the barrel of my carbine to coax Meon through asking for a report on how safe the data would be within Jiha Base.

He really dug into all the details and then expressed his pleasure at Kwon's preparation.

Wasn't sure if that was out of character and likely to arouse suspicion, or not.

I wanted to destroy Meon for sending soldiers to the lab, but U.S. Army Rangers don't shoot prisoners.

Didn't need their whole Army looking for me in five minutes, either.

So I smashed their radio and confiscated all their weapons and electronics.

When I flipped Meon over and ground his face in the muddy seat to apply tactical restraints to his arms and legs, he got out about half a word of protest before the seat made him unintelligible.

The chauffeur went easier.

Maybe I could preserve the element of surprise at Jiha Base.

"Stay here. Don't follow me. Looks like you've switched the windows with something tougher than stock, but you can try breaking out in an hour. Before then, I may hear you and come back."

Propped my ruck up against the side of the limo. Reached in the driver's side and popped the hood and the trunk.

Locked all the doors before closing them in.

Under the hood, I used my multi-tool to snip through the battery cables. No power, just in case they tried to use something inside the car.

Sliced the hoses for the centralized vacuum door lock system. They expired with a hiss.

Now the car wouldn't unlock, even with a key, even from the inside handles.

Wouldn't keep them in for long, but they wouldn't be leaving quietly.

Anti-theft features like a car's centrally controlled locking system can become vulnerabilities.

With that damage done, I tucked their spare electronics into my ruck.

Considering Kwon's description to Meon of their security measures, I walked around to the trunk and released the spare tire.

That tire would be crucial to my idea for infiltrating the base.

Appropriated the tire iron as well. Could use that to pry off the boards from one of the auto mechanic shop windows.

Time to force my way inside and start scrounging.

Needed heavy tools to crack Jiha Base.

Chapter Thirty:
Recruiting Help

Men like to think they' re in command of all they survey.

Michelle spotted Schnier hanging out on the couch next to Bishop's desk in the RRC HQ, so she went to them.

Glided down onto the red leather sofa next to Schnier.

Gave him her most alluring smile. "We never did finish our date."

Bishop put his head down and pretended to do paperwork on his laptop.

Schnier grinned back at her. "Howdy, Ma'am. We never did, you're right. Did you have something in mind?"

"Thinking a sunset cruise, maybe overlook the DMZ, have some barbecue out on the water?"

"Shore, that could be arranged. Just have to find us a nice comfy boat. May know some folks at the docks. Find us just the right level of coziness."

She ran a finger across the unit scroll on his broad shoulder. "I have it all arranged. Was thinking you could invite your platoon out on the USS Michigan with me. A submarine is always tight quarters."

Bishop guffed. "Uh... sorry, lieutenant. Must have a horny toad caught in my throat."

Schnier glared at Bishop, who looked away and coughed twice into his fist.

He'd better not interfere in her plans.

"Appreciate the invite, Ma'am, but sounds like a mite too much company, if you know what I mean. Why the whole platoon?"

"Well, the deal I made with D.C. was I could only have the sub if I brought along a spec ops platoon to man it. You fellas are man enough for it, aren't you?"

"We've used the Michigan before for covert insertions, if that's what you mean, Ma'am."

She smiled and put her hands on her knees, as if ready to leave. "Then it's all settled. Once I have the exact itinerary from the sub's captain, I'll send it to you. We'll have lots of fun!"

"Settle down there fer a minute. Not fixin' tah run off on a covert sub. Your agency have an actual mission yer recruiting us fer? Mind filling me in on that part?"

His Texas accent got thicker when he was under stress. What a delightful characteristic, to know she'd finally gotten to him.

"Oh, the mission. Yeah"—She leaned forward to invade his personal space by a few inches—"can you keep a secret?"

He leaned back a bit, but kept his voice equally low. "'Course."

Now that she had him on the hook, time to expose her cards, "Did you know Sam's across the border? We might need to pick him up. Maybe even under fire, if things go badly. You're not afraid of a little gunfire, are you?"

Schnier jerked back at her mention of Sam. "What's that dad-blasted techie got himself into now that he needs rescuing?"

"Not for sure he'll need us, but he's after the data they stole from the lab. Vital we recover the data before the DPRK can copy and use it."

"Why should I pay him no never mind? If he wanted help, should've asked for it *before* he headed north."

"Did I ever tell you how I met Sam?"

"Naw. Do I care?"

She crossed her legs. "At the end of my first day of school in 7th grade, the little brothers of the Logan Barrio Locos lined up along the path to the bus pickups. Made a barrier of arms for each of the girls. Slapped us all over. Showed everyone who ruled the neighborhood. Teachers knew better than to interfere."

"So?"

"Sam didn't. Know better, I mean. Or at least, he ignored

whatever danger-sense he had. Jumped right in. Tripped the closest Loco. Took them by surprise. Scattered them just long enough.

"We ran to the bus. Us girls, I mean. Sam got buried by their swinging fists and feet. Ended up in the hospital.

"When he got out, the brother of the guy he tripped shot Sam right outside his house. Hit his arm. More time in the hospital.

"Then they sent him to a new foster home in another neighborhood. Some Korean family looking to give back. The next time I saw him was in high school."

"So he's always been a whole 'nuther crazy, volunteering for beatings."

"Volunteering to help us. Only one there who tried to protect us."

Her story had the advantage of truth behind it.

She needed Schnier's help. "Those bullies in 7th grade weren't all bad. Even though Sam lost the fight, he won something better. A friend.

"The point is, he's counting on me to arrange backup to meet him. I don't get the sub without bringing your platoon, so you're all I've got. Please? Will mean everything to me."

Bishop cleared his throat. "You might see it as an opportunity to see how the other half lives, lieutenant. What it's like to be a support person, rather than just a shooter, for once."

"I guess. I mean, how hard can it be? Hanging out on a covert sub waiting to see if we need to pull Harper's toes out of the fire."

Bishop nodded. "Yes, sir. Used to play sports when I was younger. Coached my daughter's team one year. May find it tougher than you think, sir.

"I couldn't handle more than one season. Easier to play than sit on the sidelines and watch and hope."

Schnier grumbled. "We'll see. Either way, not gonna cross into North Korea without official orders."

Michelle uncrossed her legs and then stood up. "Great! Then it's a date. I'll send you the details."

Volunteers were the best, but if Sam needed them to cross the border, as long as they stayed covert, she'd do whatever it took to convince Schnier.

Long odds never stopped Sam from jumping into a fight.

Meon's chauffeur thudded his head against the dashboard.

Meon shifted on his side to watch him over the seat divider. "Can you break the ties which bind you?"

"I believe so, minister."

His chauffeur wriggled around and positioned his bent legs beneath him on the seat.

Back bent, arms behind, he raised his bound arms and wrists up a few feet.

Slammed his wrists down on his butt, simultaneously twisting them to maximize the pressure on his restraints.

Despite the man's obvious incompetence in leading the imperialist soldier to Meon, he was an experienced bodyguard. Meon would wait and watch him escape.

He raised and slammed his arms backward again.

This time, his wrist restraints broke.

That allowed him to pull apart his arms and crack the ties holding his upper arms.

An insufficiently paranoid political officer didn't last long enough to rise to Meon's present rank.

What if his chauffeur concluded Meon would send him to the camps for his failure to prevent the kidnapping?

With Meon tied up, his chauffeur might slice his throat and claim the imperialist killed him.

"I don't blame you for what happened. Obviously, he ambushed you, just as he ambushed me. Neither of us is to blame. If there is blame to go around, I will direct it at the border guards for allowing an intruder across the DMZ."

His chauffeur grunted once as he flipped himself over.

With his hands available to help, he split the restraints on his legs. "I'll climb over the seat. He may be out there, watching."

"Good idea. In fact, I'm not sure I'll report this incident at all. At least, not until I can order an investigation into how he got here. Help me with these bonds."

His chauffeur clambered over the seat into the rear of the limo.

"Don't want to get the leather even muddier."

He knew who would clean it up. "Never mind that. Just free me."

Meon rolled back over and presented his bound arms.

His restraints parted with a crack as his chauffeur pulled them apart. He also made quick work of those on his legs.

Meon rubbed his wrists. "Good. Do you see the imperialist coward out there?"

The American soldier probably fled as quickly as possible. If he wasn't a coward, he would've killed them both.

They peered out the windows for a few seconds. Made a visual sweep of the area.

His chauffeur finished his first. "No, sir."

Meon tried a door.

Locked.

Flicked the door lock mechanism and tried again.

Nothing. "Can you kick out a window?"

"Of course." His chauffeur lay on his back.

With a powerful thrust, he smashed the passenger side window out.

Its safety glass bent, then folded down and outward. "Easier to replace than a windshield."

Trust a chauffeur to worry more about the car than the situation as a whole.

"Let's go. Need to find someone with a radio to contact Jiha base."

Meon didn't enjoy walking long distances outdoors anymore. "You should probably run down the road ahead of me. Find us a new vehicle. I'll just slow you down."

They climbed out of the car window, his chauffeur supporting Meon as he slipped through behind him.

"Run."

His chauffeur ran as ordered. Vanished down the road, feet churning.

Meon sat on the limo's trunk until his chauffeur returned with a sergeant driving a K131 4x4 utility vehicle.

The off-road vehicle's whip antenna looked promising, tied down to its green canvas roof.

"Connect me with central communications at the main base."

The sergeant saluted and then fiddled with the radio. "I have them for you, sir."

Meon took the round dangling microphone attached to the dashboard.

"Minister Meon here. Get me Lieutenant Kwon at Jiha Base."

"Yes, minister. Right away. We've been attempting to reach you with a message from Colonel Jong-rin. This morning, security discovered the tracks of an infiltrator leading to a hole cut in the wall of the main base."

Too late to do him any good. "Message acknowledged."

"I have Lieutenant Kwon for you, sir."

"Kwon?"

"General?"

"No time to lose. I've received reliable intelligence an attempt will be made on your position soon. Need to prepare a proper welcome. Set a trap. After, we will create the ultimate insurance in the South. Something the Imperialists can't ignore."

"Yes, sir."

"Get Pahk's demolition experts over to the radio with you. I want no misunderstanding of my orders. This will be delicate work."

"Right away, sir."

One arrogant imperialist soldier thought he could knock out an entire platoon of special forces soldiers?

Between Pahk's men, Kwon, and his recently named Goshawk Device, Meon was confident things would turn out fine for him, despite this recent embarrassment.

He'd even send a reply to his contact across the border.

No, better to wait on that until Kwon was closer to being in position.

Wouldn't want to spoil the surprise.

The coward who tied them up would die at Jiha Base.

Meon would hold all the cards. He'd force the Imperialists to do exactly what he required of them.

Chapter Thirty-One:
All Wet

Best to just get it over with.

I dove into the icy river under the highway bridge. My testicles contracted.

A neoprene combat face mask and gloves protected my face and hands from the cold swishing around them. Dual-layer waterproof jacket slowed down water entry.

Designed to lock in heat to protect from infrared detection, my jacket also did a decent job keeping my tan t-shirt warm from body heat.

Was used to cold surf, but needed more layers under my pants.

Hadn't planned to swim a mountain stream before I crossed the border, but on the bright side, the remaining mud rapidly washed away.

Wouldn't die of hypothermia right away, but I'd better watch for the symptoms.

I dragged the spare tire I'd taken from Meon's Mercedes off the gravelly bank and into the river.

Climbed on top of the tire. Pressed it down with my body weight.

Too light.

Balanced on top. Picked up the toolbox I'd hauled from the mechanic's garage.

This time I sunk deeper, but remained too buoyant.

Temporarily replaced the toolbox on the bank. Strapped my full pack on my back.

Lay on my side and pulled the toolbox back onto the tire, curled into my stomach.

Unless I wanted to pull boulders from the mud, this would be my final try.

Had to work. Didn't see any other way to infiltrate Jiha base.

Enough weight to sink.

Before I needed to breathe water, I dropped two wrenches over the side, which made the toolbox just light enough I could float precariously with my head barely above the river water.

My tools, backpack, and I drifted downstream on the spare tire.

Passed industrial containers haphazardly scattered along the top of the banks.

Floated under a rusty iron footbridge, then beneath a pair of twenty-foot long concrete bridges the width of one vehicle.

Must either not get much traffic, or else take turns crossing.

No cars on the roads I passed.

The Jiha river floated me out of the Kaesong Industrial area.

My teeth chattered.

Toes and fingers were fine, the Army provides good boots and gloves, but my inner core gradually froze from the waist inward.

Up ahead, the river swept below the side of a cliff, entering through curved carved rock at the base.

No more air there.

I inhaled for five seconds.

Exhaled. Inhaled. Exhaled.

Three more times. Built up the oxygen stored in my blood.

As I floated along, closer and closer to the entrance, I fumbled at the tire's valve.

Couldn't add weight now, but could reduce the just over 60 psi I'd filled it with to a lower pressure.

Too slow.

The tire bounced off the rock.

My pack cushioned some of the direct blow, but I scrambled to keep the toolbox on the tire.

Sucked in air.

Held my breath.

Opened a short screwdriver on my multi-tool.

Pushed over the valve core with it for a few seconds to relieve the pressure.

Just enough to balance with me and everything the tire carried under water.

Released air bubbled up past my face mask.

A lot depended on how fast the current ran underground. How far the underground portion extended.

Didn't have good numbers on either of those variables.

The little light from above vanished; total blackout as I passed under the cliff's edge.

Gripped the tire valve. Couldn't lose that while underwater.

Not and live.

Counted the seconds.

Freedivers going after pearls can stay calm and under water for ten or twenty minutes. An average person, maybe two or three.

First minute went fine. During the second minute, I strained against the carbon dioxide building up in my system.

Pushed back the mental urge to breathe.

Ears clogged with water, so I squished in my protective earpieces. Turned on *California Girls*.

At least my ruggedized phone worked fine underwater. Except as an actual phone, of course.

Better to remain calm and save oxygen.

Focus on math or something.

Let's see, fast river currents are up to 3.1 meters/second. This one felt slower, call it a 1.5, a little under half that. 150 seconds, so 150 meters plus half that again, 225. Plus or minus a wide margin of error.

Maybe half that, or double that, at the most.

For some reason, my damaged right knee ached.

Come on, I constantly iced it in the river, didn't I?

Should be numb by now, not hurting.

Surely I'd break out of this watery coffin soon.

Expelled a little air.

Stuck my mouth right above the valve. Triggered the pressure regulator.

Air bubbled out like an upside down drinking fountain; air

floating up rather than water falling down.

Few seconds of high pressure was enough to give me a new gas mix with more oxygen.

Stale and rubbery.

Tire sank lower in the water.

Dumped another couple of wrenches.

Had somewhere between 12 and 20 minutes of air available from the tire.

Oxygen use depended on how calm I stayed.

How much air I lost.

Side of my pack brushed against the stone ceiling. A burst of lopsided friction spun everything in the water.

Lost track of which direction I floated.

Strained to hold on to the tire valve with one hand and the toolbox with my other.

At least I wasn't muddy.

Lost in the dark. Desperate to breathe. Balls freezing.

But not muddy.

More air from opening the valve. Tried dropping a hammer this time.

Smoother impact on the ceiling; more prepared for the contact.

Must be five or six-hundred meters now. Dim green light shone through the water. I regained blurry underwater sight.

Dropped three more wrenches. Three left; almost done with the set.

The buoyancy of the tire popped me up on top of the water again. I gasped mouthfuls of air.

Mouthfuls of diesel truck fumes. Almost worse than the compressed tire air.

A road carved out of the waterway extended the cavern to one side.

Halogen mining work lamps clamped randomly to wooden beams and crosspieces cast shadows from stalactites into the water.

A truck's headlights threatened from the tunnel road.

The river crashed into another cavern wall.

Sucked dirty air into my lungs. Hissed it out of the tire's valve.

Sank out of sight just before the light ran out again.

Using this underwater approach would've intimidated a platoon of SEALs.

Jiha base, here I come.

Kwon bounced up on the truck's passenger seat.

Shot out a hand to regain his balance.

Caught himself staring at the Jiha river running under stalactites beside the tunnel road, rather than paying attention to the truck's path.

Something dark floating on the surface of the river.

Probably his imagination, or perhaps some piece of trash sucked in.

Hopefully wasn't big enough to clog the steel netting at the entrance to the cavern, but defending that wasn't his problem anymore.

The truck's headlights picked up the entrance of the next tunnel.

The men in the back sat around the Goshawk device and the data drives.

No risk of the tunnel's roof chopping their heads off, but they reflexively ducked down a few inches anyway as the truck exited the wider river cavern.

This time, he'd gotten his orders properly updated. Didn't want to be responsible on paper for not using the special train with a secure escort.

The train they'd been waiting for.

His new orders were to ship the data on the next regular military cargo train heading north.

That'd get the critical information away from the border as fast as possible.

After their stop at the train station, Meon had special instructions he wanted to deliver in person.

Kwon would lead Pahk and his new team across the DMZ again, following in the footsteps of Team Goshawk.

Revenge for their deaths would be sweet. Meon promised that much, at least.

Kwon wondered about that, but this time his mission would

be a *complete* success and his team would return alive.

Chapter Thirty-Two:
Foreign Entanglements

Grew colder in the dark every second as the mountain swallowed the river.

Had to adjust my depth again and again.

Ran myself out of tools.

Needing oxygen, I drank more hits of rubbery air from the valve.

The underside of the tire scraped across the round pebbles on the river bottom.

Dumped the empty toolbox overboard.

Tire floated in the middle of the current again.

Last opening was at least 400 meters back. Better be another one before the tire completely deflated.

My shoulder scraped the ceiling. Not enough small weights left to make minor adjustments with.

As I floated, I removed my pack from my back.

Felt around inside my pack. Touched items in the dark with my fingers. Remembered what remained.

Had rations, weapons, extra loaded magazines, some line, half a dozen M86 PDMs.

Didn't want to lose the 21 grams of Composition A5 they each contained, but I could dump a few if I needed to.

Drew another breath from the tire.

Established a new equilibrium in the water.

Back slammed into a mess of thick steel wire. Impact forced precious air from my lungs.

Stay calm.

More air.

Triggered the tire valve again. Drank up almost the last of the remaining life.

Current pushed me up against a web of steel.

Dropped the tire for a second.

The current plastered it against the netting.

Felt around. Six-inch holes between the multi-threaded cables.

Grasped the cabling for leverage.

Swam down a few meters.

The net attached to a steel beam laid across the riverbed.

Swam up.

Anchor points in the rock above. Securely held.

Methodical placement.

Without dragging a tire with me against the current, and thus no extra air, I might swim 1.7 m/s for a while, barely exceeding the speed of the current hauling me in the other direction.

No way to return to the most recent opening.

I'd burn up all my oxygen well before that and couldn't even make headway swimming against the current if I tried to take the tire with me.

Could really use some actual scuba gear and flippers right now. Not to mention my wetsuit.

Soundtrack reached *Kokomo*.

Nice *warm* water in the Caribbean.

Dream on.

No more distractions.

Opened my multi-tool. Spread the wire cutter blades around a cable.

Squeezed.

Nothing.

Again, harder.

Tool slipped.

Felt along the cable. Nothing more than a scratch.

Too thick.

Time for a bigger persuader.

One more hit from the tire.

This time the air bubbled out weak, anemic; fighting the external pressure.

I removed a wedge-shaped M86 PDM from my pack. The mine fit into the gap between cables embedded in the ceiling.

Five more, one at a time, filled five holes in the netting near the beam at the bottom.

Couldn't take my pack with me, so at best I could control the explosions.

Removed the safety clip from the M86 PDM near the ceiling.

Once armed, the mine had a 60 second delay until it fired out four triplines designed to catch pursuers.

Normally, plenty of time to create distance if you're running madly through the wilderness.

Swimming?

At a net 0.2 m/s against the current, I'd get 12 meters away before they deployed.

Coincidentally, the official effective range of the mine extended 12 meters.

That's in open air. Water doesn't compress like air does.

Instead, the shrapnel would stop within a few meters of meeting water resistance.

Unfortunately, that same lack of compression by water increased the lethality of the explosive shock-wave. 100 meters would certainly be safe.

If the other five mines didn't explode together and increase the safety distance even further.

No way I could make 100 meters, but what choice did I have?

Running out of air. Caught like a fish in a steel net.

Had to try.

Last breath from the tire. Tucked my multi-tool away in a cargo pocket.

Set my boots against the steel netting. Bent at the knees.

Reached up. Pulled the arming strap.

Felt the rotating metal linkage inside break the shorting bar.

That forced a steel ball against the battery and broke a glass ampule holding electrolyte which activated the reserve battery, powering up the mine.

Legs are stronger than arms. I pushed off from the steel cables.

Hands ahead of me in a prayer-shape to break the water.

Angled downward.

Right knee tweaked in pain. Not recovered enough.

Glided until the current began to catch me.

Kicked with my feet. Pulled with my arms scooping water out of the way.

Reached the bottom.

Dug in with my hands, counteracting the current, pulling myself forward.

Got my feet down. Pushed off again.

Mostly used my left leg. Slight upward angle this time.

Too slow.

Pulse pounded rapidly in my ears. Competed with a desperate need to breathe.

Stay calm to use the least oxygen. Exert as much effort as possible to get away in time.

Contradictory imperatives.

My folded hands touched the rocky ceiling. I flipped over. Used my natural buoyancy to keep me against the roof.

Scrambled with my hands and feet like an upside-down mountain climber.

Shoved off through the water with every hand or foothold I could find.

Found every stone ridge not worn down by the passing water.

Any advantage to get away faster.

Sixty seconds expired.

A piston in the M86 fired.

Seven triplines released.

Three would hit the ceiling uselessly.

Four more would shoot down and out, the current pulling them into the steel webbing once they deployed to the bottom of the river.

Pulled and kicked my way another few meters. Right knee twinged every time I thrust off the rocks.

After deploying the triplines, the mine is programmed with a 10 second delay. That's to make sure the lines have time to settle after deployment.

Wouldn't want them to trigger the mine before actual movement tripped one.

Ten more seconds. Ten more meters.

Any second now, the mine would explode.

No more oxygen in my lungs anyway.

The underwater cave lit up with a flash of light behind me. Drove out the darkness for a moment.

Scrambled another half-step.

The electric detonator triggered the detcord and liquid propellant. A 21 gram sphere of Composition A5 explosive blew.

Shot fragments in all directions. A sphere of death.

Water must've stopped and cooled the hot fragments before any hit the other mines.

No more detonated.

After the flash, the shock-wave passed through my body.

Too fast to push much water. Not powerful enough at this distance to crush lungs. Earpieces protected eardrums.

Gnarly wave-front arrived a moment later. Slapped me into the rock ceiling.

Rattled my noggin even more.

Good thing I was riding this wave new school.

I *think* *Good Vibrations* started playing. Only one earpiece produced sound in my ear.

My head was somehow muddy and sharply in pain at the same time.

Tried to relax and float. Scraped along where the river met the stone ceiling.

Floated down with the current.

Must use as little oxygen as possible.

Only sharp fragments of splintered stone remained where anchors held the top of the netting before. Frayed steel cabling bunched and floated in the water; cut at my gloves.

Could've been my large and small intestines. I shuddered in the cold water.

The blast wave must've shredded my pack and the other M86 PDMs.

I thanked Archimedes and his spiritual descendants that the distance and wave reflections off the stone were enough to prevent sympathetic detonation of the Comp A5 inside the other mines.

Murky river water glowed a few meters beyond the net-line.

I swam to the surface.

Place better be empty, 'cause my carbine was somewhere on the river bottom with the shredded PDMs and whatever remained of my dinner.

Flowing cold water suppressed any residual heat. The explosion's easiest outlet had been up and into the wider cavern above.

Water still dripped from a dark gray splash pattern on the ceiling and the closer cave walls.

At least I had my phone, multi-tool, and a combat knife.

Could maybe take one guy with that, if he didn't hear my panting and gasping from when I breached the surface and ambush me.

This cave opening didn't smell of diesel fumes. More like dirty socks and a smoky kimchi campfire.

Couldn't win, but was grateful for the air, anyway.

Rolled up on the rocky river edge.

Hid behind a shattered toilet and shredded camp shower to observe.

The cavern featured a welded steel vault covered in explosives.

Cozy.

Detcord trailed from the vault to what looked suspiciously like more explosives along a steel plate wall and door exiting the room.

Dangerous.

An old camp stove, piled high with ash and twisted-melted plastic. A dozen bare wooden cots.

No one home.

What if all the explosives wired up to the vault and the door had sympathetically detonated when the mine went off?

Or if I'd tried to blow my way in through the door?

Or even used a blowtorch to cut through the steel?

Despite the relative warmth of the air compared to the river, my testicles shriveled up a bit more at the thought.

Kwon and his driver must've gotten loose faster than I planned. This wasn't random; I'd been setup.

Only lived because I'd come in via the river instead of the cave system.

Where was the stolen data?

Somewhere else in Jiha Base? With Minister Meon?

Could I still find and destroy it?

Didn't see how, not with the enemy warned and on full alert.

I'd failed.

Something metal clanked against the other side of the steel plate door leading to the rest of the cave system.

Rung out across the cavern.

Rattled the door booby-trapped with enough explosives to vaporize anything human inside this cavern.

Like me, for instance.

Chapter Thirty-Three:
Considerable Chance of Big Booms

Meon Lon-chun stared at the red phone squealing on his desk. The special line to the Supreme Leader's office.

Despite the steam radiator's struggles to keep up with the cold, Meon pulled at his green collar to loosen it.

Couldn't keep the Supreme Commander of the People's Army waiting.

He snatched up the phone. "Deputy Minister Meon here, Supreme Leader."

The woman's lilting voice didn't quite sneer at him, "Wait one moment for the Chairman."

A click as the office in Pyongyang made the final connection.

"Meon?"

The matter-of-fact way the man who held more than one nation's life in his hand spoke sent shivers through his back muscles.

"This is Meon, Marshal."

"I'm told your mission to the South failed to secure any material samples."

Failure might get him killed.

"That's true, sir, but we have the lab's data. It'll be on the way north on the next train."

"Don't argue with me. Excuses aren't becoming of a Deputy Minister. Our scientists will require additional time because of your failure.

"Even now, the Imperialists parade men they claim are your special forces in front of the news cameras. They've announced new sanctions on advanced electronics and luxury goods."

"You can trust me to make this right, sir."

"Why did I hear about the infiltration of your base from Colonel Jong-rin rather than you?"

Base security was supposed to keep quiet about that. Spies everywhere.

Meon couldn't afford to look like he was keeping secrets. "A minor incident, sir. A single enemy soldier is being dealt with. Nothing important enough to disturb you with."

"I'm disturbed by your lack of efficiency and candor. You will report to my office in Pyongyang no later than tomorrow night. We will discuss your failures in person."

Another click as the line disconnected.

What good was his political capital if society threw him out?

If he went to Pyongyang as ordered, would he ever return?

How could he forestall his fate?

He buried his face in his hands.

I'd need help to make it out of the North alive.

Put the pounding on the steel door out of my mind. Fired up my phone.

No signal, buried here in the mountain.

Wait, no cellular signal, but a local wireless network presented itself in Korean Hangul characters.

Opened the Aircrack app on my phone. Set it to capture WiFi data.

Muffled Korean voices replaced the pounding outside.

Obviously, my earlier explosion drew attention, despite its mostly underwater nature.

No time to panic.

Jogged over to the explosives wired to the door. Traced the strands of cabling from the sensors to an anti-tamper device connected to the detonators.

These guys were serious about making sure anyone breaking in wouldn't survive. Maybe infiltrating by myself wasn't the best choice after all.

My phone dinged in my remaining earpiece.

By monitoring the packets transmitted over the air between devices, Aircrack stole the WiFi network's encryption key.

Didn't have the time it would've taken to break a state-of-the-art wireless network, but outlying DPRK units get crappy outdated electronics which they then tend to misuse.

All the experts are in Pyongyang, stealing hard currency for the regime from the rest of the world.

My phone connected to the local WiFi. Ran a quick network discovery search while I walked back to the river.

A file server. Perfect.

Hadn't separated whatever they used this wireless network for from their hardwired network. Left to the end users, convenience trumps security every time.

No trace of the stolen data, but a bunch of paperwork and orders.

I compressed and slurped any text-based documents down to my phone and then deleted them.

Might have backups, but would at least lead to a little confusion as they dealt with their missing paperwork. Even more than most, the People's Army runs on forms.

If the data I needed to recover had been here, it wasn't any longer, but I had a more urgent problem.

Any minute now, someone on the other side of that door would get a bright idea, like cutting through the steel with a blowtorch. Guaranteed to set off the explosives on this side as the metal heated up.

Really didn't want to be here when that happened.

The river swept out of the cavern on the side opposite the one I'd arrived from.

No tire to provide air.

No extra equipment from my ruck.

No carbine, even, unless I wanted to figure out a way to drag the river bottom for it.

No way to know how much farther underground the freezing river went before emerging into the light.

Maybe no air.

Just a claustrophobic hole through the cavern wall.

Heavy water ahead.

I took a few deep breaths to build up my oxygen supply. Then a few more.

Stood on the stone riverbank.

Dove.

Once more into the cold, cold breach.

Meon leaned back in his desk chair and closed his eyes. Rubbed peppermint oil into his temples.

After that call from Supreme Leader, his headache from last Friday was bound to return soon.

If he returned to Pyongyang, it was possible he'd be given a reminder of why failure wasn't to be contemplated.

Might be survivable.

On the other hand, might be stripped of his rank as an example and sent to a labor battalion or the re-education camps to die of slow starvation.

Not pleasant.

Last year, the Party Chairman ordered the Minister of Education shot for his bad attitude after he failed to maintain the proper posture during a publicity event.

The embarrassment and loss of face from the recent news stories would most likely sentence Meon to an imaginative form of execution.

What could he do to save himself?

Did he have any alternatives, except to send Kwon and make a deal?

Meon tapped his desk seven times for luck.

If he made a good enough deal, he might even come out with a better material life in retirement, although it would be difficult to improve upon holding the life and death of so many people in his hands.

No self-illusions. He enjoyed wealth, but power over others thrilled him deep within.

Perhaps he could engineer a minor coup somewhere with his new wealth and take over a small island?

Probably best not to call that much attention to himself for a while.

What else could he do, except depart in style?

An efficient rap at the door.

That would be Kwon. Perfect timing. "Enter."

Kwon took up a stiff posture and saluted. "Reporting as ordered, General."

Meon screwed the dropper back into his peppermint bottle and placed it in his desk drawer. "Relax, nephew."

Kwon bowed to a respectful degree.

"Yes, uncle. I've delivered the data to the train station. The device is outside with Pahk's men in the truck."

"Good work. Your new mission requires the utmost secrecy. The data will be safe enough heading north while you're gone. Tell no one; the Imperialists can't sniff out a scent which isn't there."

"It shall be done as you command, uncle."

"We've reached a delicate stage of my negotiations for peace with the South. We need hostages, as many as possible.

"You will lead the greatest hostage taking the world has ever seen. Capture an entire city of ten million inhabitants, including tens of thousands of enemy soldiers. Historians will record your role in the key event which unified Korea."

Kwon bowed briefly. "A great honor, uncle. Thank you for your trust."

"My secretary has a mobile phone for you to use. She's pre-programmed my direct number into it. It will work here and across the border. No cutouts, we can't risk betrayal.

"Except for local tactical communication, your team will maintain complete radio silence. Ensure Pahk knows this is my specific order.

"There is too much at stake. I will communicate with you via that phone. You are to negotiate with no one; accept orders from no one else."

"Roger, sir."

Kwon stared at the red phone on the desk. He shook his head. "If I may clarify, General, I presume you mean no one but you and our Supreme Leader? As a hypothetical?"

Meon considered saying no, but if the issue ever arose, it would be too late, anyway. "Don't be an idiot, lieutenant, if you receive a direct order from his Supreme Greatness, you will of course obey it. But no one else, not even the Defense Minister himself. The risk is too great."

The risk to Meon's skin was too great, but Kwon didn't need to know that.

"My apologies, sir."

Meon removed from his desk a button on a thin stem. The stem attached to a set of wires and a box of electronics. Handed the contraption to Kwon.

"The technicians have prepared a dead-man's switch for the device. You will take it with you. Install it after you settle into position. The weak bastards in the South won't dare attack you. You will return victorious with Pahk's men after I negotiate our great victory."

Kwon turned the switch over in his hands to gaze at each side. Straightened his back. "Sir."

"The first decision point will be after you, Pahk, and his team transport the Goshawk device. Call me when you're secure on the other side of the DMZ and I'll deliver further instructions."

Kwon hesitated for a moment.

"It shall be as you command, General. I'll be right back with the mission orders for you to sign authorizing our departure across the DMZ."

Meon waved his hand at the door in dismissal. "Conquer the Dominionists with great dispatch!"

"Sir!" Kwon pivoted and then strode out of the room.

Surely even the Imperialists won't risk the destruction of Seoul?

It'll all work out for Meon, even if Kwon is required to make the ultimate sacrifice.

No turning back from destiny now.

Chapter Thirty-Four: Learning from Failure

I rode the fade, the most powerful part of the current, making minimal movements to conserve oxygen.

Icy water surrounded me inside the black hole exit channel. Periodically ran my hand over the rough stone above me.

Needed the river to reach a point where the cave roof climbed enough to clear the water.

Hunted for open air.

Flash of a glow from behind lit up the water. Two seconds later a shock-wave reverberated in the enclosed river.

Caught me.

Tightened muscles for impact.

Waves broke around me. Reflected. Put me through the dishwasher.

Shoved me into the ceiling. Scraped my left shoulder along the rocks.

Stabbing shoulder pain outbid my aching knee for attention.

Enemy soldier must've opened the door back in the cavern.

No time to rub my shoulder.

Relaxed my muscles to consume less air.

All my oxygen-fed energy must go to sustaining life and maintaining forward progress as the current ragdolled me through the underwater cave system.

Dark thoughts filled the shadowy river hollow.

Didn't set the trap the soldiers in the cavern triggered, but I bore at least partial responsibility. Might as well have been the one to move the data away, also.

Meon must've warned them. Warned them after I let him live.

If I'd brought Schnier and his team in, maybe there would've been another way.

Could've left someone to guard Meon and his chauffeur. Clean up our trail at the main base.

Ensure this visit wasn't noticed in time for them to escape with the data and leave booby-trapped explosives in their place.

Maybe there'd be something in the orders database I recovered to tell me where the data went. Some way to gain victory out of this disaster.

Light ahead grew stronger.

Probably not just oxygen deprivation, playing tricks on my mind. Actual sunlight through the water.

I cut through the water with more purpose. Could literally see the light at the end of the tunnel.

Broke the surface with a gasp.

Clean, clear, crisp winter air. Pure as the snow driven into my face by the early morning wind.

At least the cold hadn't frozen the river's surface. Gossamer snow melted as fast as it hit.

Running water takes longer to freeze.

Wasn't in any condition to bash my way out through a layer of ice.

Dumped myself onto a strip of sandy beach between two rocky cliffs. Not much vegetation, but my fire starters went down with my pack, anyway.

The horizon lit up with early morning light. A stark difference to inside underwater caves.

Sunlight caught one cliff-top, but didn't yet light all the deep shadows here at the crevice bottom.

The Army designed my clothing to wick moisture to the exterior. All I had to do was get enough internal warmth to make it work.

Needed to walk fast enough to generate heat, but not so fast I began to sweat and created new moisture.

Could use something to eat and something warm to drink to up my body temperature, but the few scraggly bushes along the cliffs here wouldn't be very appetizing and my packed-in meals were riding the river somewhere.

Climbed along the bank until the dirt widened out. The opposed cliffs were narrowest where the river emerged to create this fissure, but broadened the farther I traveled.

Water carved a higher and wider path. Left room to hike.

Used my phone to check my position.

Need to preserve it's life; spare batteries drowned along with rations and rifle.

Not much signal from the closest mobile tower penetrated the rocky cleft, but I forwarded the files I'd taken from the mountain base to Lee with a note to let me know if there was anything related to the missing data in there.

My email would get through eventually.

Crack!

Bullet whined off the cliff-face in front of me.

Too many echos to find the enemy.

Smooth is fast.

Slipped my phone into a pocket. Slid back into the freezing water. Floated away on the current.

No telltale splashing.

Three more shots. Nowhere close to me.

The shooters gave up on their lack of targets in the shadows.

Enemy guards, some kind of lookouts, on top of the cliffs.

Some idiot turned on an artificial light source at the bottom of the cliff and then lost all situational awareness by staring down at it, oblivious to the possibility of an enemy in the area.

Firing almost straight down without a ranging shot is tough, but I was still lucky to be alive.

Needed to figure out exactly where I was to know where to go, but I couldn't risk my phone screen again without concealment for the light.

Not until I left the shadows, at least.

They'd be either radioing ahead or running along the tops of the cliffs to intercept me at the only exit, wherever this river led out of the mountain.

Or both.

I needed to fix this.

All of it, not just the part where I wouldn't make it out of the

DPRK alive, but also losing the data. Of course, I no longer knew where the data was located.

Needed to get on the move to stop that shark Meon's plans, and soon.

Just didn't know how.

Prepared with the proper paperwork, Kwon's second time through the DMZ tunnel went smoother than the first.

Of course, to be polite, he had to sit through five minutes of the border guards on duty explaining how an Imperialist special forces brigade supposedly burst through and tied up their comrades before vanishing into the night.

Kwon tried to have sympathy, he really did, but he also remembered the hard time those guys had given him before.

No real evidence of large numbers of troops traversing the tunnel. Lack of footprints in the mud don't lie.

Maybe one or two guys, at most.

He had Pahk order one of his men to clean mud off the carts, then they took their positions.

Kwon in front, Pahk at the rear, the Goshawk device safely tucked in the middle, two men tasked to simply ride and secure it in place from both ends.

More work for the rest of them, pulling on the ropes with their gloved hands, but this time Kwon had a good mental gauge of how far the tunnel extended.

Cart wheels hummed. Their movements synchronized to an unheard rhythm.

He stared at the ceiling. Blocked out the repetitive scenery. Arrived at the far end quickly.

Time to "Achieve a Great Victory" once again.

He staged Pahk's men after the final left turn, inside the 50 meter tunnel to the greenhouse exit.

Left the Goshawk device behind on the carts.

Could bring it forward once they secured the area, but if they failed, it needed to be ready to return across the DMZ.

Taking the lead, Kwon slithered forward.

Peered around the stack of irrigation boxes partially blocking the tunnel exit.

One enemy soldier.

Korean military policeman, by his uniform markings. He sat on the dirt floor and leaned his back up against the greenhouse exit.

Kwon sighted his rifle on the MP's chest.

The enemy soldier wasn't watching the tunnel. Instead, he devoured some sort of sandwich in a roll.

Smacked his lips with every bite.

Kwon signed to the soldier behind him. Single unaware enemy.

The soldier handed his rifle to the man behind him.

Glided past Kwon.

Leapt out from behind the equipment.

An alarm beeped a warning when he crossed the greenhouse.

The MP looked up.

Threw his sandwich to the ground

Kwon's soldier pounced on him. The two men rolled over in the dirt.

The MP ended up on top.

Kwon reversed his rifle. Butt-stroked him in the back of the head.

MP's eyes rolled up in his head. He collapsed to the dirt floor.

No more struggle.

Kwon moved to the edge of the steel-hoop covered fabric exit into the field.

Another of Pahk's men smashed the box emitting the alarm.

One annoyance gone.

The other four spread out in the greenhouse.

These walls wouldn't provide cover against rifle fire. With them all concealed, maybe any MPs outside would come check things out.

False alarms from the motion sensor must be a frequent event.

Kwon lay down just inside the opening. Bent to the side for a quick view.

Two more MPs outside wearing plate carriers.

One stood and leaned against their military truck's hood, smoking. The other pointed at the greenhouse with his left arm.

Right at Kwon.

Drew a sidearm from a belt holster with his right hand.

Kwon slid his scope picture over to the reacting MP's face. Ten meters. Ludicrously short range for a scoped rifle.

Broke the shot with a double-tap.

The second MP dropped his smoke. Snatched at his waist.

Crack, crack, from behind him. One of Pahk's snipers took his own suppressed pair of shots.

The second MP slumped to the group before Kwon targeted him.

Their four bangs blurred together in one indistinct crash of destruction to their enemies. Great teamwork.

No mercy for the enemy.

They'd killed his last team. This trip would be different.

He maneuvered out to the gravel parking lot. No sign of anyone else; just two broken enemy bodies near the truck.

Kwon swallowed the trickle of bile threatening to escape his throat.

Pahk followed the rest of his men out of the greenhouse. They secured the rice paddy farm with a quick visual search and leapfrog.

Kwon sent Pahk to collect the enemy's identification.

They'd become MPs, at least the three of them who rode in the truck's cab. The men in back wouldn't be readily seen, anyway.

Pointed. Sent four men back into the tunnel.

"Bring up the device. Load it into the truck."

Time to call in the decision point. He unlocked the phone Meon's secretary had given him.

Called the only saved number. "Point Greenhouse secure."

Meon wasted no time. "Proceed to the tower. Next check-in there if no delays."

Risky to parade through Seoul with a nuclear device, but he wouldn't let down his team and his family these noms murdered.

"Roger. Proceeding in the guise of MPs to the tower."

Meon disconnected.

Namsan Tower in Seoul symbolized the strength of the enemy. On top of a hill, jutting 500 meters farther into the sky, any weapon detonated there would be the equivalent of an air-burst, multiplying its destructive potential.

No other way to bypass the Imperialist Army's air defenses, so only Kwon and Pahk's team could ensure the threat was real. Their threat would ensure Korea finally reunited.

Kwon's loss of his team would be the catalyst for peace.

Besides, isolated within the highest point in that part of the city, the tower would be easy to defend.

No time for doubts. Duty, instead.

Chapter Thirty-Five: Judgement Day

Not much cover, but almost complete concealment.

I rested on my back in a gully.

Stared up at a bush. The bush punished any movement with scrapes and stabs.

In my defense, I didn't discover the thorns until I was halfway camouflaged.

Just like I didn't expect Meon to get free and back in communication with his men to warn them.

Slogging through the mud and a minefield, freezing my cojones off in the Jiha river, wasn't worth these results.

I'd cleared the canyon's exit before the enemy could cut me off, but they were still out there.

Seeking me.

My backside froze to the ground.

Could try to wait until dark, but the North Korean Army, especially their border guards, had extensive experience hunting people.

No, needed to move my pile of aches off this arctic wasteland. Get back up on the board.

Hopefully, literally.

Checked my exact location on a satellite view of the area.

I'd never complain about military electronics ruggedization again, even if my phone did cost four times as much.

Jiha base would've alerted the tangos between here and the DMZ. They'd form a cordon far enough away to prevent me from slipping past before they walked the hills and canyons to flush me out.

A rock tumbled down a hillside in the distance, clanging off the stony ground.

Half-klick away.

Even if I wanted to climb back up that mountain the river just flushed me out of, going back the way I came wasn't an option.

Excited shouts in Korean echoed off the stone walls to the south.

Break time over.

Focused on the soldiers hunting me, I jumped when my phone vibrated. The screen showed Yang Hyo-jin's name and number.

"Harper", I whispered.

"Sam, I've been working on my detector. These readings don't make sense. Keep getting false positives. Could use a fresh perspective on the problem, if you'd come by the lab."

"Love to, but I'm in the middle of something here. Can it wait a few days?"

"Never mind, Lieutenant Harper. I'll figure it out on my own."

Click.

Women! I'll never figure 'em out.

Just have to explain later, assuming she'd let me.

Back in range of the cell towers across the border, my phone had service again. Time for my ace in the hole.

I texted Michelle coordinates for a spot in the Ryesong river.

Now I just had to get there, while a couple border guard battalions looked for me.

From here, could only make it farther north or west, away from the bases for the soldiers hunting me.

North took me farther into the country, so west it was.

On the map, the fastest path west would be to go back and follow the Riha river, but according to intelligence reports the conscript labor troops farmed rice along the river, using the water to flood the paddies.

Too much risk of discovery if I exited the easy way.

No, west through the canyons was my only hope. At least I had a satellite map on my phone to guide my 10k hike through rough terrain. That'd keep me out of blind canyons and dead-ends.

My phone screen died while I was staring at it, figuring out the best route west. Military electronics ruggedization sucks.

Should be enough battery remaining.

Hit my phone a couple of times.

No better.

Pocketed it. Maybe it'd work once it dried out more.

The guards would expect me to take the shortest routes. If I traveled the hard way, maybe I could evade them and salvage my life from this solo mission that traitorous bureaucrat Rhee forced on me.

A crack between cliffs to the west was the first path I remembered from the screen.

I rolled out from the bush without attracting additional notice, but scraped the side of my face across the rough branches.

Ran toward the crack.

Stayed low to avoid discovery.

Couldn't get Rhee's betrayal and losing the data out of my mind to save my life.

He'd used *my* team's report to help the North Koreans infiltrate the lab.

Who was I kidding?

The border guards might as well capture me, or even shoot me. I'd failed again.

Gone it alone.

Now my weapons and supplies were at the bottom of an underground river, the data gone. My only clue to its location the orders database I'd stolen, saved on my useless phone.

After coming to Korea, everything I'd done turned into a SNAFU.

I'd tried to rely on others for this mission without any success to show for it.

What's the point?

My bum knee failed me. Didn't retract fast enough to lift my foot high enough.

A root jutting six inches out of the dirt tripped me. I rolled on my shoulder across the stony ground.

Ouch.

Popped back up. Shook my head. Ran on.

Hazards of rapid cross-country travel.

Who could I trust, anyway?

Not my knee.

Maybe Hyo-jin, although I probably just alienated her by blowing her off on the phone.

That, I could explain, if she didn't kill me for crossing the border without telling her.

Bishop always looked out for me, even when I put him in awkward positions with the CO.

Michelle, if my eSurfboard showed up at the right time and place. We'd see about that, but she'd been my friend since high school, after all.

Lee was tough for me to read, but he'd never let me down before.

Not Schnier. Definitely not Schnier.

Not any farther than I could toss him, and that dude was too big to throw back to his ranch, anyway.

This path turned into a game trail, four inches wide. The trail curved around bushes and into the canyon.

Launched myself from a boulder. Dodged a pile of brush.

Not exactly keeping my head down.

Maybe just wasn't the right guy for this mission?

Needed a real team.

Guys to carry backup communications, weapons, ammo, explosives; cover each other's backs.

Wasn't me.

Should've turned this over to Schnier's platoon and just stayed home.

Naw, not Schnier.

SOCKOR? They could order some snake eaters across the DMZ. Plenty of SEALs lying around. Heck, had the whole 8th Army at their disposal.

A bullet whined off the boulder behind me. I ducked instinctively. The rifle crack echoed off the cliff walls to either side.

Spotted me again.

No time for distractions. *Sprint.*

Run around boulders, under thorny limbs, through openings.

Anything to escape the soldiers hunting me.

Must not catch me. Had a duty to fulfill. A responsibility.

Maybe I couldn't do that without relying on others to help me, but I also couldn't do it laying in a torture chamber, waiting for the State Department to pay them off for my return.

Lungs burned with every forced exhalation. Left side demanded I stop; feed my muscles oxygen.

A man's natural step length is about 40% of their height. Up to 135% when sprinting.

The pursuing North Koreans stood at least a foot shorter than me. Probably gained 4 inches on them with each step.

No pain.

They'd be hungry, lazy, unmotivated to do anything except the minimal required to avoid negative notice as a conscript.

Could turnover my stride faster than they would.

Maybe with more conscripts available, they'd be able to rest and set up ahead of me, but in a local footrace, I'd win.

Dodged around a canyon corner.

Chose the left fork from two different paths.

No more direct line of sight behind me. They'd radio ahead, but for now they had to have lost me.

Rather than continuing on, I slowed to a walk.

Panted back to an oxygen surplus.

Energy debt redeemed, I set about restoring my honor by free climbing the side of the cliff.

The border guards and conscripts would expect me at the ends of the forked paths, but my enemies would be out of position.

After I reached the top, I'd cut across the ridges and hilltops to the west, trading speed for risk of detection.

That risk would enable the bad guys to stay close, but a steady speed would keep me ahead of them until I reached the Ryesong river, guarded by DPRK patrol boats.

They might be out of position *if* the DPRK People's Army didn't talk directly to the People's Navy.

Not much of a plan, but I didn't know any others.

What should he do about those doggone lieutenants, Harper and Schnier?

Bishop leaned back in his chair. Propped his feet on his desk. Flipped a mk2 training grenade toward the ceiling.

Tossed it. Caught it.

Over and over.

They're like teenage girls, always staying out late and worrying their parents.

Could at least keep him in the loop. At this rate, they were gonna re-light the Korean war, with his wife and their girls in Seoul caught in the middle.

SFC Lee from Harper's MI platoon snagged the grenade out of the air, interrupting Bishop's train of thought.

"Top? A minute?"

Bishop thumped his boots on the floor. Sat up.

"Sure, whatcha got?"

Lee normally held himself ramrod straight, but now he drooped above Bishop's desk like his shoulders held a half-ton pound barbell set.

"I know I'm supposed to be in charge of my platoon, but this is way over my paygrade. Should I take it to the major or to my superiors at the KCIA? Maybe the CIA would run with it?"

"Slow down, Lee. What're you talking about?"

"Oh, I forgot, you don't know. Been negotiating with a contact in the DPRK Defense Ministry. We suspected who he was, pretty high up in the ministry, by what he could give us. Delivered promising stuff. Well, he just sent me a new message. Not only confirmed his real name, but ... well ... you should listen to it yourself."

Lee clunked the grenade onto the top of Bishop's glass desk. Pulled an Army-issue encrypted flash memory card out of his pocket. "Here's a copy."

Lee set the tiny memory chip down next to Bishop's laptop.

Bishop plugged it into his laptop's reader. Copied it over. Played the audio recording.

"I am Deputy Defense Minister Meon Lon-chun. You may

verify my identity using audio from my speeches at the most recent peace conference. I tell you this so you will take the following seriously.

"I require one-hundred million U.S. dollars: Fifty million in gold, thirty million in diamonds, fifteen million on deposit, five million in cash.

"If you agree, I will supply the delivery arrangements for the ransom and details related to my transportation out of Korea, to the island of my choice."

A pause in the recording.

"Yes, ransom. I will ransom back to you the city of Seoul and it's 10 million people. That's only ten U.S. dollars per person, or point one-six percent of the city's annual GDP.

"Quite a bargain for you.

"The city is now my hostage. A nuclear warhead is poised to destroy the city on my command, and my command alone.

"My team of special forces is armed with a dead-man's switch. They will only communicate with me. Any attempt to stop them, to disarm the device, will cause the immediate destruction of the city.

"Any attempt at mass evacuation will cause them to trigger the device.

"Don't test me. I will lose a platoon and you will lose a city, its inhabitants, your lives, and the lives of your men.

"You have twenty-four hours from this message for your intelligence services to accept my demands, at which time I will provide further instructions.

"Comply, and you can keep your city, the bomb, and I'll even throw in a special forces platoon once I'm safely away with my new wealth."

The recording ended.

Bishop's day just wasn't getting any better. "That's a real hum-dinger. How much gold is that?"

"Did the math; over 500 pounds. After our discussion about the lab data, I think he may be serious.

"Must've smuggled a trashcan nuke across the border. The voice matches Meon. Intelligence places him currently just across the DMZ.

"What do I do?"

"Any chance we can just fix this guy before he talks to his operators?"

"Assuming we get a good location on him with a drone or satellite; we'd have to attack their base across the DMZ. That's likely to start a war and get Seoul destroyed by all the artillery they have trained on it anyway, even if his men don't nuke us."

"Dang-blasted commie son-of a ..."

Bishop stopped. "Better send a copy to your bosses at the KCIA. Another to Langley. I'll run it up the SOCKOR flagpole.

"Everybody's gonna want a piece of this one. Just don't tell any of the other boots; last thing we need is panicked folks fleeing the city and trampling each other.

"Except Schnier. Call Schnier. Get him back here. Whatever he's doing out on that sub, this is more important. Once I brief the major, he's gonna want some hard tactical options."

Lee let out a long breath. "Thanks, Top."

Bishop stood and pocketed the flash drive. He rapped on the CO's door frame while Lee beat a hasty retreat for the exit.

Dag-nabbit, Major Williams would surely want to know where Harper and Schnier were.

Lieutenants! Not his day to watch 'em.

Chapter Thirty-Six:
With or Without You

Michelle wasn't impressed with the intrepidness of the USS Michigan's captain.

Late last night she'd flown with Schnier and the rest of his platoon in a 2nd Aviation Regiment Black Hawk to Busan Naval Base.

There they'd boarded the Michigan.

Now, she relaxed in a swinging hammock strung between a pair of twelve-foot navy Dry Deck Shelters (DDS).

The DDS were shaped like giant gray loafs of bread and carried like camel lumps on the back of the Michigan. They enabled special forces divers and submersibles to access the sub while underwater.

The regular motion of the submarine in the waves rocked her hammock with no additional effort on her part.

On her first submarine trip, she loved their underwater departure from port, but when they approached the border between North and South Korea in the Yellow Sea, the sub's captain insisted it was safer if they rode above the crashing waves.

With black storm clouds gathering farther offshore, she expected the captain to order them off the deck soon, once the lightning approached within a few miles.

The sub drew about twelve meters while on the surface, but the sea this close to land ran only 40 meters deep.

Too much risk of running aground to cruise the Michigan

under the surface here.

They'd just have to ride it out.

More in danger from the increased wind, a crop-duster flew from Ganghwa Peace Observatory.

Cruised well above them. Edged along the official border before turning back to begin another trip.

The plane pretended to perform photo reconnaissance, but actually waited for her orders.

Hopefully, she'd hear from Sam before the plane's pilot retreated from the approaching storm.

The sub made slow, but consistent headway against the rising whitecaps. Its course circled the Yellow Sea near the border.

A pale Navy cook grinned at her. He supplied her a mocktail Mojito on the open platform.

"The flavor will help you resist sea-sickness on these waves, Ma'am."

The cook's number one responsibility was to keep morale up on the sub, which included pleasing rare female visitors, but did not include serving *actual* alcohol.

Schnier folded his arms.

Leaned up against one of the DDS walls.

Pretended he didn't need to constantly shift his weight from foot to foot to stay balanced on the deck.

At least he properly filled out his Ranger uniform.

The rest of his men rode down below, where it was safer. Maybe she wasn't giving him enough credit; perhaps he'd arranged this time alone for them?

She took a sip. "Should try one of these. No Irish Car Bomb, but the sweet minty citrus creates a nice combo with the salty breeze."

"No, Ma'am. Last thing I need is for one of my men to catch me up here sipping mocktails. Never live it down.

"Besides, seems a mite coldhearted to relax on deck while Harper's out there on some kind of suicide mission, even if that reckless idiot deserves to get caught."

"What's wrong, nervous? Can't handle just hanging out here with me?

"After all, this is technically our date."

Schnier chuckled. "Nervous? Hardly. Learned a great technique from my Aggie public speaking course for not gettin' jumpy when talking to hot women.

"Just picture 'em naked." He winked.

Men!

Her neck flushed.

At least he saw her as hot. She could use that.

Michelle took a deliberate breath. She was in control here, not this cowboy.

Her secure phone dinged with a new message.

A text from Sam with coordinates for the air-drop he'd requested. Saved by the bell.

She showed the message to Schnier.

"Sam's on his way for extraction. Maybe even already destroyed the data."

"Seen Recon Rangers pull off ballsier stunts than that, but I bet if he had the data, he'd say it in his text. No news is bad news."

Good point. "Either way, your men need to be ready and I need to send these coordinates to the crop duster to program them into the GPS-guided chute."

She tapped a message beginning into her phone.

"Don't know what Harper sees in that thing. Just an electric surf-board. Rather have a horse under me."

"I'm sure you would. Don't miscalculate. We beat you at WARCOM on a pair of those."

Schnier cocked his head. Scratched his jaw. "Rangers aren't the kind of fellas who live on the water. Long history of Rangers in Texas. Teach the new boys all about it.

"Didn't always live to settle down with a nice family, though. Not like Bishop."

"Sam grew up in the ocean."

She hit send on the message. "Don't underestimate what he can accomplish."

"Our second deployment, my platoon hit an HVT's compound in the middle of the night. Grabbed the target, then skedaddled for the hills because the neighborhood lit up like a hornet's nest with tangos.

"Three wounded in the firefight. Made it to the primary LZ.

Marked it with chemlights just ahead of the bad guys, ready for a dust off.

"Damn Big Army bus driver refused to land to medevac my guys even after I promised him the area was secure, just because he could see tangos approaching on his IR feeds.

"Claimed they were in direct fire range of his copter.

"Without night vision, they'd never have seen him running dark, let alone been able to put effective fire into his copter, but he had a better idea, wanted us to ruck another five klicks to the alternate LZ instead.

"Lost two of those three wounded men during the egress because that bus driver didn't trust us to secure the primary LZ.

"So I don't care what nerd skills he has, Harper's gotta prove he's gonna integrate with our team before I'll trust him with my men's lives.

"Ain't about to write another letter to some guy in my platoon's wife or mother."

Michelle sat up. Leaned forward. Stared at the fiercely casual Schnier.

"If Sam flew that copter, they could've had your platoon under machine gun fire and missiles prep'd to blast at him, and he'd still land to pick-up your men. He's dumb that way."

Schnier uncrossed his arms. "We'll see if he can bust that bronc, I guess. I'll get my men ready to bail him out."

A black U-shape dropped from the biplane in the sky above them, followed by a puff of green as a parachute deployed behind it. The military dandelion floated on the breeze inland, up the Ryesong River and away from the Yellow Sea, deep into North Korea.

She hoped Sam knew what he was doing. His wasn't the only career on the line.

Doctor Yang Hyo-jin wouldn't worry about whatever Lieutenant Harper was doing.

He couldn't even take a few minutes to work on her nuclear materials detector.

With Captain Rhee under arrest, she just needed her

breakthrough to pay off. She'd prove she could run the lab unaided and be free of interference from the bureaucrats who'd always sided with Rhee before.

With no help from Sam.

Instead, she took subway trains through the city.

Pressed among the commuters.

Checked her tablet computer.

Refreshed the readings every few minutes.

Just had to figure out where these false positive alarms came from. She'd had her new conversion composite material installed in detectors scattered around Seoul, then the problems started.

The composites trapped neutrons, which pass through most matter when emitted by radioactive materials.

For each neutron trapped, her conversion composite emitted a daughter particle, which ionized gas particles, stripping them of electrons. Those electrons hit high-voltage wires.

Triggered a signal to the circuit boards built outside the gas chamber. Those circuit boards generated real-time reports of neutron sources.

Still in test mode, her tablet received strength and direction readings on any sources of neutrons from her network of detectors.

That let her software triangulate the location of a radiation source.

She'd expected lots of false positives.

Plenty of neutron radiation sources in a city like Seoul. She'd detected clusters in the labs at Sungkyunkwan University, Seoul National University, Yonsei University, and Korea University.

All famous for their physics laboratories, none of those neutron sources moved. Neither did those at Asan and Samsung Medical Centers.

Could explain all that.

Expected it.

Hadn't expected a moving source of neutrons. Doubted a particle accelerator was being hauled from place to place.

She'd considered one of her detectors was bad, but she'd received the anomalies from multiple detector locations.

No, must be something wrong with either her new hardware or a glitch in the software receiving the data.

But she couldn't find any problems at the five installations she'd checked, so that left a software issue.

Except she'd spent all night going through the software and running unit tests on each individual component.

Everything checked out fine.

Finally, she'd gotten so desperate, she thought a new pair of eyes might help.

Could spend a little time with Sam while she explained the issue to him. Maybe he'd think of something to check she'd been overlooking.

Busy resting and recovering, Sam wouldn't even come see her about it.

So she located the source of the glitch on a map with her tablet.

Tried to find it three times already, but each time she'd left a subway train and rushed outside she'd missed the source of the false positives.

But neutron emitting equipment doesn't move around like that, which is how she knew it was a bad reading.

After three attempts, she'd seen a pattern in the false positives. The detected emission spots somewhat lined up.

The distance from point one to point two was about the same as the distance between points two and three.

Scant data, but projecting it forward in time, she'd beat the source to the next detection point, or at least meet it there.

Then maybe she could figure out what was triggering her detectors which shouldn't be.

The next false positive should come from around Namsan Park, which was ridiculous, as it was just a small mountain in the middle of the city with a big stupid tower and a revolving restaurant on top.

Nothing remotely resembling a physics lab or advanced medical facility nearby.

Subway line four to Myeong-dong Station.

Shuttle bus to the little funicular, a metal elevator crowding in twenty people for each trip. The fixed angle of the funicular kept them level while it glided diagonally up the hill to the cable car terminal.

A masterpiece of engineering.

The cable car wasn't as fun. Not solidly attached to the ground, like the funicular.

Instead, the cable car dangled from wires carrying their enclosed glass box. Over six decades old, those wires might fail at any time, plunging them to their deaths on the tangle of barren trees below.

Hyo-jin knew how metal fatigued over time. Should she have hiked this last part?

People chattered. Phones rang in the close confines. Most took pictures out the cable car windows.

Weren't they scared?

A subtle bouncing up and down reminded her of the danger during the entire ride up the hill, over the brush and trees between concrete cable car towers, until they arrived at the station on top of the hill.

She pushed through the crowds at the cable car station.

Heart-shaped red, blue, and pink padlocks blanketed the walkway fences. She adored the idea of being so in love you felt compelled to lock something to a public fence.

Too bad Sam wasn't available to investigate Namsan with her.

Towering over the other visitors, she crunched across the thin layer of snow to a raised platform around the base of the tower.

Leaned over the fence.

Scanned the open plaza below.

A little Korean Army truck with soldiers in the back drove across the paved walking area below. Backed up to the side of the tower.

Strange, the park didn't allow vehicles up the road to the tower anymore. Must work on the antenna array which topped the tower or something.

Hyo-jin checked her tablet, but her equipment hadn't detected the neutron source again.

Nice view of the city from the summit of the 262 meter mountain, though. Perhaps she should ride up to the observation deck on the tower?

The spiked tower stretched another couple of hundred meters from the top of the mountain.

She'd have an even better view of her surroundings if her tablet displayed detected neutrons.

She walked toward the entrance, but families of tourists in puffy coats, wearing knit hats, began pouring out of the base of the building.

She caught something from the crowd about military police closing the tower down.

Dratz, she'd come all this way and now she'd miss the view. Hadn't even gotten a new reading.

Ping!

Too soon to give up. Her tablet alerted her to a new instance of the anomaly.

Practically right on top of it. Somewhere in the tower near that truck.

Maybe the Military Police were also here to investigate something.

She edged her way along the steel pipe railing. Let people pour past her.

Forced herself around them; into the tower entrance.

Inside, a starscape tunnel led her to the central tower shaft. The curved roof of the tunnel showed galaxies and planets, while the side displayed a night view of Seoul.

She barely noticed it as she inched forward along the edge, fighting the even thicker crowd, like a high pressure fire hose spewing people from the tower.

Reached the other end.

The people thinned out, then vanished.

She strode forward to two stainless steel high-speed elevator doors near the tower's center. A uniformed Korean soldier with an MP armband stood guard between them.

She fished her government credentials out of her lab coat pocket. Presented them to the guard. "What's going on here?"

"Tower is closed for security reasons. All civilians are to evacuate the area."

"What reasons? I need to get in there."

"One moment. I'll call my lieutenant for you."

The guard turned and reported her presence into an old beat-up radio. "He'll speak with you and clear this up. Step back from the elevator entrance."

Perhaps she could reason with his lieutenant about her readings.

If not, she'd call Sam to get an in with the military. Or Sergeant Lee, not Sam. Not again.

Maybe Captain Grant. He'd know what was going on.

She stepped backward on the black tile floor until the guard stopped glaring at her.

A moment later, the elevator dinged.

She recognized the lieutenant who stepped out. Last seen him on the security monitors in the lab's red zone.

He'd fled the lab with her data.

She bolted for the tunnel exit, clutching her tablet, long legs striding out.

"Stop!" the guard yelled behind her.

Another MP entered through the tunnel doors ahead of her. Spun to face away from her. Turned a small round knob on the metal bar across the exit doors.

The knob which locked the doors.

Trapped. Now what?

Chapter Thirty-Seven:
Railing at Storms

I ran across the ridges and hilltops. Stayed ahead of the North Korean border guards.

The hills ran out; I reached a set of rice paddies. Spotted a village of concrete buildings scattered through the paddies.

Homes for the workers.

The paddies were dry, so I plunged across them. Traded raw speed for a shorter straight line distance to the Ryesong River two klicks away on the other side of the fields.

The workers wouldn't carry weapons. Too much risk of turning on their masters.

Worse case, someone would have a radio or phone to report my presence.

I churned up the thin layer of mud on the ridges of the irrigation ditches between the fields. Followed a straight line to the river.

Six concrete huts in a line backed up to the irrigation ditch.

An older woman appeared in the glassless kitchen window. Watched me jog past, but ducked away when I turned my head in her direction.

Hopefully, they'd learned from the Party to mind their own business. To stay out of trouble.

Party officials might also have taught them to report everything. To dodge blame.

I crossed a dirt road edging the paddies.

Made it to the muddy bank of the river. Should've seen a parachute by now.

I'd texted Michelle the coordinates of the shallow mud-flat here on the edge of the Ryesong river.

Soft enough and close enough to the water to be reachable, but prevent any damage and remove any possibility of my eSurfboard floating away.

If the border guards showed up now, they'd trap me in the open against the river bank.

The parachute I'd asked her to use adjusted its cargo canopy to hit a specific set of GPS coordinates. Useful for supply drops as well as precisely targeted bombs.

Ten meters was a reasonable drift, but unless the winds were too strong for it, or the chute failed, I should be able to see it nearby.

The sky offshore shook with thunder and lightning among black clouds.

Periodic waves washed across the mud flats in front of me.

Perhaps the storm forced the plane to land?

Conceivably, a giant wave hit the mud flat before I arrived and dragged the eSurfboard out to sea by its attached parachute.

Perhaps Michelle couldn't even get the stuff I needed and had sent a reply to my message, but my governmentally indestructible phone had failed to receive it.

Maybe I was just screwed.

A pair of open trucks full of soldiers appeared at the bend where the road curved around the village.

Yep, despite the cold air, definitely in the hot place now.

I scrambled down the river bank. Ducked out of sight of the road.

Phone vibrated to notify me of an incoming message. Must be working again after drying out!

No time to look now.

Hopefully it wasn't from Michelle, telling me she couldn't drop my board to me.

The ground sucked at my feet as I ran across the mud flat. Seventy yards wide, almost a klick long, the high tide viscous silt followed the side of the river bank.

Small channels carved by the outgoing tides cut across to create ankle hazards for running surfers.

I tried to jump a channel. Landed short. Fell on my face.

Growling truck engines arrived on the road above the bank. Shouting soldiers would soon follow.

That final explosion as I left the mountain probably cracked one of my phone's internal seals.

Pulled it out of my cargo pocket. Held it up to keep it dry.

Crawled up a channel carved from the mud by a foot of water. The channel led back toward the riverbank.

The only source of cover or concealment in the area which didn't involve me crossing the kilometer-wide river.

Shouts from the border guards spread out as they organized themselves into a grid search team.

If their information was out of date, they'd head across the rice paddies instead of looking over this side of the riverbank.

I rolled onto my back. Hid in the channel. Caught my breath.

Took a moment to check my phone. Lee had replied to my email.

Searching the enemy base's database I'd sent him, he'd found a shipping order for what sounded like the stolen drive shelves full of data.

Connected the order with their railroad timetables. Sent me the train's schedule and route.

Kwon put the data on a cargo train to head north. A train that would cross this river soon.

If only enemy soldiers didn't surround me and I had transportation.

Might be able to do something about that. Again, from my time working in a warehouse attached to a train yard, I knew accidents generally came down to mass and momentum.

Right now, could barely escape, let alone move even farther into North Korea.

Enough rest. Needed to continue up this channel. Move into better concealment.

Reaching the edge of the river bank again, I crawled around a curve in the channel to where the water had pitted out swirling canyons in the mud. Up on the road a border guard grumbled about having to be out in the storm.

Prettiest thing I ever saw: My eSurfboard laying on its side in the mud.

Michelle delivered!

Either a wave washed it in here, or it landed out of sight.

Either way, all mine.

I drew my combat knife. Cut the chute away.

If anyone looked over the edge of the river bank, they'd see that splayed out, so I gathered it up. Stuffed it into a mud-hole.

Grabbed the attached controller. Tucked it into my pocket.

Picked up my U-shaped eSurfboard at its built-in balance point. Trudged back down the channel.

Needed to reach the river before the enemy spotted me.

The open river mouth to the south led into the Yellow Sea. I'd need to surf a 5k to get out of the waters claimed by the DPRK and into South Korean territory.

My only hope of escape.

Alternately, could turn north. Farther into the DPRK. Closer to their forces.

Only hope to intercept the train with the stolen data.

I'd slogged halfway down the mud channel to the river proper.

Tired. Didn't want to stay in North Korea a moment longer.

What'd I been thinking, anyway? Coming here like this.

A shout behind me from the riverbank.

I broke into a sort of jog-walk, my right-steps slow to keep from falling over, but my left-steps fast to get to deeper water.

Bullets thwacked into the mud around me, followed by the report of their departure from the border guard's rifle barrels.

Reached the edge of the mudflat. Ducked. Dove into the deeper water beyond.

At least *some* protection from the riverbank.

Rolled out of the middle of the eSurfboard. Slithered aboard.

Please start. Please start. Please start.

Hit the controller's power button. All green. Yes!

Full throttle.

Cut through the growing waves from the river's mouth.

Held on to the side rails until my board stopped bucking and pitching for a moment; long enough for me to stand.

Gain situational awareness.

I'd left the border guards on the river bank. Irrelevant now.

North or South.

Duty or Freedom.

I'd screwed up going it alone in the lab. Messed up not having any backup crossing the border, so Meon got ahead of me.

Lee and Michelle had made this last opportunity to destroy the stolen data possible. It wouldn't come again.

I leaned to the right. Turned my eSurfboard North; deeper into the DPRK.

Maybe the border guards behind me wouldn't be able to keep up with me. Maybe the road they were on didn't parallel the river for long.

Stubbornly sticking with a failed mission was stupid, but as Michelle said, I didn't always make the smart decision.

At 30 mph, only needed fifteen minutes to reach the railroad bridge.

The ancient steel span crossed at a steep and narrow part of the river, twenty-five feet above the water.

Two tiny guard tin-roofed shacks blocked out the elements, one at the top of each river bank.

Reaching the bottom of the eastern span, I parked my board at the bottom. Put it in station-keeping mode, so it'd fight the current to stay in one place.

Reached up and grabbed the edge of a steel beam. Pulled myself up.

Walked one foot in front of the other to the river bank; to where the beam connected to a concrete pad. No way to climb higher using the bridge.

No, I faced more frozen mud.

Picked a path clear of vegetation. Dug my toes into the steep bank. My shoes cracked through the thinly frozen surface, but slid down.

Not enough purchase to climb away from the concrete pad.

I shuffled to the side. This time picked a path full of bushes and reeds. Used my hands to grab them while I dug my heels into the muddy bank.

Slipped, slid, but also made progress.

Inch by inch, foot by foot, I reached the top. Peered over the edge.

The guard from the shack stood there watching me.

A conscript, the lowest of the low in the People's Army, he didn't shoot me. Spoke urgently into a brick of a radio.

I lunged forward. Tackled him at the waist.

He put out his arm, tried to stiff-arm me, to keep me away, fend me off.

Slapped his arm aside. Lifted behind his knees. Dumped him backwards. Knocked him into the gravel behind him. The back of his head bounced off a railroad tie.

Instant concussion. His eyes rolled up into his head.

Still breathed. That was something.

Stripping his belt, I wrapped up his arms and legs. Smashed his radio with my muddy heel.

Took three tries. Kept slipping.

Train due any minute. What to use to stop it?

Back in the train yard, the most common cause of a train derailment was a broken rail or weld. Didn't take much of a rail misalignment in the right location.

I picked up the guard's cheap rifle. No bayonet. The stock was practically balsa wood.

The People's Army hadn't even issued him any bullets. Guess that explains why he didn't shoot me.

Shortage of bullets behind the lines.

Examined the guard shack. Found a tall steel pipe used to carry smoke out of the roof. Some wood for a fire. Old rusted rail spikes.

With a heave, I toppled the shack over and across the tracks.

Not enough, but a start.

Twisted and turned the pipe. Broke it out of the crushed ceiling.

Took the best-looking spike. Hammered it with the pipe at a forty-five degree angle beneath the right-hand rail.

Deep into the weakest spot, the transition from dirt to bridge, where the dirt eroded, but the steel bridge stayed strong, creating a gap between the two.

Lifting the pipe, I strode back a dozen measured steps along the top of the river bank.

Ran forward.

Slotted the pipe over the spike.

Jumped. Just like pole vaulting back in high school.

The force of my run combined with the momentum of my weight.

I flew up and over.

The pipe twisted the railroad spike below it.

Forced the top forward. The bottom backward.

The spikes at the base of the rail broke through the rotten wood of the railroad tie.

I landed awkwardly, the railroad resistance turned a smooth landing into a series of small jerks and thumps.

My knee twinged. Shoulder burned.

Couldn't do that again.

Replaced the spike deeper into the gap.

Fitted the pipe over it as a lever. Used all my weight to push it down.

Expand the gap.

Got it low. Jumped up and down on it.

Winced. Refit the spike. Sat on it.

Did it all again.

Slowly, shifted the steel rails apart.

A border guard truck's engine screeched in the distance. The same soldiers from earlier; I'd know that stuck gear shift anywhere.

Didn't have long.

The rail on the bank vibrated. A low rumble approached.

I glanced over to make sure the enemy soldier was out of the path. Looked groggy, but his tied up prone body lay well clear of the tracks.

The train came around a curve. Full speed ahead.

Guess they hadn't gotten the word.

Stuck the spike into the ground in the center of the gap I'd created. Put the pipe over it, sticking straight up.

That by itself might be enough to derail the train, but the right-hand rail on the ground and the rail on the bridge no longer lined up.

Pretty sure that'd do it, as long as the train didn't stop and the border guards didn't undo my work.

No time for second thoughts. This train carried data which the DPRK's leaders could use or sell to kill millions in the years to come.

Even lead to world nuclear war.

I ran onto the bridge.

Truck a hundred meters away.

Train? Two hundred meters, clanking with a steel rhythm.

Truck's driver was more intent on not getting in the train's way than in catching me. Skidded to a halt on the gravel road.

Soldiers poured out the back.

First two out took aim.

Fired.

Bullets pinged off the bridge around me.

Air brakes puffed. Whistled.

The train's wheels screeched against the rails.

Engineer had seen the shack. Maybe the pipe.

I dove off the side of the bridge. Sucked in a breath on the way down. Splashed into the water.

My wake pushed my board from me.

I broke the surface.

The squealing hit a high note.

Climbed onto my board.

Aimed it away from the bridge.

Turned on the power. Leaned forward to counter-balance the propeller's power.

The train's cow catcher cleared the shack's debris from the rails.

Then hit the pipe.

Banged it flat. That just shifted the rails even farther apart.

One set of steel wheels fell off the right-hand rail. Scraped along the gravel.

Train's engine tilted to the right.

Collided with the steel frame of the bridge. Rest of the engine toppled in slow motion.

Gravity took over.

The momentum of the rest of the train cars pushed the engine out and over the water. Train left the bridge at about the center.

Plunged through the air. Into the river.

Each train car smashed down on those ahead of it.

A dozen meters downstream, I took a moment to watch the destruction. Needed to escape the area, but something about a train wreck is impossible to look away from.

If the data was aboard that train, they'd never recover it in one piece.

A gray patrol boat rounded the closest bend upriver.

Sixty feet long and a dozen feet wide, the speedy craft carried four indigo-clad crewman wearing orange life-preservers.

One pilot, safe behind plexiglass, controlled the water jet engines. Two crew members rode on the back, behind the radar on the roof. Carried rifles.

They'd hung a white and red flotation ring on the side of the central cabin.

The fourth member of the crew exited the hull from a hatch onto the forward deck.

Pulled an olive green canvas tarp off either a large caliber machine gun, or a small cannon mounted behind a steel gun shield on the front of the coastal patrol vessel.

I could live without finding out which it actually was. Wasn't *that* curious.

The wrecked train blocked most of the river under the bridge. The resulting ripples pushed my board away.

The crew of the patrol boat pointed at the train. Yelled to each other.

The pilot, steering and paying more attention, pointed me out to them.

An obvious figure, riding above the water. Guess the slower, older-style water propulsion, the kind you took *under* the water, still had an advantage in visibility.

I squeezed the accelerator for top speed, away from the wreckage of folded train cars.

Hopefully, it'd take the patrol boat some time to get past the bridge. Time enough for me to get away.

Fifteen minutes later, passed the area with the long mud flats. Close to the mouth of the river.

A storm gathered ahead, right offshore. Plenty of

white-capped breakers farther out.

Rounding a curve in the river, the patrol boat cut through the water behind me.

Guess it didn't take them long to clear the wreckage.

I reached the area just before the mouth of the river, at the edge of the Yellow Sea. Salt and freshwater mixed to create tall ripples where the incoming waves collided with the river's current.

The patrol boat bounced through those same ripples at about 25 mph.

At full speed, I began to pull away.

Leaned into the wind. Cut through the crests of the shallow river waves.

Crossed the open mouth of the river. Cut the power a little.

If I rode too fast into these bigger swells, I'd plunge down into the trough. Be unable to counter-balance the forward motion.

Wipe out here and that patrol boat would catch me.

It closed the distance. A rooster tail of water spewed out their rear jets.

The bow lifted into the air. The gun on the front couldn't depress enough to target me, but once they caught up to me, they'd slow down again for a steady aiming platform.

Not good.

Pushed my controller to ahead full.

Leaned left. Crossed the waves at an angle rather than straight on.

That lengthened the distance between roller-tops, but didn't cross the Yellow Sea as quickly.

The patrol boat gained on me, but slower.

Last time I'd invade a foreign country by myself again.

A gray lump on the southern horizon, hidden by the storm. I'd surf there as fast as possible.

Hope for a miracle.

Chapter Thirty-Eight:
Nothing to Fear ...

"Honey, dag-nabbit, you need to jet."

Bishop never expected this day to come. Luckily, he only lived 5 minutes from the base, but that was definitely not far enough from a nuclear warhead.

His Polynesian wife stood there in their cheap off-base apartment's living room. Gaped at him.

Two beautiful teenage daughters sat at the kitchen table. Worked on the excessive homework the local American school believed necessary to keep up with their Korean neighbors.

His oldest looked up. "Dad, no swearing!"

Bishop took a mental picture. He'd remember this exact moment.

Just in case.

"Take a flight to your parents' in Tonga. I'll explain later."

If I can.

Bishop walked over to the coat closet in the front hall. Examined the family's 72-hour emergency preparedness packs.

Each held money, first aid kits, and radios; plus enough clean clothing, food, and water for three days. He'd stored his in an extra ruck pack; that could stay here.

His wife kept hers in a rolling black suitcase. Perfect for a flight.

He pulled it out. Extended the handle. "Take the van."

"What's going on? We can't drop everything. The girls have school in the morning."

"Classified. Can't tell you. You can't even tell anyone else you're going. Couldn't do my job if'n you and the girls were here. You're my first priority."

The love of his life had been a soldier's wife long enough for her mind to finally catch up with the implications of what he'd been trying to tell her. "Married this long, I won't ask you to leave your buddies. We'll be fine."

She grabbed two pink and yellow backpacks from the closet. "Girls!"

She tossed the packs in a high enough arc that both of his adopted daughters caught their bag.

"Leave your homework. We're taking a vacation."

She was right. With her and the girls taken care of, he couldn't let down his other family, his men.

He handed her the minivan key. "Park it at the airport, don't worry about the fees. Flight leaves in less than two hours. I'll take the subway back to base."

She stopped next to him. Looked up.

He put his arms around her strong body. Planted an adamant kiss.

"Whew!" She smiled. "I love you. Be careful. Those daughters of mine have already suffered enough without losing you, too."

"See what I can do, but there's more than our family at stake. Love you, too. Call you later if I can."

Their daughters rose, backpacks in hand.

He pointed out at the family minivan, "Now go!"

Michelle felt the waves break against the side of the USS Michigan. They lifted her imperceptibly up and down.

Schnier and a pair of his men, both snipers, braced themselves against the side of the Dry Deck Shelters.

He'd rotated the men in his platoon through deck duty; kept fresh eyes up top.

They all looked for Sam on the water.

Michelle protected her eyes from the salty spray with a pair of binoculars one of the sailors on watch had lent her.

The three Rangers used the magnification scopes on their giant-bore rifles.

She'd never learned the exact caliber of their weapons, but overhearing their recent conversations, they were as proud of their rifle barrel diameters as they were of the stature of their packages.

Presumably overcompensating for something.

Schnier shouted over the rolling roar of the wind and waves, "Nuttin'. Dunno how much longer we can stay on station. Eventually, those lightning flashes on the horizon are fixin' to catch up."

Michelle leaned into a gust. Tracked her binoculars across the lines of breakers closer to shore.

"Sam should've met the chute already. Hasn't replied with a confirmation, but I'm sure he didn't abandon his baby to the enemy. He'll be out there."

"Sumpin's gotta give. Dunno how anyone can stand this. Worse'n playin' rodeo clown.

"Should we launch the inflatable? Go scour the shore yonder?

"Beats waiting here sucking our thumbs."

"You'd sink. Anyway, thought you didn't want to ..."

A figure crossed the line of breakers, dark against the white spray. Human-shape a quarter the size of the waves riding a dark line cutting through the water.

"There he is!" She pointed, "Just past the breakers."

Schnier and his men focused on where she'd detected him. "Sho 'nuff. Boy sure can ride a board, can't he?"

A compliment from Schnier for Sam?

She'd always taken for granted Sam's surfing ability. He'd surfed ever since she'd known him, but now she watched through fresh eyes, seeing what someone who hadn't grown up with him would notice.

The waves heaved away from the sub, toward the shore.

Sam cut diagonally up the face of a wave. The combined motion of his board and the storm surge tossed him into the air from the peak.

Used the spinning prop blades and electric motor as a counterweight to land at the perfect angle on the wave's backside while it dropped away below him.

Leaned to change the slant of his board before he hit the

334 | Thomas Sewell

trough ahead of the next upsurge.

Burst through a massive tube. Shot off the crest right before it collapsed.

Spun left. Landed casually sideways.

Followed the ridge on top until he dove back down to add more momentum.

Was like he instinctively knew how the water would shift ahead of time. Anticipated the breaks and the collisions between heaving liquid volumes.

A larger shape appeared on the horizon. A North Korean patrol boat bounced across the waves behind Sam.

It ran into the surf at a speed calculated to keep the hull suspended between at least two waves.

Michelle's stomach flipped with the heaving of the waves. "Yeah, but whoever's driving that patrol boat is no slouch, either. Overtaking him."

The boat supported a small cannon mounted between a gun shield on the bow. The bore four times wider than even the Ranger's sniper rifles.

Flame burst from the barrel. The explosive thud mixed with distant thunder to rumble across the water.

A shell exploded in the water a few meters away from Sam. Saltwater sprayed sideways onto him.

He veered away. Twirled down the backside of the wave. Kept the crest between him and the patrol boat.

His move took him sideways, foregoing forward progress, but out of his enemy's direct line of sight.

Stopped bringing him closer to the sub.

Schnier opened a hatch. Shouted down the conning tower.

Shook his head at the reply. Turned back to her.

"Captain won't bring the sub closer to shore. Any farther and we're out of South Korean waters and into the North."

"You going to let a few rules and the prospect of an international incident stop you from helping another Ranger?"

Schnier pretended to not hear her question, but his nose flared and his eyes narrowed in response.

Sam paralleled them. Only gained ground diagonally.

Too slow.

The boat would soon be at the same wave he was using to hide from the gunner on board.

Schnier took up a kneeling sniper pose near his men. Braced against the shelter wall. Sighted through his scope.

"Count of three. I have the gunner. You both take the pilot."

Timed his command for the peak of the slow wave rocking the sub, "Three, two, one. Fire."

They squeezed their triggers in unison.

Her ears rang.

Schnier and the two snipers wore active ear protection; it blocked out sharp sounds while permitting normal conversation. She needed to acquire something to stick in her ears.

A spark scraped across the gun shield protecting the enemy cannon.

The plexiglass protecting the boat's driver shattered into a star pattern. He slumped down on the wheel.

Schnier nodded. "Good hit on the pilot. Gunner still up."

The boat swerved sideways. Dropped into the valley between the next two waves. Only the radar on the roof showed above the crest.

Even that vanished.

The rush of the next wave rolled the vessel over. The bottom of the hull appeared at the wave's crest before rolling upright in the next trough.

No sign of the crew, just a missing cannon and swinging metal railings periodically bashing into the cabin sides.

Schnier pursed his lips and nodded.

"Put away the weapons. This is fixin' up to be a humanitarian rescue mission. Cap won't have a problem doing S&R for the crew of a boat we watched get tumped over in the storm."

Michelle grinned. "And if we happen to pick up an itinerant lost surfer at the same time, nobody will mind. Glad you didn't have to use that rubber boat after all."

Schnier's military issue phone buzzed. He read the screen.

"Lee reports the MP unit at the tunnel failed to check in. He's tracked the truck the enemy used from there via license plate scanners to Namsan Tower. TV news has a report that Namsan

Mountain Park is being evacuated by military police, but nobody seems to know why.

"The Major wants my platoon geared up and to Namsan Tower ASAP. We're the only available spec ops platoon with hostage rescue experience."

That complicated everything. What was Lee up to?

"Better hurry and pick Sam and the survivors out of the sea then, huh?"

"That sorry hombre ruins all my dates."

PART FOUR

RANGER TEAM

Chapter Thirty-Nine:
Deadly Deterrence

One of Pahk's demolition experts stretched ropes of explosives around the glass perimeter doors.

Lieutenant Kwon Chol's new team couldn't defend the doors, nor the multitude of windows around the base of the tower. Too much hard cover outside to make that tenable, but the explosives would deter any assault.

Deadly deterrence.

Standing next to the tower's central elevators, Kwon couldn't find any fault with Pahk nor his team. Goshawk team had been as efficient, they'd had the more difficult mission, that's all.

Two of Pahk's snipers carried a stainless steel table into the central lobby from the tower restaurant's kitchen.

They lined the table up on its side between the two elevators, facing the entrance.

Dragged a pair of metal box trashcans over to reinforce the barricade and provide rifle rests for the defenders.

Kwon tossed a handful of tiny chocolates from the lobby candy shop into his mouth. Excellent crunch, but a bit too sweet for his taste.

The shop held tubes and stacks and shelves and buckets of candy in every shape and color. Would supplement the food and beverages from the restaurant kitchen's bank of freezers and refrigerators.

The tower even had its own emergency generators to keep the communications equipment on the spike above energized.

If the South didn't agree to reunification terms soon, his team could survive for months in the tower.

All secure down here.

He entered the elevator. Turned the fire override key. Selected the observation level.

His men's weapons and MP identification had convinced the tower's maintenance staff to hand over all the keys and passes. Using those, they evacuated civilians from every part of the tower.

The tower's tall central tube held the elevator shafts and maintenance equipment.

Vertical air-gaps separated the three sets of circular rooms surrounding the central tube. The observation deck built atop the circle attached to the top of the tube was in turn topped by an antenna spiking into the air.

The whole structure rose a few hundred meters above the hill's peak.

Pahk's men cleared from the top down; the observation deck, the restaurant circling the tower below that, and then the shops and lobby on the hilltop.

Nobody here now except their team.

Well, except that meddling scientist, who could apparently track the Goshawk device.

How did she manage that?

Better to stash her upstairs than risk a premature panic.

The elevator dinged. The doors opened on Pahk staring out the floor to ceiling glass windows.

Even the urinals in the restrooms on this floor had great views.

Pahk's orders were to guard the woman, not gaze at the Seoul skyline. At least he'd secured her by a wrist and an ankle to the railings.

She was playing with her tablet. Some kind of game.

Anything to keep her out of their way.

Kwon strode over to him. "Need to rig up the device to ensure no one interrupts us. Take charge of the defenses below."

Pahk nodded in acquiescence. Held out a mobile phone with a black and white cat's face on it. "Her phone. She's occupied with her tablet. Already used the restroom once. Pretty shy about it, too."

Kwon took the phone. "Great. I can ignore her for a while. The dead man's switch is delicate. Don't want to do anything wrong when I arm the device and activate it."

Pahk cleared his throat, but said nothing, just rubbed the back of his neck.

The Goshawk device rested in the middle of the open floor on top of a rough-hewn table. Two of their men had brought the table up from the restaurant dining room on the floor below, along with a pair of matching benches.

"Once armed, I'll be stuck here holding that switch, so rotate the men to reduce fatigue. One of them can periodically bring me and the woman meals. If I get too tired, I'll have you relieve me on the switch."

Even as submissive as Pahk had been after Meon made it clear who was in charge, Kwon planned to limit the amount of time anyone else held massive destruction in their hand.

They needed a credible threat to achieve peace, but there was no call to be reckless.

"Got it." Pahk gestured toward the windows. "No signs of an armed response yet, but they'll come soon."

Pahk departed in the elevator.

At the first sign of a serious attack on the tower, they'd flip the emergency override to disable it. Only other way to reach this high was to climb 40 meters of steel rungs in its shaft.

A pair of snipers at the top could hold off as many men as they had rounds.

The snipers' ammo boxes each held 200 cartridges. If the enemy cleared the ground floor, with four ammo boxes stacked nearby, it'd take an Imperialist brigade sacrificing itself completely to get someone to the observation deck.

By then, they'd be able to climb up the bodies.

No, the odds of anyone confronting him here with the dead man switch for the nuclear device active were slim.

The switch also prevented the enemy shelling the tower to destroy the bomb. He'd let go before he allowed that to happen.

He tapped the photo in his breast pocket.

Better to die in an explosion, taking this city with him, than to fail his adopted family.

More North Korean soldiers in Seoul. Now what?

I'd ridden with Michelle and Schnier on the sub long enough for us to hitch a helicopter ride into Seoul. Almost dark before we assembled in the plaza at the base of the tower.

Metro Police cleared the park of civilians and enforced a strict perimeter.

Light snow drifted across the plaza's concrete pavers. Crunched underfoot as Schnier and I paced around the group in turn.

Watched for threats.

I recognized his glances around the place from my own habit of assessing infiltration points and security vulnerabilities.

The military truck backed up to the tower's rear doors sure looked like the same truck the tangos left at the tunnel entrance. Maybe if I'd disabled it on my way into the tunnel . . .

No, the MPs were responsible for securing the truck as evidence.

Back at HQ, Lee had reported two of the MPs were dead, the third in the hospital with a concussion.

The sergeant in charge of the MP detachment had explained to Captain Grant that he'd been on a food run while the enemy attacked his men.

Lee requisitioned me a replacement phone from platoon stores. We'd left him behind to hunt for more info on the attackers.

Major Williams ordered Schnier's platoon to secure the close-in perimeter. From there, they'd assess how to take the North Korean terrorists down.

The 75th RRC's sniper teams scattered themselves around the park's closest trees and stone walls.

With quad night vision, they'd see the tower's defenders much easier than they'd be seen.

Their equipment included streaming cameras to give us 360 degree live coverage of the tower.

A small team in the plaza, out of sight of the front doors,

readied a frontal assault.

I'd tagged along as a technical adviser, outfitted in fresh tactical gear from the company's lockers.

Michelle, dressed for a winter expedition in one of the Metro cop's puffy coats, stood off to the side explaining the facts of life to D.C. on her mobile phone.

She fiddled with heart locks on the fence while talking.

Told D.C. in no uncertain terms that if they didn't want Seoul to be a radioactive crater, they needed to fill our requests.

The dude in D.C. didn't sound happy, but neither were we.

Bishop stood next to me in that semi-relaxed posture a sergeant learns from hurry up and waiting for hours at a time.

Schnier stopped his pacing next to Bishop. "Start again with the basics. Why didn't they keep any hostages in the tower? Why take the tower now, and not last week, or next week?"

Bishop handed me a tiny encrypted flash card. "Play that. Can never get 'em to work on my phone."

I plugged the card into my phone. "You have to transfer the file over to decrypt it first. Can't just play it straight from the card."

We listened to the audio of Meon's ransom demands.

My heart sunk.

The timing of Meon's demands might be yet another disaster I was responsible for.

After capturing him, he'd not only warned the dudes guarding the data, but he'd sent them across the border with their lone portable nuke.

"They don't need hostages in the tower. Holding a dead man's switch on the bomb, we're all their hostages. Everyone from the tower or the park, every soldier at Yongsan base, every civilian in Seoul."

Schnier scratched behind his ear. "Why here?"

"So the nuke will be like an air-burst. The combined 500-meter height of the hill and tower means the shockwave will bounce off the ground and fold back into itself, spreading the blast wave and radiation farther horizontally.

"Gives it a much bigger effective range."

Schnier tucked his arms into his uniform jacket's armpits.

"Even if they have a dead man's switch, I need to fix up an assault plan."

"You don't get it. The fact that they chose the tower tells us they're keeping it near the top. Otherwise, they could've picked anywhere."

I stepped toward him to emphasize my point.

He stretched his arms like swords by his sides. Leaned a little too close to my face for my taste.

"I get it fine, Harper. If'n we sit here on our thumbs, this city gonna fry."

Bishop cut between us. Put his arms out like a referee at an MMA fight.

"Lieutenants, this is a good time to make use of our diverse talents as a team to figure out what we're gonna do about that nuke."

He lowered his voice to yell at us under his breath. "This isn't the time for either of you to cop an attitude."

Couldn't help myself, but at least I kept my own voice low, "He doesn't know what he's doing."

Bishop's eyebrows narrowed. He focused his eyes on mine. "Work it out together."

Schnier nodded. "Harper, don't forget, you're supposed to be my platoon's intelligence *support*."

Bishop turned to glare at Schnier. "Let it go. Your attitude is affecting the team as much as his family-history issues. *Forgive and forget*."

Schnier lowered his gaze to the ground. Kicked a small pile of snow.

Ever the diplomat, I changed the subject, "We should locate Hyo-jin. She'd be able to calculate the exact danger zone. Let me call her. See if she can join us here."

Straight to voice mail, as if her phone was off. Must've let the battery run down while she focused on her work.

Oh well, we'd ride this wave without her.

Bishop let his carbine hang loose in front of him. Braced his hands on his hips.

"Now, what about stormin' the entrances at the base of the tower? Snipers can take out anyone who fires from the edges above, so we can focus on the hallways.

"Lee is working on video footage of their entrance. That'll get us a better count, but can't be many of 'em defending the place."

Schnier shook his head. A loose strap allowed his combat helmet to wiggle back and forth. "Can get into the base of the tower, but my team's been looking at site diagrams.

"Assuming they were smart enough to put men up that middle pipe, at the top of the elevator shafts, it's a death trap to climb from the base to the observation and restaurant levels."

I hated to admit it, but, "He's right. They'll sacrifice the ground level and detonate the nuke if it looks like we're making progress up the central shaft."

Bishop didn't need to ream me out in front of Schnier, even if he knew there was no way we'd bring it up with Williams.

I could infiltrate the tower on my own. Put the defenders out of position, like Schnier's platoon in San Diego.

No defense is impenetrable.

Like the Maginot Line, I had to go around. To hit them from the other side.

Would anyone notice if I slipped away to get a ride? Maybe I could borrow a bird at Seoul Air Base.

Bet I could take the enemy tonight if I left right now. If it worked, the Rangers would have to accept me.

Bishop tapped the short range encrypted radio hanging from his tactical belt.

"They've ruled out evacuating the city. Too many casualties from the crowds of people trying to escape; too much risk it's noticed by the enemy and Meon makes good on his threat.

"The powers-that-be are experiencing a serious denial of reality right about now, but Meon's deadline isn't until the morning."

Schnier shook his head like he had rocks inside he needed to dislodge. "We'll try before then, but getting my men killed in the elevator shafts won't stop that nuke."

He reached up to clamp his helmet down and tighten the loose strap.

Michelle stalked over to rejoin us.

"Useless in D.C. Said they'd look for one of those EMP bombs you asked about, Sam, but I wouldn't hold out any hope of someone flying one to us from the States before the deadline."

I shrugged. "Long-shot anyway. That's a communications tower on top, so the place is well shielded. With an EMP we might get the bomb's detonation mechanism at the cost of all the electronics in the city, but I wouldn't want to count on that to save everyone's lives.

"More of a last-ditch effort kind of thing."

My new phone rang. The screen showed the caller as Sergeant Lee.

I answered, "You're on speaker phone with Schnier, Bishop, and Michelle."

Lee's voice echoed out of my phone like he was on the other side of a tunnel, "Reviewed the footage around the tower from the take-over. Counted eight tangos entering. What looks like a trashcan nuke was definitely in the back of that truck."

Schnier bowed his head toward my phone, "We can take eight of them, if my men can get a jump on them."

Lee wasn't done, "Doctor Yang arrived before they did. Watched it three times to be sure. She enters the tower right when the crowds start leaving, but never returns. Definitely still inside."

Hyo-jin was in there with those mass murderers? Hyo-jin?

No wonder she hadn't answered my call.

"Her detector. Must've been testing her nuclear materials detector and stumbled on them."

The detector she wanted me to help her troubleshoot, but I'd blown her off because I was uselessly traversing North Korean hills. I was so jacked up.

Maybe I *should* take off and drop in on top of the tower by myself.

I managed to mumble, "Is that all?"

"Got an ID on the guys who were giving the orders. People's Army special forces. Lieutenant Pahk Geon and Lieutenant Kwon Chol. Kwon appeared to be in charge."

Michelle pushed Schnier away from my phone, "How common is 'Kwon Chol' as a name? How much info do you have on his background?"

My phone vibrated. An alert showed a priority email from Hyo-jin.

"That'll have to wait. May have inside information. We'll get back to you."

Hung up on Lee. Opened the message. Showed it to the others.

Hyo-jin sent a brief explanation that the terrorists must not have experience with the Internet. They'd let her keep her tablet, now connected to the tower's WiFi network instead of her phone.

She'd attached pictures.

Photos of her restraints. A shot out the window of the observation deck area, so we could tell which side they'd tied her to.

Of Kwon sitting on a bench next to a table, eating dinner while holding a dead man's switch.

A red thumb-button. Spring-loaded. Wired to fire the device on the table.

The nuke holding us all hostage.

Chapter Forty:
Dead End

Jin-son's Mother put their leftovers from dinner into the refrigerator.

Looked forward to a steamy bath tonight, so she had the water running into her tub in the bathroom.

Jin-son would stay up late playing his game, like he always did, but she could relax after a long day running her seamstress business and taking care of the boy.

A fist pounded on her apartment's front door.

She forced herself to expel a long breath. Not the secret police.

No secret police here in the South, not like when she was a girl.

Probably an anxious neighbor, wanting to borrow some vinegar. "One moment."

She bustled over to her door, drying her hands on her apron. Peeked out the peephole.

A blurry pair of soldiers, carrying long black guns, one foreigner, one Korean. Someone tall in a dark suit behind them.

Did the secret police come for her?

She blinked her eyes. Squinted. Looked again.

Toby Howell.

The man behind the soldiers was that officious bureaucrat from the American embassy.

She unlocked the deadbolt. Opened the door.

One of the soldiers, a Korean, had his fist raised in the air, about to pound again.

"I said I coming. I here. What you want?"

An unannounced home visit?

Howell began to speak, but the Korean soldier held up his hand to shush him, "Ma'am? You are Yeo Min-jung. Mother of Kwon Jin-son?"

She nodded.

Howell stepped forward. "Of course she is. I told you, we've been meeting about their visas."

"I'm Sergeant Lee, from military intelligence." The Korean soldier stepped in front of Howell.

Must share her low opinion of the half-breed.

"We have a situation and require your assistance with the matter."

"Is this about Minister Meon? We need to dress for press?"

"No, Ma'am. No press at this time. If you'll collect your son, we'll escort you to Namsan Park. They'll explain everything to you there."

Jin-son rolled up to the door, laptop neglected across his legs.

"What's all this? We agreed to speak to the media if necessary, *after* we had our visas. Some trip to the park wasn't part of our deal with the Americans."

She sighed. "Must do what men say."

Looked very official.

Lee stepped through the doorway. Slipped between them. Circled around Jin-son.

Grabbed the handles of the wheelchair, but otherwise ignored her son. "It's about your brother-in-law, Ma'am. Your husband's parents died after the Party sentenced them to hard labor as dissidents, but your brother-in-law is alive and in Seoul."

My husband's younger brother? From the North?

What does this mean, that it's coming up now? Will it ruin everything for Jin-son?

She hadn't talked to the Americans much about Jin-son's uncle.

Didn't know much. He'd been a child when they ran.

She shook her head to clear it. "I go turn off bathwater. Lucky you not come five minutes later. Wouldn't have answered."

Lee gestured to the American soldier with him, who slid past them all with a smile.

"He'll take care of turning off the water. We don't have any time to waste."

He pushed Jin-son's wheelchair out the door.

They made it to the hallway when Jin-son engaged the chair's motors in reverse.

"Not so fast. You never answered my question."

Lee struggled against the powerful motors. Their contest rocked the chair back and forth in place.

"It's classified." He grunted, "Knock that off. You have no choice in the matter. Please come as a volunteer, but we'll take you under arrest if we have to."

Jin-son pushed on the chair's joystick even harder. "That'll look good on the news. Cripple dragged out of his home by the military."

Lee stopped.

The chair lurched backward, almost running over his toes, before Jin-son stopped it.

Lee leaned forward, mouth next to Jin-son's ear, spoke softly, "Want to see your uncle? Come with us. As I said, there's no time, but we'll explain everything as soon as we can."

Jin-son's Mother stepped forward to stand next to her son. "Come. Sergeant has honest eyes. Trying to do job. If he send soldier to deal with plumbing, we can take time to pay uncle visit. Discover why."

They wouldn't steal this opportunity away from her son, no matter how stubborn he was.

She knew to cooperate with the authorities. The last time she hadn't, her husband died.

1st Sgt. Keith Bishop stomped down the edge of a loose cobblestone in the courtyard outside the base of Namsan Tower.

Someone could trip on that thing.

Lee had introduced Jin-son and his mother to the Ranger leaders. Now Schnier, Harper, Lee, Michelle, and the Korean tiger mom huddled in the courtyard corner next to a fence of heart-shaped padlocks.

No love lost in that group.

Jin-son sat outside the discussion circle in his powered wheelchair. Leaned toward the group to listen.

Bishop gathered he'd been stuck without functioning legs pretty much his entire life, poor kid.

Having one of Bishop's daughters needing that much constant care growing up would've been tough. Thank goodness for his wife.

Parenting was tough enough with her to take the lead. Didn't want to even imagine having to raise a child with a major disability as a single-parent.

Trying to raise junior officers was bad enough.

What could he do to pull the shooters and the MI guys together?

To get Harper and Schnier to see they actually needed each other?

That they couldn't function as a team unless they trusted each other to do their job?

Maybe attaching Harper's MI platoon to the RRC had been a mistake.

They were fine behind the scenes, on the paperwork challenges, even as a Red Team to infiltrate friendly facilities, but during direct action missions aimed at the enemy, the Ranger Regiment's bread and buttah, Schnier's platoon needed to work smoothly with them.

To acquire real-time intelligence about the enemy and effortlessly integrate it into their battle plans.

Should fit together like a man and his huntin' dog, instead of going at each other like a hornet and a chainsaw, more dangerous to anyone else around them than to each other.

The mom raised her voice loud enough for even Bishop to hear, "This not deal! Not risk son's life. You say visa to America, maybe talk on TV about Meon, not talk to terrorist."

Schnier leaned back from the onslaught. "Ma'am, everyone in the city is at risk. You're in no more danger here than you'd be at home. We want you to speak to your brother-in-law. Help him understand the real consequences of his actions on people like you and your son."

Jin-son shook his head and muttered, "Not a Pawn. If my

uncle's here, why *not* go talk to him?"

He pushed forward on his chair's joystick.

The oversized powered wheels rolled forward. Decent traction on those, even out here.

Bishop stomped another poorly angled cobblestone. He agreed with the kid. Why not at least talk to the bad guy in charge?

He didn't even know his family was in Seoul. Knowing that might humanize them for him, hostage negotiation 101.

Anyway, it couldn't hurt, right?

They'd bring up a crisis response throw-phone, get the tangos inside talking on it, explain the family situation, surely he'd want to-

Jin-son was halfway to the glass door entrance into the base of the tower.

Dag-nabbit!

What was that fool-of-a-kid doing?

Bishop scraped the snow with his feet and sprinted all out after him, ballistic plates bouncing around on his chest.

"Hey, stop, you don't want to go in there!"

Harper and Schnier turned around, their conversation with the mom interrupted.

Jin-son stopped his chair in front of the glass double-doors.

Leaned forward.

Reached out to grab the door's handle.

Didn't he know they were booby-trapped?

Didn't he see the det-cord and plastic explosives wrapped on the other side?

He didn't have any experience on a battle-field, but common sense-

Bishop tackled Jin-son's wheelchair right as the kid snagged the door handle.

Bishop's flying tackle knocked the chair sideways and around. Instead of facing the door, it spun on its side, facing backward.

Jin-son spilled halfway out onto the ground, his legs strapped in, but his upper body lying on the cobblestones in the thin snow.

Bishop slid to a stop on his stomach, crushing white powder

into thin ice, his chest and legs behind the wheelchair, but his head and neck exposed.

Before he could pull back, the doors exploded into shrapnel.

Glass everywhere.

Glass embedded in the wheelchair's bottom. Glass cut into his neck, rattled off his helmet.

Sliced his carotid artery.

Bishop took the same basic battlefield first-aid training all Rangers got. He knew what that meant for him.

A dozen seconds to pass out. A few minutes at most before blood loss became fatal.

No way to safely tourniquet his neck.

He pressed his open hand into the skin above his collar. Blood spurted anyway, but now dripped from palm to elbow.

Stained the snow.

The patterns his life made in the crystals were gorgeous and unique, like his wife and daughters.

He glanced at Jin-son's horrified face. "You should be a lieutenant."

Jin-son shuddered, "I . . . , I . . ., I didn't . . . "

Bishop smiled to comfort the kid. "Tell 'em I love 'em. I'll see 'em in eternity, when their tour of duty in mortality is complete."

Chapter Forty-One:
Working it out

Yang Hyo-jin hoped Sam saw her email.

She'd sent shorter messages to several co-workers, but wasn't sure what any of them could do.

Her hostage situation called for a military intervention.

She leaned against the broad glass window overlooking Seoul's lights. Stuffed a mixture of weird candy and chicken into her mouth. The North Koreans chose weird food.

Her wrists zip-tied to the railing at thigh-level in front of the window forced her to bend over to take each bite.

She preferred not to prolong the meal.

An explosion thumped from somewhere near the base of the tower.

She jumped as the window vibrated with the shock.

Kwon, the lieutenant who acted in charge of the terrorists, popped up his head at the table where he'd been eating.

Was Sam attempting to breach the defenses?

Smaller pops from down below, gunfire?

Got louder when the elevator doors opened. No actual elevator, but two soldiers with scoped rifles jogged out from the two central shafts.

Spread themselves out. Lay along the edge of the observation deck platform.

Hyo-jin dropped her plate with a crash.

Huddled as low as she could get.

Her ankles were zip-tied to the railing's base. She used the tension to keep her balance as she crouched and hung from her wrists.

Ninety degrees around the circle away from her, the soldiers at the edge of the floor fired at targets on the park's grounds.

A machine gun responded. All the glass on their side of the tower exploded inward as it traversed the area.

Every few times it hit created a small explosion, something different about the bullets. The projectiles chewed holes in the ceiling above the soldiers.

Pieces of an air vent cover rained down on them. A circular ceiling light popped when hit.

She was so exposed up here, but this was as small as she could make herself. Tall is good for volleyball, but not as great for hiding.

Kwon ducked down in response to the shooting. Moved underneath the planked table with the nuclear device on it.

Spoke in bursts on his radio.

The two soldiers retreated from the edge; back to the elevator shafts.

No one made a move to free her.

After the doors exploded, I stood back up. Ran after Bishop and the wheelchair.

A North Korean sniper's first round zipped in front of me.

Bullet scraped my left chest plate at an angle. Ricocheted and shattered. No penetration.

He sees me!

Slammed into the ground. Crawled forward.

Schnier right behind me.

At least I could run faster than him.

Schnier was up. Leapfrogged forward.

Down before the sniper could fire.

I took a snapshot double-tap at the sniper closest to us. Behind partial cover; A steel table in the tower.

Sniper ducked behind the table.

Not sure I got him. Hit the table.

Scared him, at least.

I got up.

Sprinted.

Dove behind the wheelchair.

On its side, internal batteries and motors made a fine shield. As long as the high-capacity batteries didn't explode. Lots of potential energy.

Not the best place to remain.

Jin-son lay on his side, strapped in.

Bishop sprawled across the ground next to him, hand on his neck.

Unconscious. Not breathing.

Not now! Not dying today. Not ever, if I could help it.

Schnier slid to a stop.

Crouched behind the doorway's edge. Positioned out of sight from the interior.

Hidden too close to the tower for snipers on the observation deck to hit him. Not without leaning way out and back, exposing themselves to fire from our men in the surrounding park.

He pointed back at the wall around the perimeter of the courtyard, "Both to cover."

I shook my head. Pointed at the Army truck backed up to the tower's loading dock, "Faster. Get them into the back. Drive to medical."

He nodded. "Got Bishop."

A Mk 48 machine gun opened up from out in the park. Its belt of periodic spotting rounds lit up one part of the observation deck above. Added volume to the precision sniper fire from both sides.

Rained down shards of glass.

I dropped my carbine to hang from its strap.

Pulled my combat knife. Sliced the straps holding Jin-son's legs to his chair.

"Go!"

Schnier dove across the entrance. Grabbed Bishop under his arms. Lifted.

I pulled Jin-son up. He fell the rest of the way out of his chair.

Atrophied legs made it easy to pull him onto my back. Fireman's carry.

Ignored Schnier. Focused on jogging Jin-son to the back of the truck.

Schnier lugged Bishop right behind us.

When I had Jin-son on the truck bed, Schnier was only two steps away.

Helped him lay Bishop into the back.

Schnier climbed up. Held them in place.

I charged across the truck bed to the driver's door. Pulled it open.

Climbed from the bed into the cab.

The truck's push-button starter meant no keys. Engine roared.

Schnier pounded on the back of the cab.

Floored it.

Curved left and right. Threw off anyone with a scope. Crossed to the opposite side of the courtyard.

Bishop hadn't looked good. Not good at all.

Turned down an access road at the edge of the courtyard. Led behind the nearby three story cable car terminal.

Schnier pounded on the cab.

I glanced back.

He patted down on the air with a flat hand, signaling me to stop. The terminal building shielded us from the tower's direct fire.

Didn't we need to get Bishop to medical care?

I stopped the truck, anyway. Maybe he knew something I didn't.

With no more obvious targets, and no one needing to expose themselves, the shooting slowed on both sides.

Schnier tapped on the door's glass window.

One of his men ran up from the corner.

Michelle emerged from hiding nearby with Jin-son's mother. Guess they'd retreated here when the shooting started.

I rolled down the window.

Schnier leaned forward, around the edge of the cab from the truck bed.

"No use. He's gone."

No way.

Dead?

Bishop?

I flashed to my childhood, standing at the top of the stairs, in the hallway outside my bedroom.

A twenty-something social worker from Child Services huddled next to a San Diego Police Department sergeant. They bowed their heads. Wanted to look anywhere but at seven-year-old me.

They'd sent my sixteen-year-old babysitter home. Woke me up in the process. She'd been there most of the night; much later than she intended.

All I knew at first was my parents were late.

"We regret to inform you . . . earlier tonight your mom and dad died from collateral damage. They weren't the target of the blast. The police don't think it had anything to do with them.

"I mean . . . they were in the wrong place at the wrong time. We're so sorry."

Didn't know what collateral damage meant. Not then, but I hated it.

Took my parents from me.

"I'll stay here with you today. This sergeant will be downstairs, just in case."

Bishop was like a replacement parent. Took me under his big Cherry 7-UP drinking wing.

Now he was gone as well.

I took a deep breath. Shook my head. Refused to cry.

Not like that night. A grown man couldn't bawl like a seven-year-old, no matter how much he needed to.

Schnier got Jin-son out of the back of the truck. Leaned him in the dirt against the station's gray stucco wall.

His mom sat with him.

Michelle pulled me out of the truck's cab. Gave me a hug.

I tore away. Not going to let someone in again.

Hurt too much.

The dude from Schnier's platoon drove the truck away, presumably to take Bishop's body somewhere safe, not that it mattered now.

Michelle gave me space. Talked to Jin-son and his mom instead.

Schnier glared at Jin-son.

Started to say something.

Stopped.

Hammered the base of his fist into the wall. Over and over.

Must've cared about Bishop almost as much as I did. Knew him longer, anyway.

Took another deep breath. Wasn't the only one suffering here.

Couldn't think about Bishop's family. Not yet.

"We still have a job to do."

I tried to get the words out, "Bishop would want us to do our duty. To stop those guys. Otherwise more people die."

More collateral damage than the world had ever seen.

Lee stepped up. "Shooting's over. Seem content to bunker back in."

"Can we talk to them?"

He shook his head. "Not enough safe cover to toss a throw-phone where they can get it without exposing themselves.

"Could try a white flag, but then someone would have to see if they planned to start shooting or not the hard way."

Schnier growled. "Gimme a Goose and I'll personally blow the place down.

Lee couldn't help himself, "Sir, our ROE from Major Williams doesn't allow that level of destruction.

"Not in the city."

Friendly cities like Seoul suck for Rangers. A recoilless rifle firing rockets into the tower would be satisfying, but short-lived.

Schnier was using his heart, not his brain.

I needed to use *my* brain. Grief would have to wait.

"Hyo-jin is still up there, along with a nuclear weapon."

Lee cocked his head. "Standard hostage rescue tactics? Breach and disorient?"

"Naw. Won't work." Given a tactical problem, Schnier was back with us mentally, "Central tower is too much of a choke point. Don't have enough Rangers to climb 100 exposed meters in the face of enemy fire.

"My platoon can engage them from a distance. Out-snipe them. They're consolidated in the tower; no freedom of movement.

"Shoot and move. Circle the place. Wait for a good target. Eventually we'll get most of 'em."

I could make it work. Drop in from the top. Bypass their whole defenses.

Not that Schnier would care.

"Where do you want us?"

"My platoon don't need anyone but shooters near the tower. That's how good men get killed."

Should I mention my idea to Schnier?

We only had until morning. "Even if you take most of them out, they've got a dead man's switch on that nuke. Your snipers are good, but if someone hits that guy, we're all dead, along with the whole city. Even if you take out everyone else, he can release the button as soon as he decides they've lost."

"We've got to gamble he won't do it, or else it malfunctions. Got a better idea?"

Time to get real. What would Bishop want?

For us to work together and not waste his sacrifice.

"Vertical envelopment. Drop someone in from the top. Unlike our guys, the People's Army isn't in the habit of ferrying everywhere in helicopters, so they probably aren't watching the skies too well.

"Even if they are, one dude in a HALO jump could land on the top of the tower. Sneak up on the guy with the button, or talk him down enough to convince him to negotiate. Surprise 'em."

Schnier put his hand under his helmet's chinstrap. Leaned against the cable car station's wall.

"I know you want to go."

Who wouldn't?

"Of course, but it's up to you. Your command. My platoon will support in any way needed. If you send one of your dudes, I'll walk 'em through the details and photos I got from Hyo-jin.

"Hasn't responded since that first email, but I'm sure she's still a captive in the tower. Can help disarm the nuke."

Schnier reached out and tapped the unit scroll on my shoulder. "Bishop wanted me to forgive all the crap you've been putting us through. You earned that scroll.

"You should make the HALO jump. If anyone in the company

can disarm the nuke, it's you. We'll keep 'em occupied here on the ground. Focus their attention. Make sure you only have to deal with one or two at the most.

"Don't screw this up."

I nodded, not able to speak for a moment. Finally belonged to the RRC's team, even if we'd lost the best one of us all.

The man who always made me feel welcome, even when I was an idiot.

Lee pointed down the hill at the cable car towers holding its wires up above the trees and brush. "I'll call for a bus from the 2nd Aviation Regiment. Can't land in the courtyard without taking fire, and the city is too crowded, but I bet they could drop a rope ladder to one of those cable cars."

"Good idea. Make the arrangements while I go talk to our guests."

Lee got on the phone to our air support.

Schnier followed me. Stopped me halfway to the other. "Harper, here's the kicker. If you get Kwon away from the nuke, have to take him out. Can't risk that thing goes off."

"Don't worry. I won't risk the city. We'll stop that device by any means necessary."

"Good."

We walked over to where Michelle calmed Jin-son and his Mother down.

Tough enough to almost get blowed up without watching Bishop die. Damn it, even thinking about it made me use his words.

Needed to focus on accomplishing the mission. "You dudes okay?"

Jin-son's Mother looked up at me, "Sorry for your loss, but not a dude."

I held up my hands. "Not what I . . . it's just that where I'm from . . . anyway, know this must be tough for you both, Jin-son's near miss."

Jin-son bowed from the waist. Stared up at me.

"Yeah, I'd be dead if . . . I'm such an idiot."

He looked down. "Want his last words?"

At least he realized he owed Bishop. "Save them for later.

Jin-son, I'll talk to your uncle. If I can convince him to guarantee safe passage, will you come into the tower? Doubt he'll leave it."

His mother stood up. Stuck her chin out at me. "We honor memory of man who die for my son. If you need us to do, we do."

Half-expected her to not want her son to take any more risks, but I guess she finally understood.

No one would leave until we disarmed that nuke. Well, no one but me, but I was coming back.

Gave Michelle a hug.

Nodded to Schnier. Lee had made the arrangements: I was due to surf the top of a cable car.

I'm such a Barney sometimes.

Chapter Forty-Two:
Surfing a Storm

Lieutenant Kwon Chol was so useless here, tied by a dead man's switch to the Goshawk Device on the wooden table above.

He fought in the thick of the action; didn't hide and wait for enemies to arrive.

He listened from under the table until the firing around the tower died off. If the Imperialists made it up the central shaft, he'd have to release his constant pressure on the dead man's switch.

Then, oblivion.

Wouldn't come to that. He had faith in his adopted uncle to use this threat to force peace with the South.

Re-unification of Korea, on Supreme Leader's terms. He'd be a hero, the soldier who held the button which forced everyone to the negotiation table.

Pahk filled him in on the action over the radio.

They'd tried to breach the doors below with some sort of rolling robot device, but his fortified men fought them off.

The sniper fire outside would keep up as long as their enemies remained in denial about the true situation.

Kwon could wait forever for them to come to their senses.

Surfing helps balance, but I couldn't stop shaking.

The storm I'd dodged in the Yellow Sea made it to Seoul in time to catch me standing on top of the cable car.

I held on to the curved steel girders which attached the

suspension wires to the roof. Sort of a u-shape, they balanced the car below the cable, keeping it in the air.

The car dangled partway between stations. Lost some linear movement when Lee had the operator stop it, but still swayed with residual momentum.

Not exactly like riding a wave, but I shifted my balance to match the timing of the twenty-person pendulum.

Don't look down.

Instead, I stared into the gathering storm clouds. Searched for my ride.

Unlike the Big Army bus drivers, the 2nd Aviation reported to Special Operations Command. Plenty of experience with precarious pickups.

The charcoal green of the copter's bottom blended with the clouds. It flared into a hover above me.

The Black Hawk's crew chief dropped a rope ladder the remaining ten meters between us, careful not to tangle it in the cables and wires.

I stepped on the third to bottom rung.

Wrapped my elbow around the closest one. Leaned away from the cable car to ensure a clean separation.

Dangling from the sky, trusting your life to someone else, is tough, but we didn't have time to waste if this trip would make a difference.

The Black Hawk lifted a dozen gentle meters so I wouldn't get hammered back into the cable car.

I climbed the ladder.

The crew chief interlocked hands to forearms. Helped me over the side.

Safely aboard, I knelt on the deck.

He clipped me into a safety harness. Gave the pilot the wind-up signal. We gained altitude.

I gave him a thumbs up.

Chief handed me a Peltor noise canceling headset.

Put on the headset. Tapped the mic. Worked. "Thanks for the ride."

He passed over a combination altimeter/GPS in a square black package attached to Velcro straps.

"No problem. Just going up from here, right?"

I put the little screen on the back of my left hand. Wrapped the Velcro straps around my gloved wrist and palm.

"Yeah, up into the clouds where the tangos in the tower can't see us, then over top of it. I'll get out there. Can't fast-rope, this bird's blades would hit the radio tower. Can I borrow an RA-1?"

"You're jumping with whatever chute I hand you?"

"No other choice. Besides . . ." I pointed out at the storm clouds, "Trusting you guys to fly me through this junk in one piece anyway."

Chief shook his head, "Wouldn't jump with anything I didn't pack."

The wind knocked us sideways.

Bounced us up and down, but the pilot recovered with ease.

My right knee, not so much. I banged it on the floor again. Winced.

"Trust you dudes. No time, anyway. Let's go."

He handed me a clunky deployment bag containing a free-fall parachute. "At least it comes with a lifetime guarantee."

Everybody's a comedian. I slung it onto my back. Stepped into the harness. Attached it across my waist and chest.

We gained more altitude.

The cabin vibrated in time with the four-bladed rotor above. Reached the apex of the flight.

About 3 kilometers high, more of a medium altitude jump, no oxygen needed. I'd be opening low to minimize wind drift.

The pilot centered us over the tower.

I'd take all the help I could get to fight the shifting winds at various altitudes.

Besides, was cold up here.

The crew chief tapped me on the shoulder, "Go!"

I waddled to the open door. Dove headfirst into the blue-gray ocean.

Tumbled through the stored water vapor.

Stuck out my tongue to collect flakes of rainwater as they rushed past. Almost like the sea, except I surfed the storm.

What an adrenaline dump!

Head up, arms and legs extended for balance, the wind drove

my limbs upward.

No static line this time; just a free-fall chute.

Gray and black clouds swirled around me; a never-ending puff of smoke which blocked out the world.

Checked the screen on the back of my left hand. Over the tower, but losing altitude fast.

Triple bolts of jagged lightning cracked from left to right. Blasted through the sky too close for comfort.

That Black Hawk better get back to K-9 air base.

Arch. Look. Trace. Grab.

Arched my back. Looked at the main ripcord handle on my right. Extended my left hand beyond my head, palm down. Traced the main ripcord housing. Grabbed the main ripcord handle with my right hand.

Tugged the handle out of its pocket. Used it to pull the main ripcord cable. Full-arm extension.

Looked straight down.

Pilot chute deployed with a pop. Yanked the main canopy after it with a chunk.

The slider followed. Kept my suspension line groups separated.

Solid jolt. Air caught the main canopy. A good deploy.

No need for the reserve chute.

I slipped the ripcord handle over my wrist. Engaged my night vision.

Grabbed the steering line toggles.

Pulling either toggle pinched the respective corner of the rectangular chute above me down. Turned me in that direction.

Checked the back of my hand for position. Adjusted my direction to head for the tower.

In an RA-1 free-fall chute, I could glide sideways four feet for every foot I descended. Made for precise targeting, even if I didn't begin right above the drop zone.

The right altitude would be critical, otherwise I risked impaling my chute on the radio tower at the top, or worse, missing the roof of the observation deck and ending up on the ground at the base of the tower, rendering this entire trip pointless.

An occasional crack of rifle fire.

Crew chief must've notified Schnier as planned. His men kept the enemy's attention fixed on the ground, hunting for the dudes shooting at 'em.

Close, but still nothing beyond the clouds.

A moment later, Seoul's skyline of lights surrounded me. I'd dropped below the cloud cover.

Car headlights streamed along the snaking roads.

Blinking lights on top of the tower lined up beneath me.

Turned to approach at an angle. Cut across the roof of the observation deck. Aimed my chute to skim to the side of the central antenna.

That approach gave me the longest distance from edge to edge.

A gust pushed me to the side. Now my chute was aimed right at the central tower.

Pulled a steering toggle to turn left. Pulled the opposite one. Lined myself back up.

A quick jog in the air to get back on track.

Close now. Roof approached in a blur.

Flared both toggles. Slowed my descent for a soft landing.

A climate control unit on the roof loomed up at me.

Lifted my feet. Bent my knees even farther to avoid it.

Boots hit the roof. I folded over. Onto my side.

Scraped across the embedded gravel until friction ended my ride.

Dropped my now lighter pack. Only gathered the chute enough to stuff it underneath. Make sure the stiff cross breeze didn't drag it off the building.

Made it.

Now to put my hostage negotiation training to use. Needed to build a relationship of trust with the dude who had his finger on the button to destroy us all.

Assuming I suppressed my desire to avenge Bishop long enough.

Chapter Forty-Three:
The Art

Kwon sat on the rough-hewn bench, in the middle of opulence and destruction. What a waste of electricity.

City lights in three directions, blasted windows and ceiling in the fourth.

No point in responding to the intermittent sniper fire directed at his men. Not even if they became visible to the outside.

Killing one or two more enemies wouldn't complete their mission.

He'd ordered everyone to just bunker down. Prepare themselves for more close-in attacks. Each had extra ammunition, food, and water nearby.

Who knew how long negotiations would take.

The scientist woman huddled up against the window. Refused to stand again.

Made a good shield for that side.

Perhaps they could've taken hostages when they arrived. Lined them up in each direction to prevent enemy fire.

But such a hassle to feed them, take them to the restroom, and so on. Only had a limited number of men; too few to keep hostages.

She might know something useful, but perhaps he should just put her out of her misery.

Such a waste.

Something thumped into the roof above.

They weren't guarding the top of the observation deck. Again, not enough men available; they were already thin at ground level.

Not for the first time, Kwon considered how Meon tasked them at the last minute, without time for proper planning and rehearsals.

Cover. He ducked back under the table.

Radioed Pahk, "Get up here. May have a visitor from above."

All alone on the observation deck, but with a team down on the ground supporting me.

Cold wind and Bishop's death ruined it.

Three clicks of my pick gun. The lock on the stairwell's roof door opened.

Crept down two flights of stairs. Steel emergency door at the observation level barred further progress.

Fed a fiber-optic spy snake camera beneath the door. Pushed its stiff tubing past the rubber weather stripping.

The video feed on my phone from the camera showed an open room curved around the tower's central shaft.

Hyo-jin huddled next to the outer window.

Kwon Chol, whom I'd last seen while reviewing the lab's security video, sat on a wooden bench on the other side of a matching table, each piece of furniture about the length of a long-board.

The nuke occupied the tabletop; a horrendous center-piece.

With a twist of the camera's semi-rigid cable, I checked the areas on each side. One flank peaceful; the other open to the night sky. Room's ceiling pockmarked with bullet holes the size of my thumb.

Good thing I hadn't landed above that area.

The emergency exit door onto this staircase was designed to open toward me, with a crash bar on the other side, so I flipped out the door hinge popper on my multi-tool.

Using the hinge popper, a steel pin with a semi-circular guide around it, I made quiet work of the three hinges, setting each pin on the floor.

The door hung only by the friction of the zinc hinge loops.

One last check with the camera. Nothing had changed.

Tucked it into a cargo pocket.

Lifted the door. Just enough to take the weight off.

Pulled the hinge loops apart.

When infiltrating, sometimes it's easier to open a door the wrong direction.

Kwon Chol popped his head up as I set the door down. Too much noise.

Slung the barrel of my carbine in his direction. Put the laser designator on his chest.

He lifted his left fist. His thumb held down a red button attached to a thick wire.

"No closer!"

Dead man's switch.

His threat trumped mine, at least for now. Couldn't shoot him without unleashing destruction, turning the city's ten million residents plus Yongsan Base into collateral damage from our little fight.

Besides, I needed to build his trust in me, not threaten him.

Lifted my weapon horizontally to free the strap. Aimed it away from him. Rested it on the floor.

"Not here to hurt you. Let's talk, instead."

I tiptoed a few steps forward. Left my primary firearm behind.

Hyo-jin stood up. Her wrists and ankles were zip-tied to the railings, turning her normal grace into an awkward bend.

"Sam, it's a nuclear bomb!"

Kwon tucked his arms beneath his armpits, apparently satisfied I posed no immediate threat.

"Minister Meon is negotiating. I am a weapon, just as much as the one you leave behind you. You will trigger that weapon if you try to interfere. Tell your leaders to speak with Meon. There are no decision-makers here. No decisions to make."

He needed to see me as a person. Needed to cultivate empathy. Create a rapport.

I circled left for a few steps, toward Hyo-jin. "I'm aware of the enormity of the situation. Many families' lives are at stake. You hold the high cards."

Ding. Silver elevator doors opened. A barrel gaped through the gap first, aimed right at me.

I held my hands out to the side. Took another leftward step.

Another People's Army lieutenant stepped out behind his Type 88 automatic rifle. Looked like an AK-74, but with a reduced buttstock and shorter overall length to suit the average North Korean's height.

Rather than a 30-round banana magazine, curved forward like on the AK variants, he'd slung a long tube under its barrel. The helical magazine stored 150 cartridges.

Plenty deadly.

Kwon smiled. Supported his arms on the table in front of him, careful not to release the switch. He'd stalled for this dude's arrival.

"Pahk, excellent timing. I've explained to our guest that Minister Meon will negotiate, not us."

Pahk nodded, but didn't take his aim off of me as he stalked forward.

Much closer and I could risk an attempt to disarm him.

Right now he'd turn me into a poor shield for the glass behind me well before I reached him.

I lifted my hands to shoulder height, palms open and forward. Time to play a card of my own, "You may be more interested in your family reunion than Meon will be. They might embarrass him."

Kwon removed a cheap Korean pistol from a holster with his right hand. Patted his left breast pocket with it for some reason.

Maybe a cultural thing?

"My only living family are these men, Uncle Meon, and Supreme Leader."

"You have a sister-in-law. A nephew. They wait to speak with you at the base of the tower."

He pointed his pistol at me.

Now I had two gaping barrels to deal with. At least they weren't planning to shoot Hyo-jin.

"You are a liar and a murderer. My only blood relatives are dead. Dead at the hands of your soldiers, just like the team I brought to the lab.

"Were you there?

"This scientist knows you. Did you kill my men?"

"I was there."

His finger trembled on the trigger guard, but he wasn't prepared to shoot quite yet. I blessed special forces trigger discipline.

"Some who attacked me died."

"Some? You show your lies. My entire platoon died. If you didn't murder the helpless, at least some would be just wounded, or else captured."

Wait, he thought they were all dead?

"I'm going to slowly lift up my phone and play a video from the local news. Two of your soldiers from the lab are alive. They're prisoners."

Showing them every exaggerated movement, I reached down and eased my phone out of my pocket.

Pahk took a step forward like he wanted to shoot me, but Kwon held up a palm to forestall him.

Brought up a local news site with the lab story. Played full-screen videos of his men's perp-walk outside the lab, captured by news cameras on the street and from helicopters overhead.

"See, alive. One has an elbow wound, so he's wearing a sling, but otherwise they're both fine."

"Meon told me they were all killed. May have been mistaken. Imperialists lie all the time. Maybe that video is fake."

Pahk also refused to accept any aspersions, "The Juche spirit of the Party would not allow one so close to our Supreme Commander to be misled."

"Perhaps he had his own reasons for deceiving you. An attempt to bolster your morale, maybe. I can call your men. They're prisoners, but you can see and speak to them yourself, over a video chat."

Kwon shook his head, but lowered his pistol. Set it on the table next to his much larger weapon. "Doesn't matter."

"Matters to me. The only family I have and the only family you have, are all here right now. They're all dead if we can't work this out. Like you, I've already lost too much family. Don't need to lose any more.

"Not tonight."

He patted his pocket with his hand, "What family have you lost? Imperialist border guards slaughtered my only brother and his wife. My parent's grief killed them. Minister Meon raised me as his nephew.

"We have no other family!"

"A terrorist killed my mother and father when I was seven years old. I've read the records.

"A bomb, not as large as that one, but big enough to destroy its target and my parents. They were only having dinner. That's all. Innocent bystanders. Collateral damage. Not even a deliberate target."

Pahk's veins were about to pop out of his skin. "Lies, lies, lies! He seeks to prey on your sympathy, Lieutenant Kwon. Ignore him. These Dominionists are masters of deception, of shrouding people from the truth. Of shaping their past to match yours. Remember your hostage training.

"He desires you to trust him, but doesn't truly care what happens to you. Only your comrades in arms care. My team will sacrifice our lives for each other."

Kwon raised his pistol. Took aim at my nose. "You almost had me. Uncle warned me about the temptations we'd face here. If any of our men show themselves below, your snipers will kill them. No, we won't be sending anyone out into the open. You'll just die here."

Just listen once.

That's all I needed, or else Hyo-jin, my new family in the Rangers, the entire city, would all be gone together.

"I'll call them. Order a cease-fire. Tell them to bring your relatives to the door. Send them in to speak with your men alone. No risk."

I hoped Jin-son had that much courage, to approach unescorted, through the door which just exploded on him. "One of your men can search them. Bring them up. If they aren't your family, then you can still shoot me. Use them as more hostages."

Hyo-jin thrust her shoulders forward, her hip cocked to the side, "And me. You can shoot me. I trust this man to do what he says.

"He's telling the truth."

I forced down a smile, lest they misunderstand. She'd never even heard of Jin-son and his mother before.

Kwon lowered his pistol again. "How do I know they won't attempt to overpower my soldiers when they're close enough?"

"Your nephew is confined to a wheelchair. Your brother's wife is almost an old woman.

"Neither poses a physical threat."

"If you lie, you die. Call them. Give your orders.

"Pahk, take his weapon from the floor and then go make the arrangements. You know the stakes. Search them well, and then bring them to me."

"Those aren't our orders from Meon. No one is to enter."

"Minister Meon placed *me* in command."

Pahk nodded, lips tight.

He lowered his weapon. Turned on his heel.

Stooped and picked up my rifle on his way back to the elevator.

I'd miss it, but that's not the weapon I needed to wield tonight.

I made the call to Schnier. He'd trust me on this one, right?

Chapter Forty-Four:
The Deal

Jin-son's Mother overheard Lieutenant Schnier's half of his phone conversation.

With her son's life at stake, wisdom dictated she gather complete information.

Function dictated the soldier's uniforms, but like most in power, necessity ruled their actions.

The American soldiers had stashed her and Jin-son in the station lobby with Sergeant Lee and that rude military attaché, Michelle.

Lee possessed superior Korean breeding, so logic compelled a cautious mother to stay by his side. He'd already brought a new wheelchair to Jin-son from the civilian first responders stuck at the perimeter.

Schnier mentioned them four times in his conversation. He'd agreed to hand them over to the North Koreans. But first, he radioed a ceasefire order to his men.

They were no longer to target any enemy appearance.

His request was blunt, "Will you take your son into the tower? Convince Kwon Chol of who you are? Of your story?"

She preferred not to answer yet, so she picked up a water bottle. "Wait. Need use restroom."

Standing in the women's room and staring into the mirror gave her a few minutes.

Would her son be safe in the tower?

The North Koreans had no reason to kill him, specifically, but as a living relative of hers, Meon might consider him a loose end.

She was old, but remained a deserter from the North. That carried a death sentence, so they might decide to punish her escape.

Risky for them both. She couldn't lose her son! He was all she had.

Would rather lose herself.

Outside the lobby restroom doors, she filled a water bottle for her son. Took a sip for herself.

The place echoed without the usual crowds, making it difficult to think. The soldiers obviously found her son critically important, to keep them both so near the fighting.

No telling when they'd next have easy access to water. Couldn't allow her son to dehydrate.

He was important to her, too.

She strolled back to Schnier and her son. "Jin-son, record this. Send to your friend."

She turned to Michelle. Ticked off each demand with a finger, "Want American citizenship for both. Scholarship to any school in United States for son. Living expenses for time at school. Expenses for both.

"Then we will go. Have a deal with American government?"

Michelle pulled on her tacky shell necklace, as if that reminded her of something, "D.C. gave me authority for whatever is necessary, although I'll answer for it all later. I'll make it happen. You have your deal."

"Good. Jin-son shut off recording. Drink water. I'll push you to tower."

"I can use the push rims, just take off the brakes."

She released the brakes. Grabbed the cheap rubber handles. "Nonsense. Save strength. Will need if go wrong."

They left the soldiers behind.

She pushed him across the courtyard. Up to the ruined door.

The snow on the ground had either melted or turned to ice, but her grip on the chair's handles helped her balance.

After one glance, she refused to look down at the blood and broken glass. The crunch of door glass under the chair's tires mixed with crushed ice.

The American soldier saved her son, like her son's father had saved her, giving his life in the process. That was enough for her to trust his comrades-in-arms.

She pushed her precious son down a tunnel-like hallway. Silent black curved television screens echoed the tires. Parroted her steps.

They reached the barricade of steel table and trash cans.

Two snipers crouched behind cover; weapons searching for targets. A third man, an officer, stood up. "Names?"

The familiar arrogance of the North Korean military actually reassured her. She'd dealt with his kind before. "Yeo Min-jung. This Kwon Jin-son. You are?"

Her son nodded at his name, clearly not sure what to say to this icon of death, a representative of the northerners she'd warned him about his entire life.

"Lieutenant Pahk. I will search you; then you will come with me."

She stepped forward. Held out her arms. Spread her legs.

"Search old woman first. Paralyzed child next."

Her jibe hit her mark.

Pahk reddened. He understood the loss of face involved in a special forces soldier finding them a threat.

Did his duty, though. Patted her down like a pro. Even unstrapped her son and lifted him partially from the chair. Ensured they'd hidden nothing under his feeble limbs.

"Satisfied?"

"We'll take the elevator."

She pushed Jin-son in and then turned him around to face the doors.

Pahk stood to the side of the elevator where he could glare at them and also face the doors.

Never realized how frightening a long elevator ride could be, despite taking one every day in her own apartment building.

Didn't have elevators in most of North Korea, at least not for people outside the elite ruling class, so probably Pahk was even more afraid.

Doors dinged open. Pahk motioned for them to leave.

She pushed Jin-son into the room.

Lieutenant Harper and a towering Korean woman in a lab

coat formed the base of a triangle. Another North Korean officer stood at the apex, next to a table. A masculine version of his mother's looks.

"Doryeonnim?" She added, "Unmarried-younger-brother-of-my-husband?" for the American officer.

Americans spoke terrible Korean.

Harper pointed, "That's Kwon Chol."

She wasn't impressed with his grasp of the obvious. "Met when he child. Knew parents well. Doryeonnim, this your nephew, Jin-son."

Kwon Chol reached into his breast pocket. Removed a photograph. Studied it.

Stepped forward a few paces. Held it in the air between them. Examined it again.

His voice turned quiet, soft, "You're older, but it's you. And your son looks like my brother and our father. Is he alive, also?"

Now he looked hopeful.

She hated to crush him, but slowly shook her head, "Party Secretary for village, Meon Lon-chun, shot husband in back when border guard chase us. Died for me to live. To escape with unborn child."

Kwon Chol staggered back, "Meon killed my older brother?" He sat on a raw wooden bench. Stared at the floor. "What have I become?"

She pushed Jin-son forward.

After a moment of silent tears, he looked back up. "Our parents? Meon told me grief killed them after your deaths."

She bowed her head. "I ashamed. Parents starve in camps. Punishment for our treason."

Kwon Chol sighed, "Not your burden, Ajumeoni."

With that title, he acknowledged her as his older brother's wife.

Her son leaned forward. Bowed from the waist. "Glad to meet you, Uncle, even under these circumstances."

Such courage her boy had!

Her restored relative stood. Bowed correctly. Shook Jin-son's hand.

"Good to have family, even if we don't know each other."

Pahk strode forward, chest out. Stopped next to the wheelchair.

"Congratulations on your reunion, but it doesn't change the basic situation. If there is to be peace, we must complete our mission. I'm sure after we unite Korea you and your family will live together again."

Kwon Chol frowned. "He's right. Meon committed terrible crimes against our family, but I cannot betray the strength and spirit of Korea. His reckoning must come later.

"I'm sorry."

At least Hyo-jin seemed happy to see me. I watched the tearful reunion while sneaking meaningful glances at her.

Pahk, not so much.

We had maybe another fifteen minutes until Meon's deadline. Probably realized he wasn't getting a ransom yet, but expected negotiations about the timing for gathering that much portable wealth.

The family bullet had hit its mark, but we hadn't convinced Kwon Chol he couldn't trust Meon.

No more collateral damage. No more orphans today. No more losses like Bishop.

I'd wanted revenge for his death, but now I realized Kwon Chol was a naïve tool for the real villain. Meon started this chain of events in motion years ago.

Kwon Chol needed to know the truth.

Without Bishop's sacrifice, he wouldn't have his family again. I wouldn't have found *my* new family, either.

How could I help Kwon Chol understand what I'd only realized myself once Bishop died?

At least now Kwon Chol knew I was true to my word. That's an opening for trust.

I stepped forward and joined the reunion. "This is your true family. Not just Jin-son and his mother, but the men you serve with. Your fellow soldiers who risk their lives for each other.

"They're your blood brothers, not Meon. He's just using you

for wealth and power."

Pahk stepped between us. Tried to isolate me.

Ignoring him as too short to block my line of sight, I pointed down; toward the tower's entrance. "My family already lost a respected elder today. A blast killed our top sergeant while he saved your nephew's life.

"He would forgive you his family's loss. Meon wants you to set that nuke off and kill your remaining family. All of your family is in *this* city."

Kwon bowed his head. I sensed his wheels turning. "This *is* my real family, but the unification of Korea under Dear Leader is my duty. I won't embarrass my family and my ancestors by failing."

Pahk, on the other hand, wasn't buying what I was selling yet. "We have to think for the future. For the peace of our entire nation. For our relatives in the North.

"Yes, war brings great sacrifice, but peace makes it worthwhile."

How could I convince them of the madness they participated in?

What makes men obey orders to perpetrate terrible tragedies?

Avoidable catastrophes, like the explosion which killed my parents?

Couldn't they see the truth?

"Meon told you this will lead to peace? Detonating a nuclear weapon and murdering ten million civilians? Definitions get twisted in Communist North Korea, but that's what you call peace?"

Pahk spat on the floor in front of me, "You're lucky to be alive. No more of your interference."

I took a long breath. Recovered my composure. Forced myself to shrug casually, as if this wasn't the most important conversation of all of our lives.

"Call Meon. Ask him to explain how his demand for 100 million American dollars in exchange for your bomb leads to peace. To explain how wealth for himself reconciles Korea."

Pahk growled, "He's negotiating for peace and unification, not wealth."

He turned to Kwon Chol. "The Imperialist lies. Do not doubt our Party leaders."

Kwon Chol lifted his dead man's switch. "It's my responsibility. I have reason to doubt. There's no harm in calling him. You will not reveal the presence of my family. No need for distraction."

Pahk paused. Nodded.

Jin-son's mother recoiled and pulled her son's chair backward a foot before catching herself, "Let me speak to him. I have many things to say to that . . ."

Kwon Chol held up a hand. Stopped her from continuing. "No, we'll see what he has to say about this man's words."

He removed a phone from his pocket. Pushed the button for speaker-phone. Pressed redial.

Meon answered, "Status?"

"We have a situation. An American officer infiltrated the tower. Claims he's here to negotiate. That they could not reach you to attempt a diplomatic agreement. You're on speaker phone with him."

I saw where Kwon Chol was going with this, "Minister Meon, remember my voice? We've spoken before. I explained your demands to these soldiers. Been difficult to raise that amount of cash on short notice. Could we substitute more gold instead?"

Meon coughed a few times. "Kwon? You were ordered to only communicate with me, not to negotiate!"

"You told me they killed all my men. You'll be happy to know I've seen them. Alive."

Now Meon sounded like Santa Claus after he'd had 99 bottles of tequila too many, "That's great news! Must have been a mistake. Our intelligence isn't always the best from south of the DMZ. I'll insist they allow you to bring them both back with you, once this is over."

"Both? Never said there were only two."

"I just assumed. Get Pahk. I have new orders for both of you.

"Slight change in plans."

Pahk stepped forward. Bent over the phone, "I'm here, General."

"You're to take command there. I have a new mission for

Kwon, but first, kill the American. He can't be trusted. Make it painful."

I shook my head. "I can hear you. You've lied enough to these men."

Pahk pointed his Type 88 at my head. At this short range, could probably deflect the barrel to the side before he actually fired.

Unfortunately, that would direct his muzzle toward Hyo-jin, restrained at the railing and unable to even attempt to dodge.

Kwon Chol pushed Pahk's barrel down with the wrist of his hand holding the phone. "There is no proof of his words, but do you have evidence you're pushing for peace and not wealth?"

"Evidence? You have your orders, obey them!"

I drew my phone. Held it between us. Handy gadgets, these modern smart phones, even the militarized ones.

"Listen."

I played the recording I'd copied to my phone from Bishop's encrypted chip.

Meon choked on the other side of Kwon Chol's phone. Perhaps a seizure?

I didn't care.

"You'll note he identifies himself. Demands money in exchange for the city. This is my favorite part."

I rewound the recording ten seconds.

Played Meon's final words again, "Comply, and you can keep your city, the bomb, and I'll even throw in a special forces platoon once I'm safely away with my new wealth."

Cocked my head at Pahk, "I guess you dudes are the special forces platoon in his message?"

Their fearful leader made one final attempt, "Don't listen to his lies. That's a fake. Kill him, before he destroys us all."

Kwon Chol lifted his phone to his mouth, "Before he destroys you, you mean? It's all lies. Everything you ever taught me. Everything you ever said to me. Everything in my life so far.

"You killed my brother. His wife and her son are here with me. Your Party killed my parents. Betrayal after betrayal. You aren't my family, you're my slave master.

"No more!"

With those two words, Kwon Chol spun and chucked the phone.

It sailed an arc through the air. Up past the bullet-riddled ceiling. Down through the shattered window frames. Clear out the open end of the observation deck.

Impacted out of sight. Somewhere below.

The first rays of morning hit the ceiling above the opening.

I checked the time. "Meon's 24 hour deadline is over. Guess this means he won't call you and order you to set that thing off?"

Pahk took a step back from us all. Raised his weapon in our general direction.

If he shot Kwon Chol, releasing the dead man's switch, ten million Seoulites would die.

Not to mention Hyo-jin, Michelle, and the rest of us.

Chapter Forty-Five: Spiking Volleyballs

Yang Hyo-jin knew the stress-resistant properties of the vinylon zip ties binding her.

Their yield point and modulus of elasticity. Understood how weight and momentum worked, in detail.

Been a world-class athlete.

So why couldn't she break free?

Family reunions and phone calls distracted the North Koreans.

She stood in a pool of darkness at the edge of the observation platform, the only light on her from the city below, deflected through the floor to ceiling glass windows.

She twisted her wrists in opposite directions. Multiplied the strain she could apply.

Needed to exceed their load carrying capacity at the line of greatest pressure from her twist. Attack her bond's tensile strength at its weakest point.

Lifted her arms high.

Took up the inch of wrist slack.

Slammed her elbows down to generate momentum; brought her wrists apart at the apex of the force she'd generated. Used her force and her bond's friction against the steel railing's edge. Abraded the vinylon cords.

Again.

Again.

On the third try, her restraints parted. Free hands!

She flailed at the railing. Too much momentum. Her bonds

didn't hold her to it anymore.

Managed to grab on without falling on her rear. Looked at Sam, Pahk, and the others.

No one had noticed.

Except Sam. He stared at her out of the corner of his eye. She could tell, because after she recovered her balance, he winked and deliberately looked away from her.

They argued with the politician on the phone.

She went to work on the zip ties locking her ankles to the bottom railing.

With the free use of her hands, plus the greater strength of her legs, she broke those faster.

Freedom!

She rubbed her wrists and ankles. Got her blood flowing again.

As the sun rose on their deadline, Kwon Chol spun and chucked his phone out the open end of the observation deck.

Their conversation hadn't gone well. Relationships with old-Korea bureaucratic superiors didn't always go as planned.

Rhee also betrayed her, after all.

Pahk stepped away from the group. Walked backward. Toward her.

Pointed his gun at them.

Sam made eyes at her. Looked at her. Then at Pahk. Trying to tell her something, but she wasn't sure what.

She pointed at herself. At Pahk.

Sam nodded imperceptibly.

She raised her arms up. Mimicked hitting like a boxer.

Sam nodded again. Stepped forward; toward her and Pahk.

Pahk retreated until he was half the length of a volleyball court away from her. Pointed his big gun at Sam.

The biggest threat.

Hyo-jin ran her approach motion, designed to generate maximum momentum at the point of attack above the net.

Pictured Rhee's face on the back of Pahk head.

He turned his neck at the noise of her steps, but kept his weapon trained on Sam.

His face betrayed no fear.

She was just a foolish young scientist, after all. He was a trained special operations soldier.

She adjusted her approach into a curved path behind him. Leapt in the air.

Transmitted her gathered momentum and power into her arm swing.

Spiked the ball; Pahk's head, just above the ear.

The force of her blow drove him into a sideways stagger. His finger on the trigger added new holes to the ceiling.

So loud!

Sam finished his own rush. Slammed his heel into the side of Pahk's knee.

Shouldn't crunch like that. She cringed, unable to not imagine the end of a player's career in the noise.

Pahk collapsed to the deck.

Sam wrestled Pahk's rifle away. Clubbed him in the face with the shoulder stock.

Broke his nose. Blood gushed out.

Sam secured Pahk with his own zip ties.

Hyo-jin put up her hand for a high-five. He'd gotten over his emotional poison.

They'd worked together well.

Sam wrapped her in a bear hug, instead.

I released Hyo-jin from my embrace.

She blushed. Don't go much for public hugs in Korea. I didn't care.

She'd done exactly what we needed, taking out Pahk with a volleyball spike to the head.

With Pahk out of commission, tied up on the deck, that left Kwon and the soldiers guarding the base of the tower.

Kwon Chol held up the dead man's switch. "I'd surrender, but they didn't explain how to shut this thing off, just how to arm it."

I used Hyo-jin's arm to tug her over to him. Wasn't about to let her go now, not when I'd just gotten her back. We'd worry about what that meant to us later.

One mistake and we could lose the whole enchilada.

"We can leave the bomb armed. The Army EOD has specialists for that. Just need to eliminate the dead man's switch."

Hyo-jin stuck her hands into the pockets of her lab coat. "How? The spring-loaded button holds the switch closed. Can't take the pressure off of it, not reliably. If it goes to an open state, if the wires are no longer connected, boom!"

She was thinking like a scientist, not an engineer.

"There are two thick wires in that cable connecting the switch to the detonation device. Shouldn't mess with the switch. Too complicated, but wires are just wires. Can you find me electrical wire?"

She looked around. "One second."

Dragged a wooden bench over to the side of the platform where a machine gun had perforated the ceiling.

Set it under a dangling pot light. Used it as a step stool. Fiddled around up above the ceiling.

While she was busy, I'd work on a more sensitive project.

The little wire cutter on my multi-tool included a wire stripper near the handles. All I had to do was remove a tiny bit of the insulation from the wires to gain access to them.

I'd stripped wires a thousand times.

This time, I took a deep breath first to steady my hand. Grabbed a slack portion of cabling near the device. Tuned everything else out.

If I cut all the way through, it would break the circuit, the same result as if Kwon Chol released the button switch.

A little pressure on the handles. Just a dent in the wire.

A little more. The insulation on one side cut through.

A tiny squeeze further. The stripper penetrated the other side.

Access to two bare wires achieved.

Hyo-jin ripped the pot light off the ceiling, bringing strands of wire attached to twist-on wire connectors with it.

She bounced over. Swung the light fixture from a line of wire. "This work?"

"Perfect."

I handed her my tool, not wanting to release the dead man's

switch cabling.

"If you'll cut two six inch pieces of wire and strip the insulation off, we can solve this."

Jin-son rolled himself closer. "What're you doing?"

His uncle nodded, "I wondered the same thing. Experts designed the switch."

"It's great for an unexpected release, but the simplicity needed to make sure it won't malfunction renders it vulnerable. As long as you hold the switch down, it connects the two wires, allows electricity to flow between them.

"All we need to do is give the electricity a shorter path to take. Bypass the switch farther down the cable."

Hyo-jin handed me the first of the two naked wires I'd requested.

If I was wrong about how the dead man's switch worked, this is where we'd all find out. Well, we'd actually probably die before realizing anything went wrong.

Didn't matter. Waiting wouldn't improve the odds.

I put the center of the bare wire underneath and across where I'd stripped the insulation away from both sides of the cable. Wrapped it around like a coil, trying to create as much contact as possible.

That shorted the wires. No big bang.

Looked like I'd been right about how it worked. Now to make sure it remained secure.

Heaving on the wires, I pulled the coil tight. Twisted the ends together.

Held them with one hand. Put my other palm out toward Hyo-jin, "Wire nut."

She handed me one from the ceiling attachment.

I twisted it onto the bare wire ends.

"Don't let go of the switch yet, but that should actively bypass the mechanism. I'll need that second wire and another connector."

I moved up the cable, toward the switch, about a foot.

Stripped off even more insulation. Used the second bare wire to wrap the new gap.

It shorted the wires in the cable together a second time. I

twisted on another cheap wire nut.

Redundancy is always good when dealing with the lives of ten million people. The lives of those I loved, of my new family.

I took a deep breath. Held it. "Release the switch."

Kwon Chol hesitated.

Did he really trust me? My life was on the line as well. I'd parachuted onto the tower through a storm to stop this thing from going off.

That proved I'd risk my life, not that I knew what I was talking about with electrical stuff.

He put his hand out above the table.

Lay the switch and the end of the cable on the tabletop. Turned his head away, as if that would matter.

Released the button.

Nothing happened.

I breathed out. My voice came out in a high-pitched rush, "See, nothing to worry about."

Cleared my throat. "Leave the rest to the experts. They can take all the time they need. Please radio your men to surrender. I'll call our team down below. Get them to post a guard here."

Former DPRK lieutenant and new uncle Kwon Chol explained to his men that their mission was over and how to surrender safely.

I called Schnier. Explained the situation. Arranged to ensure no one got hurt who didn't deserve it.

Captain Grant would sequester Pahk and his men. Interview them to determine their status.

Michelle had one thing to add before we disconnected, "After hearing what happened, I've transmitted a copy of Meon's message to the Supreme Guard. It's the least I could do."

She'd earned her place as part of my new family, despite her occasional ruthlessness.

Chapter Forty-Six:
Crushed

The steam boiler burbled.

Deputy Defense Minister Meon Lon-chun needed to figure out how to salvage this latest blow.

He leaned back in his chair. Stared at the cheap temporary double-aluminum ceiling.

No good ideas.

Not since Kwon Chol hung up on him. Just a litany of scenarios, all bad.

He should forget all this. March out to his official car. Pay a visit to China.

By the time the secretive government spread word of his disappearance, before they noticed he hadn't shown up in Pyongyang as ordered, he'd be feasting in Beijing on what he'd acquired and stored in other countries over the years.

Yes, cut his losses.

A rumble from down the road outside. Those annoying tanks again. Their treads clanked in the frozen mud of the road approaching his temporary office hut.

A little early for them to return from their exercises. More fuel shortage excuses for laziness.

Could he get away with shooting Colonel Jong-rin, that incompetent buffoon?

Even execute him in front of his men, so they learned not to disturb his thoughts with their diesel engines?

The roar of the tank engines just got louder. Worse than ever. Sounded like they were right outside his office walls.

Oh well, he'd depart soon enough.

One had to be philosophical about these things.

Maybe he could convince the Chinese President to back a coup. They'd always considered marching in and taking over North Korea.

He could be useful to them.

A figurehead who knew the players in Pyongyang from the inside. Could bring them plenty of useful information.

The Korean people would welcome him, leader of a liberating army. Over time, he'd become the face of Chinese control in the country and return to true power, the new Supreme Leader.

Found a new dynasty of control.

The corner of a Popkung-Ho tank tread chewed through the wall behind him. Shook his Tommy Gun off of the wall.

What were those idiots doing?

The tank backed up. Its treads changed their angle. Rushed toward him.

A green laminar steel panel, the front of the main battle tank, burst through the wall. The bottom of the wall flattened under the treads. The wall's top sheered away like a hinged cabinet.

Meon picked up his Tommy Gun. Sighted it on Colonel Jong-rin, his head poked out of the tank commander's hatch. Squeezed the trigger with all his strength.

Nothing.

Never been good at taking care of his tools. Now this one let him down, just like everything else.

Jong-rin shook his fist. "Supreme Leader and my cousin the boiler mechanic have a message for you!"

He ducked into his hatch. The cupola spun toward Meon, barrel forward. The wall no longer blocked their advance.

Both treads churned forward.

Meon scuttled backward. On his knees. Under his desk.

Maybe he could get out, run away, get to his car. Drive to China.

The tank's right tread reversed direction; spun the 45 ton beast onto his teak desk.

His phones jangled. Went silent. The track ground them into spinning shards of plastic and broken electronics. The tank's diesel engine roared above him.

Maybe not.

The edge of the desk gave way. Glass shattered. Liquid leaked from the crushed drawer next to his head.

Meon huddled flat. Pressed palms into ears.

Essential oils mixed with blood.

Nobody likes a sacrificial goat which refuses to go to the altar properly.

Michelle leaned forward in her chair, toward the video conference screen. She'd spent the last hour here in the embassy's Sensitive Compartmented Information Facility (SCIF) filling in the blanks for Metcalf in D.C.

She spoke up for the microphones, "With the bomb disarmed and the data confirmed destroyed, that wraps up this incident."

The room reminded her of WARCOM's SCIF, where this all started. Same black and gray, decorated by microphones and cameras.

Probably built by the same government contractor in a hardened container and shipped to Korea.

Metcalf waved away the others from his side of the connection. A half-dozen functionaries filed out of the room behind him.

His voice boomed out of the room's speakers at her, "Dangled a lot of rope when you promised citizenship and a scholarship. You let them get you on tape?"

No one could record them here.

"Your plan to allow a minor crisis to occur and then solve that crisis failed. No, not failed . . . spiraled out of control.

"My contacts within SOCOM's Ranger Company dealt with Seoul's predicament. Any *legitimate* review will find my promises were necessary to achieve that win."

He leaned back at her attribution to him, "Perhaps. Investigations aren't always that straightforward."

Did he believe her naïve?

"If anyone knew the Agency contributed to the risk of Seoul's nuclear destruction . . ."

His eyes widened. Pupils dilated. Took a deep breath before continuing, "All's well that ends well. We'll just bury it. Forget it ever happened."

She gritted her teeth. Wouldn't get off that easy.

"Perhaps. Best if I moved on to a new assignment. Something with more responsibility, so it doesn't look like a demotion." She paused, "Doesn't imply anything went wrong."

He stepped back from the camera. The automatic tracking zoomed in on him anyway as he spoke.

"An assignment in the Asia-Pacific Region. Those decisions are within my purview, no justifications needed."

"The Philippines is hot lately, between Jihadists and the Chinese dispute over the Spratly Islands. Manila needs a new Station Chief."

"Station Chief? Maybe I can swing you as chief deputy."

"Oh, did you need me to stick around Seoul for a while? Testify at whatever inquiry they're sure to put together?"

He sighed. "Station Chief. No problem. Don't piss the ambassador off."

"I'll need military resources. Off the books. Covert commandos."

She gave him her best cobra smile. Resisted pumping her arm. Concealed her excitement. "Maybe South Korea will negotiate an end to their war and the removal of North Korea's nuclear program, now that we've demonstrated they aren't in control of their own military.

"That should free up some troops."

"Of course. Whatever you need, subject to the Army's requirements."

Would she rather have Harper or Schnier?

Decisions, decisions.

Sam was smart and loyal. She loved his naivete; how easily she could manipulate him. Besides, he needed to get into a new situation.

On the other hand, Schnier had proven more of a challenge. They never did finish their date.

Why not both? "Harper and Schnier's platoons worked well together. I'm sure you still have a few favors you could call in, especially if it's a reward for their excellent performance here in Seoul.

"Let's get them to Manila."

He paused. Considered. Made his choice.

"Consider it done."

Metcalf powered down the teleconference before she manged to assert additional demands.

Brilliant man. Harvard smart.

Not as astute as the new Manila Station Chief. At least, not this round.

Chapter Forty-Seven:
Black Granite Temple

My chest ached to see our platoons united. Unified by grief.

I hurried up and waited with Lee and Schnier on the tarmac at Seoul Air Base. Our platoons formed ranks behind us, equals in honoring the fallen.

Our whole company wore class-A dress uniforms, tan berets draped over our right ears.

Major Williams stood next to the base's main terminal. Near him, the HQ platoon's honor guard pierced the winter air with the Stars and Stripes and the 75th RRC's banner.

The eaves on the main terminal building curved upward in the Korean architectural style, supported by wide pillars. This is where the President of South Korea, or similar dignitaries entitled to a military or diplomatic flight, flew in and out of Seoul.

Civilian observers lined up opposite the honor guard.

Bishop's wife in front, a daughter on either side of her, each with an arm tucked into their mother's to support her.

They planned to see her family in American Samoa on their way back to Virginia, where they'd meet Bishop's parents for the internment.

Hjo-jin and Michelle stood at the back of the crowd with the Korean contingent. Not sure those two will ever get along.

Schnier had news from Captain Grant while we waited, "The crew of the patrol boat we picked up in the Yellow Sea all decided to stay in South Korea."

Lee nodded. "With the two from Kwon's team and Pahk's six,

that makes an even dozen. My government has a special program for defectors. They'll be fine."

Schnier looked at the northern horizon. "What about Pahk?"

I shrugged. "He thought the risk if he stayed, the risk to his parents and sister in Pyongyang, that is, was greater than if he returned without his men. Best case, he blames everything on Meon and Kwon. Maybe they'll hush it up to limit the embarrassment.

"If not, maybe he can stay free long enough to get his family out to China. Ask for asylum."

Lee's mouth shaped into a grim twist. "Intelligence reports Meon died in an unfortunate training accident while guiding a tank. No one will be around to dispute Pahk's account."

Schnier shook his head. "Risky, Pahk taking the bull by the horns like that. Speaking of which, Harper, while we're in Manila, I'll give you combatatives lessons. Train you right up."

I chuckled. At least I had Schnier's acceptance. "Bringing my board. I'll teach you how to surf."

"Anything like forkin' a bronc?"

"Yep, dude, *just* like that. You'll see."

"Anyhow, my hippie ex-girlfriend from college moved to the Philippines. Might could look her up fer you. She's hotter than a brandin' iron in Amarillo."

Dude would never change. And that was fine. I had other plans.

Just shook my head in response.

A C-17 Globemaster III taxied up the runway toward us. Its four jet engines quashed further conversation.

When it reached the terminal building, the pilot executed a 90-degree turn away. Stopped and killed the engines beneath its swept-back wings.

Lowered the rear ramp with a whine.

I double-checked my phone's sound was off. Lee returned to his position in front of our MI platoon. I took up my spot next to him.

Schnier turned. Called the assembled men of the 75th RRC to attention.

The honor guard snapped to at Major William's command.

Civilians bowed their heads. Removed their hats. Placed them over their hearts.

An Army ambulance, green camo pattern under a red cross on a white field emblazoned on the roof and sides, drove around the corner of the terminal building.

When the ambulance reached the terminal, it stopped and backed up to where the honor guard stood. A soldier inside opened the rear doors.

Exposed Bishop's flag-draped casket to view.

The chaplain and part of the honor guard, the men who worked directly under Bishop's leadership, marched with precision to the rear of the ambulance.

Slid out the casket two at a time until it rested between the eight of them.

The 75th RRC saluted on command. The chaplain led the carry detachment toward the rear of the plane. Halted them between us and the civilians.

The chaplain prayed for us all.

Full military honors would wait until Bishop reached Virginia. The detachment marched his casket up the ramp. Into the cargo hold. Lowered it in the center.

Snapped to attention.

The detachment and the air crew joined our salute.

A lone bugler marched from the terminal building. Played the mournful notes of "Taps".

The honor detachment marched with precision out the rear ramp. Major Williams conducted the vigil.

Ended it with, "As always, Rangers Lead the Way."

The entire company responded, "ALL THE WAY!"

The aircrew raised the plane's ramp.

Four jet engines roared to life. His body began its final journey home.

We released our salute to Mother Bishop.

Most of the soldiers marched back through the terminal. Many of the civilians lingered.

Schnier and I walked over to Bishop's wife and daughters to pay our condolences.

"Ma'am," Schnier saluted, "Sergeant Bishop's sacrifice, his

spirit of humility and service, well, he was a courageous personal example to me. A man to ride the range with. Kept me on the straight and narrow every time I deviated from Ranger Standards."

Bishop's wife held back tears. Nodded. Her daughters stayed strong for her as well.

Schnier dropped his salute. Stepped to the side.

I stepped up. Rendered my own salute.

"I agree with everything Lieutenant Schnier just said. Wouldn't be here today without Top's leadership and cajoling."

My eyes got some dust in them.

"Best I can do is keep asking myself, 'What would Bishop do?' He out-shined us all. I'd never surf again if it'd bring him back, but he didn't die in vain. He'll always lead us in spirit.

"Rangers everywhere will increase their devotion to the cause he shared with us."

Couldn't say anything more, but also couldn't walk away. Legs were too weak to carry me.

His wife saved me, just like Bishop would've. "I'm grateful his decision to volunteer as an Army Ranger brought him to men who became like brothers."

Her voice broke, "It may appear our family of four is now a family of three, but our family has never been larger than today."

Strength restored, I dropped my crispest salute ever and stepped to the side.

Kwon Chol wheeled his nephew up to her. Bowed from the waist.

"My family is ashamed at what our actions have cost you. We can never return your life to harmony."

Jin-son inclined forward, as close to genuflecting as he could. "I, too, am filled with deep sadness and regret. Your husband sacrificed his life to save me from my own foolish mistakes.

"His final words to me were a request to express his love to you and your daughters. To promise he will see you in eternity, when your, how did he say it? Your tour of duty in mortality is complete."

She smiled wistfully. "Sounds like my husband. You're not to worry. God sealed our family together forever. No matter what this life brings, we'll see him again. You may pay your debt with a hug."

Twice the size of the Koreans, she gathered them together and squeezed. After a moment, her daughters joined her.

When released, Kwon Chol's eyes blinked rapidly. His eyebrows squished together.

Jin-son recovered faster, "Are you sure?"

"My husband wasn't one to hold a grudge. He'd forgive you. Even better, demand you go on with your lives. What are your plans?"

"My Uncle received permission from your government to accompany my mother and I to the United States. He'll be safer there. I'm to attend the Massachusetts Institute of Technology."

Kwon Chol smiled. "His mother wasn't happy with his choice of schools, but she'll go along. Wanted to be here, but she's finalizing the paperwork to sell her seamstress business. We fly out tonight."

"Perhaps we'll be on the same flight. Thank you for your kind words. Let her know we missed her."

Yang Hyo-jin and Michelle walked over to our group. Hyo-jin pulled me out of earshot while Michelle led the two Koreans away.

As Michelle walked away she told them, "Let's leave his widow alone."

Could use lessons in grace from Bishop's wife.

For once, Hyo-jin had replaced her lab coat with a black dress. "Your friend told me you are off the hook for the court martial. They're even overlooking your trip to the mountains in the North."

She put her hands on her hips. "The trip you failed to tell me about."

"Major Williams was happy to get rid of me, although he fought and lost to keep Schnier's platoon here. Sergeant Lee is staying. He was just on loan, anyway. I've survived the bureaucracy with a little help from my friends."

She leaned forward. "What about us?"

I struggled to find the right words.

"We have to honor Bishop's example of duty and sacrifice. Now that I'm getting good at the language, now that my emotional stingray poison, as you called it, has been burned out of me . . ."

Sighed. "I'd love to stay here with you, but my duty as a Ranger requires me to leave Korea. I have my orders. They'll be a sacrifice, but . . . you can show me your work over video chat."

She frowned. "Bishop honored his duty. Sacrificed for others, but also kept a family."

"He's a better man than I am. Someday, I hope to be more like him. Started drinking Cherry 7-UP to remind myself."

I put my arms around her waist. "Losing Bishop got me over my fear of losing anyone I love all over again. It sucks, but it's not worse than not having a family in the first place. We'll have to be in a long distance relationship, for now.

"Do you have anything for me?" I leaned forward.

"Such assumptions from a foreign barbarian. As it happens, I do." She broke out of my arms.

Reached into her delicate black handbag. Removed a blue velvet jewelry case. Opened it to reveal a red ribbon with blue stripes. Red and blue yin-yang symbols surrounded by white cloth flowers decorated the attached medal and pin.

"The Taeguk Order of Military Merit, Grand Cordon. One of South Korea's highest awards. You're only the sixth American to receive one."

Not what I expected. My jaw dropped open. "They're giving Bishop a Silver Star for saving Jin-son." I accepted the case from her.

Stared at the medal.

Didn't deserve this. Not after all my screw-ups and wipe outs in Korea.

She smiled. "My country is grateful. I'm grateful. Normally, you'd receive this in a nationally televised ceremony, but the government won't allow anyone to tell how you earned it. Now I'm not the only Korean national hero." She paused. "I'll miss you."

"Thank you. For everything." I grinned back. "Our jobs keep us busy, but I hope we can talk frequently enough I won't miss you too badly."

"We've never even been on a date!"

I did my best to look wounded, "What do you mean? I arranged for us to visit the most romantic spot in Seoul together, Namsan tower at night. We even watched the sunrise from the observation deck!"

Her pale Korean skin flushed, "Now that I'm in sole charge of the lab and Rhee is in prison for treason, maybe I'll hire you as our security chief."

"Conflict of interest."

"What do you mean?"

"I don't think they let you do *this* with your security chief."

I kissed her a lingering goodbye. Hunting assassins in the Philippines could wait a little longer.

For series updates and to read free bonus stories such as the tale of Sam's *Ranger Selection*, email TR@catallaxymedia.com or visit SharperSecurity.com.

Covert Commando is next in this series.

Acknowledgements

Special thanks to those who gave pre-release feedback on *Techno Ranger* - Christi Sewell, David Parker, Belle Scharf, Victoria Watson, Lije Sewell, and Larry Kowallis.